ZEAL

ZEAL

a novel

MORGAN JERKINS

HARPER

An Imprint of HarperCollins*Publishers*

Page 58: The newspaper clipping is from the *Shreveport News*, page 2, June 10, 1865, https://chroniclingamerica.loc.gov/lccn/sn83016485/1865-06-10/ed-1/seq-2/.

HarperCollins books may be purchased for educational, business, or sales promotional use. For information, please email the Special Markets Department at SPsales@harpercollins.com.

FIRST EDITION

Designed by Nancy Singer

Library of Congress Cataloging-in-Publication Data
Title: Zeal: a novel / Morgan Jerkins.
Description: First edition. | New York: Harper, 2025.
Identifiers: LCCN 2024033262 (print) | LCCN 2024033263 (ebook) | ISBN 9780063234086 (hardcover) | ISBN 9780063435988 | ISBN 9780063234109 (ebook)
Subjects: LCGFT: Novels.
Classification: LCC PS3610.E693 Z33 2025 (print) | LCC PS3610.E693 (ebook) | DDC 813/.6—dc23/eng/20240719
LC record available at https://lccn.loc.gov/2024033262
LC ebook record available at https://lccn.loc.gov/2024033263

ISBN 978-0-06-323408-6

25 26 27 28 29 LBC 5 4 3 2 1

To James Tate, his dear wife, and the Berry family

To the enslaved who loved when separation or death threatened their bonds, and to the descendants who continue that legacy of courage and passion

ZEAL

PROLOGUE

OCTOBER 2019

A harvest moon glowed above the Manhattan skyline and Brooklyn Bridge on the evening of Oliver Benjamin and Ardelia Gibbs's engagement party. String lights stretched across the rooftop of a midtown restaurant and heat lamps dotted its perimeter. Framed black-and-white photos of the couple served as centerpieces on a dozen tables covered with white linen tablecloths, and violets and roses arched over a dessert table complete with macarons, mini strawberry cheesecakes, and a five-tier cupcake stand. Neo-soul music of the midnineties and early aughts punctuated by Sade and Anita Baker streamed through speakers positioned in each of the four corners. But the exquisitely planned, perfectly executed party would have been nothing without the people.

Just four days prior, the festivities had been in jeopardy. Mighty storms swirling in the Midwest had left Oliver's relatives in Kansas and Ardelia's Chicago clan wondering if they might have to send their best wishes instead of risking the journey. Miraculously, the storms abated and everyone important had arrived. Even Ardelia's father, Sterling—her only living parent, though that wasn't saying much— beamed with pride as he; his mother, Geraldine; and sister, Hazel, watched the couple kiss and hold hands when they thought no one was watching.

The lovers had met at Corner Social two winters ago, one night when Ardelia had needed a quick reprieve from her job at the Schomburg and Oliver had relented to pressure from his friends to go out for once. As they each sipped their elaborate cocktails, their work pulled at them. But when Oliver leaned against the bar, his hands pressed against the countertop, Ardelia found herself making a joke about how his drink order matched his outfit—old-fashioned—and after that, Oliver discovered that he couldn't quite manage to move from his spot. So they had stayed, talking till closing, and had been together ever since. The first few months weren't without strain though. Her schedule was more regular than his. Often, she'd have to squeeze into a small pocket of time with him at Starbucks or a nearby noodle shop before he had to make a mad dash back to NewYork-Presbyterian. He texted heartfelt emojis; left small, sweet notes for her to find in her purse or on her nightstand; but after a while, these gestures became less effective. He knew he needed to show his commitment. He wanted to. So he asked her to move in with him. Their relationship was young, but they were full grown, in their midthirties, confidently fleshed out in who they were, and able to take risks with both eyes open.

Now, as the party was drawing to its natural conclusion, guests were beginning to place their napkins on their tables and rise to their feet. But Oliver suddenly clinked a glass with his fork to get everyone's attention. Ardelia watched, confused. The party had gone according to plan: the seating, the eating, the speech giving, the dancing. Nevertheless, Oliver looked anxious. His cuff buttons were unhooked and his sleeves were rolled up to right underneath his elbows. He wiped his sweaty brow and took a few deep breaths.

"Don't leave!" he asked the guests again. "I have something that I want to give to Ardelia." Guests who'd been beginning to bow out, as well as those who were standing and mingling, returned to their seats.

He grinned with a closed mouth at his beloved and she beamed back at him. Then Oliver's parents walked up to where he was standing. His dad, Marshall, was carrying a large package about the width of his torso. Oliver grabbed a remote and pressed a few buttons, and the music from the speakers abruptly stopped.

"Ardelia, can you come up here, please?"

Ardelia, who'd been nibbling on a cheeseburger slider beside the buffet table, put down her small plate and obliged. As soon as they were all face-to-face, Marshall and Irene, Oliver's mother, eyed each other before Marshall extended the parcel to Ardelia.

She carefully held the object, which felt to her like a framed photograph. "What is it?" she asked.

To her left, a table was stacked high with all sorts of ornately wrapped boxes, more than one of which, she knew, was from her future parents-in-law, who'd already spent a pretty penny on the engagement party.

"It's a very special gift, Ardelia, that you have to open in front of everyone," Irene said.

"This has been passed down for generations in my family," Oliver said to Ardelia. "Now it's ours to take care of, until we have our own children and they are grown enough to do so."

Their guests leaned forward in their seats with anticipation as Ardelia slowly undid the off-white and gold wrapping to reveal a handwritten letter on yellowing, crumbling paper, encased in heavy glass. The words were so faint she couldn't read the text until Oliver hovered his cell-phone light over it.

"We think there were others, but this is the one that remains," he told her as she tried to take in the lines.

"What's it say?" a female guest yelled.

"Someone pass her a mic!" Sterling called out, then clapped when one of Oliver's friends held a mic close to Ardelia's lips.

Ardelia squinted. "Dear . . . Harri . . . Harr . . . ?"

"Harrison," Irene said.

"Dear . . . Harrison . . ." Ardelia ran her finger underneath each word as she continued.

October 13th, 1865

Dear Harrison,
It has been only a month since I wrote you last—haven't heard from you but I keep on writing letters. They will find you. I've been teaching the children, giving God glory—learning to shoot. Can you believe it? I learned how to shoot yesterday. Today I killed two quail and roasted them with some cornbread and collard greens on the side. All the while I was gathering my cornmeal and flour and such, I kept thinking about how you would've loved my quail, as you loved my other meals back at the Phoenician. I thought about what it would've been like to have a nice proper dinner with my beloved with no master around, no dogs, no overseer, no nothing. Just us sitting underneath a pecan tree with greasy mouths and full bellies. No one to pester us. Just us. I thought about it long after I ate my meal, you know. But I didn't eat alone. I admit.
I met a man here. He's a good good man. Isaac Levi is his name and it's a strong one. He's almost too good. He preaches for all the negroes in town, hardly drinks or cusses, and watches over me. I don't ask him for anything but he keeps on giving anyway: a barrel of peaches, a few ribbons for my hair, a large hat to block out the sun when I'm planting, a book. He's a sweet man but he sure isn't you.
Isaac knew that I was already in love with another man when he met me. I didn't hold my words in describing what you meant to me and what you promised me. He understands. He allows me to write my letters. He allows me to keep hope because he knows that if I don't have that, I'll have nothing left. Your love keeps my flame bright. I know you still love me even as I tell you about another man. And I wouldn't blame you if you had another woman by now. You and

I had what we had in the cruelest of times and we did the best with what we had. And we are still making it.

Make no mistake, Harrison, I haven't forgotten about you and I have never stopped loving you. I see you in my sleep and I greet the day with you beside me. I haven't stopped thinking that I'm going to see you peeking through a window or waiting for me, leaning against the trunk of some tree. I must sound foolish but I can feel you always. This letter is but a single grain to the harvest I hold for you. I'm going to try my best to make it back to you.

If it's not this life, it'll be in the next. But we will see each other. We will cross a water greater than the Mississippi together. I've prayed on it and the Bible says God gives the desires of our hearts. We will see each other again and it's going to be better than the last time we saw each other. We will see each other again and finally have rest and peace. And once we do, we are going to laugh and laugh and laugh till our babies and their babies' babies can hear the echoes. Whether you find me first or I find you. We will see each other again.

Yours,
Tirzah

Ardelia was in tears by the time she finished the letter. The crowd was moved too, with waves of "aws" filling the air.

Ardelia looked up at Oliver and his parents. "Well . . . did they ever see each other again?" she asked her beloved.

Oliver grinned. "How do you think I got here?"

SUMMER
1865

1

She was gone.

Harrison returned to Natchez after the war, and she was gone, breaking her promise. Tirzah, the love of his life and the ember in the dark nights of his soul.

Two years and twelve days before, Harrison and his beloved had stood within a grove of magnolia trees on the grounds of the Phoenician Estate to say their goodbyes. She was crying so hard that Harrison had to hold her waist so she wouldn't collapse. And he, sweaty with a dirt-caked face, had asked her to wait for him until the war was over. No matter if they were free people or still slaves, he would be coming back for her. She shook her head until her curls flopped over her face and wondered aloud why he wanted to fight a battle they would never win. Before he could answer, one of the Union officers called for him to get moving and Harrison had to let her go. He had never felt a pain so deeply wedged in his chest as in the moment he left the Phoenician. But he had to get away. He hated being who he was now that he was in love. He hated how he could not defend his beloved from the danger of being in the main house under the lustful eye of their owner's son, Spencer. Going off to war, he resolved, he would defend her, himself, and all slaves, and come back to Natchez with pride.

But the Natchez he left, with all its stunning wealth, was not the

same one to which he returned. As he and his fellow soldiers rode
their horses on a trail alongside the Mississippi approaching the city,
they saw that all the levees had been destroyed. With each step closer
to their destination, the smell of festering animal carcasses became
stronger. Weeds and swampland had swallowed up fields upon fields
of cotton.

When his regiment arrived at the area underneath the bluffs, they
found it eerily still. They passed by a well-known wood mill and a
large plantation and garden—the only one of its kind below the hill.
Before he'd left, at least a half dozen negroes would be tending to the
property at a given time, and now there were none. Hardly anyone
was mixing in the street, besides a few negroes here and there. There
were no steamboats. No sound of foghorns or carriage wheels bumping along the principal street. The relative quietness bothered him.
Harrison had to fight to smother the thoughts of the absences of many
people being a bad omen.

"You still thinkin' 'bout dat lady, ain't ya?" a fellow soldier asked,
catching Harrison's line of sight to a trail where one could ascend the
hill to the city proper.

"Still thinkin'," Harrison replied. "I finna take my horse up dere
right nah so dat I don' waste anotha second."

"You needa give dat horse a rest first. 'N by de way, what makes
you think dat she gon' even be dere? Look around you."

Harrison made a soft noise of disapproval and steered his horse
away from the rest of the group, embarking on his own path.

"You needa go 'n get you a nice one to lay up wit for all dat hard
work you put in!" another soldier yelled out.

Harrison squeezed his thighs around his horse until he couldn't
hear his comrades any longer. The horse's trot widened into a full-
speed gallop as they scaled the bluffs and made their way to Natchez
proper, where all the most spectacular plantations sat high. Cows and
pigs decomposed along the trodden path, but Harrison was undeterred
by the carnage. He knew his way. The Phoenician was only about three

miles west of the town cemetery and a hospital, two structures that were still intact when he passed, but what Harrison saw next made him instruct his horse to slow. The plantation next to the Phoenician had been desecrated. Weeds grew like outstretched hands over columns and window panels. Acres of azaleas, wildflowers, crape myrtles, and roses had wilted, been trampled upon, or shriveled up and died.

When he finally arrived at the Phoenician's entrance gates, which appeared to have been broken, he slowly dismounted from his horse and took off his hat when his boots touched soil. He stood in front of the grand expanse of his former home and closed his eyes. A cacophony of noise overtook his mind—overseers barking orders, mournful cries, music, laughter, exhausted panting. He allowed his lids to flutter open, expecting to see what he'd dreamt more than once, tossing in his disease-ridden barracks: Spencer Ambrose kneeling in agony over his lost labor, slaves dropping their cotton to dance, Tirzah running out of the main house and into his arms. But there was no one in sight.

Unconvinced that he was truly alone, Harrison walked farther into the property. Flowers that slaves had maintained so beautifully lay limp on the brown patches of grass. The roof that Harrison had worked in the blistering heat to maintain was showing signs of rot, which also explained the faint smells of animal droppings and urine; the Phoenician must be overrun with pests. Everyone really was gone, Harrison thought, because there could be no other reason why the grand estate, once home to more than a hundred slaves at a time, had reached this level of devastation.

He stood underneath the main house's now-cracked pillars and inhaled deeply, hoping to detect a whiff of Tirzah's cooking, only to have the smell of gunpowder and blood irritate his nose. He circled around to the slave cabins, where a single chair rocked mysteriously on one of the small porches. Thinking that one of his old friends must still be around, Harrison put his fingers in his mouth and blew a whistle.

"Hey! C'mon out dere! Did ya hear de news? We free!"

Not a single door swung open. No quick pacing of feet racing to see what was going on. No jubilant cries out to the Lord for finally bringing them out of their Egypt.

He made his way back around to the main house, planning another circle. While he was reminding himself that the possibility of seeing Tirzah again was worth returning to the place he had dreamt so often of leaving, he felt something small and smooth underneath his right foot. He lifted his heel to see an oxblood-colored wallet with the letter *T* emblazoned upon it, and dropped to his knees. Seven and a half by three and a half inches with a bunch of pockets to stow whatever her heart desired. A guttural wail climbed out from the depths of his belly and shook the birds clean from their nests in the trees. The wallet was a gift he had given to Tirzah one Christmas Eve. That *T*, in a golden garland motif, was the first letter he had learned to write, the first letter he requested that she teach him in their secret nightly meetings. Had he taken too long, or had she given up too soon? Either way, she really was gone.

"What ya doin' over dere?" someone called out. The voice was gravelly but not unfriendly. Harrison lifted his head and saw a portly, one-eyed negro in a wide-brimmed hat standing beside a horse and wagon outside the Phoenician's gate. "Ya don' need ta be cryin' over alladat. Stand up nah, we free!"

Harrison didn't move, just cupped the wallet in his palm, bringing it close to his chest.

"What ya doin'?" the negro asked as he drew nearer to Harrison. Harrison looked up at the stranger, and the man dropped his smile and relaxed his stance. "Aww no. I know dem eyes. Ya don' een need ta say nothin', I know." The man pulled Harrison's arm to help him to his feet, then wrapped his arm around Harrison's shoulders. "Let's go. One foot at a time nah. Dassit. Lemme get ya back down to de village and we can talk."

"De village?"

"Mm-hmm. Dere's some abandoned shacks along de river

unda'neath de hill where Natchez improper be. Been dat way since de Union came and—wait." He stopped and clutched Harrison's shoulders to take a better look at him. Noting his blue uniform, he hugged him tightly. "Thank ya," he said.

"Ya welcome," Harrison replied through strained breath.

The man let him go and extended his hand. "Name's Ezekiel."

"Harrison." He shook the man's hand. "I don' need a guide. I got my own horse."

"I saw. But it's best we stick together. Ya know dem white folk mad dey lost. Not safe to be by yaself."

"Why? Seem like everyone gone."

"Seem dat way. But we know what we know. Only a matter of time. Ya sure ya able to ride? Ya don' look too good."

Harrison paused, then sighed. "Ya don' mind if I hop in dere wit ya and my horse rides along?"

The older man smiled. "I knew I was right. You lucky I got an extra harness. C'mon." After Ezekiel attached Harrison's horse to the wagon, they climbed into the coach seat and set both animals in motion. The two men sat in silence for about a mile, until Ezekiel finally asked, "So who is she?"

"How'd ya know?"

"Boy—I know when a man go to see 'bout a woman. I may not speak fast but I ain't stupid."

Harrison hung his head. "Maybe I came back too late and she has anotha now."

"Ya don' know dat."

"Den where would she be?"

"I don' know when ya went wit da Union to fight, but some of dese old masters 'round here ran outta town wit some of dere slaves when the war got to be too much."

"Ya know where dey went?"

"Probably someplace else in de South where it was harder for de Union to get to, I guess."

Harrison shook his head. "She probably has anotha. She was beautiful. De kind of beauty dat could halt a horse."

"Mm-hmm." Ezekiel nodded. "I understand."

"All I wanted was to—"

"Be beside ya woman? I know. But ya can still take care of dat ache for yaself, ya know. Ain't no need holdin' yaself back een while ya look."

"I had befo'. While I was away. 'S just . . . I hoped . . ." Harrison tapered off.

Ezekiel shook his head. "You a handsome man, I'm sure ya had ya choices een before the army. She musta been somethin' special."

"Sounds like you know from experience."

Ezekiel leaned in and pointed to a slit where his left eye should've been. "How ya think I got dis?"

Harrison didn't so much as blink, and stayed quiet.

"Mm-hmm. I was a driver in dose days. I spent much time 'round white folk so I went out of my way to go to church just to be 'round us wit'out dem. Wasn't too much of a believer though. I thought God forgot 'bout us a long time ago. But when I saw dis woman, when I saw dis woman . . . my faith came to me. Never had I seen a person so perfect. Dat's when I knew Spirit. Dat's how God found me and I found him. Everybody thought I done lost my mind 'cause I already been caught and whipped a few times for dis woman who lived on anotha plantation. And I did. I was in love. What I need my head for? And dat woman's love—" Ezekiel shook his head again. "Her love could make de stripes on my back feel like paper cuts."

Ezekiel maneuvered the horses past the cemetery and the hospital into downtown. When they neared the city market between Wall and Canal Streets, pandemonium was ensuing. Two white women dressed in their finest coats and silk gloves, maintaining firm grips on their parasols, flailed in front of a white man in a black top hat. The crowd swelled as more white women, young and old, surrounded the top-hatted gentleman. He stood beside a placard that bore the names of plantations along with dollar amounts: $83,000, $175,000, $200,000, and so on.

"Please, sir!" one woman shouted. "My husband died in the war! This here lady's husband is crippled. Our homes are all that we have left!"

"Many men died or got crippled in the war. You think you're the only one?" the man shouted back.

"Evidently not. Look how many of us are here!"

The crowd exploded in agreement. The white men left physically unscathed by the war watched from a distance without having so much as slipped a hand into their pockets. They, too, had either lost everything or were careering toward irreparable despair.

"I am sorry for all of your troubles," the man continued. "Truly I am. But debts need to be paid. So if you don't have the money to recoup the losses, step aside."

"But how are we supposed to survive? Without our homes . . . without our men . . . without our property!"

A pair of white women on the outskirts of the crowd, clamoring to get a closer look at the drama, suddenly noticed Ezekiel and Harrison and sneered. The air ran cool. So the men lowered their heads and continued on their way. Further down the same block, negroes were roaming the street alongside the whites. Though the whites scrutinized the negroes' bodies, no one stopped them to ask for a pass. Harrison could see negro women and children struggling to stifle their grins and laughter at their new ability to move unsupervised. White women scowled at their former property, now free men and women who dared watch their former owners abase themselves in public.

"Happens every day," Ezekiel said as soon as they were a safe distance away, then lowered his voice. "I feel like a pig in shit whenever I see dat it's dem who got dere precious things on de auction block instead of us. For however long it last."

Harrison slouched and said nothing. He thought of his younger self enlisting and immediately being stationed at Fort McPherson, where he did menial labor. Weeks later, he was transferred to the heavy artillery regiment in Vicksburg, where he had to quickly learn how to operate cannons and howitzers while barely escaping small-pox from the moist, overcrowded barracks he returned to at night. He didn't want to hear about no "however long it last."

Ezekiel directed the horses one block east then one north to an establishment so modest that Harrison might have missed it: a small wooden building, with a few negroes trickling in and out of the tiny doorway.

"Where are we?"

"'Tween Pearl and Washington. Dis here de new Freedmen's Bureau. Don' know how many people dey helped so far but dey doin' somethin'. Dey'll help ya find ya woman whether she here or some-place else. Tell 'em everythin' you remember 'bout her. Understand?"

Harrison nodded.

"Den, if you still feelin' dat ache, go back in de direction dat we came. Pass de city market goin' south and you gon' see two paths leadin' to de riverfront. Take de one on ya right. When you get to de end of dat one, you gon' see a large, brick building. Das where you go."

"Where will I find you?"

"De village. At de southern tip of de riverfront where de docks and wharves be. I'll take care of ya horse while ya do what ya need to do."

Harrison thanked Ezekiel for his trouble, then opened the door to the Freedmen's Bureau. Inside, the air felt even thicker. The office seemed no bigger than a church house. There were already many ne-groes either standing or sitting in chairs, looking desperate for assis-tance. A few negroes and white men in business suits hurried from one corner to the next, papers flying in their wake, and rattling off surnames and locations with the agility of auctioneers. Harrison slid into the littlest nook that he could find, hoping to find a private mo-ment to gather his thoughts, but on either side of him, people stared. When his eyes met theirs, they smiled and nodded. It took him a mo-ment to remember he was still in uniform.

A buxom woman walked toward Harrison with the kind of command that turned his mind blank, made him forget himself. He stood at attention and realized that she was the tallest woman he'd ever seen; the top of her head reached his chin. Her hair was pulled up high on top of her head, yet tight curls hung over her forehead, and her mahogany skin was appealingly smooth.

"Can I help you?"

"Dis here de Freedmen's Bureau?" Harrison winced at asking a question to which he knew the answer.

The woman smiled. "That it is. I'm Tabithah Duncan. What is your name?"

"Harrison."

"Follow me," she said, then pivoted on her right heel and led him down the aisle toward her desk. She guided Harrison to the seat opposite her, while he kept his eyes fixed on the papers scattered across the surface.

"Now," she said. "Who are we looking for? A mother? Father? Child?"

Harrison looked up. "A woman."

He thought he saw her face fall before she said, "What's her name?"

"Tirzah. Tirzah Ambrose."

"How do you spell it?"

Harrison looked up at the ceiling and silently mouthed words. "T . . . I . . . R . . . SSSS. . . . ZZZZ . . . UHH . . ." He sighed.

Tabithah pushed a pen and paper toward him. "Can you write it out?"

He fixed his gaze on hers.

"I see."

"I do know dat her name was from de Bible."

"Tirzah . . . Tirzah, Tirzah, Tirzah . . ." Tabithah's boss, a Black man with salt-and-pepper hair, was walking by her desk, and she reached for him. "Piper! You ever heard the name Tirzah in the good book?"

"Tirzah . . . Tirzah, Tirzah, Tirzah—" Harrison repeated her name like an incantation to bring her back to him.

"Ah!" Piper snapped his fingers. "Yes. She was mentioned in the Song of Solomon. T-I-R-Z-A-H."

"Perfect." Tabithah began writing but halted before the final letter. Tirzah's name was so similar to hers, just with one fewer syllable. She looked up at Harrison, who leaned forward in his seat, and nervously smiled before continuing. "And her last name?"

"Ambrose. Dat was her—our—master's last name."

"What all do you remember about her? Who did she belong to?"

"Mercer Ambrose. But she might as well had been de owner's son's. Spencer Ambrose."

"Do you know where she has gone off to?"

"No. Not at all. I was hopin' ya help could do somethin' for me."

She nodded. "We'll start by sending an ad out through this here Freedmen's Bureau up to Washington, D.C., where the main headquarters are, as well as negro newspapers and churches in and around Texas, Louisiana, and Mississippi."

He thanked her, then asked, "How soon will I know if ya have anythin'?"

"Come back in two weeks. Hopefully I'll have something for you then."

Harrison sprang from his seat, smiling. "Thank ya, miss. Thank ya."

She nodded again. He walked out the door, and through the storefront windows, she saw him turn the corner. Immediately, she tore the sheet with Tirzah's information from the pad and held it in her hands. Every time she finished collecting information from a client, she was supposed to bring it to the back of the office for processing.

But her body would not allow her to move. Tabithah looked over her shoulder to make sure Piper wasn't near, then opened a desk drawer and closed her eyes as she slipped the note inside. Then she opened her eyes and straightened her posture.

"Next!"

2

Harrison hadn't had any intention of heading to a brothel. But as soon as he stepped outside of the Freedmen's Bureau and saw just how big the line for assistance had gotten, he wondered how many of these negroes were looking for lost lovers too. The ache sprang up.

He went past the city market and followed the winding path on his right-hand side to a spot below the bluffs where a rectangular two-story brick building suddenly appeared among wildly growing weeds and bushes. Underneath a large Confederate flag softly blowing from the second-floor balcony, a trio of women—one dark-skinned, one mulatto, and the other white—lingered by the building's front door. The straps of their dresses were falling off their shoulders, and the rouge on their cheeks was smudged. One woman held her weight on one foot to allow her other leg to escape brazenly through the slit of her dress. What existed beyond their bodies was more darkness, a darkness into which Harrison now stepped. Immediately he was taken aback by a smell so overpowering he wondered if the women bathed in perfume. But the smell was not strong enough to override his desire to press against something warm.

Inside, piano music played and the lights were so low that no specific face or body could be discerned. The anonymity disarmed him. When a circling barmaid offered him a taste of moonshine, he figured it wouldn't hurt. But almost as soon as he raised his glass, he saw the bottom and asked for another. After that glass went down just as smoothly, he tilted his head forward and saw a young woman standing in front of him. Without saying a word, she grabbed his hand and escorted him down a hallway to a small room that was partitioned from the others by only a bedsheet. Her skin was soft. Silhouettes of pleasure rustled behind the adjacent bedsheet. It was the first time in—how long?—that Harrison had felt the plushness of a mattress. He dove deep into his pockets and pulled out two dollars.

"Will dis be eno—"

She stuffed the dollars in her cleavage and straddled him before he had the chance to finish his sentence. Before Harrison could get comfortable on the bed, she was unbuckling his belt and soon unleashed a resounding moan into the humid air. He felt his eyes cross as he leaned his head back on the pillows and fully surrendered to the ride.

AS HE WALKED OUT OF THE BROTHEL, THOUGHTS OF THE MATTRESS upon which they'd rutted only reminded Harrison that he needed to find a place to stay. The village that Ezekiel had mentioned consisted of rows of shacks that looked like wreckage left over from the flooding of the Mississippi. But as he got closer, he saw more life than he expected: women hanging up wet drawers on clotheslines, children running in circles, delivery boys carrying wood and tools up and down the path that ran between the shacks, dogs barking, an older man strumming a guitar outside his home, another man observing everyone from his rocking chair.

"Hey, Harrison!" Ezekiel waved him down, pointing to a small former rum shack to his left. "Ain't she nice? Shacks for either drink or sleep been left by boatmen who wanted to join de army and now dey too dead to reclaim 'em!" He cackled. "I held dis one down for ya. Ya lucky too. Everybody tryna snap 'em up fast or dey fear dey will have to go back to de plantation. Mine's right here." Ezekiel pointed to his right. "Whenever you need anythin', come find me or my wife, Marie."

"Your wife?" Harrison asked.

"And three chirren too!"

"What happened to de woman you told me about?"

Ezekiel shrugged. "Never ya mind dat. My story ain't ya story. Now I got an extra pair of pants and shirt and soap for ya 'cause I figure ya might wanna wash up after alladat."

"Thank ya. 'S been quite a day goin' up to de Phoenician and de Freedmen's Bureau and—"

A mischievous smile grew on Ezekiel's face. "I wasn't talkin' 'bout dat."

Harrison reddened.

"Ya grown, boy. Ain't no judgment. I be back in a minute."

Harrison stood in the middle of the unpaved path as horses and wagons and groups of negroes walked past him. He expanded his chest to take in air, overwhelmed by the noise and activity around him, noticing there was not one white face in sight. Harrison felt water in the creases of his eyes. How quickly and industriously everyone was establishing their own homes and helping one another out with a piece of lumber, a new door, or a bed.

"Hey, 'Zekiel."

"Yeah?"

"Ya got any handyman tools?"

Having been a carpenter, Harrison could look at his new home as a place of possibility, even though the roof looked like it could cave in at any moment and the floor was uneven. He had to be careful with his head because with his height he could graze the ceiling if he stood up too quickly. The space was rather dark, but nothing that a few lanterns or candles couldn't fix, and the floors quite dusty, but someone around here had to have a broom. And the shack still reeked of rum, but if he kept the doors open during the day, he felt sure the freshwater smell of the Mississippi would clear the stench.

Harrison saw that he could fit a bed in the middle of the room, a stove and a few cupboards, even a small dining room table. The space was more than enough for a freedman, and adequate for two. Hopefully just right for three . . . or more. One day. The longer Harrison walked the interior perimeter, the more his imagination churned with thoughts of what to place where and how long the overall project might take.

The only window, toward the back of the house, faced the Mississippi, a view that suited him well. He wanted to be able to see the comings and goings. He stepped out the back door and let the sun beam down on him. Without thinking, he began to remove his clothes, then heard some soft giggling nearby. He turned his head and saw two young women ogling him. Instead of covering up and telling them to scatter, he gestured for them to come closer.

Harrison was surprised how quickly his stamina had returned after his visit to the brothel. He and the two women fooled around inside his new home for the better half of the afternoon. No one minded the lack of a bed. All they needed was a wall to lean against and a floor to press against.

From that day on, word began to spread through the village, and Harrison became known as the soldier who knew his way around a woman's body like the way he knew how to put a bullet in a chamber or drive a screw into a wall. After he satisfied the women, they helped him with whatever he needed: food, cookware, extra bedsheets, wood to build his own furniture. When women weren't taking him for rides, he took side jobs, inspecting other negroes' homes to make sure they were sturdy, fortifying them if they weren't. Some gave him actual money and others bartered with eggs, an extra pair of slacks, or another kerosene light.

He would think of Tirzah whenever he came home to an empty room. If a woman was waiting for him, he'd give her what she wanted but never let her spend the night. He told himself that he wasn't being unfaithful, he was having fun, something he'd had so little of in his life until now. After each release, he thought to himself that just one more couldn't hurt. His heart had not moved. But soon he began to mistake women's names for others or forget them outright. The women rotated in and out until the activity became less of a thrill and more a way to pass the time until he felt worn out, almost unrecognizable to himself.

As the months passed, his beard grew mightily, the air began to cool at night, and the sugar maple leaves turned yellow.

One night, someone rapped on Harrison's door. Expecting it to be one of his lady friends, he opened it. Ezekiel was standing there with a look of consternation that made Harrison straighten his spine.

"Come over and eat. We need to talk to ya."

Harrison followed Ezekiel into the older man's home, where Marie was attempting to wrangle the children. They abruptly halted their horseplay when they saw Harrison. The girl scrambled to sit on his lap while the two boys slung their arms around his shoulder and neck, hanging off his body.

"Aht aht aht, no!" Marie wagged a finger at her children. "You want to play like det, you go outside."

"It's okay, Marie. Dey just happy to see me."

"Naw, naw. Y'all heard ya mother. Out. Where we can see ya," Ezekiel said.

He gave Marie a solemn look and she nodded. "I'll go out dere and give you two men time to talk."

"Naw, ya need to be here. Go ask Hanna next door if she can keep an eye on 'em."

Marie glanced over at Harrison and did as she was told. Once she returned, she placed the food dishes, a pitcher of lemonade, and silverware on the small dining table and the three of them sat down. Ezekiel lit another kerosene light and placed it to the right of him, and Marie extended her hands to both men to say grace. After their unified "amen," Ezekiel leaned forward and said, "What's happenin' wit Tirzah?"

The sound of her name clanged and clashed in Harrison's eardrums. He lowered his bottom lip, but no words came out. Instead, Harrison hung his head and started to massage the back of his neck.

"I see. . . . Ya given up on her den."

Harrison immediately lifted his head. "No!" He looked at Marie and lowered his voice. "No. I haven't. I just haven't been back to de bureau. Das all."

"Why not?"

"'Cause if I was gonna hear 'bout her, I woulda by now. De village ain't but so big and I ain't too hard to find."

"Yeah, but ya runnin' up behind every skirt in de village and folk might think ya don' care."

"And I don' care what people think."

"Well, ya should. 'Cause people been talkin' 'bout ya."

"Let dem talk. Don' hurt me none. Can we just eat?"

Marie was about to pick up her fork when Ezekiel held up a hand. "Hold on nah. De food can wait."

"De food gon' get cold," Marie said.

Ezekiel cut his eyes at Harrison. "Look, I know ya been doin' what ya need to do. But ya gotta know dat time's gonna change soon. People can't keep payin' ya what dey payin' ya. Can't een do exchanges like dat no more. Things runnin' out."

"And what dat mean?"

The older man placed his arms on the table and leaned forward. The kerosene light illuminated a few beads of sweat that dotted his forehead before sliding into his salt-and-pepper beard and disappearing. Without looking at either Marie or Harrison, he said, "Dere's a lot of land wide open for farmin' right nah. We each can get our own plot, work it, den get a portion of the crop back. De Freedmen's Bureau can help us work out de details."

"What kinda crop?"

Ezekiel nervously rubbed his hands together. "Cotton."

Harrison stood, feeling his nostrils flare. He flexed his fingers before speaking. "I ain't workin' on no plantation."

"Look, Harrison—"

"I ain't workin' on no gad-dam plantation!" His booming voice made Marie jump. "I done did what I was s'posed to do. I fought in de war and we won. I ain't goin' back."

"We ain't gon' have a choice after a while!"

"Den I'm gon' wait for dat while." His stomach growled and he quickly weighed his hunger against his desire to leave.

In that silence, Marie blurted out, "Let's eat. We can worry ourselves wit dat later."

"Afraid not," Harrison said, his eyes not wavering from Ezekiel's. They were at a stalemate, neither wanting to say something he'd regret. Harrison walked behind his chair and slowly pushed it toward the table. He nodded at Marie. "Ma'am."

That night, Harrison woke up in a puddle of his own sweat. He convulsed, recalling a past life he thought he'd forgotten. All those white hands grabbing for him in the dark. Black hands bound together and ankles shackled. More white hands clawing and reaching deep into his mouth and pulling at his skin.

Harrison's fate had been sealed by his first owner, Herbert Jolliffe. Jolliffe, an Alexandria planter, had many outstanding debts, and though he promised Harrison that he'd never separate him from his family, when the soul driver came knocking for some slaves in exchange for large profits, he claimed he had no choice. Franklin Armstead was the soul driver's name. Harrison didn't have a chance to hug his mother and father before Armstead took him and threw him into a pen with other negroes. And there, in that pen, were the hands of Armstead and the other soul drivers, who grabbed at the fabric of young women's clothes, pulled them out from the group for long enough for every negro to know what was happening, and then returned the women with bloody fingernails and hands that bore the signs of the magnitude of their failed resistance.

Then there were the coffles. Their Black hands were all chained together as they marched at the break of dawn. For miles and miles, they continued until a boat was waiting for them on the Mississippi. That's when they met the darkness in the belly of that boat as they were stacked on top of one another and sealed inside without room to stretch or breathe. When the soul driver opened that door to the belly in order to take the inventory of who was still alive, the light that came in was only enough for Harrison to see Black hands floating in the air, desperate for release.

Then there was that stinging feeling of fresh air after having been left in filth for too long. The surviving negroes were stripped of their clothing, then buckets of hot, soapy water were thrown on them before they were granted a new pair of clothes. Once the boat stopped and they were transported by wagon to downtown Natchez, Harrison was in the first group to be brought out at the Forks of the Road, where they were poked and prodded to gauge their value. The white ladies, in their bonnets and petticoats, strolled the market and pointed at slaves they liked, while the men were bolder with their interest. One middle-aged man, a younger man at his side, opened Harrison's mouth, then ran his hands over Harrison's arms and penis to estimate his strength for plowing fields and making babies. It was his son's twenty-first birthday, Harrison heard him say. Twelve hundred dollars later, the father's and son's hands were pulling him onto a cart to labor at their home, the Phoenician Estate.

Now, in the darkness of his shack, the simple memory of being enslaved was what woke him. He did not want his destiny to be in the hands of someone else ever again. The desire to be autonomous was what led him to join the Colored Troops regiment in the first place. He'd believed that if the Union fought hard enough to win, then freedom would be lasting and guaranteed. White folks didn't promise him or any other soldier anything. But he assumed that after all the blood, sweat, and grime that came from the war, certain outcomes would be honored. And yet this dream felt like a reminder and a grim harbinger of his world coming undone again.

For the next few weeks, Harrison avoided Ezekiel. When the older man tried to say hello, Harrison looked the other way. Sometimes, he'd see Marie making her way to his house with a pot of food before

Ezekiel called to her to get back home and mind her business. At first, the estrangement didn't bother Harrison—until the womenfolk stopped knocking on his door. They'd pass him by without giggling or gossiping, instead looking worn out and skinny, clothes slipping off their bodies, voices devoid of any light.

And then the menfolk also stopped coming around or requesting Harrison's help with miscellaneous jobs. He'd walk along the river-bank to clear his mind and try to convince himself that work would come around again soon.

But then, one quiet morning while the sun was still low in the sky, there was a knock on Harrison's door. He practically fell over his chair to answer it. And when he did, his throat caught at the sadness in his visitor's expression.

Tabithah from the Freedmen's Bureau, all done up in a nice dress with a matching hat, held a few letters in her hands. She sighed and gathered herself. "Dese are for you." She placed the letters in his hands gently and started on her way before quickly doubling back. "Why haven't you come and seen me?"

3

The elders hadn't prepared Tabithah for how she'd feel when Harrison walked through the front door of the Freedmen's Bureau. She'd been attracted to him instantly, and when he'd sat across from her, his sweaty scent had unspun her tightly wound decorum. As he turned to leave after their meeting, questions populated her mind— Just who was that strikingly handsome man? And what did he think of her, if he even did at all? But one rose above the rest: Would she really see him again? She reassured herself that Natchez was only so big, and Harrison was so tall she would easily spot him in a crowd. And she'd bet that he would come back, if not for her, then for this Tirzah Ambrose.

The advertisement that she'd drafted for Tirzah had lain in Tabithah's desk drawer since Harrison left. Every time she went to open the drawer, she retracted her hand, telling herself that the chances of finding Tirzah were small anyway. During the few months that she'd been working at the bureau, she had yet to see a family reunited. In the beginning, Tabithah had felt for every client, walking out to the alley behind the office to cry into her sleeve when she could. But Piper promised that the job would get easier, and that it did. After a while, her body had no more tears to produce. She could finish the sentences of those who came to see her and offered automatic responses to hurry them along. But something about Harrison brought her back to her senses, igniting a flame that she didn't want to be extinguished.

One unusually chilly October evening, Tabithah was closing up the bureau when she spotted two negro women a little further down the road. They were strolling arm in arm, occasionally leaning into each other before exploding into laughter.

Tabithah chuckled. "Drunk as skunks," she said to herself.

She enjoyed watching them having fun, walking around as they pleased. Freedom was still new, though, and Tabithah slowed down her closing routine to keep an eye on them.

"I'm tellin' you! I always been told dat a man who can build know his way 'round more things den furniture 'n roofs 'n houses," she heard one of the women say.

"You don' hafta tell me, I know! Das a man who can twist, turn, and screw."

"Wit his big ol' screwdriver!" The first woman tipped her head back so far to laugh that her hat fell off.

"More like a hammer!" Their cackles were so loud that nearby mockingbirds hidden in the trees were inspired to chirp and sing in accompaniment. "Oh hold on nah. Your hat—" The shorter one walked back toward the hat, bent down to retrieve it, and stumbled a few paces to the side before falling rearfirst in the middle of the street. Tabithah opened her mouth to call out and offer assistance. But before she could, the second woman gave the fallen one a hand and got pulled to the ground herself. Together, they laughed some more as they sat in the street.

"I can hardly walk," the woman with the hat said. "Dat moonshine got to me."

"Dat wasn't the moonshine, dat was Harrison."

Tabithah's shock obscured everything the two women said next. But after she saw them get up and on their way and started her own walk home, she reflected that they spoke of Harrison like the masters did of the men before the war. Nothing about who he was as a person beyond what he could do with his body, though the labor was of a different kind.

She didn't have much time to think about what the women had said, because upon entering the all-female boardinghouse, she was met by the rest of the tenants, gathered by the fireplace in the living room, the flames illuminating the women's crestfallen faces. Their landlady, Rose Lournière, a petite Creole woman who could pass for white if she was vigilant with her parasol, sat among them in a large chair.

"Tabithah," said Rose in her honeydew voice. "Relieve yourself of your coat and sit with us. I don't want to have to repeat what I have to say."

Tabithah squeezed to sit down between two other young women on a plush chaise and unintentionally held her breath.

A pregnant silence persisted. Rose wrapped her shawl tightly around her shoulders and dabbed a handkerchief at the corners of her eyes.

"You know I care about each and every one of you. I've never allowed for my station to prevent me from having empathy for those born beneath me. But"—her voice trembled and she pressed her right hand to her chest—"this home will be gone soon." Murmurs and gasps passed through the circle, and Rose winced. "And you all will have to find new places to live."

Some of the young women were crying now. "But what about Mr. Sarpy? Can't he help us?" one of them called out.

"My beloved Thomas has fallen upon hard times and cannot afford to maintain this house any longer than he has been. I'm sure you are well aware that many men have lost much of their fortunes due to the war. He has a wife and six children, and he's worried he can't even afford dowries for his daughters!"

The woman sitting to Tabithah's left sucked her teeth and flicked her hand at Rose, refusing to take that explanation as a sensible excuse.

"Look, girls, I assure you that this distresses me greatly too."

"How? You never been a slave like us! You could go wherever, say whatever, and do whatever you please."

"Not true," Rose shot back. "I am still a woman."

"But not like us," another woman said.

Rose got to her feet and patted the front of her skirt. "I am sorry. To all of you. Understand that I've tried everything I could to make sure that this didn't happen, that you'd be able to stay for at least another year or two, but times have changed. Make arrangements sooner rather than later."

The rest of the girls remained in the living room to commiserate and begin to plan, but Tabithah followed Rose down the hall to the door of her bedroom. "Miss Lournière—"

Rose turned around and smiled. "Tabithah."

"Do you really think we'll be okay?."

"I know you will, dear. You work hard. You're one of the girls I'm least worried about."

"But why?"

Rose dropped her shoulders. "Some womanly advice: find a man. Get married."

"If where I live will soon be gone, do you think my job will be too?"

Rose leaned her head to the side and admired Tabithah. "Maybe. Maybe not. But you are a beautiful girl. Do not waste your pretty." With that, she entered her bedroom and swiftly closed the door behind her.

Tabithah stood in the darkness, a dull, persistent pain on the right side of her rib cage. Something didn't feel right. She walked up the stairs, past a few groups of women, returning to the room she shared with four others so that she could lie flat on her back in bed.

As soon as she was able to drown out the chatter from her room-mates, though, her mind carried her to the time when she labored on a plantation. Her master had hundreds of slaves, many of whom were women—and therefore, he had plenty of options to warm his bed. As soon as Tabithah's breasts began to sprout, he sought her out at least once a month, usually during a full moon. Whenever the master didn't call for her, she'd occasionally lay beside another slave in the cabins or in a mossy patch near a small creek. But her eyes would always roam. She'd look over the shoulder of the man grunting above her and watch the clouds move or a bird of prey flying over the wide fields. When they were done, no words were exchanged. He'd pull his pants up, she'd wipe herself down. The time together was done without feeling—out of boredom, or trying to see if it'd be any better when they did it themselves rather than had it done to them. Tabithah still felt like a match that could not be struck.

In the boardinghouse room, she looked toward the one small window, which framed a crescent moon hanging in the dark sky. What she was feeling was hidden, even to her. But, she thought, she was like that moon. There was another part of herself that was emerging. She knew it.

THE NEXT DAY, BEFORE THE BUREAU OFFICIALLY OPENED FOR BUSI-ness, Tabithah thought she was the first to arrive at work until she found Piper kneeling in the back room, his head in his hands. Beside him, a desk had been turned over and papers were scattered on the floor near his feet.

"What happened?" she asked as she walked gingerly toward him.

Piper lifted his head, revealing a bruised eye. "Dey came in here."

Tabithah's heart raced. "When?"

"Early dis mornin'. I came in and found 'em."

She remembered locking up last night but now she wasn't so sure. After hearing those drunken women brag about Harrison, could she have closed the door without securing it?

"For what?"

"Because dey can. A bunch of hoodlums. Wanted to see some of our records and I showed it to 'em. Dey burnt them right in front of me and laughed. Weren't sent on account of de governor, mayor, nothin'. Dey might come back too. Just got word that all our books are gonna be reviewed soon anyway so dere can't be anythin' outta place."

"Want me to fetch someone to come and look at your scars?"

"Naw, naw." Piper waved his hand in front of his face. "I'm fine."

"Okay," Tabithah said, unconvinced. She turned her back on Piper and started toward her desk.

"Are you lookin' for dis?"

Tabithah spun around and saw him holding up a folded sheet of paper. She felt the color drain from her face as he opened it and asked, "Who is dis Tirzah Ambrose?"

She couldn't say a word. Her tongue lost its direction somewhere between the back of her throat and her teeth.

"When I saw dis, I was just as speechless as you 'cause you never put dis kind of information in your desk drawer. You know we keep our records clean and thorough. We make sure nothin' gets lost 'cause folk countin' on us. De white folk don't hire enough of us negroes to help our own people out in dis here bureau. Dey don't trust us—rather leave our business in dere hands still. We got lucky. So what was you thinkin'?"

"I wasn't."

"Damn right you wasn't. You tired? D'you need rest?"

She shook her head.

"So was dis just an oversight?"

Tabithah shook her head again.

"Is she a relative?"

"No."

"Who is she den?" Piper said, raising his voice.

Tabithah looked to the ground. "She someone else's lover."

Piper sucked his teeth. "Lawd have mercy. I always knew you were smart and dat's why I taught you how to read. You still a young girl and you gon' make stupid decisions, but dis"—he raised the paper in the air—"ain't stupid. It's evil. You don't mess wit people's destinies. And if you love 'em—whoever he is—you let things happen. What is meant to be will be."

"Easy for a man to say," Tabithah retorted, her cheeks burning. "Y'all always take things into ya own hands. When a woman does it, you tell us to stand down." She snatched the paper from his hand and thumbtacked it to their bulletin board. "I'll add it to de books and send it up to Washington."

"Don't bother. I already done it. I got letters in de back from de same woman. Can't trust dat dey'll be here another day after what happened dis mornin' so I'm gonna deliver to dis Harrison," he said, making for the door.

She trailed behind him. "I'll do it."

"Oh no. I won't have you workin' here no more. You can't keep up with de records 'cause your feelings got in de way and I won't have dis bureau go down 'cause of you."

"Let me at least go wit you," she said, but Piper was already grabbing his hat and coat. "Please!" she yelled with an intensity that made Piper halt in his tracks.

Piper sighed. He went to the back of the bureau office to grab the letters and hesitated before handing them off to her. "I'll be watchin' you while you do it. Den after that—" He reached in his pocket and gave her three quarters. "Dis be your last payment. Understand?"

Tabithah nodded. "Yes, sir."

The letters were painful to touch. Each one with the return address of a Tirzah Ambrose of Shreveport, Louisiana. Even her cursive was beautiful. Tabithah had only seen writing like that from white people and knew that Tirzah worked in the house. The muscles in her fingers tensed up as she held the envelopes. Piper and Tabithah made the two-mile trip down to below the bluffs at the wharves where the negro village was. There, Tabithah randomly stopped a woman who crossed her path.

"Excuse me. Can you tell me where Harrison lives?"

The woman scrutinized Tabithah with a scowl, looking her up and down, then twisted her neck and said, "Just a little further down from where we standin' . . . on de right-hand side. It has de strongest-lookin' roof 'cause he done fixed it wit his God-given hands. Ya can't miss it."

Tabithah thanked her and continued a little ways in that direction before the woman called out, "Don't expect nothin'! You heard it from me!"

When she knocked on Harrison's door and he answered, Tabithah saw that he was more handsome than she remembered, but he looked more irritated too.

There was a brief silence before Tabithah looked to her right, to where Piper was watching her, his foot turned outward to intervene if need be.

She took a deep breath. "Dese are for you." She placed the letters in his hands and started on her way before quickly doubling back to stand right in front of his face. "Why haven't you come and seen me?" It didn't matter if anyone around could hear her. She needed to know or else she'd go crazy from regret, confusion, or both.

Harrison blinked. "I . . . I already knew what de answer would be."

"What answer?"

"'Bout"—he took a deep breath—"Tirzah."

"Take a look at de letters. Dey from her."

Harrison looked down at them and back up at her. "I can't read 'em."

"Do you wanna know what dey say?"

Harrison took a moment. "I know betta den to ask a woman to read sum'n dat another woman wrote. 'Specially one like you."

"One like me? What you mean?"

"Ya like me."

Tabithah puffed out her chest. "You don't know me."

"Ya right, I don'. But thank ya for dese." Harrison took the letters and placed them off to the side. "I'll figure it out."

"Okay. G'day."

"Do ya want to come inside for a bit?"

Tabithah paused for a moment on the threshold, fingering the coins on her pocket. Then she steadied herself and took Harrison's hand. The last image she collected before the door closed was Piper disappointingly shaking his head and walking away.

• • •

Tabithah didn't know exactly what to expect when she was invited into Harrison's home because the offer alone filled her with excitement. But when he pushed her back up against one of those walls and smashed his lips into hers, she knew that it was not what she wanted. His tongue deep into her mouth was making it impossible to speak, and she pressed both of her hands on his chest to give herself a moment to breathe. Then his hand went underneath her dress from the bottom, and without thinking she pushed him so far that he fell backward and landed flat on the second set of cheeks God gave him.

He looked up at Tabithah in shock.

"S-Sorry," she stammered. "No. No, I'm not. I'm not sorry. Why you do dat?"

Harrison rose and dusted off the back of his trousers. "I thought dat's what ya wanted."

"Listen. I heard 'bout what you been doin' wit de women 'round here unless dere's another Harrison who's good wit his hands. Dey may like it but I'm not dem."

Harrison blinked. "Even de way ya speak outside of de bureau is different."

"'Cause I was bein' professional conductin' business in an office and such. We inside now talkin' personal, I can talk straight."

"Hmm."

In the beginning of his freedom, sure, he'd make small talk with a female visitor and even offer her a drink or a small bite to eat. But once his name began to circulate under the bluffs, the women who came by didn't want none of those niceties. They asked why he was taking so long or baited him by wondering aloud if the rumors about him were true.

"Ya came all dis way just to give me letters from anotha woman? Ain't no job make ya do dat," he said at last. "I thought ya came here 'cause ya like me. Since we talkin' personal . . .'"

"You don't know my boss. But I thought . . ." Tabithah said, and sighed. "I thought it might make you happy."

Harrison started to walk toward the basin in the far right-hand corner of the shack. "I don' know 'bout dat."

"But . . . you love her, don't you?"

Harrison turned back around. "Yeah, I love her. I never stopped. But it's gonna take me a long time to know what dem letters say and she might be married off by now. Pretty as she was."

Tabithah stepped toward him. "You know how many negroes would give dere life to God again and maybe een the devil himself to hear from someone who dey thought dey lost?"

Harrison looked away.

"You hear me talkin' to you?"

He met her eyes. The light that beamed through between the wooden planks of his roof emphasized the dewiness of her skin and the soft, plump nature of her lips. There was also something about the shift in her voice, her directness, that made him strangely curious about this woman.

"I hear ya," he finally responded.

"And you ain't answer my question from before."

"Which one?"

"Why you do dat? Kissin' me like dat? I know you ain't really want to."

"How ya figure dat?"

"Because . . ." Her voice dipped. "You looked bored."

Harrison blinked. "Woman—" He held up his calloused hands. "I been workin' all day. What ya mean, 'bored'?"

"I've known men before you and I know bored when I see it. Won't no feelin' wit what you did."

Harrison tsked.

"And besides, I worked in dem fields before," she continued. "I've seen dose kinds of hands, and dose calluses been dere for a while. Ain't dat much jobs to go 'round."

He lowered himself into his rocking chair, then leaned forward. "So why ya still here den?"

Tabithah's eyes roamed to the back window and the undulating of the Mississippi. "Maybe I do like you." Her eyes shot back to Harrison, wanting to catch his gaze as she made herself clear. His face, she believed, would tell her everything she needed to know.

The scrunched lines in the space between his eyebrows loosened and his jaw relaxed. His eyes, once full of scrutiny, were now calm and disarming. "And what ya want me to do wit dat?"

"What?"

"Ya know about anotha woman. Das een how we met. Ya come here, gimme her letters, push me when I kiss ya, and den tell me ya like me. I can't hold much, Tabithah. Ya right dat dese calluses old. But dat crackin' and peelin' ya see ain't just from buildin' and hammerin'. Das from a body dry and thirsty for de one thing it can't drink. So how ya expect me to fill ya up wit anythin' other den what I been doin'?"

Tabithah scanned the room. "Well, I can't expect nothin' from a man who ain't even offer me nothin' when he let me into his home. Not even dat chair right beside you. You may have let me and other women all close up in here, but you as far as can be."

When Harrison frowned and said nothing, Tabithah took it upon herself to sit beside him. He turned his face away from her as she spoke.

"I see you, Harrison. And you sad. You real sad. You don't have to tell me but I see it." Even though he was still refusing to look at her, she smiled. "You wanna tell me about her? I wanna know more 'bout de woman who got you like dis."

Harrison scoffed with a smirk. "Ya sound like 'Zekiel."

"Who's that?"

Without thinking, Harrison leaned his body toward hers. As he told her about the bond he and Ezekiel had in the relatively short time they had known each other, he was impressed by how easily Tabithah had summoned him from a low place. Once he started speaking, he couldn't stop. He talked about the war, the people he'd seen die in front of him, and how he and his fellow soldiers improvised their fun in order to survive. Before he knew it, the crickets were chittering and it was time to light the kerosene lights.

4

The next morning, Tabithah woke up alone in Harrison's bed, still wearing her dress from the day before. The room was empty. She looked out the back window and didn't see him bathing or hanging up clothes, and wondered where he could have gone. When Tabithah opened the front door, a small woman was approaching, her breath coming in fits and starts, and shaking all over. Tabithah wanted to offer the woman a place to sit or something to drink, but she wasn't the lady of the home; it would have been inappropriate. She wished she could take the woman in her arms—do anything to ease her trembling—but she had never seen her before.

"Ma'am?" Tabithah said. "Are you all right?"

"I can't find my husband," the woman said, her teeth chattering loudly.

"I can take you down to de Freedmen's Bureau, Missus—"

"Ligon. My name's Marie. And no, he ain't gone like det. I just ain't seen him in two days. I done walked up down and 'round dis village and no one ain't seen or heard nothin'. Harrison ain't say nothin'?"

So the woman knew Harrison too. "What's your husband's name?"

"Ezekiel."

Tabithah's eyes widened. "Harrison did tell me dat he was a good friend. He say he worry too much for his own good but a good friend."

Marie wheezed as her chest expanded to take in more of the

humid air. "Worry too much? He was bein' smart 'bout what's comin'," she said.

"What's comin'?"

"We all gon' be back on de plantation soon enough 'cause dere ain't no money. Harrison walked outta our house when 'Zekiel tried to warn him. Den 'Zekiel thought he mighta been afraid too much and refused a contract with one of dem white men for a job pickin' cotton. De boys need new shoes, Millie got a hole in one of her best Sunday dresses, and I"—Marie extended her arms by her sides, then slapped her hands on her thighs—"I wanna have enough hominy and meat and grits to last till spring."

Tabithah looked at the older woman sympathetically. "When you hear of him last?"

"Two days ago, ain't you listenin'? I ain't seen him in two days. We got into an argument 'bout dat contract. He was tellin' me he was tryna bargain. Tuh! Bargainin' wit dem white folk. When has det ever happened? Aw Lord . . ."

Tabithah felt compelled to comfort Marie, and had just pulled her into an embrace when Harrison came down the path, clutching a few envelopes.

"Harrison!" Marie ran over to him and placed her hands on his chest. "Please tell me you saw Ezekiel."

"No." Taken aback, Harrison gently took her hands away from him. "What's goin' on?"

"He missin'!" Marie yelled.

Harrison's bottom lip quivered and he rubbed at his eyes. He started toward his front door while saying, "Not now, Marie. I'm sorry." He went into the shack and left the two women standing in shock at his brusqueness.

"I can come and check on you later," Tabithah asked.

"Please. Thank you. I'm right across from y'all." Marie pointed to her shack. "What is your name?"

"Tabithah."

"Well, Tabithah, hopefully anotha woman can talk some sense into dis here man 'cause we tried!" Marie threw up her hands and marched farther down the path to ask other passersby about her husband.

Tabithah went back inside to find Harrison fixing himself some hibiscus tea. She stepped in front of him as he was stirring the ingredients. "You just gon' keep on doin' what you doin'?" she asked. "What was dat?"

"Tabithah . . ."

"Dat lady is worried sick about her husband, de man you talked up so much last night and you actin' like you don't care."

"I do care."

"You have a strange way of showin' it!"

"I already have one missing person to deal wit and I can't have two! Understand?" Harrison's voice boomed so loudly that Tabithah took a step backward. "He fine. I know it." Harrison sniffled and Tabithah stood in disbelief that he would think that he could fool her again by acting unbothered.

"She said he turned down a contract 'cause of you."

"I don' know nothin' 'bout dat. He can work on a plantation all he want. I ain't doin' it. I done told him. Not every negro need to be workin' with cotton. Look at you. De Freedmen Bureau still dere."

Tabithah stepped aside to allow Harrison to finish making his drink and dug her fingernails into her palm. "I don't work dere no more."

Harrison dropped the pitcher on the counter with a clang and raised his left eyebrow.

"It's a long story. But de bureau might not be for long. White folks almost busted Piper's head in. I only got seventy-five cents before he saw me out."

"So what ya gon' do?"

Tabithah shrugged. "Do what I can to stay alive, I guess. Ain't we all?"

"Hmph. Dat we are."

Tabithah switched her attention to the folded sheets of papers and torn envelopes peeking out from Harrison's bulging right pocket. "Where you been at anyway?"

"I din' wanna wake ya. Found someone to read de front of one of de envelopes and it say Tirzah in Shreveport. Tried to ask around 'bout how I can get dere, and some white men told me I'm gon' need a pass. I ain't hear nothin' 'bout no pass. Den dey asked where I work and I told dem I work for me and dey laughed at me. Said I need to get me a labor contract and work till I can get on de boat to see 'bout her. Dey een gave me one."

"Well . . . where is it?"

"I ripped it up in front of dere face."

"You what?" Tabithah yelled.

Harrison sighed. "Mm-hmm. And now I'm gon' drink my tea and enjoy de rest of my day. Ya can stay and have yourself a glass or leave. Make me no difference."

"I'm goin' but I'll be back. We still got things we need to discuss."

Tabithah had no things to gather, so she marched right out of Harrison's home planning to leave the negro village for the boardinghouse. Once, as she walked past the wharves to the middle part of the riverfront by the lumberyards, her feet skidded on the dirt path. Whites mounted on gigantic horses stood on every corner. They were randomly stopping every negro man, woman, and child, asking where they were going and why they were going, who they lived with, who they worked for. Every time one of the negroes spoke, a white man took notes. Before Tabithah could turn around, a white man on horseback blocked her from going any further. She quickly told the white man that she worked at the Freedmen's Bureau, and he laughed until spit speckled the top of her lips. He didn't write down anything about her identity, then flicked her away like an irksome gnat.

As she approached the boardinghouse back in Natchez proper, just a few blocks north of the Freedmen's Bureau, she saw that the front door was wide open and papers and various articles of clothing had spilled out onto the porch. A few horses had been hitched to nearby trees, their ears twitching at random intervals. Tabithah had a bad feeling and was tempted to turn back around. But she needed her things. And she'd be damned if she let a white man confiscate her possessions. She straightened her posture to walk right into the foyer and halted. Rose's artwork on the walls was all gone. The throw pillows on her living room sofas were gutted and thrown about, the cotton strewn all across the floor. Furniture had been flipped over, pools of wine stained the rugs, and there was a faint smell of piss coming from somewhere else on the main floor.

Tabithah was thanking God that none of the other tenants seemed to be home and witnessing this when a groan shook her to her core. She closed her eyes, hoping it wasn't real, then heard it again. She followed the sound all the way to Rose Lournière's bedroom, tiptoeing inside and shutting the door behind her. The room had been turned upside down, and Rose lay on the rug, her arms and legs twisted grotesquely, but the sound coming from her indicated that she was somehow still alive. A large red knot was swelling in the middle of Rose's forehead, and long lines of dried blood streaked her inner thighs. Her hair was bedraggled and matted. One of her breasts—inflamed and punctuated with bite marks—hung out of the top of her shredded dress. And the smell—Tabithah recognized it too well. It was the smell of iron, sweat, and a woman turned inside out.

"Miss Lournière," Tabithah whispered as she knelt down beside her. She reached out to touch her, but Rose hissed at the hand coming toward her. Her eyes rolled in the back of her head before redirecting to Tabithah. "I done told you to leave."

Her neck jerked. It was the first time she'd heard Rose speak like one of them, and she could tell that Rose meant every word.

"I had to come back for my things."

Rose's eyes fluttered. "Git outta here before those soldiers come back."

"Soldiers?"

"Wearing their Confederate uniforms. They lost and now they're angry and they're going to do whatever they can to satisfy that anger." Rose suddenly spiraled into a coughing fit. "Don't come back here no more. They might not be done with me, and I can't bear to imagine what they'll do to you if they find you here."

Tears welled up in Tabithah's eyes. "But—"

Rose shook her head. "Go. Go, I say!"

Tabithah ran out of the boardinghouse back down to the negro village, where the roads were completely empty. Just the day before, the neighborhood had swelled with the noises of music playing, loud conversations, and food sizzling. The eerie quiet only meant one thing: it was safer inside than out on the streets. No clothes hung on the clotheslines. No chairs rocked back and forth. Even Marie, who'd been roaming the streets looking for Ezekiel just a few hours ago, was sitting stock-still in her street-facing window. Her face was grayish and ghostly, seemingly hovering behind the dirty glass.

She pushed on the door to Harrison's shack and it opened easily. He wasn't inside, but two dinner plates and cups were on the table. Fresh bread sat on the table, two slices already cut. Rice and black-eyed peas were soaking in separate large bowls in the basin. He'd been preparing for both of them, she could tell. But where was he? Was he safe? She could not go back outside to look for him. She couldn't risk someone grabbing her, especially now that she had no clothes but the ones she now wore, no possessions with which to barter for her life.

After being unable to ignore her hunger and helping herself to some of the bread, Tabithah's eye fell again to Tirzah's letters, which Harrison conspicuously left behind on a stool near his side of the bed. She needed something to distract her from Harrison's absence, but that wasn't the only reason she was drawn to the letters. The man was still an enigma. Who was this lady that he loved, yet not so much that he would risk flinging himself into the river to get to her the moment he knew where she was? And what could Tabithah learn from her?

One of the letters was not in an envelope. If she wanted to take a peek, Tabithah thought, Harrison would never know. She hesitated, then moved closer to that naked letter, one step at a time. Once Tabithah held it with both hands, she glared at the door and held a breath, hoping the knob wouldn't turn. After a few moments, Tabithah exhaled and started to read. Besides having beautiful handwriting, Tirzah was a compelling storyteller. Some of the lines made Tabithah blush because they were so intimate. Other times she marveled at how thoughtfully the words were strung together, like a string of pearls glimmering in its sophistication.

She read the letter over and over. By nightfall, however, the words had started to blur together. Harrison had still not returned, and she didn't know where to place her anxiety. She had too much pride to go knocking on doors to look for him—a small part of her was worried he was with another woman. But Tabithah knew that she was afraid more than she was jealous, and the fear did not go away, even as she occupied herself with tidying up the shack.

Finally, the silence was pierced by the sound of hooves on the ground, growing closer and closer. Looking through the window, Tabithah couldn't make out a single person, just the yellow glow of the many lanterns that appeared to float in the dark, letting her know that there was a crowd. The trotting continued to get louder until it stopped right outside Harrison's door. She saw the rider, a negro teenage boy, crying and sliding off his saddle. Tabithah, shaking, opened the front door slightly and saw a crowd forming around the horse and the rider, who could not pick up his head when asked what afflicted him. Then, one elder Black man shone his light on the wagon attached to the horse and gasped, dropping the lantern on the ground, others quickly stamping it out to avoid a fire.

"I didn't wanna bring 'em!" the young rider yelled. "I didn't wanna bring 'em but dey made me! Dey told me I needed to show him to y'all for your own good and if I didn't, I'd be next!" He moaned into a lady's bosom and she covered his head with her shawl.

Still full of trepidation, Tabithah walked slowly out the door to join the crowd. They peeked into the carriage and then quickly looked away. Some gagged and covered their mouths. Others burst into tears.

"What's going on?" Marie asked as she pushed through the crowd. Some tried to shield her face, but it was too late. The scream that came from her small body could have ripped a woman like Tabithah in half.

The image of her Ezekiel's gutted corpse would haunt his wife the rest of her days.

5

The dream came for him again. The darkness surrounding Harrison was so deep and black that he began to lose his connection to his body, though not so much that he didn't realize that the slightest movement would make the shackles around his wrists and ankles rattle. Or maybe those sounds were coming from another part of the room. He did not know how many others were around him—wherever he was—but judging by the clanging that echoed from one side of the room to the other, Harrison knew that he was far from alone. When the door opened and a light from a large lantern penetrated the space, Harrison looked around and saw about twenty negro men in coffles. So much blood ran from their bodies that it was impossible to tell where one man's wounds ended and another's began. Harrison wondered how long they would be kept there. How long it would be till they would be told to march somewhere else and be sold again. But Harrison blinked and realized that this was no dream. He was fully awake, absorbing everything. Perhaps this wasn't slavery, but whatever it was, it was close. Everyone groaned and wept. An unspeakable heat, coupled with a horrible stench, permeated the room. Harrison hung his head low and bit down on his tongue until his mouth tasted of iron. Ezekiel was right, he thought, and all he wanted right now was to tell his friend that.

The forceful knocks at the door had come soon after Tabithah left that morning. The men carried whips and blackjacks, and their hands caressed their weapons when they ordered Harrison out into the street. It turned out that all of his asking about how and when to get to Shreveport got back to a few officers, who were informed that a negro Union soldier was carrying himself with too much pride and authority.

"A vagrant nigger at that," one of them yelled while the others cackled.

"Who do you work for?" another asked.

"I don' work for no one," Harrison responded, looking his interrogator straight in the face, then a brief flash of light obstructed his view. When his vision returned, his cheek was on the ground and his face lay beside a boot raised a few inches off the ground. Next thing he knew, he was being dragged by his legs along the dirt road. They slapped shackles on his wrists and ankles, then threw Harrison into a cart like a sack of flour, where his elbows and legs hit other detained negro men. He could not move to sit upright, so he lay across the wooden planks lopsided. From what Harrison remembered of the bumpy ride, the white men were saying that there couldn't be too many niggers walking in and around Natchez with nothing to do.

The cart eventually stopped and all the detainees were grabbed one by one and ordered to walk in single file to a jailhouse, where an officer with a huge rifle hoisted over his right shoulder was standing at the entrance. They walked inside, where only a sliver of light came from a window too tall for any of them to reach. Harrison could tell from the incessant loud groans and sounds of metal impacting a surface that there had to be dozens of men already in the cells. Traces of their silhouettes rendered them ghostlike; the echoes of their dissent were all too familiar.

Harrison was directed to an already crowded cell, where the heat from other bodies radiated from one corner to the next. The jailhouse opened again and more negroes were brought inside Harrison's cell. The heat had risen so much that Harrison was struggling to breathe.

Time passed by slowly. Harrison's senses were overwhelmed as he drifted in and out of consciousness, unable to discern if the noises reverberating from one side of the room to the other were as thunderous as they sounded, or if his memories were overlapping onto the present moment. The jailhouse door eventually opened again and Harrison silently pleaded to God that he would not suffocate. Instead, one of the officers who first seized him at home came over to Harrison's cell and unlocked the door.

"Come with me, boy," the officer said, and grabbed ahold of Harrison before he could center himself on his own two feet. "You sure are a lucky nigger," he added before relieving Harrison of his shackles.

Harrison was brought outside under the light of the full moon, where he saw Tabithah standing between two white men, a black shawl covering her head. She'd slackened her posture, perhaps to make herself look smaller than the two officers, whom she matched in height.

"This here negress done saved your life, I reckon. You two git on outta here before I change my mind and lock you both up."

Tabithah cupped Harrison's left cheek. "C'mon, dear. Let's go home."

They'd taken a few paces when one of the officers called out, "Work starts on Monday! I better see that you reported there."

Harrison stopped.

"Just keep walkin', please," Tabithah begged him.

Harrison looked around and saw that the city market was adjacent to the jailhouse. He recalled on his first day back in Natchez, the two white women begging not to have their homes taken away. The joy he felt then. The stupidity he was burdened with now, thinking that he once believed in a different world—one that he fought for. The shackles that bound him as a slave were the same that bound him as a freedman, if any negro could even label themselves as a freedman.

As they made the half-mile journey down one of the trails leading to the riverfront, Harrison asked, "What did ya do?"

"Let me get you home first," Tabithah said as they walked further along the docks.

"What did ya do?" Harrison repeated as soon as they approached his home.

"Look," Tabithah snapped. "Your mouth has gotten you into more trouble den you realize. Now you hush up and get inside and I'll tell you." She helped Harrison into his shack and propped his legs up in his bed. She was about to fetch some water when he grabbed her wrist.

"What . . . did ya do?"

"I freed you, das what. I paid for you to get out of jail but dey also wanted you to start workin' or else dey would keep my money and you wit dem. So I promised dat you would start work next week. We both would. Chicory Plantation. We till the land, get a profit of de shares, and give some to de boss. Das how I got you out, and how we'll make our livin'."

"Ya signed me up to be a slave."

"I signed you up to live!" Tabithah's voice cracked. "How can you say dat after all I've done—ungrateful!"

"How much did ya pay to free me?"

Her eyes dropped to the floor. "Seventy-five cents."

Shocked, Harrison released her wrist and Tabithah left the shack.

When she returned with water, he looked at her gently. "Ya spent your earnings from de Freedmen Bureau to free me?"

"Yes. Now please drink." She held the glass up to his lips, and he sipped from it.

"Did 'Zekiel ever come back around?"

Tabithah's eyes sank to the ground.

Harrison sat upright in bed and leaned toward Tabithah, moving his head around to get a good look at her though her eyes refused to meet his gaze.

"What's wrong?"

Tabithah covered her face, crying into her hands. "Oh Jesus . . . I can't. I can't, I can't, I can't."

"Can't what?"

Once Tabithah was able to compose herself, she wiped her cheeks and said, "Dey killed him, Harrison. Over tryna bargain for better wages on de plantation. Dey ruined his whole body. Even had a young boy ride in his body here to mark him too as a message. De whole village saw it. And poor Marie—I fear she turn crazy now."

"No." Harrison lifted himself up and began limping toward the door.

"Harrison—" Tabithah tried to reach out to him, but he brushed her aside.

He flung open the front door and stepped outside, Tabithah close behind him. He saw that the light was on inside Ezekiel's home. At this time of the night, Ezekiel would usually be drinking moonshine or dancing with Marie while the kids slept. Harrison peered through the window and saw Marie on the ground, shaking her head feverishly while a group of elders crowded around her, fanning her forehead and praying. The children were huddled together in the corner and crying. When Marie raised her arms in the air and opened her mouth to scream, the agonizing sound rendered Harrison breathless. He couldn't stand it anymore.

"Help me to de river," he said to Tabithah.

She led him down to the bank, holding on to him tightly, and when they reached the Mississippi, Harrison knelt down and closed his eyes. His body rocked in rhythm with the waves lapping around him. His chest heaved until the tears came out like a deluge. Tabithah put her arm around him, and Harrison shook his head. "Naw, naw, naw. You don' understand. Dat was my friend. Dat was my friend. Dat was MY friend!" He hit his chest with his fist to punctuate each word. Tabithah encircled his neck with her arms and pulled him closer. "Why do dat to him? Why do dat to him?!"

She shushed and nodded. "I don' know, dear. I don' know."

"I can't—" Harrison inadvertently touched his face, his right eye puckered shut. Possibly from that boot, he didn't remember. But what he could recall was Ezekiel pointing to his own missing left eye as he spoke about the love he had for a woman way back when.

"Can't what?" Tabithah asked.

Harrison drew another breath. He looked out toward the expanse of the Mississippi, where no boats were arriving or departing. He thought of Ezekiel and he thought of Tirzah. He thought of her letters, he thought of the ad he'd placed, and he thought of the white men who'd come for him. Then he caught sight of Tabithah, who never left his side—loving, doting, but most of all . . . here. The sadness in the muscles and lines of his face melted away into a poised resolve. Tabithah noticed it too, how his profile transformed. Under the moonlight, she felt the tides swell in her body.

He looked at Tabithah with determination in his eyes and said, "Marry me."

JUNE 1865—
TIRZAH

6

Some 160 miles from Natchez near the banks of the Red River in Shreveport, Tirzah was tidying up her mistress's vanity when she heard hysterical weeping coming from the first floor. At first, Tirzah rolled her eyes—her mistress Athéné's inability to hold back water could rival the Mississippi's. She cried over the most trivial matters: a stain on her bodice, a wrinkled linen tablecloth, missing a note or two at a Chopin recital. Tirzah stopped fluffing the dust from Athéné's perfume bottles when she heard a loud thud, and she raced down the stairs. Athéné was lying on the floor with the back of her hand on her forehead. She looked so ridiculous that Tirzah covered her mouth. After a beat, Tirzah composed herself and affected concern. "Miss, are you all right?" Athéné groaned and waved her other hand in the air. Tirzah fetched her a glass of water and lifted the woman's head to rest on her lap.

"What's the matter?"

Athéné gasped for air, and Tirzah fanned a hand in front of her face. Her mistress sat up and gulped down the water, then coughed. "The war! It—it's over! Our world has come tumblin' down!"

Tirzah gasped and struggled to breathe.

Beside Athéné lay a newspaper opened to page two. Tirzah snatched it and read:

As all resistance to the United States authorities have ceased throughout the length and breadth of the late Confederate States, it behooves every citizen to conform his actions to the new order of things. Further resistance will be fruitless, heartburnings and a rancorous hatred impotent, and a retirement from all interest in public concerns impolitic. The country is still our home and must be that of our children through all future years.

New Labor System.

Gen. Herron's General Orders No. 20, dated Shreveport June 3rd., 1865, says "there are no longer ony slaves in the United States." Slavery was destroyed by the "Emancipation Proclamation," January 1st. 1865,

A different system of labor has been adopted, the negro will hereafter receive a moderate compensation for his labor, and

Tirzah dropped the newspaper. She couldn't read any further. For months, she'd heard rumors from other negroes that the war was coming to an end soon, but she dismissed them as wishful thinking. Tirzah had resigned herself to the belief that she'd always be a slave—same as her mother and the mothers before her. But now, she felt as if her body and its possibilities were expanding so fully and quickly that she might burst, if not for her new status, then for the exhilaration of reuniting with her beloved Harrison.

Delirium from the news set in. With no one but Harrison on her mind, Tirzah stopped consoling Athéné, rose to her feet, and started toward the front door.

Her mistress shot up. "Where do you think you're going? I haven't told you that you could leave."

Athéné couldn't have been much more than a hundred pounds, and Tirzah, while petite, had more meat and musculature to over-power her. Tirzah stared at Athéné until her posture crumbled as Tirzah wouldn't defer to her even in gaze. Then, Tirzah removed the apron strap from around her neck and studied Athéné's face. She was afraid that if she stared any longer at her hazel eyes, she'd either start to pity her or cackle at the sudden shift in circumstances. So Tirzah left Athéné standing there, hoping that she wouldn't come after her.

When Tirzah stepped outside, the heat almost pushed her back in. The air was imbued with the heaviness of expectation. Even the passerines flying in formation above Tirzah's head appeared to be full of purpose. The tightly knit neighborhood was situated on the lower-numbered blocks that ran between Fannin and Caddo streets. West of this area were the Texas and Pacific Railroad tracks, which served as the dividing line between the wealthy and the common. The former lived on elevated ground near the western part of the Bayou Cross, where breezes were abundant, whereas the latter sat low in muddy, mosquito-ridden areas.

This famed enclave was now unspeakably quiet. There were no drivers pulling carriages down the semipaved roads, no women gossiping underneath the canopies of their umbrellas, no children frolicking. But there were negroes poking their heads out from behind the pillars of estates and out of second-floor windows. They were afraid to speak, but language still found its way through their collective wide-eyed expressions toward one another. Is it true? Is it really true?

Their unspoken connection was interrupted by a wave of cries that exploded from every home. Several women, young and old, were sobbing. Some unlatched their windows to scream into the air, and others traipsed onto their verandas. A few almost fainted in the same fashion as Athéné—the back of one hand pressed to their forehead, the other hand dangling the newspaper. All bemoaned the fall of the Confederacy and what might become of their lives now. Tirzah beamed and bit down hard into her knuckles so that she would not scream for joy.

There was no time to waste. If she was free, then she was leaving Shreveport to go back to Mississippi to reunite with Harrison. She would go in the opposite direction and head south toward the railroad, where she'd demand that the conductor put her on the next train to Vicksburg, so help her God. As Tirzah began walking, she realized that she had no money. She lowered her head as she remembered the most precious thing she once had: her wallet. Harrison had given it to her one Christmas Eve so that she'd always have a place to save the money he was confident she'd make on her own after the war. But Spencer had made her and other slaves march from the Phoenician without any possession besides the clothes on their backs. Upon arriving in Shreveport in June of 1862, a month after Natchez surrendered to Union forces, Tirzah realized with sadness that the wallet was gone. Now as a freedwoman, the possibilities the wallet held—to hold money or even to pawn for a train ticket to Mississippi—damn near made her want to stamp her feet in anger at its loss.

No one was present at the rectangular-shaped brick-and-stone depot upon Tirzah's arrival. After completing a full revolution around the structure, she spotted a negro man on the tracks, heaving items onto a cargo car. The outside of the car was dusty, and there was no conductor and no passengers either. No ticket sellers. No carriages pulling up outside the station to drop anyone off.

She waved at the negro man with a "Hey!"

He stopped what he was doing when he caught sight of Tirzah's beauty. He approached her and tipped his hat once they stood in front of each other. "G'day, ma'am."

"Good day. I need to get to Mississippi. Natchez, specifically. But I hear this railroad can take me to Vicksburg, and I'll manage once I get there. Now I don't have any money on me but I was wondering if you could find it in your heart—"

"Can't do that, ma'am."

Tirzah cut her eyes at him. "Oh. You're one of them."

He shook his head. "Ain't nothin' like dat. See, dere ain't no route to go to Vicksburg. Not no more."

"What do you mean?"

"You ain't know, ma'am? De war ruined alladat. Any railroad line east of Monroe de Yankees messed up, tore up, blew up. You wanna go to Mississippi den you gon' need a driver and dat's a long, long way. I reckon no negro would take you dere and een if he did, he a fool. I guess he'd only git 'bout fifteen, twenty, twenty-five miles wit you before some of dese white folks grab ahold of him."

Tirzah was beside herself from the man's words and stepped backward. "Are you sure? You're not lying to me, are you?"

"Ma'am," the negro said, pulling the visor of his hat forward to block out the rising sun, "what reason would I have to lie? Now you g'on back to where you stay. 'S not safe for a woman to just be walkin' 'round right now. Free or not."

Tirzah turned to leave but only made it a few paces before looking back over her shoulder. "You sure? I mean, are you really sure?"

"Yes, ma'am. My people from Delhi. If I knew I could get to 'em, do you think I'd be standin' here talkin' to you?"

Tirzah stayed quiet.

"Dat's right. I'd be folding myself into one of dem bags I put on de car and smugglin' myself dere."

Tirzah thanked him as sincerely as she could, and as she made her way back to town, she wasted no time wallowing in self-pity. Harrison would've wanted her to keep going no matter what, and there was one man in town who might risk being a fool in order to make her happy. A free person of color even before the war, this man was commanding and tall, with laughter that brought the rain in and anger that made the trees listen. Some people believed he was the closest thing to High John de Conqueror, maybe even one of his grandsons, though he denied it, even if he never knew his own father. He also was Tirzah's first friend in Shreveport.

AT THIS TIME OF THE DAY, THAT MAN WOULD USUALLY BE MAKING deliveries to the well-to-do whites in town. Tirzah crossed the railroad tracks to Texas and Fairfield Avenue in a neighborhood that negroes referred to as "the Bottoms," called such because it was the southernmost, lowliest part of Shreveport. It was here where Tirzah heard the cries of negroes coming from inside the town's only negro church. The building was no bigger than three or four slave cabins put together, and had been built by the man she sought and a few of his friends with their bare hands. In those days, Tirzah would work quickly in the Bringier home so she could have time to go out into town—under the guise of completing tasks for Athéné—and watch the men as they worked. Tirzah would observe how gently they'd pick and move lumber—no throwing, grunting, or cursing even when the air was wet and muggy. She wondered what else their hands could touch as gently, and silently asked her beloved Harrison to forgive her.

As she approached the church house, it looked as if it were quaking. Cries and singing were interspersed with the preacher's towering voice rising above the crowd. When she carefully opened the church doors, she saw women lying on the floor with white cloths over them, men young and old kneeling with their hands raised to the cross at the altar, and folks of both sexes speaking in tongues. The whole congregation was slain in the spirit. The Holy Spirit took over and warped everyone into ecstasy.

In the back of the sanctuary, Tirzah found herself smiling at the blissed bodies all around her. She started to tiptoe around a few heads to advance to the front and catch the preacher's attention, but that wasn't necessary. The man she sought, Isaac, stopped speaking as soon as he spotted her. High above the others at his podium, he stared at her until some elderly woman saw fit to sing louder to fill his absence. Tirzah stopped, and the two watched each other from their respective places. The longer his brilliant green eyes stayed on her, the more pliant her body became.

Instead of moving closer to the podium, she sat in a nearby pew and bowed her head. Her knees would not bend, and the spirit didn't come to her. She was too ashamed. Too ashamed to raise her hands in gratitude. Too ashamed to pray out loud because she suspected someone knew about their connection. When Tirzah lifted her head, Isaac was still staring at her. The right side of his mouth lifted into a boyish grin. Isaac's deliberate pause had some congregants shouting for Isaac to take his time preaching, believing that he stopped because of the Holy Spirit overwhelming him.

"The book of Matthew tells us that the faith of a mustard seed can move mountains—whew!" He tapped his podium and shook his head. "But I know this congregation had the faith that could smite the institution of slavery and all those who upheld it! And that's why we are here today, because God has not forgotten us! Just like he hadn't forgotten the Israelites in the wilderness. We have been brought out of Egypt and we can rejoice!"

Then Isaac began to hop and shout around the pulpit. The crowd cheered him on. Tirzah remained silent, knowing that it wasn't just God that made his spirit move like that. She squirmed in her seat and pressed her inner thighs together so forcefully that by the end of the benediction, her skin started to chafe.

She was still sitting with her eyes closed and her hands clasped in her lap long after the other congregants left the church house. Eventually, she felt a gentle touch on her shoulder and opened her eyes.

"Isaac," she said. He stood close to her, a white man beside him.

"I didn't think I'd see you after—"

"Shh!" Tirzah shushed him, not wanting the white man to hear the rest. "Let's not talk about that in the house of the Lord."

Isaac glanced over at his companion and said, "Albert, I would like to introduce you to Tirzah. Tirzah, this is Albert, and he is going to be assisting us around here."

Tirzah shook the man's hand. "It's nice to meet you."

"Likewise. I've heard so much about you."

Tirzah glared at Isaac. "Well . . . hopefully it was appropriate and about good and godly things."

"Indeed it is. Isaac, I'll be back later." With that, Albert hurriedly left the church.

"What all did you tell that man?" Tirzah's voice echoed in the empty space as she spoke.

"Not what you think. I promise. Tirzah." Isaac smiled and sat down beside her in the pew. "We did what we did and it felt good. I mean . . . I hope it felt good to you."

Tirzah blushed, then assumed a more serious demeanor. "Yeah but . . . we weren't married."

"I would've married you, and I still would. But you know why I didn't ask." He shook his head. "We found each other there that night and . . . the flesh is flesh for a reason: It's weak, vulnerable, and desiring of touch."

Isaac was right that she knew why he wouldn't ask. Tirzah didn't love him, not the way she loved Harrison. But he damn sure wasn't a simple friend either. There was no language for the way her heart held space for Harrison, but also for Isaac.

Back in May, there had been an extraordinarily high yield of beans, potatoes, and berries. The harvest season had coincided with the church's annual revival to renew the devotees' faith in God through repentance and to bring in new converts. The cooks worked with the sugarcane laborers to make the most potent pies and rum for their masters. The cotton laborers helped one another exceed their daily quotas, and the maids of every main house cleaned, fluffed, and washed down all its surfaces before sundown. When all the full-bellied white folk were sound asleep, completely sated of food and liquor, negroes from the plantations of Caddo Parish headed to the woods to hear Isaac preach by the light of just a few lanterns. Standing next to a tree stump, Isaac spoke about God's everlasting glory and love for all his children, then he referenced the book of Exodus. Some of the congregants, who obsessively looked over their shoulders out of fear that Isaac's words might be overhead by a passing white man, left the gathering. Then he turned to the war—that he knew that the South was losing, and they'd all be free soon—and more people trickled out after that. By the time Isaac moved to the importance of the negro vote, Tirzah was the only one who remained.

She'd sat down beside him on that stump, placed her hand on his left knee, and said, "I believe you. Even if I think you're crazy and asking for trouble."

"If that is so, then why do you continue to believe me?" he asked, his expression changing from confident to uncertain.

Tirzah shrugged. "Because believing is better than thinking this is it. You think Christ was on that cross, in spite of all that pain and suffering, thinking that there had to be something better?"

Isaac looked straight ahead. "No one's ever asked me that. But yes, I do."

"Sure you do. Because if not, why would you be up there preaching?"

Isaac returned his attention to Tirzah and did a double take.

"What?" Tirzah asked.

"There's this strange, white light around you." Isaac shifted his lantern from left to right and his jaw slightly hung open. "Huh."

"What?"

"I thought it might've been just the lantern, but the light is still there and it's getting bigger."

"Where?" Tirzah looked behind her.

Isaac laughed and said, "It's gone."

Tirzah stopped and pursed her lips. "Were you lying to me?"

"You think a pastor would lie? Soon after giving a sermon at that?"

"Maybe not."

Isaac shook his head slowly. "Harrison is a lucky man, boy, I tell you."

Tirzah suddenly shot to her feet and patted down her dress. She hadn't been giving a single thought to Harrison and hearing his name filled her with sorrow. She looked up at the loblolly pine trees that seemed to touch the edge of the moon and tapped her feet on the dirt and mulch beneath them to stop the dam from breaking. Suddenly, she burst into tears. Isaac took her hands in his and tried to look at her face, but she turned away from him.

"What's wrong, Miss Tirzah? You can talk to me."

Her limbs felt heavy, but she eventually stopped hiding. She regarded Isaac and said, "Here I am talking about faith tonight without realizing how much my faith's been on its way out."

"I don't understand."

"What if how it is now is what it will always be? What if I never see him again?"

"You will see him again. I'll take you myself if I have to."

Tirzah laughed and wiped her nose. "Why are you so kind to me?"

Isaac took a beat. "Because when you've been visited by an angel, you take heed."

"An angel? Where? When?" She laughed.

He touched the bottom of Tirzah's chin and moved her face closer to his. "I'm talking about you, Miss Tirzah. That light I saw around you meant you're an angel to me. Do you believe me?"

Speechless, Tirzah raised her eyebrows. Finally, she nodded.

"Then believe me when I say you'll see him again."

"But why would you believe that for me and another man?"

"Because you're a good woman, Miss Tirzah. You're beautiful . . . divinely so. Your smile makes the sun seek shade from embarrassment."

After that, everything happened quickly. Perhaps it was Tirzah who moved her face closer to his, but their lips met in the middle. Isaac knocked the lanterns over so that not even the foxes and crickets could see as he kissed her all over her face while removing her clothes. Very soon, there wasn't a part of her body that his lips hadn't touched. Tirzah lay flat on her back and watched the stars expand and pulsate until she thought her mind had run loose from her head. He climbed on top of her, and something inside her shifted each time he touched a place she thought no one else could reach. She clawed at his back, half afraid of her own pleasure. He could feel her tightening and contracting around him and gently pressed a hand over her mouth. When she pushed out that final scream, it surged to the heavens before reaching like roots back deep inside her body so that the memory of this night would always remain there. After they finished together, Tirzah stood up, giving Isaac one last glimpse of her: same as when he'd first seen her, all dirtied up, though this time, it was his doing.

Since that night, Tirzah had been able to avoid Isaac, but now, in the church house, they sat awkwardly side by side, their bodies tense.

"You know . . . a Freedmen's Bureau is coming here soon," Isaac said at last.

"Freedmen's Bureau?" Tirzah asked.

"Yes. That's why Albert is here. He and a few other well-meaning white folk are planning to set up an office and they're employing a bunch of people, including myself. We'll start a school and help other negroes find their loved ones with ads and all of that."

"Ads?" Tirzah thought of Harrison.

"Yes."

"I see . . ."

"You should consider becoming a teacher, you know. You can read and you can teach others. Folks around here are going to get jobs . . . real jobs with pay."

"I'm not trying to stay here, Isaac. I have to go and I have to go as soon as I can, but the railroads are ruined. I need to find another way, which is why I wanted to talk to you."

"I'll ask my boys."

"Thank you."

"Do think about the teacher job. You can save up money. You're going to need to take a steamboat at some point."

Tirzah winced as she ran through estimable numbers of how long she'd have to work to afford a steamboat ticket and how much patience Harrison could maintain after years of being in a war without her.

"What's wrong?" Isaac asked.

"I know working is the most reasonable plan, but I don't want to keep Harrison waiting any longer without even a word to him to hold on."

"The railroads may be torn up but the post office isn't."

Confused, Tirzah leaned her head to the side and pursed her lips.

Isaac patted her on the shoulder. "You have an ability that not many negroes in town have. You can write him a letter."

Tirzah sat up straight, her body animating with renewed hope.

1

Tirzah wasn't sure of the actual day that it happened, but she knew it had been in August, when the field slaves were planting corn before the cotton bolls came in. The heat showed out that day, and all the windows in the main house had been lifted because everyone was beginning to smell. Tirzah was in the kitchen preparing duck stew for lunch when she realized that she was alone. Neither the head maid nor her underlings were nearby. She didn't hear their whispers in the pantry or their footsteps approaching. For years to come, Tirzah would turn this uncharacteristic quiet, the feeling that something was wrong, over in her mind.

Maybe, Tirzah wondered in the nights to come, she'd been too focused on not burning the roux when she felt a coolness on the back of her thigh. Then a hand crawled up her dress from one side. She intended to ignore it because he always did this when no one was around. But this time, he curved his hand around to reach her private parts, and flexed his fingers to spread her apart, and then curled them again, planting nail marks into her skin. She whirled around to gently protest but the strong smell of wine coming off his body had her at a loss for words. He placed his free hand over her mouth and leaned forward. His wavy brown hair tickled her forehead, and his lecherous member poked her in the middle.

In that short and still moment when neither of them moved, Tirzah pitied him, even with that wicked grin on his face. Spencer had barely scratched twenty-three, and his entire family already recognized that he would not live up to a sliver of his father's shadow. He'd lasted only one semester at Princeton, and upon his return, overplayed his hand on horse bets, which surely would have seen him dead if he hadn't been Mercer Ambrose's firstborn. His unsavory reputation clung to him like a stench—everyone in town knew about his activities at the saloons along the river landing. His mother, Catherine, worried aloud that someday an unpedigreed woman would knock on their door with his baby in her arms. Tirzah would nurse her mistress's fevered head as Catherine dreamt up ways to get rid of such a woman: send the child to Paris to be brought up properly before introducing him to society, send them both away to a convent, or set the wheels in motion for them to have a boating accident somewhere near the Mississippi. The third option seemed the most likely, as Catherine was no stranger to violence. Tirzah once saw her tie up a slave who'd lain with her husband and rub snuff into her eyes. That slave, now partially blind, was sold the next week. She'd poisoned Tirzah's own mother, Fortuna, for the same reason, leading to a slow and painful death. All the house slaves knew Catherine had done it. Evelyn, the head maid, taught Tirzah the art of the root to protect herself when she noticed that the master's eyes lingered too long on Tirzah's body as she served him dinner. It was plain as day: Tirzah grew up resembling the Ambroses more than any of their white children. And now, Tirzah thought, what would Catherine do to her if she discovered that her son inherited at least one thing from his father: a hunger for negro women?

Tirzah whimpered as she leaned against the stove. Spencer held her waist and placed his dominant foot behind one of her ankles to knock her down to the ground. She stayed completely still, learning from previous occasions to refrain from resisting. There was a burning smell emanating from the cast-iron stove where the roux was surely ruining, and she wrestled to get up to remove the pot from the cooking surface. In retaliation, Spencer pushed her hand onto the stove and she yelped. In a knee-jerk reaction, Tirzah shoved him with all the strength in her, and he fell flat on his back onto the wooden floor. He sat up slowly and wiped spittle from one corner of his mouth. She held out her hands in front of her.

"Please," she said. "Please."

He sprang up, grabbed a chunk of her hair, and dragged her into the scullery in the back of the house. About half of the way there, Tirzah stopped kicking and screaming and went limp. She was supposed to not fight back. Now it was too late. Inside, Spencer slammed the door and the dishes on the counter near the double-chamber sink shook. He grabbed a chair from the pantry adjacent to the washing area, forced Tirzah to sit, and tied her arms around the back post using a few dish rags that he pulled from the storage shelves. Then he took off both of his socks and stuffed them deep into her mouth, though she was too confused to scream anyway. If he wanted her, why would he tie her up? Spencer left the room, soon returning with some deer horns, bells, and men's trousers, which he laid down at her feet. He lifted a pair of scissors from his pocket. With one hand on the shears and a fistful of her hair in the other, he cut. When she began to cry and shake her head, he cut more sloppily. Once he seemed satisfied with the heaps of hair on the floor around them, he stripped off all her clothes, dressed her in the man's clothes he'd brought in, and placed the deer horns and bells on her head.

Tirzah couldn't feel anything by the time he finally removed the socks from her mouth.

"I think it's time to show everyone your new look," he said with a grin. "Don't you agree?"

She didn't say a word.

Excitement in his voice, Spencer helped her to her feet as he said, "Go outside."

"Outside?" Tirzah heard herself asking.

Spencer guided her all the way to the foyer, in front of the large mirror near the entrance door, and Tirzah made the mistake of looking up. She screamed at the boy who stared back at her. She fell back into Spencer's arms and pulled at his collar, begging him to not open the door—that she would do everything, anything if he would let her stay inside. But Spencer flung it open and pushed her out onto the porch, then slammed the door behind her.

"You don't come back in until I say so!" he yelled from the inside.

Tirzah wiped her eyes and faced the fields. For her entire life, she'd observed them like they were a foreign country. In the main house, Tirzah knew everyone, all their gestures and quirks. But those in the open field were virtual strangers to her.

There was nowhere to go but forward though. There was no indication that Spencer would come out to retrieve her anytime soon. He might be drinking more, or he might have passed out in some room on the first floor. But he'd still need to eat. There was still work to be done around the house. Tirzah abandoned the thought. It didn't matter if she remained outside or managed to make her way back to the kitchen, she was going to be punished. With each step she took as she walked out from underneath the portico, the bells rang so loudly that one of the household staff from above called out, "Say, girl, what dat ya got on?"

Tirzah tried to look up, but one of the deer horns pierced her right temple when she moved, and she lost her balance down the steps. She fell into the grass on her side, and a shock wave rippled through her body, either from the impact or the way one of the horns had pricked her skin.

She was lying there when a sudden shade was cast over her body and two hands took her arms and helped her to her feet. She wondered if the goodness of the almighty had interceded to give Spencer a change of heart, and was more than willing at this point to yield to any one of his desires. But this was not Spencer. Before she could make out the man's face, she smelled him, and couldn't detect a hint of alcohol. Instead, his breath smelled of cabbage and meat. A damp cloth was now being dabbed over her eyes, nose, and mouth. She blinked twice, and the gentlest set of eyes met her gaze. The sweat that slicked the man's neck and limbs accentuated his muscles. His tattered trouser pockets were stuffed with tools, and when she looked down at his hands, she saw that they were thick and calloused.

A closed-lipped smile emerged on his face as gradually as the sun stretched over the horizon. Then he spoke: "Ya all right, miss. Ya all right."

The encouragement made Tirzah believe that she actually was all right, if only for a moment. The longer she stared at him, the more the rows of cotton in her periphery faded away, until she felt like they were the last two people on earth.

It was then that she understood the pleasure of being touched by a man with kindness and without aggression. There'd been times when she would eavesdrop on Mercer and Catherine Ambrose holding each other in some private corner of the house, in the dead of night, and she'd wondered what that kind of belonging felt like. Now she wanted this man's name so that she could carry it with her always, and be reminded of the fullness of the world beyond the house, which now seemed so small and insignificant.

But then the man was smacked upside his head by an overseer who had some harsh words for him: "Boy, if you don't leave that wench alone and get back to work."

The man who'd helped her up nodded before climbing the ladder back onto the roof, keeping his eye on Tirzah the entire time. The white man, gripping the whip at his side, sneered. "Just what have you gotten yourself into, huh? You look crazy."

"I—"

The overseer yanked her arm and pulled her out into the fields where the rows of cotton pickers raised their heads to see her arriving. Tirzah closed her eyes, not sure she could take any more embarrassment. When he let go of her arm, she opened her eyes to see that she was standing in the middle of the field, where everyone could see her. It could've been five dozen—maybe even a hundred pairs of eyes on her. She expected someone—everyone—to laugh, but they all stared at her with pity and exhaustion.

"Y'all want some entertainment?" the white man asked. "You." He pointed to one Black man and whistled at him. "Go get the banjo. You." He pointed to an older Black man on the opposite side and clicked his tongue. "Do that thing with your hands. You know."

When the banjo player returned, he and the old man stood a few paces on either side of Tirzah. The white man held his hands up like a conductor and curved them into a downward swoop, and so the banjo player strummed an upbeat tune, which the old man complemented with syncopated claps. Tirzah shifted her weight to one side uncomfortably before a slap on her back informed her that she was the main attraction.

"Dance," the white man growled at her.

Tirzah looked up at him, tears in her eyes, mouthing "please" because her voice could not travel from her diaphragm, but he unfurled his whip.

"Hey!" A Negro woman with a white scarf tied around her head lifted her dress above her knees and kicked out her feet to dance. "C'mon, suga. Dance wit me." She took ahold of Tirzah's hands and spun her around and around. Then pulling Tirzah close to her, she said, "Just keep spinnin'. Y'hear me? Do what I do. Smile. Go 'head and smile." After a few more rotations, Tirzah became dizzy, and the ridiculousness of the scene did in fact make her smile. The claps multiplied. Soon, everyone joined in on the dance, singing and clapping, until the white man sat stewing at their enjoyment.

What followed next existed only in shards of her memory. The music stopped as the overseer violently grabbed Tirzah and dragged her to a nearby chinaberry tree. He ripped her shirt open and walked behind her. Suddenly she heard a huge whooshing sound, then a cracking before her skin was cut open. Screams emptied from her body until sound could no longer be produced. Blood geysered upward. Her back was torn to pieces as she lay on the ground, motionless.

A few negro women carried Tirzah to one of the slave cabins, where they cleaned her wounds and placed sassafras leaves over the skin ruptures. Spencer was waiting right outside the quarters to finish educating Tirzah with the cruelest lesson.

Tirzah yelled herself out of the dream and looked around as dawn began to break. She wasn't at the Phoenician. She wasn't there. She was back in the present, in a shack along with several other freedpeople who decided to leave their masters' house and get work elsewhere after being declared free. This is where she'd sought refuge after leaving the church after Isaac's service. Once Tirzah caught her breath and recognized that she was all right, she rose to her feet to go outside and stretch. But as soon as she stood upright, a sharp pang afflicted her pelvic area, and she yelped at the way it smarted. She attempted to massage her stomach, but the pang came again like the crash of cymbals, and when she closed her eyes to wait for it to pass, she saw a bunch of colors on the inside of her head. Lightheaded and slightly dizzy, Tirzah knew who she needed to go see.

Sena was an old mother of the community, one with whom Tirzah became acquainted through church. With silver hair braided down to her ankles and gray eyes that could pierce through anything, she was only consulted for the most serious of matters. She was a midwife for many of the negro babies born in Shreveport and a healer to the white families too, which is why she was allowed to live alone and unbothered deep in the woods across from where a line of bluffs flanked the Bayou Pierre.

The shack in which Tirzah now lived was equidistant from the negro church and the forests, about a mile in length from west to east. Tirzah always knew that she was on the right path to Sena's home via the forest when she passed by a half dozen lopsided gray tombstones. Sena was the unofficial guardian of this cemetery, her home neighboring the burial grounds. Jewels and chimes hung in the trees surrounding her property. Fresh lilies and tulips blossomed in her front yard. And there she was: sitting in her rocking chair on her porch as though she had been waiting for Tirzah all along. She greeted Sena by grasping the hand that Sena kept firmly on her cane and kissing it.

"Mornin', Miss Sena."

Miss Sena spoke in a honeyed voice that sounded like that of a much younger woman. "What brings you here dis mornin'? You in trouble?"

"No-no-no." Tirzah shook her head. "Whenever Spencer comes for me, I chew the root."

Sena tapped her cane on the ground and stood to size Tirzah up with her eyes. Though the older woman's curved posture made Tirzah tower over her, Tirzah started to sweat under her scrutiny. "C'mon in hea." She opened her front door, and Tirzah entered Sena's home, where hibiscus tea was already brewing. A white votive candle burned on the windowsill. Like always, Sena had partitioned her home so that her own bed, nightstand, and altar were separate from the small cot upon which she motioned for Tirzah to sit down. Then she rinsed her hands in a large bowl of basil-infused water.

After shaking her hands dry, Sena pulled up a chair in front of Tirzah and sat down across from her. "Now . . . what seems to be goin' on?"

"The dream I used to have started up again."

"De one wit de bells?"

Tirzah nodded.

Sena sighed. "Was it brought on by somethin'?"

"Nothing, I don't think. Besides the end of the war, and being free now . . ."

"Maybe you afraid you not really free 'cause he'll come lookin' for you."

"What am I supposed to do to avoid him? Shreveport ain't but so big."

"It's not you who should be avoidin' him, it's he who should be avoidin' you. But he won't 'cause dat boy loves danger more than a pig loves shit."

"And how am I a danger to him?"

"Lie back." After she did what she was told, the older woman touched Tirzah's stomach and felt around with her eyes closed. "Mm," she grunted. "I can feel the memory in your body. 'S tight like a grapefruit. Dat's what happens when pain don't get released. It swell up."

"How do I get rid of it?"

Sena felt around a bit more. "Take off your draws so I can inspect betta."

After Tirzah did as she was told, Sena said, "Deep breath." Once Tirzah's chest rose, Sena reached inside of her with a few fingers and said, "Dere's anotha man, ain't it?"

Tirzah lifted her head. "What?"

"Dis ain't Spencer I'm feelin'. Someone else knows you, and it wasn't too long ago."

Tirzah didn't say anything.

"Hm. You quiet 'cause I'm right, huh. G'on say his name. Might as well now."

"Isaac," Tirzah said reluctantly.

"I knew it. Ah! You feel dat?"

"Feel what?"

"De grapefruit shriveled a bit. Das how you let it go. 'Cause whatever dat man did to you is gon' be lasting whether you know it now or not."

"But I don't love him."

Sena shook her head. "Who said anythin' 'bout love? All I'm sayin' is you betta stick beside him for a short while. Somethin's happenin' and you gotta learn somethin'."

"Learn what?"

"Sit up fa me."

Tirzah sat upright and her eyes caught a pair of carpetbags lying beside the front door. "You leaving?" she asked.

Sena looked over her shoulder and sighed. "Dat I am. Another woman who came and seen me yesterday told me de Black Codes goin' into effect soon."

"The ones from before the war?"

"Unh-unh." She frowned. "New ones. One of dem say no negro can rent or keep a house in this parish and if a white person sign off on it, dey gotta pay a fine of five dollas."

"Five dollars?!"

"Mm-hmm."

"Where are you going to go?"

"I dunno but I ain't stayin' here. I don't trust dese white folk to keep dere word to leave me alone. I already read de signs in my tea leaves. I'm too old. Soon dey gon' have us in slavery all over again. Dey also say we gotta be employed by a white person so if you have anotha option den Spencer before it's too late, I'd say don't be a fool."

"But I don't know no other white person besides Spencer and Athéné."

"Look to Isaac den. He ain't white but he dat gens de couleur type. He got power too."

AS RECOMPENSE FOR SENA'S SERVICE, TIRZAH ALWAYS COOKED Sena a muscadine cobbler. The fruits were already grown on Sena's property and her cabinets were always stocked with spices, butters, and large portions of flour. At noon, Tirzah was walking west out of the woods back to the Bottoms when she saw that there were over a half dozen officers patrolling the area where freedpeople lived and communed with one another. A few white men on horseback gripped the whips riveted to their gun belts. Though no one stopped to interrogate any negro, it didn't matter. Their presence alone was enough of a message, and everyone knew in the stark silence that they may've been free in name but not in reality. Her intuition sounded the alarm from all this surveillance. The codes were coming sooner than expected, Tirzah suspected. She decided to run to the church instead of returning to the shack where she could've caught up on more sleep after last night's nightmare.

Once she was safely inside the church house, she found Isaac,

Albert, two white men, and a few negro men in the middle of a conversation.

The men all lifted their hands at Tirzah's arrival. She peeked out one of the church windows and saw a few patrol officers strolling by on their horses. Then before any of the men could say a word, Tirzah nodded at Isaac and said, "I'll do it."

8

Albert Peachy must have been the most compassionate white man in all of Caddo Parish. Quakers from Chester County, Pennsylvania, Albert's folks had disagreed with slavery long before the war and permitted runaways to hide in their home en route to Canada. Albert and about another handful of white folk, both men and women, arrived in Shreveport at the tail end of the war to set up the Freedmen's Bureau, and they stayed to help sustain it, hoping to provide education and employment for the formerly enslaved. Peachy and his friends also snapped up a few small homes that had been confiscated or abandoned after the war to provide shelter to freedmen who didn't want to live on the plantations where they once labored.

For $1.15 a month, Tirzah would earn her keep as a teacher. Some of what she had left after food expenditures and stamps for her letters to Harrison, she pitched into a pot along with other freedmen to maintain the shack in which they lived and saved the rest for her departure. She'd watched Isaac and his men quickly build the one-room Freedmen's school with funds from the U.S. Department of War. The school was situated just a few feet behind the negro church. Those who lacked brawn had provided lemonade to the workers and made chalkboards with several wooden boards painted black for the teachers and pupils.

In the beginning, Tirzah taught only about ten children, but in a matter of a few months, that number ballooned to fifty-two. When the heat became unbearable, she and another literate freedwoman divided the class in half, keeping one group inside and taking the other out to sit underneath the shade of a pecan tree. Sometimes a Northern white from Albert Peachy's group would come by to help with materials and provide suggestions for lessons. Children were taught in the mornings, adolescents in the afternoons, after they spent the mornings supplementing their parents' work. In the evenings, when the adolescents could take care of their younger siblings, it was time for the adults to learn. Everyone received instruction in reading, writing, and basic arithmetic, and during their rare break times, they shared stories for entertainment. Tirzah found the job rewarding, not least of all because she no longer had to hide her fondness for the written word. If she was not in the classroom, she was in her shack writing or at church strategizing with Isaac about how to stretch their food rations into hearty meals for those who needed them.

Every morning, the women and children would line up behind their front doors and open them only when they heard the signal: four knocks in eighth notes, a rest, then one final knock. Freedmen would come to escort them to either their former masters' homes for paid work or the Freedmen's school.

No freedman or woman found it safe to walk anywhere in Shreveport alone, because white people were raving with anger at the way their former property moved and chatted without their say-so. Many made their disdain apparent with cursing, spitting, and even gun wielding. Others, Isaac told Tirzah, were more discreet. Rumors of disappearances reverberated throughout the community.

One day when Tirzah exited the shack to be accompanied to the schoolhouse with a group of fifteen, Isaac's face wasn't brimming with its usual optimism. He shifted his weight from left to right and demanded that the men do a second and third head count before they got to moving.

"Something wrong?" Tirzah asked.

Isaac took a moment to respond. "I just woke up with a bad feeling today," he said at last. He looked behind Tirzah at the children, who were too busy giggling and swinging from their mothers' hands to notice his concern, then continued, "I've been having these premonitions since I was a little boy. My mother said that was how she knew that I was supposed to be a preacher, because they were God-given. But anything God-given is a responsibility, and it can make even the strongest of men crumble under the weight of it if they don't stay ready."

"Ready for what?" Tirzah asked.

Isaac grinned. "I used to ask the same thing to her. You wanna know what she said?"

"What?"

"If you have to ask, then you ain't ready," he said. He nudged her arm, and they laughed together. The sound of her laugh was the music he most cherished, aside from the praise and worship part of service. Whenever Isaac could make Tirzah smile or turn her face to hide her blushing cheeks, he felt pride in how he could have that effect. He was a man down to his most basic self. Whenever her presence reminded him of this fundamental fact, he felt so seen that the clothes on his back might as well have disappeared.

Their laughter evaporated as they drew closer to a swamp. Something was drifting in the water. Multiple objects, it seemed. A little girl named Josie yelled, "Duckies!" and ran ahead of the crowd. Josie's mother called out her name and ran after her, then stopped suddenly. When the group turned the bend to catch up with them, Tirzah saw the child's mother covering her daughter's eyes and pulling her away from the shore. Several dead negro bodies were floating in the swamp, fruit flies feasting on their flesh. Tirzah dry-heaved at the sight and stumbled off to the side to retch.

"Close your eyes and walk the other way!" Isaac yelled to the group while swinging his hands wildly in the direction they'd come from. "Now!" his voice boomed.

A few of the women sang and clapped their hands to distract the little ones, and the rest of the adults joined in as the group rerouted.

Isaac placed a hand on Tirzah's shoulder. "Lord have mercy," he said.

Tirzah took in as much air as she could so that she could stand up straight. She walked further up the bog and discovered a green wine bottle wedged in soil. It was small enough to fit inside a trouser pocket. A coat of arms was printed on the label. The name itself was fully visible from where Tirzah stood. Her hands balled up into fists before flexing them like claws.

"Madeira Sercial," she read aloud.

"What?" Isaac asked as he approached.

Tirzah repeated herself as she pointed to the bottle.

"What about it?"

Tirzah looked uneasy. "Spencer Ambrose did this. I know he did. He's a violent brute. And a drunk."

"How you figure? White men are known to be violent brutes who drink a lot like every other Southerner."

Tirzah closed her eyes and the rapid and fleeting image of the bells being planted on her head startled her back to the present, where Isaac leaned toward her with concern.

"Because no negro or regular white can afford that liquor. The rich drink it like it's whiskey. It makes them feel better that it comes from Europe—makes them regal. Trust me, I poured it for him plenty of times. I know." Tirzah stretched her neck to look around, and her pupils dilated. She thought of the bells ringing, the alcohol swishing in the bottle, the filthy hands over her body. Isaac reached out to touch her to get her attention and she instantly swatted his hand away.

"I'm sorry," Tirzah said. "I . . . I just got lost in my head."

Isaac shook his head. "It's all right. Don't worry."

The rest of the way to the freedmen's school, Isaac didn't say a word. He clapped in unison with the others, but his eyes glinted with rage. Tirzah stole a glance at him; the muscles in his face were tight, as if he were gritting his teeth.

As soon as they reached the school, he leaned toward her. "Come to my office." He led her to the storage room in the back of the church, where stacks of papers were piled high on top of shelves and desks.

"Watch your step. You may have to squeeze a bit, apologies."

Isaac and Tirzah were pressed practically chest to chest, and they both laughed nervously, trying to move past each other only to knock over a pile of papers.

"Don't worry about that. I'll get it later."

"Is that why you brought me back here? To help you with all of this?"

"Not at all. I wanted you to have a moment to calm yourself before you went into the school."

Her nerves softened at Isaac's compassion. "Well, thank you. But I've seen worse. I know you can say the same."

"I can. But I don't want that to be the case now."

"Indeed."

Tirzah felt desperate to change the subject and looked around at the stacks of papers. "So what's all this?"

Isaac was glad for the question. "Templates for labor contracts, lists of school supplies. Then there are the advertisements from family members. First the ads were sent up to Washington and then down here, but I wish they would've given us more time to prepare before they sent all of this. The other men started sorting through them." He walked past her to a board cluttered with all kinds of notices. "Now I've been spending my free time just tacking them up here."

Tirzah stopped hearing what Isaac was saying as she slowly walked over to the bulletin board. She started at the top left corner before her eyes went down and across.

"Do you see anything?"

"Shh!" She held up her right pointer finger, then pressed it onto the board.

There it was: her name in fine black ink and a large font.

Information wanted for Tirzah Ambrose. She was sold to Mercer Ambrose but last belonged to his son, Spencer Ambrose. Last seen in Natchez, Mississippi. Would like to know the whereabouts of the above-named person for a Harrison Ambrose. Any information may be sent to Piper Carlisle, Freedmen's Bureau of Natchez between Pearl and Washington Streets.

Tirzah tore the ad from the bulletin board and held it in her palms, then clasped them to her heart.

"He hadn't written me back after all the letters I sent him. Now this . . ."

Tirzah held the notice out to Isaac, and once he was finished reading, she saw sadness fall over his face. He struggled to feign a smile. "Oh Tirzah . . ."

Isaac stopped what he was about to say next when he heard some chatter in the sanctuary. One man's voice rose above the rest, spewing threats. Isaac started toward the door, but Tirzah pulled him back. With only a few inches between them, he was able to see the terror in her eyes, the color of her irises altered in the light. He pushed her gently back into the storage room, locked the door behind him after he exited, and went further out into the sanctuary, his back straight, his eyes fixed forward.

Isaac saw five members of his flock standing at attention, watching with plaintive eyes as three white men sneered and laughed while looking around at the sanctuary. The one who disgusted Isaac the most, standing between two gun-carrying henchmen, he recognized immediately as Spencer Ambrose. He reeked of alcohol, and the sweat trapped in his hair emitted an offensive odor.

"Can I help you three gentlemen this morning?" Isaac asked.

Spencer moved his tongue around in his mouth. "I'm looking for

Tirzah." He raised his nose to the ceiling and took in as much air into his lungs as he could before continuing: "Tirzah. Mm." He sucked his teeth hungrily. "Where is she?"

"She's not here. Did you try Sprague Street? I've had people search for open land there for the possibility of a second church. It's getting a bit too small in here for our community."

Spencer stumbled closer until his rancid breath rustled the hairs in Isaac's nostrils. "You lyin' to me, boy?" He raised his nose toward the ceiling again. "I know there's a woman in here. I can smell her."

"I'm sorry?" Isaac said.

"Oh, you will be if I find out you're lyin', boy. We all know the smell of a woman, don't we?" He stretched his arms at his side and guffawed.

"I'm afraid I don't understand," Isaac said.

He closed his eyes and adjusted his trousers. "I can feel her like a dog sensin' a storm. I know she's here, and we're not leaving until I can see her."

As Spencer spoke, Isaac fantasized about ripping out his throat and using the blood as fertilizer for his garden. He strained to keep his hands from balling into fists, but he didn't know how long he'd be able to hide his rage and his fear.

"You can look around if you like."

Spencer's two henchmen rolled up their sleeves, but he held them back, his hands to their chests. "No. I got a better idea. I want your men to do it. I want them to flip over every single pew in this here church until I've got her."

Isaac looked at the five men caught in the crosshairs of this scene. Some rubbed their arms, a few scratched the back of their necks, others shifted from side to side. The demand recalled their deepest shames and regrets, what they had seen or been forced to do to the most vulnerable members of their community at a time when they could not protect them. And here they were, once again stripped of all that made them feel like men, in the house of the Lord, no less.

Isaac nodded for them to proceed, and they spread out across the sanctuary and delicately began turning over each oak pew.

"They ain't movin' quick enough. I'm a busy man. Faster!" Spencer yelled, and the men painfully contorted their faces as they knocked down the remaining pews, strewing flimsy Bibles, fans, and tambourines all over the sanctuary. When there was nothing else left to upset or overturn, Spencer seemed about to give up, until he saw that one of the pulpit curtains was moving. He tiptoed over to the curtain and swiftly pulled it back to reveal a door.

"What's this here?" Spencer asked.

"Our storage room. I also use it as my office."

"Open it."

"There's nothing but papers and papers in there."

One of Spencer's men shoved Isaac and said, "You heard 'im. Open up that door." He felt something hard brush against his backside and froze. If he moved, Isaac thought, he just might kill the other man, not just for this time, but for all the other times. He just might kill him even if it cost him his own life. Suddenly, the two men grabbed ahold of his arms and pressed his face against the door's surface, nearly hard enough to break his nose.

Isaac wasn't sure if he and Tirzah could communicate without sound, but he hoped that she'd receive his apology for what he was about to do. He fidgeted with the lock and closed his eyes when the door creaked open. But something strange happened: he didn't hear a gasp, a shuffling of feet, or a satisfied exclamation from the ringleader. Quite the opposite: Spencer growled.

When Isaac opened his eyes, he saw Spencer and his men rifling through the office, throwing books and folders around just because they could. None of it mattered though. Their frustration brought a smile to Isaac's face. Spencer might be quick, but Tirzah was quicker.

Spencer ocked some phlegm onto the ground. He turned to his men with downturned lips and a crinkled nose. "Let's go."

The men followed Spencer's orders and left while launching dirty looks at Isaac the whole way out the door. Isaac waited for relief to come to him, but instead he worried that those thugs might find her at her home and drag her off to someplace where he couldn't reach her. He didn't want to leave the church and his men, whose wounded pride expressed itself through their groans and expletives. But Tirzah and her dignity were holier and more worthy of protection than any temple he could think of at the moment.

At Tirzah's, he made the signal—four knocks in eighth notes, a rest, then one final knock—and said, "Tirzah, it's me. It's Isaac. Are you in there?"

Silence.

He made the signal again and stated his name a second time. When he didn't hear anything, he pressed his right hand on the door and leaned forward. His voice cracked as he said, "Please say that you're in there." He almost fell over when the door was flung open. Tirzah tried to catch him, but they both tumbled onto the floor. Before Tirzah could straighten herself out, Isaac wrapped his arms around her and caressed her hair. "I'm so glad that you're okay," he said.

"You came back for me," she said quietly. The last man who'd promised to come back for her hadn't made it before she was forced to leave for Shreveport. Now the man sitting in front of her had returned as though it were as natural as him breathing. She couldn't help but be moved at how much he was mindful of her.

Isaac pulled away from her and held her face in his hands. "Of course I came back for you. I will always come back for you."

She rose to her feet and walked to a window to gather some air. Sadness engulfed her.

"As long as I stay here, Spencer is always going to be after me."

Isaac looked confused while rising to his feet as well. "But why would a rich man who had many slaves come for you and only you?"

Tirzah pursed her lips and leaned her head to one side. "Now you know better than to ask a woman that."

He bowed his head. "I apologize."

"With all due respect, Pastor, you don't know what it's like. When a white man wants to control you in ways beyond your labor, they want to see what the rest of your body can do, and none of your parts is safe."

No matter how much Isaac blinked, he could not stop the tears from welling up. He closed his eyes and took a deep breath. "I do know what that's like," he confessed before blinking his eyes open.

Tirzah's eyes narrowed in confusion just before her entire face expanded, her mouth gaping wide in shock as she comprehended what he'd just said to her. He had never shared it with anyone and likely never would again. "I wasn't born free, you know. I hope you don't think less of me as a man for it now."

Tirzah shook her head. "As long as you don't think of me as any less of a woman."

"Never."

"But you know, Pastor, you can't be in two places at once and protect me all the time. He may come back around tomorrow or three months from now. I don't know. But I know that I hate that man. If God would allow me one exemption of sin, it would be to hate him for the rest of my life, and I hope he goes before I do."

Isaac stepped back from Tirzah and saw her hands balled up into fists. "So what would you have done if it was Spencer who broke through the door?"

"By himself?"

"By himself."

"I'd fight 'im."

"You can't bring a fist to a pistol fight."

Tirzah's shoulders dropped. "You're right. I can't."

"Follow me."

Isaac grabbed Tirzah's hand and led her out of the shack and deep into the woods. She wasn't sure what direction they were walking because she did not see the cemetery that Sena monitored, and therefore Sena's home could not be a point of reference. They walked far enough that Tirzah could feel the fabric on her armpits moisten and her throat get dry. The sun was noticeably higher and stronger than when they first started. And just as soon as Tirzah was going to ask how much longer, they exited out of the woods and arrived at a large cabin near the Red River, which demarcated the boundary between Caddo and Bossier parishes.

A horse stood chewing on a plant next to the house. A lush garden full of desert petunias, marigolds, and dianthus grew along the front. Other sections of the land abounded with vegetables—cabbage, tomatoes, and sweet potatoes.

As they approached the front door, Isaac reached deep into his pocket. Tirzah started to get nervous. He placed his key into the lock, and she quickly released his hand.

"What are you doing?" she said.

He laughed as he twisted the knob. "What does it look like I'm doing? I'm opening the door to my house."

"Your house?"

"Yes. Come in." She remained on the doorstep. "Please," he said. "I promise it's all right."

As soon as Tirzah entered, her eyes went to the study on the left-hand side of the first floor. Classics that she only heard of in passing lined the shelves: the *Iliad, Odyssey,* a thick volume of Shakespeare's plays, *Paradise Lost, Moby Dick.* She thought about what it must feel like to read for leisure, not to teach or study or devote yourself to God, but simply to enjoy. She found herself fantasizing about cooking here in the mornings and reading in the afternoons.

"You like it?" Isaac asked. He enjoyed seeing Tirzah's wonder at his home.

"I knew gens de couleur lived nicer than negroes, but I never would've imagined this."

Isaac laughed. "After being manumitted, I saved my earnings and was able to get a few of my people to help build this once I got grown. All the wood outside—we chopped down ourselves from the forest we just walked through."

"But you're out here all by yourself. This is a lot of space for one man."

"For now. Not forever, I hope."

Tirzah cleared her throat and turned her face away as her cheeks flushed. Neither of them spoke for a moment, and then Isaac walked over to the desk and opened the drawer, pulling out a King James Bible, then a revolver.

"Where did you get that?" Tirzah whispered.

Isaac laughed. "As Moses carried his staff to part the Red Sea, I carry a gun in support of us against them."

"I never would've thought of you as a violent man."

"I'm not violent, I'm cautious."

"Hmm."

"Ever held a gun in your hand, Miss Tirzah?"

"What?"

"I'm serious. You ever felt the metal warmed within your palm, the marks on your hands after you grip it, your finger pulling the trigger?"

"'Fraid not."

"Would you like to try?"

IN THE BACKYARD, TIRZAH PERCHED ON A STOOL WITH HER LEGS crossed as Isaac readied the training. He removed the ammunition and magazines from the revolver and filled them with snap caps to prevent an accidental discharge, then proceeded to arrange several stools in a row ten feet from Tirzah. One by one he placed one object on each stool—an orange, a watermelon, a tin can, a head of cabbage. It was hours, though, before he let her pull the trigger. During that time, he taught her the anatomy of the gun, demonstrated for her different stances to get a good aim, and made her practice withdrawing it from her dress to shoot until she was confident in the motion.

Eventually he said, "Now, go ahead and shoot."

"Which one?"

"Any one. If multiple people are coming at you, does it matter?"

Tirzah closed her eyes and pulled the trigger, hitting the leg of the middle stool.

He chuckled. "I knew you were going to do that, which is why I didn't pack the gun with real bullets."

"Do what?"

"You closed your eyes. Keep your eyes open at all times. If you pull your gun, you better mean it. So take your time. Reholster and try again."

Tirzah drew the gun with her arms fully extended and pulled the trigger only to hit the leg of another stool.

Frustrated, she reholstered and said, "I can't do it. It's too hard."

"But you see what you just did?"

"What?"

"You reholstered quickly. You didn't point the gun at the ground or flail your arms or hit a bird or something. Your body is getting used to it now." He inched closer. "If I may?"

Tirzah nodded.

Isaac placed his hand on the small of her back and whispered into her ear. "Best way to get better is to focus like a hawk does on its prey. Remember, you are not the prey, you're the hawk. He's not in control, you are. Control your body here"—Isaac pointed to her temple—"and here," he said as he indicated her dominant hand.

"I am in control of my body."

"Yes."

"I am the hawk and not the prey."

"Not anymore, you're not. That's it." Isaac inched backward and folded his arms across his chest. "Whenever you're ready."

The harder Tirzah focused, the quieter everything around her became, until all she could hear was her heart thumping in both her ears. She silently repeated to herself, *I am the hawk and not the prey.* The phrase helped her to withstand all the memories of powerlessness she carried with her, recollections that usually converged and morphed into one large specter of shame. Once she acknowledged the ghost, though, the shame was overtaken by a sharp rage. She held the gun up to eye level and pulled the trigger. The bullet penetrated the watermelon, causing a dazzling explosion of rind and flesh.

Isaac clapped exuberantly, but Tirzah took the time to reholster the gun and feel the leather next to her skin. The texture didn't feel simply good, it felt liberating. For a minute, she thought of that leather wallet, long lost to her now. One by one, she shot each of the other targets with either one or both hands. Then she asked Isaac to add new targets, but the temperature had now cooled and the sky was a mélange of azure, magenta, and tangerine.

"I think it's time to get you home," said Issac.

He went back into the house, returning with a long black cloak that he placed over her shoulders. Afterward, he jumped into the saddle, then lifted her onto his horse.

Before Tirzah could say a word, Isaac squeezed his calves and heels against the creature's powerful body and lengthened the reins so that the horse could pick up speed. Tirzah held on as tight as she could. Her right cheek pressed against Isaac's back, and the friction triggered by each gallop caused a burning sensation on her face as the pair sped through the evening air.

Once they arrived at her shack, the sky was bronze and the sun's rays were dim as it passed beneath the horizon. Isaac dismounted from the horse and gently helped Tirzah down. Once on her own two feet, she asked, "Why did you go so quickly?"

He replied, "Not safe to be outside at night for a woman like you . . . given all that's happening."

Tirzah nodded.

"I'll see you tomorrow?"

"You will. And thank you for today. I—I've never felt so powerful in my life."

"You're a natural with that gun."

"Thank you."

He kissed her right hand and watched her retreat into the shack.

Once out of her line of sight, he relaxed his posture and took a few deep breaths. He rubbed the horse's snout and thanked it for its patience, and decided to reward it with a short trip to a well in the center of town, where the animal made so much noise as it sloshed around with glee.

"Liar."

Isaac spun around to find Spencer Ambrose emerging from the shadows under the lone streetlight.

"I knew you knew where she was." He pressed his finger to Isaac's chest. "I knew it." He tapped to punctuate each word. "So now we're at a stalemate, and I don't believe in draws. Someone's gotta win or lose. But since I am a charitable fella and I see that you two have a fondness for each other, I'll make you a deal: You get Tirzah to come on back to work for me, and I won't get my boys to handle you for trying to start an insurrection."

"What insurrection?"

"Teaching a negress how to shoot a damn gun. You have three days. And if you care about her, as I'm sure you do, you better do it."

With that, Spencer dissolved into the shadows. Isaac leaned over the well to catch his breath. For a drunk, Spencer was a keen observer. He was right: Isaac would do anything for Tirzah. And so, though it was late, he did not return home.

9

The corpses they came upon in the swamp that morning were not the first that Isaac had seen in a local body of water, and he knew they wouldn't be the last. Seemed like every week he and the other men would come across them on the way to the shacks in the mornings. Sometimes they'd have enough time to properly bury them, other times they'd just have to allow the water to carry the bodies upstream. Whenever Isaac would pass a white man while tending to business affairs or performing his duties to the negro community, he had to force himself not to stare too long, not to search the lines of the white man's face or the depths of his eyes for any signs of murder. But Spencer was different. Isaac didn't need to search his face; Spencer reveled in his barbarity, which made Isaac all the more terrified of the fate that awaited Tirzah. And that was why, after his confrontation with Spencer, he found himself in Albert Peachy's home.

Usually, whenever Isaac would visit, Albert would offer him something to drink or a light meal. This time, however, Albert looked harried when he opened the door, a bundle of wrinkled clothes in his arms. He quickly ushered Isaac in.

"Are you going somewhere?" Isaac asked after he spotted a large mountain of stacked carpetbags on the floor.

Albert stopped moving for a moment. His hair was unkempt,

matted with sweat and pasted all over his face, and his sleeves were rolled up to the elbows. Isaac's smile faded.

"I'm sorry," Albert replied at last.

"Sorry for what?"

"Sorry that I can't stay here any longer."

"You mean . . . you're leaving? I don't understand."

Albert sighed, then motioned for Isaac to sit down beside him at his table. "It's becoming too dangerous for me or any other Yankee to stay here. And you and I both know that the Freedmen's Bureau is only going to be around for so long. The white people around here are getting more fed up by the day, and the local government has been threatening to shut us down anyway."

"Which is why we need you here. I don't want to be discourteous with my words, but—"

"Say what you feel."

"You know if admirable white men like yourself are a part of our projects, other white men are less likely to attack the members of my community."

"I wouldn't be too sure about that."

"How do you mean?"

"You remember Pennock Farlow? That boy with the long hair and clothes too big for him?"

"I do, yes."

"He's dead now. He along with four negroes who were a few miles outside of Shreveport. Some say they were talking to people about voting, and they were on their way back home after a long night. Others say they weren't doing anything at all. I went down to the coroner's office to see him and—" Albert choked up and briefly held up his right pointer finger as a request for patience. "How am I going to tell his mother, Isaac? I've never seen anything so terrible in my life and I don't believe I ever will again!"

"What about the others who were with him?"

Albert's tears subsided and he lifted his face slowly from his palms. "We haven't been able to find them. But after what they did to Pennock, I think it's better that we don't."

Isaac leaned back in his seat and massaged his temples.

"I'm sorry, Isaac. It's just not safe for us anymore."

"And what about the freedmen? What are we all supposed to do?"

"I don't know. None of us do. But my first order of business is getting out of Shreveport."

"Pennsylvania is a long ways from here."

"That it is. Now—" Albert stood to his feet and started making his way to the bedroom. "I wish I could be a better host, but I have much packing to do and no time to waste."

"It's about Tirzah!" Isaac called out.

Albert pivoted on his right heel. "No. Please don't tell me—"

"No, no, she's fine. But she has to leave too, Albert, so help me God."

"Isaac—"

"It won't take long. Now I thought about it while I was on my way over here and . . . I just need you to sign some documents stating that she can leave the town and the parish."

Albert frowned.

"It would only take a few minutes to do."

"Isaac . . ." Albert held up his hand while walking toward him, which only made Isaac accelerate his speech.

"She's under Spencer Ambrose's eye, Albert. She—"

"Spencer?" He shook his head. "Absolutely not. No. I'm not getting involved with anything to do with him. I value my life too much."

"And what about hers?"

"How dare you ask a question like that?"

Isaac lunged at Albert, gathered his shirt with both hands, and pinned him against the wall, raising him so his feet were dangling over the ground.

"You know I can't fight back," Albert managed.

Isaac looked down at the white of his own knuckles and the

tightness of his fists before letting him down slowly so that he wouldn't fall to the ground. He rubbed the back of his neck. "I'm sorry. I . . . I lost myself for a moment."

Albert slowly nodded. "You're forgiven. Look, I know you think highly of her from how much you talk about her. But forging papers isn't the way to do it. Because if he's watching her, you best believe he's got his boys watching her too. Papers aren't going to do anything."

Isaac held up his hand, his fingers shaking. "Take her with you instead. She just needs to get to Mississippi, and you need to pass through it on the way to Pennsylvania. I know the routes—I can help you. Take her." Isaac knelt before him. "Please."

10

Tirzah sat by the window under the moonlight because she could not sleep. Yesterday, she wrote and sent a letter to Harrison, telling him of her most recent news: a negro woman learning how to shoot in broad daylight. She hoped that Harrison would be proud of her. Then again, he might be jealous that another man was teaching her something. But the excitement was like steam from a brewing pot; she had to tell someone. Even now, two days after her shooting lesson, Tirzah could not stop thinking about how the gun felt in her hand or how proudly Isaac looked at her when she hit the target, until both memories merged together. Eventually, Tirzah could not stop thinking of Isaac no matter how much she tried to push him out of her mind.

All of a sudden, Tirzah heard a rustling. She told herself it was just an opossum and ignored the sounds. But once the rustling stopped, it was replaced by a silence that caused all the hairs on her arm and neck to rise. She squinted through the window, and a man in a black, wide-brimmed hat appeared to be walking toward her. Tirzah jumped and the man held a finger to his lips. He removed his hat and the face was Isaac's. He held up both hands in front of him, then cocked his head to the right to signal for her to go to the front door. As soon as she did so, she saw Albert with a large horse and covered wagon a few paces behind Isaac, who placed an extremely large coat across her shoulders, caressing her arms as he stared at her. Eventually, he whispered, "It's time to go, Tirzah."

"Now?" Tirzah whispered back.

Isaac covered her mouth. "Please. We don't have much time before sunrise, not even for you to gather anything. Here—" He grabbed her hand and placed a small pistol into her palm. "Just in case. Don't tell Albert. Remember, he's Quaker," he said with a half smile.

They stared at each other until a breeze moved past both of their bodies. Isaac couldn't restrain himself, and took her into his arms one last time. Her embrace felt different though; her body seemed sturdier and fuller. He pulled backward and looked at her, taking in her whole self.

"I love you, Tirzah," he said. "You hear me? I always have and always will." She opened her mouth, but Isaac shook his head. "Come on."

Isaac lifted her into the wagon bed behind the driver's seat. There, she was shielded by an arched, overhead canvas that was supported by a frame of hickory bows tied to the sides of the wagon bed "Lie down," Isaac instructed her, then moved some of Albert's bags around her body to conceal her. Tirzah was thankful that although the bed was hard, narrow, and short, her body snuggled perfectly within its parameters. "Do not lift your head at all until Albert says so. I don't care if you feel the sun on it or you hear what sounds like friendly voices around. Do not move one bit until Albert tells you. Understand?" Tirzah said nothing and the bags around her stayed in place. "Very good."

Once Albert's wagon pulled out of sight, Isaac reached into his shirt and pulled out the cross hanging from his neck. He recited the Lord's Prayer until his emotions had him tripping over his words and tears wetted his clasped hands.

Full-out weeping now, he was more afraid than he had been in a long time, and he was relieved that no one in his congregation could witness how broken he was. And yet even in his brokenness, he was reminded of Jesus in the Garden of Gethsemane—alone, doubtful, and terrified. And so light found its way back into Isaac's heart because he knew that only the most divine of love could have him in this condition. And maybe there was no need to be afraid. For death, he reminded himself, is never final, and his love would be resurrected in some shape or form. In the midst of his pain, Isaac smiled and counted it as a blessing that he could feel these sensations, that he could love at all.

TIRZAH WASN'T CERTAIN HOW LONG THEY'D BEEN TRAVELING. SHE wished that she could've gone to sleep to make the time go quicker but her anticipation wouldn't allow her. She could no longer feel a breeze and the temperature was starting to rise, indicating that day had broken. They had to be out of Shreveport by now. If Caddo Parish was behind them, even better. But she couldn't ignore how famished she was. Her mouth had begun to water, and she couldn't move her arms to soothe her stomach's rumbles. Tirzah figured that the best thing she could do was to remain calm and envision what it would be like to cross the Mississippi and be back on Natchez soil again. Squeezed between and physically strained by two large bags at each side, another pressed on her chest, and three on her legs, Tirzah could do nothing but imagine. She wondered if Harrison had grown a beard or become stockier during his time in the military. She hoped that he wasn't too upset with her for having left—she'd explain to him that she'd had no choice—and that her letters served as a harbinger of the warmth that her body would bring to his bedside.

"You are some woman, you know that?" she heard Albert say above her. His voice rang in her chest, but she dared not reply. "Good for you for not speaking. Very good. But I know you're awake. I don't think anyone can sleep with all those bags on top of them. Besides, you must be excited." Albert chuckled. "But you are some woman, and I hope you know that. Not many men would risk their lives—and minds—for their woman." He took a beat and continued, "But what I

can't seem to figure out is why Isaac would not go with you. You don't know how much that boy—I mean . . . you don't know how much he would talk about you. I mean, I've never heard him talk about any—"
Albert stopped.

She felt the horse slowly coming to a stop.

"Good day, gentlemen," she heard Albert say.

Tirzah closed her eyes and began to pray.

"Good day," a hoarse voice replied. "What's a man like you travelin 'round here with all these bags?" Tirzah could hear other footsteps circling around the wagon. There were shadows on the canvas. This man wasn't alone. There were three, four . . . maybe five of them.

"Goin' home," Albert said. "Pennsylvania."

"Hmm. Pennsylvania's a long way. What business you have down here anyway?"

Albert paused.

"He asked you a question," another one yelled out to Albert.

"I was down here working with the Freedmen's Bureau."

"Freedmen's Bureau? You hear that, boys? This here Yankee been workin' at the Freedmen's Bureau! And what made you stop?"

"Gotten to be too dangerous. I'm going home to my wife and children where I belong."

"Where you belong . . . hmm." The hoarse voice took a beat. "This sure is a lot of stuff for one man. You sure you not carrying something else?"

"No." Albert's voice went up in pitch.

"I see."

"You don't mind if we take a look, do you?"

Albert stayed quiet.

The hoarse voice spoke in a deeper, more menacing tone. "You have trouble hearing?"

"N-N-No, sir," Albert stammered.

"You look scared. What you scared for?"

Silence.

"Well, if you ain't doin' nothin' wrong then you ain't got nothin' to be scared about. We just two men talkin', ain't we?"

Tirzah held her breath for as long as she could and tried to exhale little by little, but the bags shifted.

"What's that sound?" another man asked.

Silence.

"Did y'all hear that?"

Tirzah tucked her lips into her mouth.

Before she could pray again, light beamed down on her as bags were yanked off the wagon and a patchy-bearded man stared directly into her eyes. Four other white men crowded around him to have a look themselves.

The patchy-bearded man scowled at Albert. "You a nigger lover."

"No! No, I'm not—honest."

"You a nigger lover trying to smuggle his nigger wench out of here."

"No, I'm not, please—"

"If you love a nigger so much, we should treat you like one. You already made your stance clear," another said.

Before Albert could offer another plea, the patchy-bearded man snatched him from the driver's seat and pulled him to the ground, pummeling him with the heel of his boot. As he cried and begged for his life, each of the other men took their turn.

Tirzah didn't have time to waste. Whatever was going to happen to Albert would be finished soon, she could tell; it didn't sound like he was fighting back. The adrenaline catalyzed her as she grabbed the gun on her person and flung herself onto the front seat of the vehicle. One of the men yelled, "Hey, wait! Stop her!" She fired three gunshots in the air, startling the horse enough to whinny and stand on its two hind legs, causing Tirzah to drop the gun while grasping for the reins. The horse began to gallop at full speed toward a canopy of nearby cypress trees, racing so vigorously until it lost its balance. The world turned sideways as Tirzah fell from the driver's seat and everything shuttered into darkness.

When Tirzah opened her eyes again, she could taste blood seeping from her mouth. She saw a few pairs of men's boots standing in front of her face. Before anyone could seize her, Tirzah said the name "Spencer Ambrose" and saw the boots back up a little. In that brief moment, before everything returned to black, Tirzah felt herself giving up. Whatever the men were going to do, they were going to do. At least it wouldn't be painful, she thought, because she couldn't feel anything at all. In the darkness, she waited to hear the earsplitting screams of hell or the trumpet sounds of heaven. But she heard neither.

TIRZAH'S EYELIDS TWITCHED. SOMEONE WAS LEANING FORWARD in front of her, wherever she was. As her eyes adjusted to the light, she could hardly believe that the person before her was Sena. Her silvery braids had been shorn to a thick, cropped nest that barely grazed her shoulders. She wasn't wearing her own clothes but instead an apron with stains streaked across the bib. There was half-eaten food at the head of a table a few feet from where Tirzah lay. On the other end of that table, a bottle of Madeira. Tirzah turned her head to the side and saw a steaming teapot, a white candle dressed in oil, and a crucifix, and knew that this was really Sena. Second by second, minute by minute, her view grew wider and wider until her surroundings became devastatingly clear. She knew that coat draped over one of the chairs. She knew those patent leather shoes. Her lips began to flap, but no tears fell. Only moans came out of her mouth.

Sena placed a warm compress on her forehead and dabbed a bit. "You a strong one, indeed. You know dat?"

Tirzah said nothing. She stared at the blood Sena was wringing out of the compress and into a large wooden bowl of steaming water and loose herbs.

"You a strong one," Sena repeated. "You should be dead. Good 'n dead. Like dat white man dat tried to take you outta here."

Tirzah blinked and winced as she tried to sit upright, then Sena helped her into a seated position. With her hand still holding onto Tirzah's arms, Sena said, "You probably wonderin' what happened, yeah? Well, once those white vigilante men heard you say de name Spencer Ambrose, dey spared your life. Smart girl you are for callin' his name out. Turns out despite his drunken ways, he still feared in and out of Shreveport. And dey brought you back here believin' dat you still belong to him."

"Back?" Tirzah's voice cracked. She looked around and realized that they were in Spencer's kitchen. She repeated with a lowly resignation, "Back."

"Someone's here to see ya. But I can go to de door and get de message for ya."

"Help me to my feet."

"I don't think you should be walkin' just yet, Miss Tirzah. You had a nasty fall."

"I said, help me to my feet."

"All right nah, take it easy." Sena wrapped her arms around Tirzah's waist and helped her down the hall.

Tirzah opened the front door and saw Isaac standing outside at the gate leading to Spencer Ambrose's home. He didn't come closer and neither did she. He slowly took off his hat and pressed it to his chest. He blinked and gritted his teeth to keep from crying, but a single tear fell from his left eye, and he did not wipe it. Isaac's eyes begged for forgiveness and Tirzah responded with the blessing of grace.

She looked down at her body and began to lift her dress. Isaac placed a hand on the gate. Tirzah exposed the bump in her stomach to him and placed a hand at its center. His mouth opened. She didn't know what compelled her to do such a thing—hope, love, resignation. There would be no more Natchez. There would be no more Mississippi. But whatever was taking place in her body had survived death itself and Isaac had a part in that. If this entity were that strong—and had been for months in secret—then it anchored her in Shreveport and the focus would be on settling here.

Tirzah stood at the threshold of the door and gazed upon that man to whom fate brought her. And as she imagined what life they'd have together, she experienced a flutter.

WINTER
1882

11

Everline's baby boy, Cato: A boy who had turned all of thirteen at the start of the harvest season. A gap-toothed child whose voice had yet to drop, but whose commanding stride rivaled those of men three times his age. A confidence that had sentenced him to lying here on this Saturday morning, at the altar of Shreveport Baptist Church, inside a closed casket.

The sanctuary—which had doubled in size since Emancipation— was filled to the brim with over two hundred parishioners. People needed a place to gather and mourn a continuous loop of death. In the years following Tirzah's failed escape, more blood drenched the Shreveport soil than rain. There were hardly any songs sung during Sunday service about the love of Jesus, but rather about the afterlife, since the current one was hard to bear. The names on the sick and shut-in list for prayer grew from one line to several. They had to be written smaller and smaller in order to fit on the page in the bulletin each week.

Tirzah sat in the front row, with her legs crossed, a white cloth over her lap, and a wide-brimmed black hat shielding her face. As first lady of the church, she was required to attend each and every funeral, comfort the grieving mothers and wives, and offer prayers for solace and healing at all hours of the day and night. She'd scorched her fingers baking so many sympathy pies, and her hands ached from holding all the people she consoled, keeping them from falling into fits. She sat in the cleanest pew, a row especially reserved for her, with the wives of assistant preachers on her left and the wives of deacons on her right.

"And I say death!" Isaac boomed from the pulpit, dressed in a black cloak with golden trim.

"Death!" the congregation replied and whooped and hollered for Isaac to continue.

He leaned over his podium and stretched out his left hand. "Death!" Isaac echoed, then shook his head. The pianist struck a key and the room fell silent.

"Death . . . is not the end of the story. Mm, mm, mm. For Christ has taught us that we overcome death and we!—"

The pianist struck another key.

"We get the final glory because of Him!"

Tirzah wanted to be anywhere but here, in this hot and sticky church listening to the familiar message about a death that should never have happened. She remembered when Cato was just born. The boy wasn't even two days old before Everline brought him over to Tirzah for a blessing. He was a good boy who always minded his manners and greeted elders with respect. He should be out catching fireflies at night with his friends. He should be playing his harmonica, singing words too mature for his age before being caught by his mother and spanked for acting too grown. He shouldn't be dead. And yet here was his mother, falling to the floor in grief.

Cato should be alive like Tirzah's own son, who was sitting proudly behind his father's podium. She knew that since her son managed to survive her failed escape, he was a special one. And that he was—handsome, charismatic, a joy. She named him Free because that's all she wanted him to be. His name held more in its one syllable than any other English word she knew. But he was no freer than other negro boys in Shreveport. She lost count of how many friends' funerals Free attended in the past year, and thanked God that her instinct to continue chewing the root after his birth was spot-on. She couldn't handle another child, even though Isaac wanted another badly. The worry over the life of one was enough.

The deacons and assistant preachers sitting to Isaac's right eyed Tirzah. Isaac beamed down at her, then slid his gaze to Everline. This was the moment that Tirzah was supposed to part the crowd that had quickly surrounded Everline and lay hands on her. But she could not move. She would not move. Even as Free beamed at her too before mouthing to please get up out of her seat. Free always sought to copy his father's ways. Whether it was the gestures, the horseback riding, or card playing, at times Tirzah wondered if Isaac, not she, birthed him.

The veins in Isaac's neck bulged as Tirzah remained in her seat. The wives on either side of her craned their necks to see what she would do, knowing they should not be first to lay hands on the grieving mother. Free started to rise, and though Isaac's back was to his son, he motioned for him to stay put, then for the choir to give everyone another song. Isaac nodded at the eldest of the elders in the church, indicating they should move toward Everline, then gave the first-pew wives permission to do the same. Everyone in the church—the choir, the deacons and assistant preachers, the musician, Free, and Isaac—inched forward and leaned toward Everline until layers and layers of hands obscured her body. Finally, Tirzah slowly rose and approached Everline to bestow a gentle touch to her shoulder. Once the crowd returned to their seats, Tirzah lifted her seething face to Isaac, and he hurried to segue into the benediction.

By the time the last "amen" was uttered, Tirzah was halfway down the sanctuary to the exit. She sat in the family carriage to write in the journal that she pulled from her carpetbag. Writing was her only refuge in stressful times such as these, when she fantasized of being in another place and with another person.

After the service, Isaac climbed into the carriage and Free hopped into the back. Isaac breathed heavily, the hot air touching Tirzah's forehead as she craned her neck over the journal.

"Well?" he asked.

Tirzah looked up and sighed, then stowed both her pen and journal away in her bag. "What?"

"What?" Isaac steered the horse away from the crowd outside the church in the direction of their home. "You owe Miss Everline an apology for your behavior back there."

"I comforted her."

"But you took too long. And you hardly touched her," Free chimed in.

"I don't need assistance, Free," Isaac quipped.

"I am tired, Isaac . . ."

"Ma, we're all tired . . ."

Isaac looked over his shoulder at his son. "What did I just say?" He sighed and continued, "But the boy is right. You don't think the rest of us aren't tired? But we still have our responsibilities. And what you did back there was not becoming of you."

"Death takes a toll, you know. It's hard to comfort the grievers all the time. He was just a child, Isaac."

"Indeed he was! And he deserved a better service than that!"

"What he deserved was a longer life," she shot back.

Isaac scoffed. "He's in a much better place now."

Tirzah turned quickly toward Isaac with widened eyes. She could not believe that he used the same line, but with a flat inflection, as he'd done with those who grieved. Was there nothing else to say? Nothing creative at all? She wondered if the number of times he'd uttered these words placed him at an emotional remove from the tragedies that surrounded them, and she secretly wished for him to return home on foot while she took the carriage.

For the rest of the ride, no one spoke. When Isaac stopped the horse outside their home, Tirzah jumped out before Free had a chance to walk around to help her out, as he usually did.

"Cato would still be here if it weren't for you!" Tirzah shouted in Isaac's direction.

Then she ran into the house and sprinted up the steps. Isaac instructed Free to stay downstairs, then followed her to find she had locked him out of the bedroom. When his pleas for her to open the door were fruitless, he used a penknife from his pocket and undid the lock on his own. When he swung open the door, Tirzah was standing with her arms crossed like she'd been waiting for him.

"What did you mean by that?"

She answered him with silence.

"C'mon now. Speak. You had a lot of mouth in front of our son. I want to hear you finish."

"They castrated that boy, Isaac. Castrated him! While he was still alive! Then they hung him with his pants down so everybody could see what they did. Like they were proud of their handiwork." She sighed and continued.

"How can you sleep at night? It's your fault, you know. It's you putting silly dreams into these young boys' heads, that they'll ever vote like white men. And nobody else is going to tell you, because they want to be respectful of the town preacher. But I'll tell you right to your face: he died because of you, Isaac Levi. You."

She tapped his chest and he caught her hand, caressing it. From the periphery, a peculiarity stood out to her amid this tense embrace. She moved her head to the side to inspect his right hand and found liver spots. The older Isaac had gotten, much to his chagrin, the more liver spots would appear indiscriminately over his body. Like rings around a tree, Tirzah cherished them, for they were histories of their length of time together. Some were circles, others looked like clouds, wings, hearts. But these spots that graced his ring finger in a vertical design were a constellation of stars.

"What?" Isaac asked.

She held up his hand. "How long have you had these?"

Isaac shrugged. "You know I never know when they come. They decide on their own."

"Indeed they do." She took a breath but held herself back.

"What's wrong?"

She took a beat.

"They just look like how the stars looked when we first made love."

Isaac straightened and fought to hold back tears. "Back when you used to have hope in me. You remember that?"

"Of course I do. But . . . we were younger then. Don't you see? It's already a miracle that our freedom hasn't been snatched away yet. This is as good as it's going to get, and you're only making things worse."

Isaac cupped her face in his hands. "Nothing happens without struggle. 'Weeping may endure for the night but joy—'"

"I have to get ready for work." Tirzah stepped away from him and grabbed her maid's uniform. Their tender moment was broken the moment Isaac slipped into common, overused biblical verses as placeholders for accessing the hard reality of his actions.

Deflated, Isaac walked down the stairs, his hands deep in his pockets, and found Free drawing up some more posters. "Free. G'on and take your mother to work. I'll finish up with the planning."

Instead of sitting down on the chaise with the posters and maps, though, Isaac went through the kitchen and into the scullery and shut the door behind him.

Tirzah was fastening her apron while walking down the steps and expected Isaac to be near the front door waiting for her. "Where's your pa?" she asked Free.

"I'm taking you today."

"Well, try not to look so sad about it," Tirzah joked. They walked outside and Free helped her into the carriage before taking his place in the driver's seat.

Tirzah attempted to thaw the awkward silence. "Seems like we hardly have any time to ourselves now that you—"

"Why did you really act like that in church? I know you've been acting a kind of way for a while but this was different," Free blurted out.

Tirzah didn't say a word.

"Are you sick?"

"No, I'm not sick. I'm tired and I don't feel like having the same conversation with you as I had with your pa."

"Seems like you've been tired a lot lately."

Tirzah looked over at her son, who puffed out his chest while keeping a hold on his reins and his eyes on the dirt path. "What do you mean by that?"

Free shifted in his seat. "Well . . ." The sound of the carriage wheels rolling over rocks and mulch got louder the longer he hesitated.

"Go on."

"Sometimes when we say grace and Pa holds his hand out for you, you lean back like you can't stand his touch. And when he gives you kind words from the pulpit, you can't even smile. You're sad, Ma. Tired and sad."

Tirzah blinked. She couldn't deny it even if she wanted to. Her isolation had felt so dense that she'd forgotten anyone else might notice it.

"Is there someone else?"

"Excuse me?" Tirzah snapped her neck at him. "How dare you ask your ma something like that?"

Free shrugged. "We're talking, aren't we? And I'll be seventeen soon. I'm almost a grown man."

"But you are still my son, and you owe me respect."

What Tirzah couldn't say was that there was always going to be another man. But she'd promised Isaac that she would never say Harrison's name in their home. And for a while, she'd preferred it that way. The silence afforded her privacy to maintain an ancient part of herself that had nothing to do with her work or being first lady at Shreveport, a mother, and a wife.

"Well . . . do you love Pa?" Free asked gently, and she softened.

She didn't hesitate. "Of course I love him. He's an example for how any husband should treat his wife. And if you've been watching him, any woman out there would be blessed to have you too."

Free lit up, making Tirzah smile, but her smile faded as she leaned back in her seat. She knew what her son dreamt when he thought of love. He thought love meant automatic devotion. He thought love was the high notes with none of the bass and rhythm with which to sustain them. He thought love was unconditional. And that was beautiful. For a child. She wanted him to remain in ignorant bliss; her adolescence had been devoid of such small pleasures.

"Free, I know it's going to make you upset, but I need to ask a favor of you."

"What is it?"

"I want you to take a break from canvassing for a while."

Free halted the horse in the middle of a busy intersection of the Bottoms before maneuvering to the side after other drivers voiced their frustration at his abruptness. He turned to stare at his mother. "What? Why?"

"What do you mean 'why'? We buried one of your friends this morning!"

"Cato would've wanted us to keep going."

"He was only thirteen. He didn't know what he wanted beyond following you and the rest of the older boys around."

"That's not true. If anything, he was more outspoken than a whole lot of us."

"Yes, and look where that got him."

A look of scorn passed over Free's face, and he parted his lips to speak, but instead shook his head and motioned to the horse to carry on.

Tirzah recognized that kind of head shake. Isaac did it whenever she asked him to hang up his clothes or come home at a decent hour for dinner. She saw other husbands do it to their wives too, and not always when the woman was asking for something. Free was growing up more quickly than she would have liked, and now he was at that age where he realized the power he had over her simply because she was a woman.

Free eventually directed the horse toward a gate where camellias were in full bloom by its side. He leaned over and said, "I love you, Ma." His lips trembled and his jaw slackened with the weight of suppressed vulnerability. She sensed he wanted to say more but didn't press.

Instead, Tirzah cupped both of his cheeks in her hands, pulled him forward, and was about to kiss him on top of his head when Spencer came storming out the front door. After the end of the war, returning to Natchez hadn't been an option for him since his family's plantation, like many others, had been ransacked and abandoned. His parents, Mercer and Catherine, along with many of their peers, cut their losses knowing that the social hierarchy would never be the same, went to Europe, and never came back. Spencer, however, stayed in Shreveport, preferring to socialize and drink far from their watchful eyes. Though his reputation as a womanizing drunkard preceded him, and the years of hard drinking had devastated his body, the considerable fortune he was set to inherit made him quite the eligible bachelor.

At some point Spencer decided to choose a wife from the array of Shreveport war widows, and Athéné Bringier had managed to fight her way to the top of the list. Widowed young without any children of her own, her only asset was the house in which she was living, and Spencer moved right in. Though he and his family would've preferred a woman of higher status, Athéné was beautiful, and she didn't ask too many questions.

Now, Spencer approached Free's side of the carriage. He had a large potbelly that jiggled whenever he walked, his skin had become leathery, and his once thick head of hair was now just a few strands clinging for dear life to the center of his crown.

Tirzah leaned forward, one hand gripping the seat and one the dashboard.

"Whoa, whoa, whoa, now," Spencer said in response. "I'm just saying hello to the boy. How ya doin', son?"

Tirzah could feel the anger burning behind her eyes as Free took a beat and looked Spencer straight in his face. "I'm doing just fine, Mister Spencer."

He leaned closer and Free averted his face to avoid the reek of alcohol from the older man's breath. "My, my, my, aren't you a fine-lookin' one." He glanced over at Tirzah. "I'll be back later. Have my dinner ready for me before I arrive."

Soon after Spencer took his own horse from beside the front gate and left the neighborhood, a female voice yelled, "Hi, Free!"

Novella, Spencer and Athéné's second maid, stood at the door, excitedly waving to him with one hand and holding the newest Ambrose baby on her hip with the other.

Tirzah nudged Free, encouraging him to speak to the young woman, who clearly liked him, but he just flashed a boyish grin and waved back at Novella.

When Tirzah and Isaac had first married, Athéné said she thought it was best for newlyweds to spend their time together with the intention of building their family. But Tirzah knew better. Athéné wasn't a good liar, no matter how wide her smiles or how saccharine her voice. The new Mrs. Ambrose was aware of what Spencer would do with Tirzah. Athéné thought that if she were the only woman in the house overnight, her husband could focus on expanding their brood, and that they did. Nevertheless, Tirzah was watchful. Novella was still a pretty girl—and a naive one at that. For as long as she was working under the Ambroses' roof, Tirzah wanted to protect the younger woman, which is why she obliged Spencer a few times until all the drink gradually destroyed his ability to get and stay stiff. The fifth Ambrose baby was nothing short of a miracle.

Tirzah often worked at the house till dusk. She scrubbed dishes, floors, and baseboards, made his bed, cooked his meals, and did all his laundry. Most days, Novella tended to the children, and Tirzah would be left alone because Spencer spent most of his time at the saloons, coming home only to play chess by himself or write telegrams to his father begging for more money. But some evenings, she'd smell the metallic odor he emitted and know he was nearby, and he'd have come home carrying a keepsake: some bloody teeth, a severed ear, a penis stored in a glass jar. He'd line his souvenirs on the mantel and smile at his display whenever she'd come into the living room. Initially, Tirzah prayed for those who'd suffered at his hands, until she became so tired of the ubiquitous violence that she gave up petitioning to God for help.

On this day, Tirzah was dusting off his keepsakes while scrutinizing the jars' contents for any sign of Cato. When she couldn't find anything, she sighed loudly, just as Novella walked into the living room.

"I already looked dere," the younger woman said.

"Novella, I told you before that I didn't want you anywhere near this mantelpiece. It's my domain. I clean this."

"Cato was like family. I had to see if he been disgraced and parts of him left dere rottin'."

Novella gestured for Tirzah to follow her, and led her into the kitchen. She looked around to make sure none of the children were lurking behind a corner, then reached deep into her uniform pocket. She pulled out a wrinkled sheet of paper and unfolded it to reveal in large, bold lettering:

HO FOR KANSAS!
Brethren, Friends, & Fellow Citizens:
I feel thankful to inform you that the
REAL ESTATE
AND
Homestead Association
Will Leave Here
December 15th, 1882
In pursuit of homes in the Southwestern
Lands of America, at Transportation Rates cheaper than
ever was known before.

**For full information inquire of
Benji Singleton, better known as Old Pap
NO. 5 North Front Street
Beware of speculators and adventurers, as it is a
dangerous thing to fall in their hands**
Nashville, TN, November 15th, 1882

"Why are you showing me this?" Tirzah asked.

"Ain't it obvious? Kansas de land of opportunity! De white folk movin' out 'cause dey done drove de Injuns away and now dey grabbin' up dat land somewhere else."

"Kansas?"

"Yes, ma'am. Things gettin' too crazy 'round here. I know folk who went up dere and never looked back. Heard a lot of other negroes doin' de same. Just thought I let you know."

"Good for you, Novella. You should go."

Tirzah began to wipe down the countertops, humming a melody. Novella rustled the paper in her hands. "I was thinkin' you might be interested."

Tirzah turned to face her. "Me?" Novella nodded. "How are you even planning to go?"

"We take a boat down to Baton Rouge before headin' back up to St. Louis. Den from dere we can take another boat to Atchison in Kansas. Dere all kinds of negroes willin' to help us along de way. Food, a place to sleep, whatever we need. We can take a couple pieces of jewelry—Mistress has baubles dat she hasn't touched in months and dey collectin' dust—and any silver you might have and dat be enough to see us through."

Tirzah's heartbeat quickened. Her ancient self, though dormant, was now being reactivated with the temptation to dream again. She'd never be able to convince Isaac to go, but if Novella and Free were attracted to each other, that might be enough for them all to escape. Her eyes burned with thoughts of a new life, one that she secretly believed she deserved. But just as soon as she felt this excitement, her face hardened with the remembrance of how much time had passed and how much more dangerous Shreveport had gotten. She judged herself foolish for wishful thinking, as if she were still Novella's age. She'd never make it.

"Why are you telling me this, Novella?"

"Well . . ." Novella slid the paper back into her pocket. "I know who you was. I heard 'bout you . . . from de older folks. Dey say you tried to escape and almost got killed doin' it. All while you was pregnant wit Free. I seen de way you were at Cato's funeral. I thought maybe . . . you still had it in you."

12

Tirzah was still plagued by nightmares of Albert Peachy's death; she had never forgiven herself for what had happened to him. She hadn't tried to escape again once the entire town caught word that she was carrying Isaac's child, and she wouldn't risk being responsible for someone else dying to get her back to Natchez. Her desire for another life was sublimated into the commitment to a prosperous family life as a Levi. But now, she was tired of her responsibilities as first lady, how she was expected to be a pillar of strength for the families whose mournful bellows left her paralyzed at the end of the night. How long could they stay in Shreveport before her son would be put in the ground? She beat the eggs for a vanilla custard pie too roughly and silently asked God to calm her worries, but the what-ifs continued in her mind.

For the next few Sundays, whenever Tirzah delivered the weekly announcements at services, her mind was stuck on Novella. She wasn't too hard to spot in the pews with her reddish-brown hair always plaited and tied together with a large, bright ribbon. They exchanged discreet glances within which Novella hoped that something in Tirzah's demeanor would indicate that she was thinking about Kansas. Tirzah, on the other hand, never held her gaze for long, afraid that Novella would see her clearly in such a way that no one else had for years. After service, Novella would always stay behind to pray as the rest of the large congregation filed out, and she and Tirzah would say a few polite words, but none of them about Kansas.

One Sunday, Tirzah sat in her own pew and persisted in silence long after service was over. She loved that the longer she even considered Kansas, the more pleasurable her small and secret rebellion was. Once Tirzah snapped out of her daydreaming, she walked outside and saw a bunch of girls literally lined up to talk to Free. But Novella wasn't among them.

Tirzah went straight to work thereafter and found Novella preoccupied with the children. At first Tirzah didn't mind. There were more than enough household tasks to keep her busy for the rest of the afternoon into the night. But when the women crossed paths in the hallway next to the kitchen, Novella turned sideways and cast her eyes at the floor, and Tirzah wondered if she had done something wrong. Throughout the day, Tirzah suspected that Novella was avoiding her, as every time they were near each other, Novella would flee to another room and busy herself with some tidying matter. Furthermore, she was less chatty than usual. As dusk settled in and the children were put to bed, Tirzah grew impatient. As soon as Novella entered the downstairs bathroom, Tirzah hurried to push open the door. Inside, Novella was leaning on the edge of the bathroom sink, soothing her inner thighs with the halved interior of an aloe vera leaf.

Novella looked over her shoulder and turned around slowly. "Mister Spencer din't get me. He tried but he din't get me."

"When?"

"About a week ago."

How could that be? Tirzah thought. He was damn near impotent. Yet his impairment still remained secondary to his obsession with exerting his power. Tirzah opened her mouth to speak, but when she heard the creak of the front door opening, she hurried to the entry foyer. Her head bowed, she waited for Spencer to give her his jacket, but his nostrils flared when he caught wind of the aroma coming from the kitchen. He tossed his jacket on the ground before sauntering into the dining room. When Tirzah went to pick it up, a rolled-up sheet of paper spilled out of the right pocket; a few exclamation points on one side were visible through. She only had a moment while Spencer untied his shoelaces and kicked his heels up on the table, so she used her pinky to gently unroll the paper. There it was: Isaac's thick penmanship reminding negroes of their citizenship and the right to vote it conferred. She folded the paper until it was no bigger than her thumbnail and stuffed it inside her pocket.

That night, she sat next to Isaac in the carriage on the way home, full of nerves. As they ventured deeper into the woods, she could stand it no longer. She unrolled the announcement and placed it in her lap.

"What's that?" he asked.

"You know what it is. Mister Spencer got ahold of one of them."

"Well, why wouldn't he? They're not hidden."

"They're not?"

"The interest is there. We have people."

"Evidently you do."

"Did he say anything to you?"

"Nothing at all. As a matter of fact, he barely said anything tonight, and you know he's a man of many words."

"Indeed he is."

Isaac pulled Tirzah closer to his chest and squeezed the horse's sides with his legs so that they'd speed up. He was relieved that the dark night concealed the disquiet on his face. Spencer's silence could only mean one thing: a plan was already in the works.

As they neared the house, they saw that there were several horses and carriages lined up near their garden. Oil lamps burned in the windows, which illuminated people moving about inside. She could hear lively conversation and pots and pans clamoring.

"What's going on?" she asked Isaac, who held her hand as they approached. When he opened the door, twenty or so negro men and women and a sprinkling of white folks were communing in her living room while their house staff whirled to and from the kitchen with pots of food and glasses of mint lemonade or brandy.

"There's a meeting tonight."

"Since when?" Tirzah yelled above the din.

"Since today. We had to do it."

"Why are you only telling me this now?"

Isaac sighed and flagged Free, whose tie and cufflinks were still undone, to come tend to his mother. Tirzah and her son sequestered themselves in his bedroom on the second floor, where he paced from side to side so many times that dirt traces of his feet overlapped one another on the wooden floor, beads of sweat dotting his hairline. Without saying a word, Tirzah tilted Free's neck toward the ceiling to knot his tie and extended his arms to hook his cuff links. No matter how tall he was or how deep the bass in his voice stretched, a boy still needed his mother.

"I told you to stop canvassing," she said sternly.

"Ma—"

Tirzah held his chin toward her face. "What did I say?"

Free scoffed and looked at the ground. "But Pa—"

"But Pa—what about me?"

"Why don't you believe in me and what I'm doing?"

"It's not that I don't believe in you, son." Tirzah took his hands into hers. "It's that you want a different kind of world, but that world isn't here yet."

"And it won't be here unless we fight for it."

"You sure are hardheaded. You must understand that as much as a person seeks to fight, no mother wants her son to be sacrificed for the cause."

Free dropped his shoulders. "Well, I can't argue with that. You done put me in a corner where I can't have a response."

"Good, because I need you to listen to me. I know you got big dreams, Free. Big, big dreams. But your generation doesn't know what me and your father have seen."

"Why did you name me Free then?" he said suddenly.

Tirzah dropped his hands and backed up to sit on the edge of his bed. "Now you got me. Wish fulfillment, I guess."

"I have something to tell you," Free said, perching next to his mother. "Today, Pa and I were posting and passing out flyers when Mister Spencer came around."

"I know."

"How?"

Tirzah pursed her lips. "Go on."

"Well, I thought he was gonna do something. Maybe whip my hide a few times or wave his gun around."

"And?"

"He asked me to read what was on the flyer, because he wasn't sure if I knew what every word meant, and I did it perfectly. Then—" Free looked down at his lap.

She shook his shoulder. "What, Free? What did he do?"

"He asked for a flyer, I gave it to him, he put it in his jacket pocket and left."

She opened her eyes. "That's it?"

Free nodded. "That's it."

They stared at each other in shock before erupting into laughter. She pulled Free into her bosom and kissed his right temple. "Oh, my son. My son, my son, my son."

WHEN FREE AND TIRZAH REACHED THE FOOT OF THE STAIRCASE, Isaac was finishing a speech at a makeshift podium set up in the middle of the living room. He motioned in their direction and the crowd began to clap. Tirzah had every intention of retreating into the kitchen or scullery to help with the hostessing, but Free pulled her to stand next to him on Isaac's left-hand side.

"I want to tell you about my son. My son who makes me and my wife, Tirzah, so very proud." As Isaac spoke, Free raised his eyes to his father and hung on to every word as though it were a crown placed upon his head. Isaac was God manifested to Free, and there was no other person he wanted to emulate more. On another occasion, Tirzah might have been envious; Free never gazed at her so reverentially. But tonight, when Free delighted in the uproarious rounds of applause, appearing to be on the verge of tears as Isaac shook his hand, then kissed his forehead, Tirzah understood. And not only did she understand, she felt lucky to have created a family like this for herself.

Free had never delivered a public speech before. He looked toward his mother and father, then grabbed both sides of his podium and leaned forward toward the audience. From his first sentences, Tirzah was transfixed. Her son, who had been mimicking his father from the time he could walk, had developed his own oratorical style, one that inspired even as it acknowledged challenges. He was clear-eyed, forthright, honest. With the fluidity of a skilled dancer, he spoke of the importance of organizing, fair pay, shorter working hours, better working conditions, and, of course, voting.

Tirzah observed how their guests responded with the kind of enthusiasm they usually reserved for Isaac's sermons—perhaps even more for her son. Then she spotted Novella in the third row of chairs, positioned a few feet in front of the podium. She was wedged between two men twice her size, crying silently as she gazed ahead. Tirzah followed her line of sight to Free and noticed that he was staring at Novella in such a way that confirmed what she already suspected: romance was brewing between them.

Tirzah eventually retired to her bedroom to reflect. When Isaac came upstairs, she could still hear the sounds of merriment from below. "Where did you go?" he asked.

She sighed and turned toward the threshold of their bedroom where he stood. "There is no place for me down there. You know how all that loud carrying on scares me. White people are always lurking, remember that."

"But I need you to support me. Be my helpmeet. The people—they don't just look up to me. They look up to you too."

"When are you going to be my helpmeet?" she asked as she began to walk from her bedside over to him.

Isaac blinked. "What do you mean? I've been supporting the family. I've been doing my share."

"But you're not listening to me. Even now. Doesn't my fear mean anything to you?"

"It does. I'm sorry." He looked briefly past Tirzah's left shoulder and saw two small, wrinkled pieces of paper lying on their bed.

"What?" Tirzah followed his line of sight, then gave Isaac her most regretful eyes.

Isaac suspected the papers' contents but walked over to her side of the bed just to be sure. Tirzah walked quietly behind him.

"Isaac . . ." Tirzah gently said.

He gathered the papers in his hand and subsequently tossed them into the air in anger. Isaac saw the words—"Information wanted for Tirzah Ambrose" on one page—and then a faint, brown letter addressed to a Harrison on the second—and whatever penitence he sought from Tirzah had evaporated.

"You held on to these all this time?"

Tirzah nodded. "Why would I throw them away?" For years, Tirzah kept pages and pages of handwritten entries to Harrison that she had no intention of sending. She couldn't. The Freedmen's Bureau had been dismantled; there wasn't a trustworthy system in place to deliver the mail. And she was the pastor's wife. If someone saw her down there, mailing a letter to another man—the community scorn would not be worth the trouble. Isaac didn't deserve what would be whispered behind his back. But then again, he didn't deserve what he discovered here in their bedroom tonight either.

"I just thought—" Isaac shrank away from her. "I thought after all these years of marriage . . . having Free, expanding our church . . . you just wouldn't care anymore."

"But you knew I loved him when we got married."

"That I did. But I thought that with time, you'd love me more and . . . I don't know, leave it in the past."

Tirzah dropped her shoulders. "I'm sorry."

Isaac sighed and looked at the door. "You are so selfish," he said, an unfamiliar spitefulness in his tone.

She stared at him. "What?"

"You only care about yourself and your feelings."

"Isaac—" Tirzah rose and approached him but he held up his hands. "How can you say that to me? I married you. I—I gave you a son."

"A son who you hid from me, who you wouldn't have told me about had your escape been successful."

Tirzah sat on the edge of the bed. Isaac's blow siphoned all the energy out of the room, and for a moment, she could not recognize the man in front of her. How long had he been holding this in? Had all of their disagreements been steadily building to this moment?

He frowned and shook his head at her before quietly leaving the bedroom. Tirzah sat there feeling that something much deeper had shifted between them. He'd left her to sit in the wreckage of all that lay unspoken between them, years' worth of arguments never voiced, only imagined. Was their union born of love or of obligation, freedom or fear? As the gathering downstairs proceeded without her, Tirzah wondered if the life that she'd made for herself was about to change.

13

Early in the morning, before the sun came out or the cocks crowed, Isaac migrated to Tirzah's side of the bed and slipped a hand under the covers. She turned around to face him before his fingers could touch the fabric of her nightgown. Isaac's heart began to race, but his apprehension dissipated when he saw that Tirzah was moving closer, so close that the tips of their noses almost touched. Like teenagers, they gazed at each other almost shyly, their bodies illuminated by the moonlight.

"Are you awake?" Isaac asked. His voice was always deeper first thing in the morning. That sound, full like a bass, slow like molasses, and rich like mousse, made Tirzah's inner thighs throb.

"Mm-hmm."

"Do you still want to be together?"

"What? Why would you even ask that?"

"I just worry that I don't make you happy any longer."

"Oh, Isaac. That's not true. I worry for you, that's all. Your bravery was a part of the reason why I fell in love with you, but I don't want you to leave this earth yet."

"I didn't plan on it anytime soon," Isaac said. "But husbands are supposed to go on to glory before their wives anyway. So it's been said."

Tirzah shook her head. "Please stop. I don't want to hear any of this kind of talk."

"C'mere." He pulled Tirzah closer into his chest and kissed her with an open mouth so that she could take his breath into her own body.

Isaac was not usually interested in making love during the week, when his working hours were long and hard. He would kiss her lips and caress her waist in an up-down motion a few times before falling asleep. But now, he lowered his hands and touched her in all the places that made her forget time. When her breaths became short and labored, Isaac climbed on top of her and made love to her more vigorously than he ever had before. As he mounted forward, the moonlight blessed his grunting and relentless face. He stared so deeply into her eyes that she briefly imagined him piercing through to the other side of her body. He held on to her so tightly that his fingernails made impressions in her sides. She wanted to tell him that there was no need to hold so tight, she was right here, but the sex had left her breathless and sore. This was a man whose emotions she could read by how he held his fork in the morning or how tightly he held the reins during carriage rides, yet now she wondered what had caused his sudden desire to keep her so close. Was he holding something back so as not to undermine the intimacy?

When Tirzah woke again later that morning, it was to the kind of perfect calmness that put her on edge. The sun was shining, a comforting breeze subtly blew through the trees, and the hummingbirds sang their song. That's it? Tirzah thought. After Isaac's powerful speech and their fight followed by intense lovemaking, everyone was just going to go about their day? Maybe, Tirzah thought, she didn't have anything to worry about. Life was moving on. She had held anxiety in her body for too many years and her family remained intact regardless. Counting her blessings seemed more valuable to her spare time than worrying.

"So about Novella—" Tirzah said during the family's ride into town for work.

"What is there to talk about?" Free said.

"I saw the way you were looking at her last night. You have something you want to tell us?"

"Ma . . ." Free groaned.

"Leave the boy alone, sweetheart," Isaac said, shooting her a mischievous glance.

"Fair enough," Tirzah said. "I think it's beautiful though, honey."

"C'mon now, Tirzah. You heard the boy."

"You're going to be calling him man in a minute." She looked over her shoulder and winked at Free, who smiled despite himself. Then she looked up at the sky. "What a beautiful day it is today, isn't it?"

"Indeed it is," Isaac said.

When they dropped her at the Ambroses' home, a man was fixing himself up with a spring in his step and a melody on his tongue as he descended the front porch. It took a moment for Tirzah to realize that Spencer had transformed himself into a gentleman. He had groomed his bushy beard, and his normally greasy hair had been washed, cut, and styled.

"Well, I'll be," Tirzah said while approaching the front door. "What's the occasion?"

"A special business affair." He whirled Tirzah around and held her face to kiss her. Her blood ran cold. Roughness was the standard for him, and Spencer had no qualms about doing whatever he wanted with Tirzah whenever he felt like it. This softness was much worse. He left Tirzah standing exactly where she was underneath the portico, dumbfounded.

"Good mornin'," Novella called out from the second floor as soon as Tirzah entered the home. She was floating down the staircase happily. Tirzah knew the reason, but also knew her place, so she decided not to pry about Novella and her son.

"Good morning. Where are the children?"

"Visitin' family in Vivian. Dey gon' be gone for a week."

"Okay. Then c'mon down here and keep me company."

Novella and Tirzah moved through the first floor like clockwork.

The china was shined to perfection, Spencer's watches were dusted, the floors were scrubbed, and all the dishes were put in their rightful places in the cupboards. The emptiness of the house allowed the two women to work quickly and efficiently, so much so that by the afternoon, Tirzah suggested that they sit out on the veranda and have a glass of lemonade.

"Really? We can do dat?" Novella asked, incredulous.

"I think so. Mister Spencer won't be back for a while, I reckon. He looked like he was going somewhere important: 'a special business affair,' he said."

"I hope whatever dat 'affair' is lead to a job so he stop dressin' just to drink."

They giggled.

Tirzah pulled out the lemons and sugar, while Novella gathered the glasses and a few napkins to set up outside. Once they got comfortable on the veranda swing, Tirzah observed the backyard with its variety of azaleas and phlox and irises, the peach and cherry trees, the birdhouses. She and Novella had grown and maintained all these beauties, but this was the first chance to be still and absorb all that they had done.

"A beautiful day today, ain't it?" Novella said between sips of lemonade.

"I was just saying that to Isaac and Free."

"I wish I could go swimmin' or have fun on de trails in de backwoods."

"Yes, that would be nice," Tirzah said noncommittally.

Novella took a beat and said, "Have you thought more 'bout what I said?"

"I have . . ."

The younger woman straightened her spine expectantly.

"I can't, Novella. I can't. I have to stay here and be there for my family and the church. But you're young, and I think you should go."

Novella frowned and stared at her feet. "I din't want to go alone."

Tirzah touched Novella's left shoulder. "I understand, especially seeing as how you don't have your parents."

"You like a mother to me and it ain't just 'cause I have heart for your son. You watch out for me and care for me. I don't wanna leave wit'out you."

Tirzah placed her glass on the ground and pulled Novella in for a hug. Afterward, they indulged in each other's company without conversation and time melted away. The wood warblers' song lulled them to sleep until the sound of the front door opening and closing had them springing to their feet. The sky was now overcast, and the regular afternoon breeze had turned into a strong wind. The two women hurried and gathered up the pitcher and glasses before moving into kitchen to feign busyness.

Spencer stumbled into the living room—shirttail hanging out of his pants, trousers loosened, and red streaks all over his front. The women froze with dishrags in their hands, horrified over what Spencer might have just done. He tripped over his dragging pants and spilled onto the floor, and once he pulled himself up, cursing, he flung his dirty shoes into the living room. Right before his body appeared as if it would finally give out, Spencer placed another souvenir on his mantelpiece. He plopped down on the linen settee and immediately began snoring.

"I just cleaned de fabric of dat thing a few days ago," Novella whispered to Tirzah.

"Come help me get him upstairs and then we'll just have to clean that again as well as the carpet."

Novella went for the legs and Tirzah was able to get her arms around his back to pull him up on the count of three. He groaned and mumbled as the women winced at his offensive smell. Just as Novella was about to move backward so that they could make their way to the staircase, Tirzah froze and said, "Wait."

"What's wrong?"

Tirzah lowered Spencer's back onto the settee and started walking toward the fireplace.

"But—"

"Shh!" Tirzah held up a finger to her lips, not taking her eyes off the mantelpiece.

She wanted to not look at the contents. That would've been the wiser decision. Whatever was there was none of her business. But her need to know took over.

In the jar sat mangled negro fingers. Wishing herself not to see it, convincing herself she wasn't seeing it, she saw the constellation of stars along the skin cut off from its original source, signaling the end of her dear husband and the end of their time on earth together as one.

14

The world around Tirzah evaporated once she saw parts of her husband in that jar. She staggered toward the front door, holding on to chairs and leaning against walls so she didn't collapse. When Tirzah flung open the door, there was already a small crowd of negro men gathered outside the Ambroses' gate. Their hats were pressed to their chests, their heads slightly bowed. Her heart could've bolted straight out of her chest as sheer panic spread through every limb of her body. With the door left open behind her, Tirzah took a few more steps, down the porch and out the gate. The crowd closed ranks around her.

The men murmured to her, but their words and faces blurred together and Tirzah couldn't make out who any of them were. She didn't care. She snatched a man by his collar and asked, "Where is he? Where is he?" When he didn't answer immediately, she smacked him across his cheek. "Where is he, huh?" She started to beat on another's chest, crying out, "I want to see my husband!" before someone's hands clamped over her mouth. She screamed into his palms, and would not relent no matter how much everyone pleaded with her, telling her it wasn't safe to make a scene.

"I'll tell ya but ya have got to calm down, Missus Levi, or we'll all be strung up," Clarence, the man with his hand over her mouth, said quietly, and she finally nodded. He released her and continued, "We already got some men from de church cuttin' him down now. The last thing we wanted was for the whole town to see him all cut up and swingin', wit'out any dignity."

Tirzah's mouth dropped as she wilted into Clarence's arms. "It was such a beautiful day too. Why now?" She looked around at all the men with woeful faces, none of whom could look her in the eye because they were on the verge of weeping themselves.

"We will honor 'im as best we can, ma'am," said Percy, a young man about Free's age.

Tirzah gasped and turned to Clarence. "Did you see my son?"

"No, ma'am. It . . . it was only him. We only found him."

Tirzah pushed past the men and started down the path leading toward the center of town. She could hear that men were following her and said, "Find him. Search the woods again, high and low. And the river. And don't come back until every corner is covered."

If there was a maid outside cleaning her boss's front porch or watering the flowers, Tirzah asked her if she'd seen Free. Every negro horseman riding past was flagged down and interrogated. For hours, she circled through town asking any negro who was in her line of sight, until everyone knew that Isaac had been lynched and the first lady's son was missing.

When the sun was beginning to set, Clarence offered to take Tirzah home, to which she agreed.

During the ride, Clarence said, "Me and a few of my boys gon' patrol de outside of your house all night in case dey come back for more. You in too much danger to be left alone."

"So is my son."

Clarence didn't say a word as he navigated through the woods.

Five men were already standing outside of the Levi home, guns by their sides. Chairs had been set up on the edge of Tirzah's garden, and nearby a few blankets were folded neatly.

Tirzah barely looked at any of them as she quietly entered her home.

"Ma?" a faint voice asked.

Tirzah rushed around the left corner to the living room, where Free was shaking uncontrollably on the chaise.

"My God!" She wrapped her arms around Free with a force that would've knocked him to the ground had he not braced himself. He stared at some imperceptible spot near their fireplace, shivering and inconsolable.

The relief of finally being reunited with her son came apart with the recognition that her son was broken. For such a young man who had grown quite tall, he now shrank and was coiled within himself. There was no light in his eyes, no spirit in his posture. And for the first time in her motherhood, Tirzah didn't know what to do. The damage had already stretched far too deep inside of him.

"It happened so fast. We were putting up signs and they surrounded us. Before Pa could talk them down, they grabbed him, and I could hear them whooping and cheering. I asked for them to have mercy and—" Free showed his entire face to Tirzah, revealing his busted lip and blood in the white of his right eye. "They held my face and made me watch. Then they—" Tirzah hurriedly shushed him up and pushed his face into her chest, where he fell apart. He cried and cried and screamed into her bosom until the front of her dress was damp with his tears. She silently cried as she rubbed his back. There was nothing to say, nothing to do to quiet him—she rocked him gently as she once did when he was a child, until his body relaxed in her arms.

Moments after Free had miraculously fallen asleep, the front door opened and Novella stood at the threshold with flowers in her hands. "I came as quick as I could."

THE NEXT MORNING DAWNED AS BEAUTIFUL AS THE PREVIOUS DAY. Tirzah slept in her marital bed, and came downstairs to find Novella, who'd stayed downstairs all night with Free, trying to get him to drink or eat something.

"Good morning, son," Tirzah said.

He didn't respond.

"How's he doing?" she asked Novella.

"He's . . ." Novella shrugged.

Tirzah nodded. "Best to leave him be. I just was getting ready for work."

"Work?" Novella asked.

"Yes," Tirzah said curtly. She stuck out her arm. "Shall we go together?"

Novella looked at Free, who was staring off into space.

"Why are you looking at him? He doesn't make the decisions around here. I do."

And Tirzah was already out the door, Novella behind her, leaving Free alone. Clarence was waiting outside with his horse and carriage. Beside him Isaac's horse was tied to a poplar tree and an unattached carriage was tipped to the side, centimeters away from the azaleas in Tirzah's small garden. Without saying a word, Tirzah unhitched Isaac's horse and climbed into the saddle. She sat up proudly and extended a hand toward Novella. "Are you coming or not?"

"You sure you feel okay ridin'? I mean after all dat just happened? Clarence been kind enough—"

"My horse ain't dead, my husband is. Ride with Clarence if you feel safer with a man."

Novella looked over at Clarence, who nodded at her. Then Novella grabbed on to Tirzah's hand, placed her left heel into the stirrup to swing her right foot over the horse's back, and held on tight to Tirzah's rib cage. Clarence trailed behind the women, but Tirzah's eyes kept to the dirt roads in front of her, refusing to acknowledge him.

"You should think about leaving soon," Tirzah said when they were halfway out of the woods. "You should've been left already but I suppose love got you in a stronghold." Novella lowered her head and Tirzah looked over her shoulder. "You hear me talking to you, young lady?"

"Yes, ma'am."

"Then make a plan. Go before Athéné comes back. Mister Spencer will be out doing whatever and he will be drunk a lot of the time. He'll be too watchful over how I react because Isaac is dead, and it'll be distracting enough for you to get gone."

"Yes, ma'am."

"How often does the boat leave?"

"Every Sunday . . . folks think it is better on de Lord's day, dey think God almighty will be more merciful to dere travels. And white folks too busy relaxin' wit dere families too."

"Hmm." Tirzah steered the horse into town, her expression stoic as she passed by negro townspeople on their way to work, who stared up at her in awe. Even if any of them had had it in them to greet Tirzah, she wouldn't have said a word back. Her husband was dead, and she had no time for pleasantries.

By the time Tirzah and Novella approached the Ambrose household, there must have been several pairs of negro eyes glued to their backs. Tirzah could feel the anticipation hanging in the air. But there would be no show. She dismounted from the horse and helped Novella off the saddle, then she patted down the back of her dress and entered through the front door, Novella trailing behind. There was no sign of Spencer, so they set to work quickly. Tirzah got on her hands and knees to clean the baseboards. Novella tried to wash the windows, but she was so distracted by Tirzah that she got more suds on her sleeves than the actual glass. How could someone who had lost their husband just a day ago be so concerned with dust?

Eventually Spencer came home at dusk, took one look at Tirzah, and uttered a firm hello.

Novella held her breath, but Tirzah repeated the greeting back to him without any tension in her body. Her body was relaxed, her temperament even. Novella was astonished at how Tirzah could even speak to the man who murdered her husband, much less look him in the eye. In secret, Novella wished that Tirzah would retaliate—do something. She wanted to experience the fearless woman who negroes in town spoke about. The longer Novella silently watched Tirzah, the more she wondered if that woman was a myth, because Tirzah was too restrained a person for Novella to see any trace of that former self.

The days that followed were slow and excruciating. Tirzah got up each morning from her marital bed, bathed and dressed, and headed out the door. She allowed visitors to stay at her home to keep her company and do housework for as long as they wanted—even if she'd much rather be alone. Once her feet touched the welcome mat of her home at the end of the workday, she marched upstairs to her bedroom and wasn't seen or heard from till the following morning. Meanwhile, Free paced the house at all hours of the night to outrun the sleep that tried to claw its way to him, afraid to dream of his father's death, of all he'd seen. During the day, he did not leave the house.

On the Sunday morning following Isaac's death, a terrible storm fell over Shreveport, which made Isaac's funeral even more melancholic. The older folks assured the younger ones that God had sent the rain to make the route slick so the chariot carrying Isaac's soul would get to Him sooner. Inside the church, which was packed to the brim once again with negroes from all over Caddo Parish, Tirzah heard all of the chattering about the downpour from behind her wide-brimmed black hat and fan. She managed to stay composed when a hand would clutch her arm or pat her shoulder for consolation. With the pews filled, some attendees stood on the side to catch a glimpse of the casket of the great Isaac Levi, if only for a moment.

During the service, the heat swelled in the sanctuary alongside the organ playing and choir singing. Free sat behind his father's podium as the first assistant pastor delivered a rousing speech about Isaac's commitment to "his family, church, and the people" but never delved into his fierce advocacy for negro rights as workers and human beings. Tirzah wasn't shocked. Everyone was afraid, as they should have been. Their beacon of light had been snuffed out, leaving their community even more vulnerable to white violence. When the assistant pastor turned around to ask if Free wanted to say a few words, he rose slowly, then fell back down into his seat before a few deacons surrounded him, affording him the privacy to cry. The benediction closed out the service, and Isaac was then buried behind the church in a cemetery for members. In order to avoid too much pandemonium over a famed preacher and activist, which might provoke whites in town to act violently again, he was put into the ground quickly, with no singing accompaniment—only the Lord's Prayer to send him off. Afterward, some men and women from the church returned to the Levi home with baked goods and drink as condolence gifts and sat around the living room to share warm memories of Isaac.

Hours later, as if it were a day like any other, Novella and Tirzah went together to the Ambrose house for work. Spencer was in his study with the door closed. Eventually, he emerged, went to one of his bar cabinets, and poured himself a large glass of cognac, which he downed in one swallow. Then he threw the glass into the fireplace, where it shattered loudly, and shouted, "Tirzah, cut me another slice of your famous vanilla custard pie!"

Tirzah obeyed and went over to the windowsill to fetch the dish, while Novella busied herself with the place setting. Spencer sat at the dining-room table and placed a crusty boot on the tablecloth, then leaned back with his hands behind his head. As Tirzah plated the pie, he reached forward to caress her backside. She winced silently. With his other hand, he patted Novella's bottom as she placed his silverware beside his plate.

"Y'all are some fine nigras. You know that?"

"Thank you, sir," Novella said quickly, but Tirzah had started to walk away when Spencer grabbed her wrist and pinned it to the table.

His bloodshot eyes monitored her. "I know you must be angry with me. But I couldn't allow Isaac to start giving any of the niggers around here ideas." Tirzah's pupils dilated, her body inflamed after hearing Spencer invoke her husband's name. "I gave him a chance. And he didn't listen, unlike you—"

Spencer held Tirzah's face, and before she knew it, she flashed a gun out from her inner apron pocket. A noise rang out and blood splattered everywhere. Spencer's chair fell backward as parts of his brain slid down the damask wallpaper. Tirzah and Novella stood over his body, watching his fingers twitch even when life was no longer in him. Novella touched Tirzah's right hand, whose index and middle fingers were still on the trigger, and slowly took the gun from her to set it on the dining-room table.

Suddenly, Tirzah burst into hysterical laughter, and Novella grabbed the rag in her right apron pocket to cover the older woman's mouth. When Tirzah had finally stopped, Novella wiped Spencer's blood from Tirzah's face and threw the rag at his corpse.

Novella leaned forward, smiled, and whispered, "Dere you are, Tirzah. You still dat girl from long ago. Now let's go."

15

Free did not object to leaving. He was no longer a preacher's son, after all. For as long as he stayed in Shreveport, there wouldn't be a negro who didn't pity him for what happened to his father. As his father's body had swung from that limb, Free's dreams of suffrage for negro people died along with it. Voting, he suspected, was not going to change anything, and even if it did, he wouldn't live long enough in Louisiana to find out. That's why when Novella and Tirzah hurried him to get ready to leave, he asked no questions and did what he was told.

As their carriage bumped along the road, Novella reached into her bag and gave Tirzah something to sip on to calm her nerves, but even after drinking, Tirzah just laughed until tears fell out of her eyes. Her head surged with fantasies of witnessing the look on Athéné's and the children's faces when they walked through the door and saw their father's head blown off. If only she could've danced to the sounds of their wailing and screaming. Then, suddenly, Tirzah quieted down and stared blankly ahead.

"What did you give her?" Free asked.

"Valerian and kava. She'll be good for a while."

Beneath the bonnet of the wagon where the Levi family hid, Novella clutched Free's hand and rested it on her lap. She considered, gazing at him, what their lives in Kansas might be like. With arms like his, he could be a carpenter, blacksmith, or a farmer. They'd raise a family on acres upon acres of land, and the only white they'd see for miles would be that of the fresh linen drying on the clothesline. In time, she figured, his love for her would return. Her unyielding faith would have to suffice for now, because at the minute Free could not be any less interested in her. All he could do was stare straight ahead, possibly more fixated on the journey than anything else.

"Natchez," Tirzah mumbled.

"What, Ma?" Free asked.

She began to rub her temples and groaned. "The bells. It's just—" She didn't finish.

The wagon slowed, and Free peeked his head out from the bonnet. They were approaching a section of the Red River where the trees shielded boats arriving and departing. The storm had thankfully abated, and the river had miraculously not overflowed. Only a handful of negroes were scattered about along a makeshift boarding area, and they were bartering with the white personnel to get a place on the ship. Only two families had enough to board, one of them being Tirzah's. Free offered three silver spoons and trinkets and the personnel snatched them all before urging them to move quickly onto the vessel.

Inside the boat, scores of other negroes huddled together, their hunger and thirst made visible by the hollow pockets of their cheeks and the cracked skin of their lips. A foul smell filled the air, but the thick heat was more offensive, without any ventilation to provide even a modicum of relief. Free wanted to relieve himself of the two bags that he'd had to pack in a terrible rush, which contained only a fraction of what he and his mother possessed. But he didn't trust that they'd be safe once he set them down. The other passengers stared at him and his mother with a curiosity that unsettled him.

As soon as Novella spotted a vacant corner, she tugged Free toward it, and he pulled his mother along. But when Free saw Novella placing her one bag onto the ship floor, he shook his head, and so she sat down and placed it on her lap. He bent his knees, holding his and his mother's bags against his chest. As for Tirzah, still groggy from what Novella had given her, she could barely see where she was in the dim light. Her tongue was heavy and her jaw slack. Free worried her expression would make the other passengers think she was slow and perhaps easy to deceive, so once she sat, he draped a cloth over her head and pulled her closer to him.

To pass the time, Free reached into his right pocket and took out a deck of cards his father had given him and began shuffling. When the Joker flew out and floated toward the floor, Tirzah caught it, studying the figure. In his red-and-yellow trousers and matching jacket and silver bells adorning his head, he held a mask in his right hand. She closed her eyes and clenched her fist around the card. "I was this person once. A long time ago," she said. "But he saved me. He saved me." She opened her eyes and pointed to her chest. "I love him. I never stopped. Not even after all these years."

"Ma, do you remember who you are and where we are? You are Tirzah Levi. I'm your son, Free Levi."

Tirzah cast sorrowful eyes at her son and announced, "My name is Tirzah Ambrose." The self-assurance in her tone contradicted Free's assumption that the herbs were still doing their work. His mouth turned dry, and he could feel anger welling up in his body, with no space to release it. Novella massaged his arm and said, "'S okay, Free. She just goin' through her thoughts. She'll come out soon enough. Just practice your game."

Free loved his mother. Unconditionally so. But he was frustrated and offended. Why did she insist to go by the name of her former master? Why was she so adamant not to claim the name Levi after Free's pa died? Who was the man she never stopped loving?

16

Novella leaned against the wall and allowed the small rocking of the ship to calm her, stealing glances at Free. She vividly remembered the day she met him: Easter Sunday 1881. She'd made her first appearance at Isaac Levi's church after a grueling week of learning her new home and mistress. Her original boss was a finicky white man who was weak in the face of any vice that might kill him, and the future of his family's estate lay in the hands of the many men to whom he owed money and favors. Spencer Ambrose was one of the men he owed. As a measure to break even, Novella's former employer decided to send her to Spencer to work for him until all debts were paid, leaving Novella with hardly any money to save for herself.

She'd never forget the day she arrived in Shreveport from Coushatta. She entered her new mistress's home through the back door and up into the attic, where the heat could've killed her. Her mistress started working Novella until blisters and sores all over her body spread faster than the weeds she pulled from the family garden. But four hours of church every Sunday was nonnegotiable, because her mistress had recently come around to the idea that niggers had souls and that Scripture could provide structure even without masters to guide them.

Novella was not the slightest bit religious, but she wasn't going to miss the break from her mistress's house, or the opportunity to be in the presence of pomp and circumstance. Born during Louisiana's last gasp of slavery, Novella remembered less and less of her parents the older she got. A man and a woman cared and loved her once, and then one day they disappeared. Just five years old, Novella woke up one morning in her family's cabin by herself. Their clothes still hung in the closet. Shoes still by the front door. No kin claimed her. Instead, she was left to the will of other adults, who were often too busy with their own affairs to give her instruction, such as basic hygiene. In the aftermath of her parents' disappearance, Novella began to develop a stench that was hardly improved by the Louisiana heat. She wanted to be in the same condition she was in the last time she saw them, believing that somewhere within her stink, there was a hint of her mother and father.

But the other sharecroppers soon tired of the assault on their noses, and one morning, some of the heftiest women in the community dragged Novella to the Red River and scrubbed her skin with lye and oils until it became raw and red, a baptism of the worst kind. Novella came up from the water with her body cleansed but her spirit discontent. From there on, she was taken in by other sharecroppers in the community—a week here, several months there, a year or two over yonder. She spoke less to others, never played with the other children, and worked the land while her neighbors sat in church. She wouldn't have recognized God if He stood in the middle of a well-beaten path.

But the Easter she first saw Free was different. She walked in the direction of the sounds of praise and worship and entered the sanctuary just as Isaac was concluding his sermon. The two front doors creaked open, and even the most devout parishioners struggled to keep from turning to see who had the audacity to arrive this late. Free, who sat in the first pew, failed to control his curiosity and looked over his shoulder. Novella caught his eye and half smiled at him before taking her seat all the way in the back, and he turned his gaze forward to continue praying, but his inward eyes saw only her.

As time went on, she started to attend services weekly, and the glances they exchanged became more obvious. Their connection was hardly welcome news to all the eligible young ladies in the church, who would dress in their Sunday finest and make a beeline for Free immediately after benediction. He knew, though, that the women who surrounded him did not solely like him for his looks or his spirit. He was the son of Isaac and Tirzah Levi, and any negro in Caddo Parish knew what that meant. He was the closest thing to royalty. When Novella first came to church, Free wondered why she didn't chase him like the rest of the girls. Truthfully, as an abandoned child who never had a stable home, she was always careful about being a burden to others, and Free looked pretty preoccupied. But to Free, her cool demeanor made him want to approach her. Soon, he was a fly to her light, always wanting to know that she was watching him as he was watching her. Her commitment to wait inspired him to undertake what the other girls didn't require: a pursuit.

A DAY LATER, THEY BOARDED A SECOND SHIP AT BATON ROUGE, AND Tirzah had gone from quiet to silent. Two more days dragged on as the ship traveled up the Mississippi, then into the Missouri River once they passed St. Louis. Tirzah's sense of smell had become more acute as she sniffed and surveyed the other passengers. When the horn blew and the door to the bottom level of the ship flung open, she bumped aside the other passengers as she clamored for the open air. The saltwater called to her. She vaguely recalled her confession to Free about wanting to return to Natchez, but where and when she had said so evaded her.

But as soon as Tirzah climbed the stairs to the top level, she was certain that there'd been a mistake. No seagulls flapped overhead, and she saw no crawfish or crab traps at the water's edge. She looked for the familiar bluffs overlooking the Mississippi, and the markets in the lower part of town, but saw neither. A hand touched the crook of her right elbow, and Tirzah stared back at Free, who was nudging her to follow the current of the movement off the ship.

"Where are we?" Tirzah asked him, alarmed.

"Kansas," Novella said. "Remember?"

Tirzah hesitated to step forward, but soon the rest of the passengers shoved past her, and her body was subsumed by the frenzy. Free and Novella could not hear her calling out to them above the shouts of the crowd, but finally Free saw her arm flailing in the air and ran over to prevent her from being trampled. Tirzah's hair flopped into her face and her clothes were dirtied, but they were getting off the boat. Novella took the bags while Free held on to his mother and didn't let go until they reached steady ground.

Tirzah and Free barely spoke to each other after he dropped her hand. Not even when they traveled westward via railroad to Topeka and wound up in a shelter for other negro refugees. Not even when they had to share a blanket as they weren't acclimated to a Midwestern winter night where the breeze off the nearby Kansas River was strong and unrelenting. And not even when they loaded themselves and their bags into a wagon from that shelter to a town that supposedly had lots of land for transplants. Novella sat in between mother and son for several hours as they traversed dirt roads through cornfields, afraid to say the wrong thing while trying to ease the tension between the two.

Once everything felt calm and Free had enough time to process all that they experienced on this long journey, out of the blue, he asked, "Why did we really leave so quickly?"

Novella and Tirzah exchanged secret looks with each other.

"I mean, I know we weren't safe but—"

"That's right, son. I didn't feel safe being in that house after your Pa died, so I thought it was best to leave. That's all."

Free leaned back in his seat, dissatisfied at the response but too exhausted from all the traveling to press further.

When the wagon finally screeched to a halt, the driver instructed them to transfer to another carriage that had eased up alongside them, then grumbled to himself until Free, Novella, and Tirzah disembarked, before hurrying out of sight. Once the dust cleared and they'd loaded themselves into the other carriage, the trio saw a wooden sign carved with words "Nicodemus Established 1877" staked into the ground on the road, clearly leading to a village.

Nicodemus could've been a mirage for all they knew. There'd been nothing but acres of corn for miles, but now homes began to emerge from the horizon. The skies overhead had very few clouds and the air was less thick. Their carriage went along, passing by the homes of negro families. Women outside hanging up clothes or supervising children waved at them as they approached the center of town. The landscape felt wide and the town full of possibility. Novella felt excitement, and Free was determined, but Tirzah felt only guilt. She gazed out the window and saw tenderness between these new negro citizens: an older negro couple walking along a dusty road, a new mother strolling with her baby, a woman animatedly talking with her husband on the porch of their log cabin. Tirzah finally made it out of Shreveport, yet she could not share this moment with Isaac. She would not cry, because her body had nothing left to give. The fog of her medicinal haze had faded, but her grief became ever more present. All Tirzah could do was exhale to push out the sadness. Exhale in gratitude that she was alive, and knowing that she'd keep on for Isaac's sake.

They followed the flow of carts into the town square, where she saw hundreds of negro people bustling in and out. But she saw no white men on horseback or white women eyeing their every move. There was a bank, a drug store, a milliner, three general merchandise stores, and a schoolhouse all packed within this lively public square.

Right near the center of town, two men dressed in their Sunday best stood on opposite sides of a door leading into First Baptist Missionary Church. Tirzah felt the carriage slow to a stop and the driver let them out and gestured them inside, where female parishioners wearing plain white uniforms sat at tables ready to help new arrivals.

As they hurriedly oriented themselves inside to escape the cold temperature, a woman dressed in a copper polonaise dress with pink stripes, lace-trimmed heels, and a high-crowned bonnet—a stark contrast from what the female registration volunteers wore—approached them. She smelled of tuberose and jasmine, scents Tirzah recognized because she'd regularly spritzed them onto her own skin back home.

"Welcome to Nicodemus," the woman proclaimed exuberantly. "I'm Elodie Williams, first lady of this church."

They shook hands.

"It's a pleasure to meet you," Tirzah said. "I figured from your style of dress, you had to be a first lady."

"Ah, you're a woman of God too?"

Tirzah took a beat. "Indeed, I am."

"What was your church home?"

Tirzah's eyes glazed over when she deliberated over how much to divulge. "Somewhere way down south. In a town neither you nor anyone else might've heard of, I'm sure."

"I see," Elodie said, still smiling. She noticed that these three people were shivering and said, "This weather must be a lot if you're coming from down south. I'll have some of my people fetch you some appropriate coats."

"Thank you so much," Tirzah said.

"You're welcome. I didn't quite catch your name."

Tirzah scanned the room and spotted the letterboard on the wall across from them, which read "1 Samuel 9:21: Saul answered, 'Am I not a Benjamite, from the smallest tribe of Israel, and is not my clan the least of all the clans of the tribe of Benjamin?'"

The smallest and the mightiest. The name Levi was different, a prominent and priestly name from another tribe of Israel. Now this same name, once of a proud, God-fearing lineage in Shreveport, would be no more. It would have to be cast aside for a humbler one so that they could begin again and avoid who might want to avenge Spencer's murder. Everything that came before would have to be erased, in fact. Tirzah silently thanked God that Free's bloody eye was all cleared up so that no one would ask questions as to how he had gotten hurt. She couldn't be certain that he'd be tightlipped about what truly happened.

"Benjamin," she proclaimed. "My name is Tirzah Benjamin."

As Free heard his mother lie, his nostrils flared and he tried to catch her eye, but she wouldn't look at him.

"This is my son, Free, and this here is Miss Novella."

Novella smiled and said how do you do, but Free was silent.

Elodie nodded. "Pleasure to meet you all."

For such a seemingly proper and well-to-do woman, Elodie wondered, why had this Tirzah Benjamin arrived with so little? But when Free shifted his weight, she saw the shimmer of a silver spoon sticking out from one of his pockets and realized they must have some wealth in their past. So she guided the trio behind the pulpit, pulling back the curtain into a back room where she took down their names herself. With the newcomers' consent, a few men briefly looked through their carpet bags to estimate how many more valuables they had. Alongside rumpled clothing and undergarments, they found a few jewels, more silver, and a Bible. No sooner had the men finished their search, their eyebrows raised in fascination, than Elodie whisked the trio to the largest suite on the highest floor of the St. Francis Hotel, where uniformed bellboys carried their few bags for them.

"Now these accommodations are temporary," Elodie said as she sat with Free and Novella in the main room. "First Baptist Missionary has been working tirelessly to help all our new neighbors, especially those who can contribute to our town's vision of economic growth and opportunity. The Osage Indians have also been helping us with timber and other resources for years, so we will find you a piece of land. You're lucky you're here now. Once the railroad comes, you might've been stuck."

"Why a railroad?" Free asked, the first words he'd spoken to Elodie.

"We're campaigning to have a main railroad come through

Nicodemus to bring in more business and more people. We're the largest negro colony in America, dear. And we intend to be even larger." Free grinned, which she took as an invitation to continue. "Now, Free—are you okay with me calling you Free?"

"I don't go by any other name."

"Son—" Tirzah interjected from the other room where she was already reclining on a loveseat.

"What's your vocation? What are you good at?"

"Well . . ." He paused and massaged the nape of his neck. "I'm pretty strong, or so I've been told."

"How about carpentry?" Elodie suggested.

"No!" Tirzah marched into the living room, surprising the others. If Harrison hadn't rushed to the forefront of her memory, she might've remained composed, but she couldn't shake the image of him at work on the Phoenician the day they first met. She took a deep breath and said, "Anything else. I won't allow carpentry."

"Understood." Elodie nodded. "What about blacksmithing? Jericho offers apprenticeships at his shop and if you pay attention, he'll prepare you to be a fine craftsman."

"I'll try—I mean. I'll—" The word hung awkwardly in his mouth. "I'll try it out."

"Splendid. And what about you, Novella?"

Novella, whose mind had wandered off to someplace else, snapped up. "Me? Oh. I suppose cookin'. I do maid work and cookin'."

"Is that what you *want* to do?"

Novella blushed and placed a curl behind one of her ears. "Dat's a question I never been asked before."

"Then we'll start now and find something for you." She leaned over and touched the young woman's shoulder before rising to her feet. "Tonight, I would be honored if you all could join us at my home for an event hosted by the Prince Hall Order of the Eastern Star."

"Order of de Eastern Star?" Novella echoed.

"The Eastern Star. Freemasons, sweetheart. Be there at seven.

My home is between Adams and Second Street. You'll know it from the number of carriages outside." Elodie bowed slightly and turned to walk out of the suite.

Once the door closed, Free and Novella began to unpack their bags, but she soon realized that the one dress she packed was far too plain for tonight's event. She clutched one of Tirzah's slips close to her chest and stared off into space.

"What's wrong?" Free asked while folding a pair of trousers.

"Nothin'."

"Yes it is." He turned to Tirzah, who'd settled into a nearby chair to supervise. "And Ma—why do you have them call us Benjamin instead of Levi?"

"Because we're starting over here, that's why."

"But why does that mean we have to change our name?" Free just stared at her.

Tirzah sighed. "Free, just stop back-talking me for once, and let's get settled."

"It feels like you are shutting me out about something and I have no say about anything."

He shook his head while Tirzah retreated into the bedroom to peer out the window at the Solomon River. Nicodemus rested on low-lying terrain, and on a clear day like this, she could see several miles in any direction. But the land was not as lush as it was back in Louisiana. She saw no pine forests or wetlands or fields of cotton. Here, wheat was king. Tirzah knew all the ways in which wheat could be used in the kitchen: breads, all kinds of pastries. She started to dream of all she could make, the bounty that'd be available to her here, but a dull pain grew in her chest at the thought of settling in and actually enjoying the place.

"'Scuse me . . ." Novella spoke in a low voice, joining her at the window.

Tirzah whispered, "Do not tell Free about what I did to Mister Spencer. He's too emotional to hear about that right now. If he finds out about that, God knows what he'd do. You hear me? This is between you and me."

"Yes, ma'am."

"Good. Now what is it?"

Novella inched forward. "I only got one dress and it ain't good enough. Do you have one dat I can borrow? I plan to get a job first thing in de mornin'. I get my own clothes, promise."

Tirzah sighed and placed a hand on Novella's shoulder. "Yes, I can lend you one. I like you. You're hardworking and you want to work for your own things. Never lose that. Always have something for you and you alone. No matter if you're by yourself or you have a man. Understand?"

Novella nodded.

Before Tirzah could continue, Free stepped into the room, a Bible in his hands.

Tirzah chuckled. "What now? Are you planning on giving us a Word?"

He opened the Bible and removed a wrinkled brown paper from between two pages, then recited: "Information wanted for Tirzah Ambrose. She was sold to Mercer Ambrose but last belonged to his son, Spencer Ambrose. Last seen in Natchez, Mississippi. Would like to know the whereabouts of the above-named person for a Harrison Ambrose. Any information may be sent to Piper Carlisle, Freedmen's Bureau of Natchez between Pearl and Washington Streets."

A sad smile started to curve across Tirzah's face.

"Ma? What is this?"

"This"—she said emphatically—"is an advertisement for someone looking for me."

"I know that," Free said. "But is this the man you were talking about on the ship? The man you said you loved, the one who saved you?"

Tirzah pressed a hand to her heart. "On the ship? Wh—what man? I wasn't talking about any man, I—"

"You said it!" her son said, raising his voice. "On the ship. You told everyone who had ears that you loved someone before Pa and you thought you were going back to Natchez."

"I—" She looked to the ground, searching for the memory, but she could not find it. When she finally raised her face, she asked him, "What did you do to me back in Shreveport?"

"What are you talking about? I didn't do anything to you."

"Valerian and kava," Novella intervened with a frustrated sigh. "It was to calm you down after you was . . . actin' all crazy once you k—"

"Do you still love him?" Free asked in a quieter but higher-pitched voice.

"Yes, I still love him. And I still love your Pa. I have had and lost two great loves in my life. I was wanted and I was cared for and looked after. I am lucky. Even in the face of death."

Novella was moved by Tirzah's words and grabbed her right hand with both of hers, but Free dropped the Bible on a table and left the room again, mumbling to himself. Soon, the women heard the door to the suite slam, and Novella felt the impulse to follow him, but she realized she would have to be patient with him. He didn't understand the language of women. He wanted to live with certainty, with hard and clear truths. She was especially thankful for Tirzah's company in that moment.

FREE'S ANGER WITH HIS MOTHER WASN'T GOING TO STOP HIM FROM accompanying her and Novella to the gathering that evening. They had to present a united front. Indeed, they saw as they approached that Elodie Williams had been right: no passersby could miss her home. Besides the carriages outside, it was the largest property on the block—a limestone, two-story structure surrounded by vast wheat fields.

An older gentleman, who introduced himself as Budd, Elodie's husband, greeted them at the door and took the trio's borrowed coats. When they entered, the party was not as crowded as they'd envisioned. Little groups were spaced out around the house, which smelled faintly of tobacco smoke and dark liquor. Boisterous men seated at a round table argued among one another and threw down card suits simultaneously. A banjo-playing gentleman in a porkpie hat and a tuxedo-wearing piano player strummed notes and sang, the result a blend of gospel and some kind of sound she'd never heard before. Tirzah regretted not having an extra shawl to cover her sweaty armpits as this indulgent environment was quite new for her, and she was unsure of how she'd fit in, especially as a single woman. She glanced over at Novella and Free, who were visibly starstruck by all of the happenings, and wished she felt more secure within herself.

"Well hello!" Elodie emerged from a corner wearing a silk damask gown. She floated over to the Benjamins and stretched out her white-gloved hands to shake theirs. Tirzah wondered if her bare hands were inappropriate for this occasion. "I'm so glad that you all could make it, especially after such a long journey."

"We are honored by the invitation," Tirzah said. "Right, children?"

Tirzah looked at Novella, who nodded vigorously, and Free, who remained stoic.

"Would any of you like something to drink?" their hostess asked.

"Whiskey, if you have it," Free said, and Elodie nodded. A waitstaff person was fortuitously walking by and Elodie stopped him to deliver Free's order.

Tirzah's eyes bulged—Free knew he had no business ordering alcohol, especially in front of her—but she refrained from protesting; she and Free had been against each other long enough. "Forgive me for saying this but—"

"Please," Elodie insisted.

"I'm surprised that you men and women of God are drinking. I expected this to be a more conservative gathering."

Elodie nodded. "We are conservative, which is why we're doing this in our home. The Order of the Eastern Star is a wonderful organization that brings religious folks together. Our lodge is just right on the outskirts of this township, but we come here from time to time because I have the bigger space."

"And dis all of Nicodemus?" Novella asked.

"Heavens, no."

"I dunno why anyone would turn down a gathering like dis."

Elodie smiled. "You all have never heard of the Prince Hall Order for where you come from, I take it."

"You're correct," Tirzah said.

"Well, I brought you here to tell you all about it. Miss Tirzah, I'd love to show you around my home. Walk with me?"

"Of course." As Tirzah left with her host, Novella turned to Free.

"You never told me dat you drink whiskey," Novella said to him when the older ladies were out of earshot.

"I don't," Free said, and laughed.

Novella coquettishly pushed his chest. "You gon' turn her head gray if you keep this up."

"She'll be fine."

As the women moved toward the other side of the floor near the sun-room, Elodie leaned closer toward her new neighbor and said, "May I ask you something a bit more personal?"

"Sure," Tirzah reluctantly replied. Feeling what was coming, Tirzah blurted out, "May I have something to drink as well?" Another server was moving in and out of the kitchen with champagne glasses and Tirzah waved him down to grab two for herself. She downed both quickly. "You were saying?"

"You're married, yes? I see a ring on your finger but no husband, and you have all these valuables . . ." She trailed off.

"My husband's dead." Tirzah immediately regretted the flatness of her tone when she saw Elodie's face change. She didn't want to hear any sympathy but, Tirzah thought, at least her tipsiness would lessen the impact.

"Oh I'm so sorry," Elodie said. "How long has it been?"

Tirzah swallowed. "A few months. Excuse me." She quickly

walked away from Elodie to hide the shame of her lie. She found a column in the hallway and pressed her back up against it while she counted her breaths. Grief flooded her body, and she ached for her husband's presence. Isaac would have loved to have met other church members, probably would have had some whiskey or champagne himself or socialized with all the men here. But aside from Isaac's interpersonal skills, Tirzah missed his resounding laughter, his touch on the small of her back, the way his fist banged on the podium when he delivered hope to their congregants. She missed her north star. Isaac would have wanted her to ingratiate herself into this churchly milieu, she knew. Now she could be a woman of standing without the duties of being a first lady—the best of both worlds—but she'd have to move strategically.

On the other side of the room, a gentleman approached Free, who was shuffling his card deck absentmindedly.

The man sized Free up. "You play?"

"Blackjack," Free responded, feigning an air of cool.

"Blackjack?" the gentleman asked in mock disbelief. "Say, you hear that, fellas? This youngblood said he knows how to play blackjack!"

The other card players snickered as the smoke from their cigars serpentined upward into the air.

"One game." Free dug into his pocket and pulled out a silver spoon, and a murmur went across the room.

"Free, no," Novella whispered, touching his free hand. She pulled him toward her. "You can't do dat. Dat's too high of a wager."

"I know what I'm doing, Nov."

"But Free—!"

"Hey!" one of the players called out. "Are we negotiating with you, or do you have to get permission from your woman?"

"Deal me in," Free said without hesitation. He pulled up a chair, and a new game began.

All the guests crowded around the table to watch, and soon the rhythmic breathing of the game participants was its own music. The players placed their bets and the cards were dealt. The men glanced over at one another and leaned back in their chairs to assess their choices, grunting or mumbling along the way. Free remained silent and steady, the world fading behind the perimeters of his cards. Some of the men wanted the dealer to give them another card, and a few folded. All expected that they would have no trouble taking the silver spoon from that youngblood's hand. But Free won the first round, and the crowd burst into an uproar. Beginner's luck, the men agreed after throwing down their cards. But when he won a third and then a fourth time, they began to perspire in their seats and pull at their scalps in disbelief.

"That boy is sum'n'!" one of the players said, both excited and dejected.

"Damn right he is."

"I know that's right!" a woman's voice called out while several others giggled from behind their fans. All the while, Tirzah massaged the nape of her sweaty neck over what her son had gotten himself into with these strangers.

Feeling as though there were no place for her, Novella had backed away slowly until she became indistinguishable from the rest of the crowd. Eventually, she found herself all the way in the back, standing on her toes, straining to catch a glimpse of her beloved's face or neck. He was still whenever cards were dealt, but each time he won, she noticed, he'd lift his head to watch a woman in the crowd. This woman wasn't Novella, and he didn't look lovestruck in the way he had looked at her months before. This stranger had skin the shade of brown one revels in at sunset. Her cheekbones were defined like God sculpted them with his own hands, and her almond-shaped eyes were lovely and intense.

Free looked ravenous. Novella wondered if anyone else saw what could only be called the sin in his eyes. When she scanned the room to see if anyone noticed, Tirzah came up beside her and pressed a hand on her shoulder. Novella turned halfway to see that Tirzah's eyes were fixed on the same woman, her mouth was half open, and her breaths large and deep. As she walked through the crowd toward this stranger, Novella followed.

When Tirzah finally reached the young woman, she stared directly into her face. Feeling awkward, the woman looked at the ground, but Tirzah reached out a hand and gently lifted her chin.

"I know you. Or at least I think I do. What is your name?"

FEBRUARY
1882

17

Almost nine months exactly to the night when Harrison asked Tabithah to marry him, Miriam was born. Her arrival was nothing short of dramatic. Shorebirds from the Mississippi had flown far inland—a sign of an imminent storm—while folks in the negro village along the river worried that they didn't have enough plywood to protect their windows. Her father was out making repairs around town, while her mother was wobbling to and from the bedroom to the kitchen with a midwife monitoring her every breath.

The first and only child of her parents, Miriam was deeply wanted. Her mother had her father build a crib the moment her blood didn't arrive at its usual time. Names were thrown around and dreams of what she could be, a member of the first generation born out of slavery, filled her mother's head before she even felt the first kick. When the birth workers announced they believed the child would be a girl, though, Tabithah felt a sharp tinge of disappointment before her last labored push. This daughter, Tabithah presumed, would only go so far in life, as most negro women did.

When Miriam slid out of Tabithah and heard her mother's voice earthside, she immediately stopped wailing, already familiar with the sound. But with Harrison—who arrived, sweaty and late to the birth—it was different; his presence sent her into a crying fit. Much time passed before she quieted in his arms. She just didn't want to be

held by him. Folks believed it to be a terrible omen for a man to be farther than the other side of the door from where his wife was birthing.
The village doctor and midwife told him that the baby could feel his
stress and frustration, which only made things worse.

As a young child, Miriam could not help but feel imbalanced,
vulnerable to the slightest shift of Tabithah's moods and her mother's desperation for her father's attention. Harrison loved Miriam and
was always spoiling her with compliments and physical affection.
However, she always detected a mystery behind every gaze and every
smile he bestowed upon her, to where she assumed that she'd never
fully know him. Between the push and pull of her parents, Miriam was
quiet and never gave them much trouble. She followed her mother's
advice on cooking, cleaning, and other womanly duties, and obeyed
any order from her father. But there was always a deep sadness about
her—something that neither her parents, the village doctor, nor the
preacher could place. Nor could she.

When she was allowed, she would wander along the Mississippi
or through downtown and lose her way on streets that should have
been familiar to her. She'd rest underneath a tree and wake up, hours
later, not knowing where she was. There wasn't enough turpentine or
anointed oil to fix whatever ailed her.

As she moved toward adolescence, Miriam's random bouts of
crying led many in the community to believe that she had too much
water in her, likely from being born by the river during a torrential
downpour. What she needed, some suggested to her mother, was
to be dried up: more spices and astringents in her diet, more exercise to sweat out the excess, a move further inland. The last was an
impossibility—her father breathed the fresh water into his body every
morning and couldn't imagine leaving.

But the problem with Miriam wasn't just that she was sad. As
she aged, she became more suspicious of her parents' relationship.
Her parents didn't know how acutely she observed them. Something
was missing between them, almost like they were strangers to one

another. It caused her to develop a fierce streak of independence, a yearning for a larger life, more than what they'd endeavored to build for her. And yet her sadness seemed to eclipse her ambition. By the time she was fifteen, after many episodes of heartburn, chest pains, sleepless nights, and seemingly unprompted bouts of sobbing, Miriam concluded that this was how her life was always going to be. The resignation eradicated almost every shred of her desire for something more, something different.

That was until the storm came, and it stayed, and stayed, raging for several weeks on end and sending all of Natchez into a frenzy. Dogs howled on roofs, people mistook day for night and failed to show up to work and earn their pay, even food didn't cook right. On one particular Saturday morning, the wind blew through Miriam's home, sending miscellaneous papers everywhere. Her father was already outside cutting timber, and Miriam was trying to fall back asleep from her perch across the room, as she saw her mother frantically running around to catch every paper in midair, stuffing some of them between her large bosoms. Miriam had never seen her mother move that quickly in her life. The shift in her behavior sparked Miriam's curiosity.

"Do ya need any help?" Miriam lifted her head from her pillow.

"No. Just mind your own," her mother shot back.

Miriam would have if she had any business to mind. The front door creaked open, and her mother quickly stuffed the papers away before patting the back of her head to make sure her hair looked right. For a woman who'd been married for many years, Miriam thought, she sure acted like she was still in the early throes of courtship, like her husband's intentions for her were still to be determined. Her mother was beautiful in her morning slip and robe. But her father walked right past her into the kitchen and plopped down to collect himself. Tabithah followed him and began loudly opening and closing all the cupboards as she prepared breakfast. He turned his head away from the kitchen and grinned at Miriam, who could not help but smile back.

"My Miriam," he said, beaming. "My Miriam, my Miriam, my Miriam. Good mornin'.'"

Her mother turned around with a pitcher of orange juice in her hand and a furrow in her brow.

"Mornin', Pa. You out workin' early already again?"

"Of course. A man dat don' work, don' eat. Dat's in de good book."

"Which is why ya need to eat up righ' nah." Miriam's mother had found a way into the conversation at last.

Miriam laughed as she made her way to the table, where her mother loudly plopped a full plate in front of her. She sat in her usual chair, and the family held hands and said grace before they dug in. Her father took vigorous bite after bite while Tabithah eyed him, exhaustion sinking into her face, and Miriam observed how loudly his utensils clinked together.

"Pa."

"Yeah?" He finally lifted his head from his plate.

"Ain't ya gon' say thank you?"

"I ain't hear a thank you from you either, young lady," Tabithah said.

"Apologies." Her father lifted his head. "I'm sorry. You right. Dat was very impolite of me."

"Me too. I'm sorry," Miriam said before her eyes wandered to the colony of seagulls squawking and flapping outside the kitchen window.

"Miriam," her father said, his tone a mix of admonishment and admiration. "Girl, ya seen dem birds all ya life. Why now of all days ya so distracted?"

"She always distracted," Tabithah cut in.

"I don' know. Just—can't explain it, sorry." Miriam dropped her head and picked at the grits on her plate.

"What you see out dere?"

"Birds," Miriam said dryly.

"Obviously," Harrison chuckled. "Das all dat's keepin' ya distracted is de birds?"

"What is dis about, honey?" Tabithah asked Harrison.

"Let her answer." He held up his hand and nodded. "G'on."

She looked out the window at the nimbus clouds shifting across the morning sky and the unwieldy tides of the Mississippi. "I can't explain it." Miriam shook her head. "I'm sorry. I'm just lookin' beyond myself, dat's all."

"'Beyond,' ya say," her father responded, his eyes gazing out the window as well.

Tabithah's gaze bounced from her child to her husband and back again. She knew that the two people she loved most in this world were right next to her at this table, and yet she felt like they were far from her and moving farther, removing themselves from their home. She leaned to the side and touched her husband's back, but he didn't acknowledge her. Then she broke the silence by slamming her hands on the table and shooting to her feet. "I had enough of dis silly talk. It's not makin' any sense and I don' like it."

"I had someone in my life who always looked beyond demself too," her husband said.

"Harrison," Tabithah said in a warning tone. She held her breath and pressed a hand to her chest, but he just chuckled. His wife's shakiness almost amused him. After all these years building a life together—well, she was the most unconfident architect he'd ever met. He wasn't going to say what she thought he would say, though. Unlike other men, he wasn't the type to test a woman's patience. But he could not help but feel an unrighteous degree of satisfaction in seeing her panic at a threat that was no threat at all.

"What's goin' on?" Miriam looked from her mother to her father, searching for an answer.

"I wanna show ya somethin'." Harrison got up from the table and pulled out a large chest from underneath the bed he shared with Miriam. He took out a smaller chest inside of the larger one, with a lock to unlatch. Then he walked back to Miriam's side and handed her a leather wallet.

"Here," he said. "Take it."

"For what? I don't have no money and it's not like I'm goin' anywhere."

"Who's to say dat ain't gon' happen?" He extended his hand until the wallet grazed her chest.

She held the wallet and saw an engraving on its surface. "*T*?" She asked. "What do it stand for?"

Tabithah interjected: "Dat don' look like any one of mines. I don' remember you givin' me somethin' like dat."

His back was to his wife, and only Miriam could see tears forming in the corners of his eyes. He pushed out a long breath, and then his smile returned, and the tears receded. "Tomorrow," he said.

"Tomorrow?" Miriam asked.

"Yes. The *T* stand for tomorrow as in lookin' forward to tomorrow and not knowin' what will happen next in de best of ways."

Miriam didn't believe him, but didn't want to push him further.

Tabithah turned her back to them and began to furiously scrub the dishes, hoping that the racket would obscure her sniffling. Harrison was lying. She could tell by the sadness in his voice. Harrison hadn't told Miriam about Tirzah, but he had been dangerously close. Even if Harrison hadn't spoken her name, after all these years of Tabithah's love and devotion, was that enough? Had that been enough, if his memory of Tirzah still haunted their home? Immersed in these thoughts, Tabithah scrubbed a plate so hard that it slipped from her hands, crashing to the floor. The sound of it shattering caused Harrison and Miriam to crane their necks with concern, but she rubbed her eyes with the end of her apron and nervously laughed as she bent to pick up the pieces of the dish.

Before she could say a word, someone knocked on the front door and Tabithah raced to answer it before anyone could ask her what was wrong. Marie stood in their doorway carrying a large split-cane basket full of vegetables: carrots, sunchokes, fava beans, spinach, and turnips. Tabithah greeted Marie with a wide hug and relieved her of her bounty.

"Hi, Aunt Marie," Miriam said, embracing Marie, who kissed her on the right cheek.

"Hey, baby. Thought I'd stop by wit some gifts from my li'l garden."

"Dat's very nice of you," Harrison said. "You always comin' wit somethin'."

"'S only right. Y'all been dere for me ever since Ezek—" Marie pressed a hand to her chest. Tabithah and Miriam each held on to one of her shoulders to steady her balance while Harrison pulled out a chair from the dining table and guided her to rest. "Sorry. 'S been all dese years and I still get dis way."

"No need to apologize." Tabithah touched her hand.

"Anyway—I wanted to talk to y'all about your plans."

"Plans?" Tabithah asked.

"Y'all ain't hear? A storm's a comin'. Everybody's talkin' about it and figurin' what dey gon' do, who got cousins here, who got an uncle or an aunt dere . . ."

"A storm always comin', Marie," Tabithah said. "Why dis one have all de village shakin' and quakin', I don' know. But y'all gon' find out dat you worryin' for nothin'."

"I wouldn't be too sure 'bout dat, Tabithah. Look where we situated. Nothin' but shacks 'long de river. Ain't got nothin' to really protect us if de river get to floodin'. We either build better or move on."

"And you gon' use all dat timber for nothin' more den drizzle when you could be usin' it on gettin' us a better juke joint or church," said Tabithah.

Marie turned to Harrison, hoping for a different answer. "What say you, Harrison? You de head of de household."

"I have to agree wit my wife. We seen floods before and we made do. Doomsday thinkin' don' hurt nobody but ourself."

"Yeah, well, don't be mad at me when you find out I'm right. Even de white folk livin' above on de bluff scared 'bout it. Dey packin' and goin' far as La Salle Parish. Over dere in Louisiana? Some place called Jena? It ain't near water. We need to take heed."

"And leave Natchez so we can wind up wit no home? No." Tabithah shook her head. "Dis town done seen dem some rumors, nah. 'Member back in de day when dey thought we was plottin' to kill our masters and dey was killin' and jailin' every Tom, Dick, and Harry dey could? Won' nothin' true 'bout it. Now dere's a rumor dat white folk leavin' 'cause of a storm. Tuh!" Tabithah ranted. "Ain't nothin' but a scheme to see what we do when—or if—dey leave and den dey surround de city and lynch us all for insubordination or whatever kind of charge dey can trump up."

"How far Jena from here, Aunt Marie?" Miriam asked.

The three adults stared at her.

"Now see look what you done started," Tabithah said. "We best get goin' and start our day and not think about any of dis foolishness no more."

With that, Tabithah snatched all the dirty dishes and cups from the table and ordered Miriam to get dressed and Harrison to wash up. Marie held up her hands in surrender and abandoned the subject.

Every day, Marie would walk with Miriam and Tabithah to work. It was safer for the womenfolk to travel in groups—especially widows whose grown children had homes and families of their own. They worked the same plantation together, planting throughout the seasons. Sharecropping was what they called it.

Usually, Tabithah would compensate for what she believed to be her daughter's laziness by working extra hard to meet their quotas. But today Miriam was doing so little work, Tabithah wasn't sure she would be able to make up for it. Clearly, Miriam's wandering spirit had kicked into overdrive, and she just couldn't focus on twisting the cotton from the bolls. She stomped on Miriam's foot, elbowed her, and even grabbed the back of her neck, but nothing could get her to remain in the present.

Meanwhile, the sky grew darker and darker. Whenever Miriam looked up, she'd lose her balance. As the clouds grew heavier, so did her body. During the lunch break, she ate nothing and said nothing; she was trying to ease the tempest raging in her belly. As the winds became stronger and the trees roared with the rustling of their leaves, Miriam vomited water into the fields where she toiled until she wheezed. She fell on her back lightheaded, entranced by the low-hanging clouds. She imagined them enveloping her in its mist.

She saw the front door open and feared she would be chastised for lying down by whoever was coming outside. It was indeed her farmer boss, but his hands were too full with luggage to give her a whipping. His wife, two children, and servants followed behind with enough trunks to fill up several wagons. Each time they moved back and forth from the foyer to the wagon they looked up at the sky and hustled a bit more quickly. The rest of the planters watched their boss and his family, even as their careful hands separated the cotton from the bolls. Then the patriarch, his family, and his servants left without making any kind of announcement. The lady of the house pulled the curtains of the wagon to shield them, their driver gave a horse a good old kick, and that was it.

Miriam had been working the fields since she could walk, and she had never seen her boss do something like that. Murmurs spread from rows to row, the workers' voices ultimately reaching a volume that challenged the winds' howling.

"Ma, do we keep workin'?" she asked.

"I don' know." Tabithah lowered her burlap sack full of cotton slowly down to her side. "I don' know."

A couple of men took it upon themselves to walk over to the nearest plantation to see what was going on there and discovered sharecroppers standing around in a stupor because their bosses and their families had just up and left too. A few men from that plantation joined them, and together they went to the next plantation down the road, to find the sharecroppers there had been deserted as well. After this, everyone agreed to stop working and take shelter.

But shelter didn't necessarily mean home. Plenty of white folks were gone, and no one knew whether to fear the storm or laugh at how it was only their kind who could weather it. By midday, the negro village was strangely abuzz with activity.

People had to do something with their nervousness, and so it seemed like a good time for a party. When night fell, the juke joint would be open. Come early for the best seat in town, the word spread. If you come late, continue the revelry out the back door. As Miriam rested in her bed, Tabithah bathed herself in the communal shower in their backyard. She beautified herself with the only mirror they had in their home and alternated between seeing to her face and looking down at the ground.

"You okay, Mama?" Miriam asked.

"Hmm? Oh . . ." Tabithah said distractedly. "Yeah, I'm fine."

Miriam swallowed. "Ma . . . about what happened dis mornin' wit de plate . . ."

"What about it?"

"I just—"

Tabithah shook her head and waved her hands like window shutters in front of her. "Never you mind," she said. "Ain' ya gon' wash up? Ya don' wanna get nice and clean after a long workday?"

"What long workday?" Miriam joked.

They laughed, and then Miriam obliged her mother and bathed.

Harrison returned home at his usual hour, already aware of the white folks' exodus. All he wanted to do was rest in his chair for the remainder of the evening, but the smell of lavender extract greeted him before he opened the front door of his home.

"Don' y'all look and smell pretty. What's goin' on'?"

"We wanna go to de juke joint like everybody else and dem," Miriam told him.

"De juke joint?" Harrison asked.

"Just for a short while," Tabithah added.

"Y'all g'on 'head," Harrison said. He took off his coat and carelessly threw it toward the dining-table chair, missing the top rail completely, and walking right past the mess to kick his feet up on the small table in the living room. "I'm tired," he groaned, soothing his temple with his hand.

Tabithah looked over at Miriam, who pouted and lowered her head and blew a huge, audible gust of wind out her nostrils in frustration. Tabithah bent down to grab the jacket and threw it to Harrison's chest.

"Get up, Harrison. We goin'."

He wasn't a fan of the juke joint and hadn't been since before Miriam was born, when he still thought of himself as a Union soldier worthy of honor. But an honorably discharged serviceman such as Harrison still maintained a sense of duty—this time to his household. With his wife on one arm and his daughter on the left, he accompanied them down the road without saying a word. Tabithah walked into the joint with her head held high, but Miriam felt uncomfortable. The deep lines and creases in her father's face signaled to her that he was unhappy. Again. His eyes pointed straight ahead. Maybe he was thinking of the potential flooding, even though he was skeptical of its danger. If that was not the cause of his tight cheeks and chin, what else? Seemed like he could not help but look beyond himself too.

A ramshackle building that looked as if it would slide into the river at any moment, the juke joint was a place for the negro men to drink, the negro women to gossip, and for both parties to slow drag until the pianist closed his instrument's lid. People packed into the joint so tightly it was a wonder that the walls didn't burst. Shutters had to be open at all times to keep the heat from being unbearable. Tabithah yanked Harrison's arm and pulled him toward the bar in the back while Miriam trailed closely behind.

"Two orders of moonshine, please," Tabithah said.

"One, actually," Harrison said. "I'm taking water instead."

"You sure?" the bartender asked, and seductively leaned over the counter, her breasts spilling over onto the surface. "We got de best moonshine out of any tall ridin' boot in Adams County."

"I'm sure," Harrison said.

There was a thick silence, one in which Tabithah estimated the risk of saying how she felt or holding her tongue and dealing with the pain of swallowing her expression later. She tucked her lower lip into her mouth and shook her head.

"You ain't never given me no wallet," Tabithah said as they walked back from the bar, glasses in hand.

He sipped his water. "So?"

Tabithah's eyes bulged. "'So'?"

"Tabithah, let's just enjoy the night, okay? Ya wanted to go out, so we out."

She took a swig of the moonshine to calm her nerves. For a brief moment, she pictured herself whacking Harrison over the head with her jug. It might have gotten her a better answer.

"Well . . . ain't ya gon' ask me to dance?"

He raised an eyebrow. "Awright. Don't get yaself out of sorts nah." He extended his hand, which she took, and they found a small pocket of space on the dance floor to press their bodies against each other and sway from left to right.

From another corner, Miriam watched her mother lean her head from side to side to meet Harrison's eyes. He would pacify her for a second and a half before moving on past her earlobes as though he were looking for someone else. She walked over to the counter where the bartender and a few of her girlfriends were having themselves a good laugh. Miriam was just about to ask what was going on, when she followed their line of sight to find the subject of their mockery.

"Dat Tabithah . . ." The bartender shook her head as she inspected her face for any scars as her friend held up a compact mirror.

"After all dese years, she still gotta get her husband to pay attention to her."

"Don't know what else he gotta pay attention to since he done had every woman up in here befo'," the lady holding the compact mirror chimed in with a tipsy slur. The rest of the women started drunkenly giggling and trying to shush one another up only for more laughs to spill out from behind their fans.

"What do you mean?" Miriam interjected.

"Be quiet, Pearl," one of the girlfriends named Gussie said. "Ya know we talkin' in front of dey daughter."

"Tsk," Pearl replied. "She old enough to know. She a smart one. 'S not like it's a secret or anything."

"What secret?" Miriam asked.

The bartender's neck jerked. "Lissen li'l girl, ya daddy don't love ya mother."

"Mercy!" Gussie touched her chest in shock at the bartender's brazen comment.

The bartender carried on: "He never had. De woman he really wanted to be with won' nowhere to be found and she was de only one who made it her mission to be his. Dat's why she act de way she do. But chile, look at me sayin' too much."

So that's why the love was missing between her parents, Miriam thought. Now everything started to make sense—her father's lack of acknowledging her mother's cooking, her mother breaking the plate, her mother being in a daze when alone, her father throwing his jacket on the ground, her dad not even wanting to be around her enough for a night at the juke joint. And that was only today. What about yesterday, last week, last month, all her life? The recollections of the push and pull, the neglect made her head ache.

"You'd think someone with dat good of a face and all dat for a body would be comfortable but she ain't. Dat's what she get though. Can' ever claim what's never rightfully yours, 'specially not no man heart . . . no matter how much she been gone," Pearl said.

"Mm-hmm," the ladies agreed in unison, nodding their heads and lowering their eyes, the memories of their own dalliances and affairs suddenly remade fresh.

"You want some moonshine? Best to come out of any tall ridin' boot in all of Adams County?" the bartender offered.

"No, thanks," Miriam replied, deflated. "Y'all have a good evenin'."

She weaseled her way to the door through the outer borders of the crowd so her parents wouldn't catch her leaving. When she didn't hear her mother's voice above the music calling out for her, she hurried home with the moonlight guiding her path.

Once Miriam arrived, she intended to do what had to be done quickly. The winds were picking up speed, and each time they swirled, the knob on the front door pounded, as if someone was fixing to walk right in.

She looked over both of her shoulders and walked up to her mother's nightstand drawer. She took a deep breath when her fingers grazed the handle. A slight tug led to dozens upon dozens of envelopes bursting from the bottom. She held as many as she could in her hands and sat on her mother's side of the bed to flip through them. Some didn't take long to cast aside—notices, bills, church announcements, sales—but in between all these insubstantial papers, a name kept reappearing in the upper-right-hand corner of some of the fattest envelopes: Tirzah Ambrose.

Miriam assumed she was a relative, until she saw that the letters were addressed only to her father. The dates listed at the top of the letters stretched far back before Miriam was born. Each one was torn open at the seal flap. The temptation to know more was too heavy to withstand. She held a few of the letters close to her chest and read a few lines here and there in each one without finishing any of them in its entirety. The words were intimate, inappropriate for anyone's eyes except the addressee's. Miriam stuffed the envelopes back into her mother's drawer and walked in circles around her home. The bartender and her women were right. Her daddy was in love, but not with her mama.

And if he never loved her mama, could he really love her? Was she another substitute for what he could never have? She wondered whether her restlessness, her sadness, her dreaminess, if these aspects of her character were not her burden to carry but rather a curse inherited for what had not been done right before. Maybe, she thought, she looked beyond because she wasn't meant to be born, just like her father was not meant to be her mother's husband.

A large bead of water smacked her forehead and yanked her out of her thoughts. She raised her chin and saw water leaking from the ceiling. Seconds later, thunder boomed directly above the village and shook the house. Lightning briefly struck the Mississippi River. How the weather changed so quickly after Miriam returned home had her worried. She leaned on the adjacent wall and held her stomach, which was full of a maelstrom of its own. Her neighbors were yelling about the rising of the tides, screaming at the storm to get back and have mercy on them all.

Then everything stopped.

The water beads didn't drop from overhead. The winds receded, and the thunder moved away from the village.

But Miriam vomited water anyhow. She was sick until her throat burned. She waited for the storm inside her to pass too.

18

The next morning, though, the river widened its mouth to collect her people. She spoke clearly through the raging of a heavy rain and the trembling of every shack in the negro village. Miriam could not stop shaking and sweating in her bed. Tabithah was too flushed with moonshine to notice how her daughter suffered; she was still in bed herself. Harrison stood outside, his mouth agape at how the Mississippi reached his feet before receding and then surrounding him once more. His legs couldn't move. He didn't know what to do. If he and his family stayed, they could be swallowed up. If they ran and the Mississippi eventually returned to her place, then they would have left for nothing. And who knows how far they'd get before someone called them back to work? Which was worse: submitting to nature or the tyranny of white rule?

The decision was made for Harrison when Tabithah started screaming. The screams shocked his body enough for him to regain the mobility to sprint back into their home. But when he did, he froze again as he saw Tabithah grabbing both of Miriam's shoulders, her neck violently jerking with each shake. Harrison immediately pulled Tabithah from their daughter, giving Miriam enough time to grab the envelopes off the floor.

"What's goin' on?" Harrison asked.

Tabithah screamed and extended her curled fingers to tear at Miriam's flesh, but Harrison placed a foot in her path and restrained her.

"Let me go!" she yelled, and thrashed in his arms till she couldn't see straight and her head ached. Then, she closed her eyes, refusing to look in Miriam's direction while she mumbled, "Oh, Lord. Oh Lord, oh Lord, oh Lord."

Harrison kept hold of her wrists and shook her loose to fix whatever was in disarray in the mind that was making her act like this. It wasn't the moonshine that'd done this to her. He'd seen her drunk six ways to Sunday. This was a different kind of temper.

"Pa, look—"

"No!" Tabithah sobbed. She turned her face toward the door and shook her head.

Miriam opened the envelopes and held a few of them up to his eyes.

"She been keepin' dese letters from a woman named Tirzah!"

Harrison and Tabithah didn't say a word.

"Is dis her? Is she de woman you truly love?"

"Enough," Harrison's voice boomed.

Harrison unintentionally released his grip on Tabithah, who seized the opportunity to swing around with the fullness of her strength and slap Miriam hard across the face. Miriam saw nothing but a flash of light before her right cheek hit the ground.

Harrison turned toward Tabithah and asked, "Why did you keep de letters all dese years?"

The blood ran cold in Miriam's face as she soothed her inflamed cheek on the floor.

"Yeah," Miriam said softly. "Yeah! Mama, why d'ya keep dem?"

"Because!" Tabithah shot back. Her breath accelerated and she could not manage to focus her eyes on either Harrison or Miriam for long. "I wanted to know 'bout de woman who got to see a side of de man dat I never got. De man I married and gave a child to. De man I made a home wit. I gave you more years den her and she still got to see your sweet, your tenderness. Not me."

"What all did you read?" Harrison asked Miriam.

She was afraid to speak up.

"G'on nah! Ya wanted to know somethin'."

"Dat . . . she was gonna come back to Natchez. Dat she was in Shreveport."

"I know. I was gonna go lookin' for her."

"Harrison!" Tabithah yelled.

"She sent two letters, den . . . things changed," Harrison said.

"No." Miriam shook her head. "She sent more. Way more."

Harrison faced Tabithah again. "Is dis true?"

Tabithah cut her eyes at Harrison. "What difference does it make now? You married. She married too. Much time had passed."

"But befo' it didn't. I still coulda had time," Harrison said. Miriam held her breath. So he did love her, she thought.

"Not after you went to jail you didn't! You coulda died!"

Harrison sighed. "Storm's comin'. Y'all do what y'all must to prepare." And he stalked out through the back door.

Once Tabithah was distracted by watching Harrison leave, Miriam got up from the ground and flinched when she walked past her mother to get back to her bed. She wrestled underneath her mattress for the wallet so that she could hide the letters there. After folding the letters into eighths, Miriam placed them inside the wallet and kept it close to her heart.

Tabithah walked up behind her and Miriam jumped at the same time that lightning struck. She spun around to witness how her mother's disposition had become much gentler.

"I'm not gon' hurt you," Tabithah said in a small voice that Miriam struggled to hear above the rainfall. "I . . . I can't believe you did dat but I know why you did. You a curious li'l girl. I was curious like dat too once. Dat's how I got ya daddy." She laughed cynically, but Miriam couldn't bear to smile. Tabithah's mouth hung open, and she slowly sank to her knees. "I love him, Miriam. I always have. He woulda made himself sick waitin' for anyone knowin' good and well dey don' come back and if dey do, dey ain' de same. It was best for him to be here. To stay here. And focus on what he could build here and wit me."

"But . . . she was waitin' for him too."

Tabithah pulled in a deep breath and exhaled. "Times were different. Dere was too much, too much killin' and roundin' up for dem to even try. It was safer for him to stay here."

"You said dat already."

"If he didn' stay we wouldn't have had you. And I couldn't imagine life like dat."

"Ma . . ." Miriam noticed the water snaking through the cracks of the doors and the hairs along her arms began to rise.

"I'm serious. You my baby. I loved you before you even knew me. If you don' believe me 'bout nothin' else, believe dat. But now you know what you know and I can't change dat. So don't be like me."

"Huh?"

"I see de way you look at me and your dad. I see de way you want more, and I ain't wanted nothin' but Harrison. Don't give yourself to a man fully. Or don't give yourself to a man at all. Maybe in your life you'll get more den I ever had, and what mother could ask for more?"

In that instant, the wind tore the back door off its hinges and water began to flood the Ambrose home. Tabithah and Miriam jumped as plates and glasses fell off the kitchen shelf, shattering to the floor. Water submerged Miriam's thin shoes and then covered her entire feet.

"Run!" Tabithah yelled.

Miriam began to run faster and faster down the waterfront until she could reach a trail to take her to an elevated area above the bluffs. She ran farther and farther until both sides of her abdomen developed stitch pain. She was young, but she was tired. Her breath became harder to regulate, and the humidity was exhausting. She was just about to climb but she stopped for a spell on a road that was still dirt, not yet mud.

The angle at which Miriam stood gave her a wide view of the negro village, which she now saw being swallowed in front of her eyes. The Mississippi was grayish white and relentless, hurling its power upon whoever was in its path. It kept running. Snaking its way through every shack and breaking it down, plank by plank and stick by stick. Miriam could see a pair of bodies, frantically waving for help before disappearing under the water altogether. She searched all around for a sign of her mother and father's shack—even just the roof, anything that proved her father's peerless skill as a carpenter could withstand the greatest of storms. But all of the negro village was underwater.

Sorrow coursed through Miriam's body as the Mississippi continued its destruction through the small town. Was that it? Were her mother and father gone? Just like that? Were the neighbors who shared their extra sweet potatoes swallowed up too? The juke joint where everyone danced? The small bazaar shops where people bartered and traded? The resident musicians who played small melodies after long workdays to soothe the community? Were they all just gone like that?

The sky grew darker, and the Mississippi was close enough to hiss its water at her. Miriam could hear someone was calling out from somewhere above the hill, and began to run up the trail in the voice's direction. But the water soon grabbed Miriam by the ankle and pulled her in, in one quick motion. Her body spun in several directions as the water raged all around her, taking her wherever it chose. Miriam felt herself being pulled downward.

Time slowed underwater. Everything was silent. Miriam's chest rose and fell.

MIRIAM TURNED ON HER SIDE TO RELIEVE HER STOMACH; SHE WAS lying atop dirty blankets. Her body was covered in open wounds; long streaks of blood streamed down her arms. She struggled to lift herself up enough so she could better take in her surroundings. To her right lay a body beneath a pile of wood chips. She knew the person was dead because she saw a limp arm protruding from the heap, buzzards circling around it. She chose not to look to her left. Judging by the rotten smell in the air, it was more of the same.

Beyond, a fire burned in the middle of what appeared to be a large campsite. The sky was pitch black. No crickets chirped and no owls hooted. Even they avoided the wreckage. The raging water from below had simmered down to a flood. The water slithered through the avenues and open roads, carrying remnants of homes and disparate limbs in its own body. The air was stickier and more humid than Miriam had ever experienced. If it were at all possible, she would have shed out her own skin to make being alive more bearable.

Someone lying a few feet from Miriam hissed and struggled to breathe. By instinct, Miriam turned toward the person—an older woman who was shivering so badly that Miriam could not hold her still with both hands. The woman kept her eyes on Miriam and flashed her teeth as though she were going to snarl, or say a word, but she did neither. She shivered and shivered until the small light in her eyes that was illuminated by the nearby fire extinguished itself. Then she stopped moving altogether. Miriam sat with the lady's corpse and thought of her mother. Her mother could've been this woman—shivering, helpless, alone. Her father could've been this woman—shivering, helpless, lovelorn. Out from the depths of Miriam's stomach issued a soul-tired bellow that stirred every survivor in that campsite up on the cliffs to stare at her. Soon, another bellow followed, and then hot tears streamed down her face.

A trio of women approached Miriam with sassafras leaves in hand and pressed them on every one of her wounds. Another woman came around with a large ladle full of decocted willow bark.

"Sip it," she instructed. "For the pain."

Miriam swatted away the offering and pointed at the two dead bodies on each side of her. Someone whistled for a few men to come over, and the bodies were removed.

"Disease," one of the women said. "We can't have 'em spreadin' disease."

With every stranger that joined the camp over the course of the night, Miriam's heart broke a little bit further down the middle. None of them were her mother, or her father. Indeed, each time Miriam heard approaching footsteps and twigs snapping underneath the weight of someone's feet, she sat upright, faced their direction, and hoped to find her parents. She scrutinized every newcomer's face, bloodied, swollen, bruised, and tried to find her mother's and father's features within it.

The following morning, seagulls squawked overhead. By now, the river herself was quiet and unassuming. There was no vestige of the grave sins it had committed, no one floating in its waters, no part of anyone's home coughed back up onto shore as proof of what had happened. Most people at the camp were alone, shivering on the damp ground with no family beside them. Barely anyone communicated with anyone else, except the occasional head nod, hand hold, or a brief exchanging of names. But it was not silent. Throughout the camp, people were coughing and sneezing. There weren't enough blankets to go around so some huddled together, but the sickness only seemed to get worse.

Finally, a figure whom she recognized appeared: Marie. She sat down on the ground a sizable distance from Miriam and said, "Awww baby. . . ."

Once Miriam heard Marie's consoling tone, she realized she'd never hear from her mother again, and she burst into tears. "Why ain't God take me wit 'em?"

"Hey, hey, hey, don' talk like that. God ain't take you 'cause he has a purpose for you."

"And what purpose he have for my parents?"

Marie became tight-lipped. "I would put my hand on you right now but I know it won' make it right. Besides, I assume dat dere's yellow fever goin' 'round in dis here camp. Always happen when places get flooded and it's hot and sticky and de mosquito buzzin' 'round."

Miriam lowered her head.

"I thought you was gonna be as good as dead. But den again I remembered who you were."

"What do you mean?"

"De water child. Dat's who you are. De water been speakin' to you. She won't gon' hurt you. Everybody know you special in that way. Besides . . . you wanted to go. You grabbed all your things ready before your dad said a word. You already made up your mind."

"My things," Miriam said. She straightened her legs out in front of her and patted down her body before closing her eyes. "Oh my God," her voice trembled. She reached deep down into her bosom and pulled out her soggy leather wallet that contained a few folded letters inside.

"Mercy," Marie said.

Miriam rocked back and forth, holding the wallet to her chest. She opened her eyes to Marie, who looked back at her.

"Aunt Marie, you believe my father loved my mother? And don' lie to me, please. I'm not a baby."

"I believe your father loved your mother de best way dat he knew how to."

"'Cause he was in love wit another woman?"

"Yes. 'Cause he was in love wit another woman."

"Aunt Marie?"

"Mm-hmm?"

"I remember you sayin' dat you knew of people leavin' here. Even before de flood."

"I did."

"Is dat still an option?"

Marie looked out toward the river, then back at Miriam. "Follow me."

19

Kansas, honey," was what Marie said before putting a reluctant Miriam on a boat.

"Don't worry about me or yourself. You gon' be fine. I must stay behind to help others, 'specially other orphans like yourself."

Orphan. The word tasted profane on her tongue. "Orphan" felt like a permanent mark upon her person. Though no one could see or would care about this new shame as she sat in a crowded corner on the boat, Miriam shrank deeply into herself, worried that she would never see her Aunt Marie again, that no one would ever call her "baby."

After a week of traveling by boat from Natchez to St. Louis, arriving ashore in Atchison, followed by sleeping in a refugee shelter in Topeka for a night, Miriam boarded the first wagon she saw and traveled hours further inland until the pain of her formative years in Natchez became a faint memory. As they rode, Miriam looked around Kansas and wondered how the grass was so green, the air so clean, the crops so bountiful, without any water for miles and miles. Even the sky was broader than Miriam had ever seen it. She thought it seemed like the sky in the book of Genesis, like it was the first sky, the sky as it was meant to be. The sun beamed through the dense clouds to bless sunflowers and wild violets. Miriam was awestruck. Never before had she appreciated flora and fauna, but now she did not want to blink, fearing she might miss something in nature that she never had the time to appreciate while she worked the fields. In her previous life, every plant and every seed were for labor and had a calculation of what it could yield; the crops they produced were not to be beheld as beautiful. For the first time, she could sop up all of nature's grace.

In Nicodemus, Miriam was so astounded by the volume of well-dressed and well-spoken negroes who possessed an air about them that she could hardly put her amazement into words. The women carried parasols and wore gloves, the men sported pocket watches and leather shoes. Every establishment—from the schoolhouse to the church—was strongly built and properly maintained. She sensed ease and saw gaiety in this new place, perhaps because there were no white people monitoring their every move. These people hardly even sweated, she said to herself. Was it due to the lack of humidity in comparison to Natchez? Was the labor not as strenuous? Was life . . . better?

Miriam and a bunch of other new and female arrivals were taken into the lower parts of the St. Francis Hotel where there were sleeping quarters. During the days, they were expected to work either in cleaning, entertainment, or administration to earn their keep. Miriam was open to any task, but Elodie, the first lady at First Baptist Missionary Church who greeted Miriam upon her arrival in town, said that she had a face for the public. That was how she found herself yanked from the kitchen and hidden compartments of the hotel to the bar and lobby to greet and tend to people.

Weeks on end, the St. Francis Hotel sang with the activity of patrons and newcomers alike, and Miriam was thrilled by all the excitement, feeling like she might never have to be alone again. The names, the faces, the smiles, the gestures, the gossip, the fights, the bedtime giggles with other girls—she found herself struggling to go to sleep, afraid that she'd wake up and find she had to fix herself up for another day of picking cotton. But when the morning came, she'd open her eyes to a dozen other girls, a large smile on her face, happy that this was her new life.

It was an otherwise mundane weekday afternoon when Free and his family walked into Elodie's home that first day. Miriam was on a rare break, laughing with one of her girlfriends in the powder room, so she didn't see him then. By chance she'd accepted Elodie's invitation to her home that evening. Most workdays exhausted her to the bone marrow, but something told her to go. When she arrived, she felt like a fish struggling for air. She was dressed appropriately but not elegantly enough. When someone asked her a question, she obsessed over whether her response had been articulate enough as soon as the person walked away. She never had to worry like this in Natchez.

Still, she made an effort. She spoke so much and to so many people that her jaw ached. And she found she was delighted with this world full of new people, who proved to her just how small and cloistered her life in Natchez had been. She wanted to belong here, she decided. And if she was going to ingratiate herself with this crowd, she thought, she would have to work longer hours at the hotel to afford more dresses. Exactly how to dress required observation, which, luckily for her, was something she was good at. As the night carried on, she gradually shied away from making light talk and instead took some time to observe the color patterns, jewelry, perfumes, and gestures of some of the women guests. She hadn't realized that the spot from which she stood, examining her fellow partygoers, placed her directly in Free's line of sight.

As soon as Free was dealt his cards, she looked past his broad shoulders with a dull sting of secondhand embarrassment. He was nothing but a boy compared to these men with salt-and-pepper hair, smoky laughs and wheezes, and crow's feet on the side of their eyes. The game would be over before it even started, and judging by the mocking looks of the bystanders surrounding the table, she was not alone in her prediction. But the longer she tried to look beyond Free, the more forceful her desire to watch him grew. She wasn't here to learn about him, and yet she admired his gumption and confidence. Just a peek, she thought.

When she slowly moved her eyes back over to his face, she saw that he was staring back at her. She swallowed and quickly averted her gaze, but it was too late. He saw her and she saw him. His eyes were serene, his posture assured. Briefly, she wondered if he could hear her thoughts.

Free returned to the game and flashed an ace and a ten. The crowd roared and more people gathered around, but Free never lost her, no matter how many women flocked to his side to flirtatiously lean over the table. And she never lost sight of him.

That was until she realized that someone else had been watching her, a woman who looked a great deal like Free. Before Miriam knew it, the woman was walking toward her.

"I know you," she began. "Or at least I think I do. What is your name?" The authority in this woman's voice made Miriam shrink as she shuffled her weight from side to side.

"Miriam."

They examined each other for however long it took to make everything around them blur together. This woman squinted to take in all of Miriam's features, and Miriam stood still, unsure what this lady expected to find.

"Miriam what?"

Miriam's eyes roamed around the room for a second and then she directed her attention back to the lady. "Waters."

"Oh." The lady's voice dipped. "Must have been my mistake then. . . . You just looked like a man I once knew. And you're not married?"

"No, ma'am."

"Where are your people from?"

"Jena," Miriam lied.

"Jena?" Tirzah asked. "Your accent gives me someplace else . . ."

"Where?" Miriam asked.

"Mmm . . . toward the bottom half of Mississippi, I reckon."

Miriam raised both eyebrows in astonishment, his chest jutting out and her shoulders raised. How would she know southern Mississippi if she hadn't visited or . . . lived there? Miriam silently questioned. "What is your name?" Miriam asked.

"Tirzah. Mrs. Tirzah Benjamin."

Miriam opened her mouth, but stutters tumbled out. How many Tirzahs were there walking around? But her last name was Benjamin, not Ambrose, as was written in the letters addressed to her father. No, Benjamin had to be her married name; she did say "Missus." But where was her husband? Unless she was lying just like Miriam was?

"You okay, dear?" Tirzah leaned forward. Miriam's body felt electrified when Tirzah touched her shoulder. "Let me go and get you some water and hopefully pull my boy Free from this nonsense."

The crowd of people naturally parted as Tirzah made her way to the drinks and small platters section of the party. As soon as Miriam could only see the top of Tirzah's head, her feet took off as her mind struggled to catch up. Soon, she found herself outside, gasping into the cold, dry, evening air.

This was the woman. This had to be the woman. She wasn't some ghost casting a presence over Miriam's family. She was an actual, real person, full of flesh and blood, beautiful and disarming, intelligent and independent. No wonder her father had loved her. Hell, Tirzah's presence took Miriam's breath away.

Miriam steadied herself. She had not wound up in the same place as her father's beloved because of coincidence. There was something she needed to investigate, if not for her father, then for herself.

She recollected herself and returned to the party. Guests were already filing out, but Tirzah, Free, and another woman were standing in the middle of the living room. They all watched as she returned, and Miriam deduced that they had been waiting for her: Tirzah with a glass of ice water in hand, Free with a wad of cash won from cardplaying in his right hand, and the unnamed woman with a face scorched with contempt.

The four decided to walk home together once they learned that they lived in the same hotel. Miriam listened more than she spoke. By the time they made it to the lobby, she learned where they came from, what kind of house they lived in in Shreveport, and of their church community there too.

And when it was time to part ways, Free offered to walk Miriam to her room, much to Novella's chagrin. Before Novella could protest, Tirzah grabbed her hand and led her back to their room on the upper floor.

Miriam and Free stood in the hallway right in front of her living quarters and remained silent. He took her in with his glances. She did the same. Then, she looked down at the floor, but Free took her face into his hands.

"You are beautiful, do you know that?"

Before Free could say anything else, Miriam wrapped her arms around him and kissed him. It was the first time she had touched a man in this way.

She looked up at him and said, "I do."

20

Free could barely feel the floor underneath his feet once he got to the hallway of the floor where he stayed. Once he got a handle on himself, he reached into his pocket and pulled out his earnings from the night. It was not lost on him that he had grown up in a family of means back in Shreveport; but to actually see money in his hand that he earned through his own skill was something else. Adrenaline coursed through his body. The image of his dying father waited behind a small door in the corner of his mind, but the excitement of having won several rounds of blackjack made sure that the door didn't so much as creak open. It was the first time since his father's death that grief didn't flood his whole body, weighing him down so that everything he saw and every person he met burdened him even more. His hand on the doorknob to his suite, he waited to go in. What would he say to his mother? Hell, what would he say to Novella? He didn't have to think too long because the door swung open, and Novella stood behind it with eyes that could have seared the entire hotel floor.

"Where you been? Get inside now." She pulled Free into the dark living room, and they sat side by side on the couch, small candles burning on the coffee table beside them. Free had enough time to see the light in the space between his mother's bedroom door and the floor. He hoped that she would emerge to intervene in what was about to be a fight he had no interest in participating in.

Novella sat on the opposite side of the couch from Free and turned her body toward him. One of her breasts almost peeked out from her slip, and he strained not to look any lower than her sternum. She propped her elbow on the arm of the couch and her right pointer finger and thumb hoisted the right side of her face.

"Well?" Novella asked.

"Novella, I'm tired."

"I'm tired too. I been waitin' up for you. Had no idea where you gone, but I figured it musta been somethin' important."

"No one told you to wait up for me."

Novella's eyes got bigger the longer they kept quiet, and the audacity of Free's comment fully sank into her heart.

"I mean," Free relented, "you could've gone to sleep. It's been a long journey."

"Dat it has. And you be best to remember who brought you on dis journey."

"What you mean by that?"

"Free . . . I saved your life. And dis de thanks I get?"

Free burst into laughter. "Saved my life?"

"Y'all wouldn't have known 'bout Kansas if it wasn't for me. I was de one who made sure everythin' was in order for us to leave. But I ain't think as soon as we'd get here, you would start actin' like dis."

"Acting like what?"

"Gamblin'. What's gotten into you? You ain't like dis. You ain't never been like dis."

Free sank into himself. Novella was right: he had never been like this before, but no sooner did he hear what she said than his grin reemerged before he could register he was smiling.

Novella became flustered and her cheeks swole up with frustration. "I don't like you like dis, Free. You still your father's son no matter what—"

"All right, I've had enough." Free got to his feet and kicked his shoes off before starting to walk back toward the door.

Novella picked up his shoes and walked up beside him. "No, I'm not done—"

"I said, 'Enough!'" Free got so loud that he spooked his own self and Novella, too, who scurried over to the second and last bedroom in the suite and slammed the door behind her. Not too long after her exit, he heard sniffling from behind the door. He didn't have it in him to apologize. All he wanted was to be alone in his own thoughts. So he lay on the couch and hoped that euphoria would come back to him, until he drifted into sleep.

When Free woke up the next morning, both Tirzah and Novella were already fully dressed. He noticed that Novella was wearing another one of his mother's dresses, and even the way she swayed her hips to and fro across the suite was just like his mother.

Novella caught his reflection while she was putting on earrings in the mirror and said, "Oh thank God, you're up. Hurry and get yaself togetha. Today's de day we gotta both get jobs."

Free groaned and turned his body toward the inside of the couch. Novella threw a pillow at his head. "C'mon nah."

"Ma . . ." Free croaked to Tirzah, hoping she'd save him.

"Leave me out of your lovers' quarrel," Tirzah protested. "I need to go see about getting involved with the church and the Order of the Northern Star or whatever they call it. We all need to busy ourselves with something to do instead of arguing or sleeping like vagabonds."

Free sat upright and reached deep into his pockets. He pulled out the bills and placed them on the table. "Will this at least give me another day or two to rest?"

"No," Novella shot back. "Dat's gamblin' money. You need to make money de right way."

"What do you mean 'the right way'? I won it fair and square."

"You got lucky!" she said, and Free sucked his teeth and put the money back in his pocket. "I won't have a husband who gambles!"

"Who said anything about marriage?" he asked.

"C'mon, Free. We been seein' each other for some time. We gonna get set up here nice, get jobs, and start our lives togetha."

"Seems like you've done all the planning without even including me. I'm not thinking about marriage. I don't even know if I want to get married."

Free's eyes met his mother's, and Tirzah's face dropped when she saw grief written on her son's features.

"Miss Tirzah!" Novella called out to her. "You ain't gon' say nothin'? As a woman of God? As a first lady!"

Tirzah sighed and said, "I'm not a first lady anymore."

"But you're a wife!"

Tirzah shook her head. "No longer."

This angered Free. She still wore her wedding ring. She still belonged to his father no matter what. He couldn't help but wonder why she hardly said anything about Isaac—that she still loved him even if she was a widow. Instead, Tirzah fixed a wide-brimmed hat over her head, cupped Novella's cheek with one hand, and said, "Give him time, Novella. Give him time. He just lost his father."

"I lost my parents too!" Novella shouted.

Free had begun to feel claustrophobic, watching the two women in his life go back and forth, like he was in the audience watching a play about some other family.

"That is true. But that was years ago. This loss is much more recent. Let him have his time." Tirzah curved her arm toward Novella. "Come on. Walk with me and shake off some of that anger. It's too early for all of that."

Free had every intention of lying on the couch for as long as he wanted once he saw the backs of Tirzah and Novella leaving out the front door. But as soon as the door closed behind them and he could no longer hear their steps receding, Miriam came to his thoughts again. Was this who he really was: a man who gravitated toward whomever he pleased, a man who didn't feel much obligation toward anyone besides himself?

Later on that afternoon, he fixed himself up and went downstairs to see about her. She was working behind the desk when he caught her eye. Her curly hair fell over the top of her forehead in an updo. Her painted lips spoke to whoever passed by her station, and her delicately pink cheeks raised and beamed whenever someone's conversation delighted her. Small crowds of people passed by him as he stood in the lobby watching her do her job. Everything else slowed down. People's faces blurred, the sounds of chatter and the soft piano playing near the restaurant and bar muted. Before Free knew it, there it was, that euphoria. It was not as strong as the moment right after he'd won several games of blackjack, but nevertheless, he leaned toward the light.

As Free was approaching Miriam at her work area, some of her coworkers passed by her and stared, wondering just what these two were doing.

"Good mornin'," Miriam finally said.

Free blinked and then chuckled like a small boy. "Good morning."

Another full stare.

"Can I help you with anythin'?"

"There you are—" Free felt a thick hand grip his shoulder. He turned to see one of the players who lost to him at blackjack the night before. "That was a good game you played at Elodie's party," the man said. "A good, good game. Me and the fellas are impressed."

"Thank you, sir," Free replied.

"We play again next Thursday. Nine p.m. at 8203 South Street— not too far from First Baptist Missionary." He gripped Free's shoulder harder. "Be there," he finished in a less friendly tone. Then he tipped his hat toward Miriam with a "Miss," and went on his way.

"Can I come sometime?" Miriam blurted out when the man was out of earshot.

"Seeing me gambling last night wasn't enough for you?" said Free. "That doesn't make you upset? Like I need to make money a different way?"

Miriam shrugged. "It looked fun. 'Scuse me—" She had to assist a couple, leaving Free standing there in disbelief.

• • •

The days leading up to the next blackjack night were long and dull. Every morning and evening Novella managed to slip the prospect of marriage into conversations as unrelated and far-reaching as ironing clothes or inclement weather. Usually, Free would remain quiet because Novella and her dreams took up enough space in the room. He wanted to admit to her that yes, he did feel indebted to her for being by his and his mother's side on the journey to this foreign land. But he wasn't ready to be the man that she wanted, one who stayed close to home and settled down. During the day, she worked as a traveling stenographer to any preacher, doctor, or entrepreneur who needed help documenting records, which lent Free a bit of reprieve. Other times, she stuck close to Tirzah's side, attempting to learn what it meant to be a mother and a wife. Though the quotidian rhythms of their lives orbited around one another, Free couldn't help but think about Miriam. He wondered why she never came looking for him. Why didn't she want to talk to him? Or maybe she expected him to pursue her? He'd pass through the lobby acting as though he had someplace to be and they'd lock eyes. Like drawing water from the well, Free went downstairs to get his fill before returning to his suite to sit around and think and dream and dream and think again.

When Thursday came around, Free had a spring in his step that didn't escape his mother's and Novella's notice. He had the plan all figured out. Supper was at seven. They would finish around 8:30 p.m. He would freshen up and go downstairs to find Miriam.

"Going somewhere important?" Tirzah asked Free while he was fastening his cuff links.

"Out."

"Dis one of Miss Elodie's parties tonight too?" Novella asked.

"Both of you would've been invited if that were the case."

"Den where you goin'?" Novella asked.

"I said I'm going out," Free shot back. "I'll be back."

Novella faced Tirzah with the most pitiful, shining eyes. Tirzah sighed and said, "You're not going out to be with that Miriam Waters, are you?"

Novella spun back around again to Free, who didn't immediately deny it. Her nostrils flared in tandem with the anger welling up in her body. "Out of all people? Dat's who you gettin' dressed up for?"

Free held both of Novella's arms as she looked like she was about to cry. "Novella, listen—"

"That girl is a strange one. She looks so familiar to me and I can't put my finger on it," Tirzah said. "She said she was from Louisiana but not Shreveport. I can't help but feel like I've seen her before."

"We're just passing time," Free said. But the words felt bitter on his tongue, and Novella was still on the verge of tears. Still, he repeated the phrase and rubbed her arms. This time, he was shocked at how easy the lie turned from bitter to sweet when Novella's breathing became steady.

"Can I come too?" she finally said.

Free stammered out, "You wouldn't like where we're going."

"Where you goin' den?"

"I'm going to play cards, Nov. That's what I'm doing."

Everyone silently stared at one another. Free was dripping sweat from his pits down to his navel at the prospect of Novella tagging along with him and Miriam.

Novella sighed and sat on the couch. "Fine," Novella said. "G'on."

"What?" Free looked over at Tirzah, who was already preoccupying herself with reading her Bible. He wondered if she was studying Scripture or that ad he found between the Bible's pages.

"G'on. You said you just passin' time, and I believe you. Dis ain't no different den de girls back at Shreveport Baptist, and I outlasted dem all. I know she probably fancies you and why wouldn't she? But she ain't me." Novella fixed her skirt over her knee and lifted her chin. "You still grievin' like your mother said. I ain't gon' hold you."

Free smiled and dashed out the door before Novella could say another word. How everything aligned for the women in his life to allow him to do what he wanted, he didn't know. He didn't care to question it, or to figure out what he wanted. The only wants he was sure of was Miriam and some more money in his pocket. That certainty gave him enough direction. He raced down the stairs to find Miriam standing by the entrance doors. The wind blew through her curls and caught the edge of her navy jacket, which gave her an ethereal appearance. She turned toward Free the moment his feet touched the floor of the main lobby. Almost as if she knew when he would arrive. They looked at each other from across the floor with straight faces that gave way to childish smiles.

He approached her slowly, saying, "I hope you weren't waiting too long."

"Not at all."

Free squinted at her.

"What?" she asked.

"My mother said you look familiar and that you say you're from Louisiana. I don't think I ever met you before. But could you have met my mother somewhere?"

Miriam's face dropped and she looked down at her right foot drawing circles on the floor. "No. Maybe she knew my people from long ago though. Did she ever guess that?"

"I didn't ask. She was in Shreveport for most of her life and before that . . ." Free trailed off. "It's not important. That was before you and I were even born. Besides, she probably didn't ask because Novella was standing there. She's been pressuring me to marry her and be like my father and I'm not like him. Not anymore. Even though she wants me to be and my mother does too. I know it."

Miriam immediately recognized the sadness that seemed to cover Free's whole person. She decided that she wasn't going to tell Free that his mother had loved someone else before his daddy. Her own daddy. He didn't need to know that. At least not for a while.

Then Free took Miriam's hand and together they walked out into the open air to seek an adventure detached from their respective pasts—a present full of promise.

1912

21

Kansas was a playground for two passionate youths like Miriam and Free. During the day, they were often separated by physical walls—he inside a gilded suite on a high floor of the St. Francis Hotel, and she in the lobby. Sometimes, she would see him passing to and from the entrance doors either alone or with Novella on his arm. Miriam waited for jealousy to sting her chest, but what she wound up feeling was sympathy. When Novella clung to Free, Miriam saw how she stared at him lovingly while he always looked elsewhere—just like her father had done to her mother. If she saw Novella by herself, Miriam felt the urge to tell her that it was best for her to keep her eyes out in front of her rather than on any man. But who was she to strike down anyone's fantasy? They were young, after all, and they were allowed to dream.

Miriam wanted Free, but not in the same manner that Novella wanted him. They would find each other at night either in a secret hallway near the kitchen or behind the hotel near the trash bins. Sometimes, they would do nothing but sit there and count the fireflies together; other times, they'd talk about their former lives. He told her that he was the son of a preacher and that he saw his father get killed right in front of him. She told him that she was the daughter of sharecroppers and her parents got swept away in a terrible flood. He asked no questions. Instead, he wrapped his arm around her and said that he was sorry for her loss. Within his embrace, Miriam found it extraordinary that someone like Free could still have enough warmth in him to get close to another woman. And when his eyes only sought hers, she couldn't help but feel special. Then they would return to their respective rooms without knowing when or where they'd meet again. Miriam never asked anything of Free—and that made him feel larger than himself, made him think that perhaps he loved her.

Every step he took toward his suite was like a pang in his chest. He knew that the following morning, Novella would be wondering when they'd be getting married or asking him about work. Half the week, Free worked for the postal service, and the other half he worked at nearby railroad depots, the latter coordinated by Tirzah and Elodie in hopes that Nicodemus would become an important transportation center. He hated both jobs. But he kept quiet, and divided some of his earnings between his mother and Novella so they could be kept in the best outfits. Whatever money that was left over, he used to gamble; it was his release. He'd offer to share some of his earnings with Miriam, but all she wanted was Free and his stories. She wanted to know about his father and, more importantly, his mother, whose eye toward her became more and more inquisitive as time went on.

Meanwhile, Tirzah was too busy acclimating herself with the Nicodemus elite to worry about affairs of the heart. She attended church every Sunday for service, Wednesday for Bible study, and Friday for noonday prayer. She was present at every inaugural business opening and charity event. When migrants came to town, she stood right beside Elodie to welcome and document them all with a smile and a proper introduction. At first, she surprised herself by her adherence to the social calendar. But the more Tirzah became well-versed in all the mechanisms that kept the community well-oiled and the deeper she forged bonds with others, however, she realized that she liked church and she liked tradition. What she hadn't liked about church back in Shreveport was being first lady, but once she wasn't required to do anything, she wanted to do it all. And besides, she wasn't surrounded by death here; she didn't have to hold the grief of others and tell them their children were in a better place. Life was different in Nicodemus; but she would not quite say it was better, because how could it be, without Isaac?

Yet she was not stupid when it came to Free. She knew her son's eyes just as well as she knew Isaac's. After all, it was through Isaac's glances that she knew he wanted her more than any other woman in Shreveport. And sometimes at night, when her house was quiet, she'd lie in bed and dream that Isaac was still watching her from an incandescent pulpit, and she was still a young woman in the back of the sanctuary, attempting not to draw attention to herself. But somehow, he always found her, even in her dreams. In her waking life, however, if she happened to see Miriam in passing, she couldn't help but feel like Harrison was somewhere close by. But why would this young girl have reason to lie to her about her last name or where she was born? Once or twice, Tirzah smiled at Miriam and asked her a friendly question, but Miriam would deflect and change the subject, leaving Tirzah embarrassed.

This went on for a while, until people started talking about Free and Novella. In the eyes of the town, he had gone from "that handsome, young man" and "that good girl" to "that man" and "that poor woman," and Tirzah heard every bit of it—almost as if the townspeople wanted her to know. Churchgoers gossiped about how and why Free wouldn't do the right and godly thing by asking Novella to marry him when they were almost certain that the two were sleeping together. Tirzah tried as best she could to ignore everyone's judgment because, truthfully, she was not concerned about her son or his girlfriend. She didn't desire for either of them to rush into a union until they were ready, although Tirzah did observe how Novella's personality had changed from adventurous and spirited to disillusioned and obsessive. Her eyes knew only of Free, while his wandered to card tables and parties. He became a showboat while she became an island in herself, waiting for him to arrive at her shore.

Eventually, Tirzah couldn't stand the discord. Late one night, she waited for him to come through the front door of their suite at the end of the workday and called him into her bedroom. Once he situated himself inside and locked the door behind him, per Tirzah's orders, she said: "Do right by Novella or leave her be. Your father never made me question my station in his life and I'm counting on you to follow his example and have respect for yourself and the woman who loves you." He was taken aback by his mother's earnest tone and serious countenance. He had been running around on everyone's time, hoping no one would say a word. But eventually, he had to face himself and his responsibilities so he nodded and said, "I'll do right, Ma. I will."

That same night, he proposed to Miriam, who rejected his offer.

Miriam feared that she would wind up like her parents, and besides, she said to him, "If you are marryin' me out of fear from de town and your mother, den dat's no reason to marry at all." Free didn't know what to say, so he said nothing at all. Instead, he walked home in the dead of night, believing that he loved her even more for refusing to be beholden to him. He wanted to understand her and this strength she had to be a single negro woman. But Free didn't like being rejected. It was then that his mind went to Novella and how she assisted in saving all of their lives by encouraging them to move to Nicodemus. He thought of how her eyes glowed whenever he entered a room and how there was nothing she wouldn't do for him. He owed marriage to her. And besides, he reasoned, Miriam could stand on her own unmarried. Novella didn't have the heart.

By the following afternoon, Novella was squealing and prancing around the town center, telling everyone that she was going to be Missus Free Benjamin. The townspeople breathed a sigh of relief; there'd be a wedding after all. Many of the elder women offered to help with flowers, music, and ceremony attire.

Their engagement period was the happiest that Tirzah and Free had ever seen Novella. A smile never left her face, a spring and a skip were in her step, and she giggled throughout every sentence she uttered in daily conversation. Her revival was infectious; the excitement had many believing that these nuptials would be the wedding of the century.

The wedding party would be exceptionally large—fourteen bridesmaids and fourteen groomsmen, the reception, hundreds of people, and the food—of red beans and rice, and cornbread and catfish, and macaroni and cheese—was a feast fit for King Solomon. Their vows would be proof that Novella's patience eventually paid off and that she and Free would live a long, healthy life together.

Tirzah could see vestiges of her husband in Free as he stood at the altar, waiting for his bride. He was sweating in his suit but knew he was doing the right thing, believed he was doing the right thing . . . right? If that were the case, why was he still thinking of Miriam?

At the close of the day, after the wedding reception, when he was alone with Novella, why did he feel like he was doing, yet again, what was expected of him as Isaac's successor and Tirzah's son? He loved his father and he loved his mother. Yet all this oscillation had him questioning which were truly his own desires and which had been imposed on him. He was bound to find out.

It was about a month into the marriage when Free sought Miriam in the middle of the night, while Novella was fast asleep, and they began their affair. Their romance not only remained but intensified.

FREE AND NOVELLA'S MARRIAGE WAS A BANDAGE OVER A GUSHING spout. Vows did nothing to control Free in the long run. The first few years of their union found Novella often waiting up near the front windows for Free to return from wherever he chose to spend his time when not working, or going outside to hunt him down herself. He never gave many reasons for why he'd been gone and for so long, but he always returned with a little more money than when he'd left. Novella didn't ask any questions.

Her first pregnancy was quick and deliberate, happening just a year into the marriage. She figured that a newborn would be enough to tether Free to the marital home. But soon, even a baby wasn't enough to keep him from returning to his old ways. So Novella cooked another one, then another, until the gaggle of children only gave him more excuses to stay away in search of peace and quiet.

Tirzah felt blessed to be a grandmother—she had moved to a congenial home on Madison Street, a few paces away from her son and daughter-in-law's—and was always available when Novella needed her for support. She was impressed with Novella's ability to get pregnant and tend to twelve children, since Free spent more time outside of the home than inside. Most days, Tirzah saw her son's back more than his face. And during those brief moments when she could see the front of him, his eyes never met hers. Whatever she wanted to say to her son would be pushed back down her throat to rest like sediment in her belly.

When Free stepped out, he either went gambling or snaked his way down a mossy path along Solomon River to Miriam's back door. They weren't going to stop seeing each other. Not even as older women in the community warned her to stay away from Free and get her own husband. Not even when she eventually did get her own husband, and Free was heartbroken, reminded of the first time she didn't choose him.

His name was Corinthian Sterling. When Corinthian expressed his intent to marry Miriam, she turned him down too. He was handsome, kind, and good. Good enough. He had broad-enough shoulders to make her feel physically safe and enough money to ward off any envy she might have from her neighbors. But he didn't excite her. Somehow word got out about Miriam refusing Corinthian's proposal, and older women returned to her again to warn her not to be stupid. She ignored them until the judgmental stares and rude comments beneath the breath of passersby got to be too much. Only two months after his second proposal, they wed. Even Miriam was surprised at how easy it was for her to acquiesce, and to realize that she was already breaking away from the scorn she'd received from her dealings with Free.

Corinthian arrived at the church on their wedding day in a finely designed suit, while Miriam wore a tailored wedding gown and some boots, slicked with mud from the pouring rain.

During their marriage, he allowed her to do whatever she wanted. If she wanted to come home late from a party, he'd be up waiting for her. If she didn't feel like cooking, he'd fry fish for dinner. If she didn't feel like loving, he'd turn on his side and gently rock the bed with his rubbing until he relieved himself. Eventually, she realized that no matter how much she tried to test him, Corinthian was patient and kind. She resented how much she wanted more when any other woman would consider him enough.

Despite this, she tried: She rarely flinched from his affection in the early morning or evening. Each time they loved, she drained the liquid from his body. When she cooked, she always left the bigger piece for him. She soothed him when he was tired and prayed with him when he needed help. They spent the first several years of their marriage learning about each other, and he liked what he saw. She was beautiful, kind, calm, and good. Enough.

But their first several years weren't without difficulty. He knew what the town said about his woman, but he never showed his concern. Not even when the back door creaked at random hours of the night and he couldn't discern the difference between human whispers or the wind coursing through the trees.

There was the inability to get pregnant followed by years of stillbirths. By the time Corinthian and Miriam were deep into their thirties, they were afraid to try again—disappointment did a lot to marriage—but then, unexpectedly, their daughter Temperance came into the world. A miracle. Temperance looked like Miriam, and they were delighted. The child was nothing like her name. She carried Miriam's idiosyncrasies and took pride in being a daddy's girl. She liked to take risks in a way that added to the gray stubble in his beard. She picked up snakes without thinking about whether they were poisonous, took on any dare that a boy in town challenged her to, and easily won any game where money was on the line. She'd come home with all kinds of trinkets, and Corinthian would interrogate her, assuming she'd been stealing. But she'd won whatever she brought home fair and square.

Their second and last child, Vera, was the one who stirred Corinthian's emotions. She didn't look anything like him, and where he was from, girl babies always looked like their fathers. Unlike her sister, Vera was quiet. She only spoke when spoken to and never gave any adult in her proximity trouble. Often, Vera would be outside sitting on the grass feeding a meadowlark or watching the wind blow through the cornfield, completely satisfied by her own company and that of nature. Miriam thought Vera was most like her, connected to the elements in ways that most people wouldn't understand. Of course, locals made their comments about the children and everybody's else children; as the population thinned, the line between outside and in-house business became virtually nonexistent. Gossip became the engine that kept the community together and was a way to show care and concern. Aside from their vibrant rumor mill, the townspeople were sometimes able to consolidate their attention on more useful things, like the watch night service, the religious gathering performed to ring in the New Year. It was Tirzah's year to preside over the logistics of everything related to the night—from the church service to the subsequent festivities—and she reminded everyone that they needed to help her out more than ever before.

So Miriam found herself at Tirzah's doorstep on the afternoon of December 31, with a bouquet of flowers, ready to help her with final watch night preparations. She announced herself before stepping inside, and saw Tirzah standing over several steaming pots in the kitchen. Miriam guided the older woman to sit down.

"Thank you," Tirzah said, and quickly pulled out a handkerchief to cover her mouth while she coughed. She folded it back up and stuffed it in her apron with a weak smile. "It's gonna be a long day and I have so much to do."

Miriam shook her head. "No you don'," she said as she noticed flowers in a vase on a table, almost identical to the ones she'd brought. "I'll help out."

Tirzah was about to answer when the back door swung open and Novella entered the kitchen, eyeing Miriam without speaking. Interactions between the two women always began this way—the staring, the awkward silences, the odd shuffling around each other.

"Novella!" Tirzah greeted her daughter-in-law, a rasp in her voice. "I forgot you were back there, you were out so long."

"Dere's a lot of preparation for today, Ma. Some of us don' have de luxury of sittin' on our hides. We have our priorities." She cornered Miriam with her eyes again.

"That we do," Tirzah replied, her hands in a firm fist on her chest. "Tonight needs to be perfect. Y'all hear me? Can't be a strand of hair or a stitch of fabric out of place. Understand?"

"Yes, ma'am," Miriam and Novella said in unison.

Tirzah smiled. "I know I don't have to worry about you two. Us women always seem to have it together."

"Dat we do, Ma." Novella leaned over and kissed her on the cheek. "Ain't dese flowers lovely, Mrs. Sterling?" She pointed to the vase and made no mention of the ones in Miriam's hands, a slight jab that Miriam decided to ignore.

"Novella, you known me for years before I became a Sterling. It's not necessary to call me Missus, you know dat."

"How your huhs-band doin'?'"

"He doin' fine. Fine as ever."

"Dat's good. Dat's very good. He comin' to the celebration tonight?"

"Perhaps. I haven't asked."

Something passed over Novella's face. "You haven't asked ya own husband to come to de social event of de year? Wives shouldn't be wanderin' 'bout wit'out dey husbands. It get people to talkin'."

"And what do dey say, Novella? Seems like you'd know firsthand."

"All right, enough," Tirzah interjected. "Y'all are too busy lolly-gagging in my kitchen when y'all know I got things for you to do. Where are my grandchildren, Novella?"

"The older ones watchin' de young'uns back at de house. Clothes already picked out."

"Good. Where's Free?"

"Out," Novella said.

"Obviously he's out. He's always out. But where is he?"

Novella sighed. "Must be handlin' business. He gotta pick up de cake, bring de decorations to de hall, and help de band set up."

"Are you sure?" Tirzah asked.

Novella dropped her head and her voice. "No . . ."

Tirzah placed both hands on her hips. "You two have been married for twenty-something years and you still don't know where your husband is. What time did he leave this morning?"

"Before sunrise, I think."

"Before sunrise?" Tirzah asked.

"Yes'm," Novella replied.

"I see," Tirzah said, knowing full well Free should've been done with his errands and back home by now. She looked down at the flower pattern on her tablecloth and traced the petals with her eyes.

Novella wrapped her arms around her mother-in-law and rocked her from side to side. "Den it must be a surprise, Ma. Don' you worry your pretty li'l head. Free got you."

Miriam, impressed by Novella's quick thinking to protect the older woman's feelings, half smiled. "I best get a move on," she said. "It's gonna be a long day."

"Dat it is," Novella said, nodding.

As she headed to the back door, Miriam reached into her pocket for her wallet, where she kept her errand list for the day; in a split second, she felt the wallet leave her fingers and fall to the floor. She could feel Tirzah's eyes on the wallet as she hurriedly reached down, hoping that after all these years Tirzah wouldn't recognize the billfold.

Miriam used it often, but made sure to keep it out of sight, especially when Tirzah was around. Miriam looked at Tirzah, who'd lost all the color in her face.

Novella's eyes bounced between the two women, confused and impatient. She was about to bend down and pick the wallet up herself when Tirzah lifted a hand to stop her. With her eyes locked on Miriam's face, Tirzah took the wallet in her hand, running her fingers along the curvatures of the single letter *T*.

"Where did you get this? This . . . looks like something I had a very long time ago," she stuttered, her eyes fixed on the wallet.

Miriam could've told her that it was her mother's, the only keepsake of hers that she had. But the older she had gotten, the harder she found it to lie. She studied the deep lines in Tirzah's face, her sunken eyes, and the slight quiver in her lip, and dropped her shoulders in surrender.

"Tirzah," Miriam began, only to be interrupted by Tirzah's incessant coughing. Her spasms were violent, causing her to double over and hold on to the nearby table to keep her balance, therefore dropping the wallet as she did.

"G'ON, MIRIAM!" NOVELLA SAID, RUSHING TO TIRZAH'S SIDE AND waving Miriam away. "Just g'on wit what you need to do."

Miriam didn't know whether to take back the wallet or leave it. She landed on a compromise: she took out all that she needed, left the wallet on a counter, and hurried out the back door.

"Why didn't she take her wallet?" Novella asked Tirzah as the two women held each other.

Tirzah shook her head as it swarmed with all sorts of questions—about the long-lost wallet, her son, and now Miriam. But her chest was feeling stiff and her body was getting weak. While she knew the best thing to do would be to rest, she thought of all the things she still had to do before watch night. She didn't want to talk about Miriam or the wallet anymore.

"Never you mind that," she replied to Novella, and she rose herself from her chair and headed to the front door. "Could we make another stop before we go?" Tirzah already had one foot outside the house.

"What's dat, Ma?" Novella asked.

"Can we stop by the apothecary? I got this cough that I can't shake."

AFTER LEAVING TIRZAH'S, MIRIAM HEADED TO TOWN TO RETRACE Free's steps. When she went to the town bakery and asked about the watch night celebration cake, Mr. Mills, the head pastry chef, was puzzled. "Which cake, Mrs. Sterling?" he replied.

Miriam blinked. "De one dat Free Benjamin put in."

"Ha!" Mr. Mills threw back his head so far to cackle that his toque fell off. "Free Benjamin ain't put in no order."

"You sure?"

"Yes, ma'am. But donchu worry. I know what day it is. Trust me, dere'll be enough."

Miriam ran over to the general store and asked the cashier if Free Benjamin had stopped by to order the candles, balloons, and table-cloths for the night's event. The young boy at the counter sensed her nervousness and flipped several times forward and backward through the notepad nailed to the wall behind him. When he turned back around, it was with a slight grimace. "I don' see nothin', Mrs. Sterling. But donchu worry. We got decorations for tonight. We wouldn't miss it. Let me go show you what we got."

"I'm gonna kill him," Miriam said under her breath.

"Huh?" the boy asked.

"Never you mind."

Miriam dashed out of the store. She started off back in the direction she came from in a rush, and in her haste, found herself butt first on the ground without a clue as to how she got there. There might have been a foot that planted itself directly in her path on purpose. Maybe a shoulder that suddenly jutted outward to curve into hers and propel her backward. That would explain the sting in her clavicle. When the dust smoke cleared, three women eyeballed Miriam and disarmed whatever barbed words she had prepared for whoever had bulldozed her.

"You Tirzah Benjamin kin?" the shortest and stoutest woman, Lavinia, who wore a deep red lip and a large, wide-brimmed hat, asked.

"Who askin'?" Miriam said as she rose to her feet and dusted off the flounce of her dress.

"We are. Obviously." Lavinia outstretched her arms to the rest of her company and poked out her chest with a snobbish insincerity. "We are newcomers to Nicodemus and we wanted to talk to de main ma'ams of dis here town."

"Newcomers?" Miriam asked. She couldn't remember the last time anyone new came to Nicodemus, and a whole group of people at that.

Nicodemus lost its luster as a thriving community for refugees and migrants when the railroad failed to come through town. Its residents had never mobilized for anything more important in their lives than this opportunity. Certain as the waterfowls flying through every fall, the people of Nicodemus petitioned the Union Pacific Railroad with letters and invited any rail official to tour businesses and private homes whenever they chose, and even issued sixteen thousand in bonds to help close the deal. But in the end, the company ultimately withdrew their offer and established a new town called Bogue, located only four miles west from Nicodemus.

As a result, Nicodemus was not the bustling town it once was but rather a peninsula of clipped dreams—isolated, neglected, and stagnant. Entrepreneurs who could break even in their profits were seen to have been favored by God. Employees lost their verve for labor. The droughts turned neighbors into foes when one believed that another was not being mindful of the town-mandated water restrictions when the well turned out empty. Hailstorms tore through Nicodemus and left fields of bruised and broken corn crops in their wake. Year after year the wheat harvest dwindled, then followed the farmers who trickled out of Nicodemus into other parts of Graham County, like ants lured with the smell of molasses nearby. Those who stayed either rooted themselves with smug pride in their loyalty for the town or burned with regret over not seizing the moment to leave with others.

As a response to Miriam's inquiry about these newcomers, another woman, Verlean, held up a notice in front of Miriam's face and snatched it back before Miriam could fully read the paper in its entirety. Nevertheless, she recognized the content by the style of the words, and thought about how this material landed in this woman's hands.

When the announcement was given that the railroad would not come to Nicodemus, Tirzah had taken it upon herself to form a task force to get the word out to any negro who was searching for a new home. She and the members wrote ads in newspapers, sent notices to churches all over the Midwest and South, and posted flyers on unmarked trees in Graham County. Some arrived and took advantage of the church people's hospitality, but they never stayed. They'd be on their merry way with a full belly, leaving folks with the sense that that was all they really wanted, since they never seemed to come with any of their belongings. The pattern became so common that people would place bets on how long a visitor would stay. But even those visits had dried up in recent years.

"You come on a very busy day," Miriam said. "It's our watch night service celebration tonight and dere's a lot of planning to do. If you'll excuse me."

"Where de party? We'd like to attend." The third woman, Beatrice, asked. Her expression seemed friendly, yet Miriam intuited somehow that it was anything but.

"First Baptist Missionary," Miriam reluctantly disclosed.

"We be dere." Beatrice smiled even harder. "We didn' get your name."

"Miriam. Miriam Sterling."

"Miriam Sterling. You related to de Benjamin kin through blood? Marriage?"

"Neither. We related through de passage of time."

"Oh." Beatrice let out a sharp exhale.

The women left Miriam standing there, just as confused as she was offended.

22

At half past six in the evening, the town gathered into First Baptist Missionary for the watch night service that would commence at 7:00 p.m. sharp. The pastor began the event with the history of the tradition that commemorated the enslaved waiting for the new year to begin and the Emancipation Proclamation taking effect. Those who were born enslaved shared brief memories of their time picking cotton, receiving cruel punishment from the overseers, and their newfound freedom. Tirzah chose to speak of her short time as a teacher and wouldn't go any further.

Then, a large choir sang renditions of negro spirituals like "Wade in the Water" and "Go Down Moses" with such strength that many thought they could've shaken the church's foundation with their voices. Everyone hoped that the extended praise and worship followed by an impassioned sermon would keep Tirzah distracted enough not to recognize that her son wasn't present. But her eyes roamed around the sanctuary nevertheless. She was cordial and appreciative to those who complimented her on the good job she had done planning watch night, which she accepted graciously. But by the time Tirzah had made it to the hall beside the church for the social part of the celebration, she had had enough of keeping up appearances and making small talk. Everyone smiled in her face and asked her about everything under the sun except her own son until the omission became too glaring to ignore. Where was Free? Was he okay? The more hours that passed, the more she figured that Novella and Miriam were lying to her about his so-called surprise for her.

"Where is Free?" Tirzah finally asked Novella, who directed her to sit at the head of a long banquet table.

"He'll be here, Ma. He'll be here."

"That's not what I asked."

"Should I get you some sweet tea, water, lemonade?"

Tirzah slammed her hand on the table, and a few of the female ushers, serving today as party volunteers, paused what they were doing, as did the musicians who were tuning their instruments.

"I'm sorry," Tirzah said and slowly retracted her hand. "I just—no one is telling me where my son is. I don't like it when I don't know where my family is. I don't like when I'm separated from them to do busywork. The last time that happened my husband died."

Novella remained quiet.

"Well?" Tirzah said.

"What am I s'posed to say after you say somethin' so awful as that?"

Tirzah sighed and rubbed Novella's shoulder. "I'll just take water. My chest isn't feeling right."

"Yes'm."

Novella turned away from Tirzah and headed to the kitchen. That was when she saw Miriam coming through the main door with the cake.

"Thank goodness y'all here!" Novella motioned for some volunteers to relieve Miriam of the cake and grabbed her hand to pull her toward the side of the hall as more and more guests poured into the venue.

"What?" Miriam asked.

"Shh!" Novella said.

"Novella, I promise you no one can hear us wit all de talkin' and music playin' goin' on. Now what you want? And hurry 'cause more stuff gotta come in."

"You know I never asked you dis in all our years of knowin' each other."

Miriam raised her eyebrows. "Well?"

"You know where Free is at?"

Miriam relaxed her shoulders. "You mean to tell me he still not here?"

Novella shook her head slowly.

"Dat son of a bitch."

"Miriam!"

"I'm sorry. What you want me to say? I'm mad. Dis ain't right."

"Sure ain't."

Miriam's eyes drifted in Tirzah's direction. "Wait a second."

The trio of women Miriam had come across earlier in the day was making small talk with Tirzah. They were smiling, nodding, and gesticulating with their hands, until they took it upon themselves to sit right beside her! Without saying a word, Miriam marched over to the long banquet table with her hands on her hips.

"Oh!" Tirzah delightfully leaned back in her chair and smiled. "Miriam, I'm so glad to see you. I wanted to introduce you to—"

"We met already," Miriam said coldly.

"Dat we did," Verlean said. "But Miriam looked to be busy, and we can see why. Dis party looks fabulous and we can tell dat a lot of work was put into it. 'Splains why I can smell your sweat from here."

"You still haven't told any of us who you are and what business you have doin' here." Miriam was anxious; something didn't feel right about these women.

"They're here because they want to be in Nicodemus!" Tirzah smiled and clasped her hands together. "I knew that all our work to lure people to town would bring in a harvest. It was all in the timing, at the appointed hour. Praise God."

"You Free's ma, right?"

Tirzah and Miriam fixated on Lavinia, who caught a swift elbow to her side from Beatrice.

"Yeah," Tirzah said with reluctance. "Yes, my son is Free. How did you know his name?"

"Well . . ." Verlean said.

"Don't do it, Verlean. Not yet!" Lavinia said.

"'Not yet' what?" Tirzah looked around.

When no one responded, Tirzah eyeballed Verlean and said sharply, "Look at me." When Verlean did as she was told, Tirzah asked, "What's going on with my son?" She pushed out the last word as her voice was faltering and took out her handkerchief to catch a wet cough.

"He . . . ain't no good." Verlean shook her head. "He ruined our homes. Destroyed our families. Put checks in our husbands' names so he could pay back other people he owed until dere won't no more left."

"We came here 'cause we heard you a good woman wit somethin' to your name and we tryna get back what was stolen from us," Lavinia said. "By de looks of it, you ain't doin' too bad."

"Excuse me!" Novella yelled.

Just then, the doors of the hall swung open. Standing there, at last, was Free. The pockets in his dirty trousers were turned inside out and he was muttering incoherently. His bloodshot eyes struggled to focus on one subject at a time, and he kept shifting his weight from left to right, hardly able to stand straight.

The room was so silent that Tirzah's heels echoed when she approached her son. She placed one hand on his cheek. "Free," she whispered, smiling uneasily. "What happened to you, baby? Look at me. C'mon, you can tell me."

Free avoided her eyes because he knew she'd find the truth there. But looking past her wasn't any better, as his slow gaze landed on the female visitors, and Miriam and Novella standing at a banquet table. He started to make a run back out the hall but was stopped by two white police officers who had arrived at the door.

"What's the matter?" Tirzah asked the men, who had grabbed Free by his arms.

"Ma," Free said. "Ma, I'm sorry."

"Gambling," one of the police officers said flatly. "This here boy's got a gambling problem and he forged checks, committed fraud. We should lock him up for life for all the mayhem he caused in Graham County."

Tirzah looked around the room to see her friends and neighbors murmuring about how Free's wandering was finally catching up to him. She grabbed his shirt collar and shook him. "You found a way to disgrace me tonight," she said with both anger and sadness in her voice. "Tonight, of all nights."

"Ma, I didn't know that they would be coming."

"And we come to collect what's ours!" Beatrice yelled across the room, shaking her fist in the air.

"I don't discuss this with women! You have your husbands talk to me!" Free said, his voice booming at the three women.

"Dey gone!" Verlean chimed in.

Beatrice crossed her arms in agreement. "Mine's too! Left for work elsewhere den chase you all around Kansas for de money!"

Lavinia marched over to Free so quickly that the other two couldn't keep up to restrain her. She spewed, "My husband would shoot you dead if he wasn't out in Ohio tryna make a livin' out in dem factories 'cause you ain't worth de bullet to do you in or de dirt to cover you over!"

Free lunged at Lavinia, but the police officers held him back, thrusting him out the door to be put in the back of their motorized wagon. He called out for his mother, begging her to come and help him, but Tirzah had lost all feeling in her body. Her son was no good. She loved him still, but she couldn't move as his cries for her crescendoed into a childlike pitch. When she was at last able to follow after him, coughing and panting, the police wagon had driven off, leaving a thick cloud of exhaust smoke in the wake. Tirzah shielded her face and coughed inside of her blouse.

With a heaviness in her heart that she had felt only one other time in her life, Tirzah returned to the party slowly, where the music and the conversation had quickly resumed, and took her seat at her table. Novella—shell-shocked and fatigued after seeing her husband in this state—set a plate of food in front of her, and Tirzah began to eat.

"You okay?" Miriam asked, placing her hand on Tirzah's shoulder.

Tirzah lifted her head to see the three visitors now socializing with her own neighbors. And here she was, staring down the banquet table, feeling more alone than she'd ever felt in her life.

She nodded and continued eating in silence.

As the revelers headed out of the hall to prepare to count down to midnight, Novella took Tirzah by her elbow and guided her outside to join the others. Miriam saw that Tirzah had forgotten her handkerchief on the table, and picked it up to bring it to her. The handkerchief unfurled in her hand to reveal a deep, moist patch of blood.

23

All the grandchildren were crammed into the back room of Tirzah's home and were told to stay put unless they wanted to pick out their own switch from the sycamore tree outside. No one cared if the children went to sleep or were cutting up, so long as they stayed there. When their voices got too loud, no one bothered to check up on them. After all, their daddy had been hauled off to jail, and no one was going to be able to make sense of that sight in one night's time. Although Nicodemus was silent, as it always was at this hour, there was a strong, energetic hum in the air that tensed everyone's shoulders. The three out-of-towners sat on chairs enclosed in their own circle. Novella went back and forth between the living room and kitchen to put more leftover potato salad and peach cobbler from the watch night service celebration on the table so that people could occupy themselves with food to make up for the silence. Tirzah rested her elbow on the arm of her sofa and dolefully rubbed her veiny forehead. Miriam, who sat on the other end of the sofa, stole looks at Tirzah and the handkerchief in her right fist.

Tirzah's shoulders lifted up and then she flexed her chest. The women leaned forward and braced themselves for another hacking cough before they realized that she was laughing.

"You all right?" Miriam asked.

Tirzah placed both hands on her knees. "I couldn't get any of you to shut up just a few hours ago and now not one of you can say a thing. Especially y'all." She pointed her finger at the three female visitors, who shrank deeper into their seats. "Y'all come here under the pretense of wanting to live here. Y'all showed up to the watch night service. Y'all knew exactly what y'all were doing, and here y'all are in front of everyone without so much as a simple apology?"

The women gazed at the lines of their palms.

"Look at me when I'm talking to you! Agh!" Tirzah hacked again into her handkerchief and held up a hand when Miriam leaned forward to assist her. "Y'all are funny. Dressing up nicely, being pretty, smelling good, but no decency. But judging by your long faces, at least there might be a bit of shame. Tirzah held her handkerchief close to her heart. "I can't believe this."

"We just as shocked as you are, Ma," Novella said.

"I don't know why you're shocked, Novella." Tirzah straightened her spine. "You see Free as often as I do, which isn't saying much."

Novella lowered her head and pressed her hands together in her lap.

"And you—" Tirzah turned toward Miriam. "We all know where Free goes when he's not with his own wife."

Miriam stared.

"Don't stay quiet now—we're talking as women! How did you not know where he's been and you've been lying up with him all these years?" Tirzah asked.

Miriam shook her head. "He don't tell me everythin'."

"Evidently he doesn't!"

"Besides, he don't spend all his time wit me either. Sometimes he goes out of town . . ."

Novella and Tirzah leaned in toward Miriam.

"Where out of town?" Novella asked.

Miriam averted her eyes and said softly, "In and around Graham County. Sometimes Bogue . . ."

"Bogue?!" Tirzah yelled.

"She's right," Beatrice chimed in.

Soon afterwards, the three women told Tirzah that for years, Free wrote checks under different names and justified this approach by saying that he wanted to avoid his wife finding out about his gambling since she maintained the books of their home. The transactions, according to Free, were all okayed by the names he used, and for a while, everything checked out. He'd beaten their husbands in blackjack games fair and square, and that had been their arrangement. But then he lost his touch. Started losing and took advantage of his new friends' trust. The scam could only go on for so long.

"How much does Free owe you?" Tirzah asked with trepidation.

"'Tween de three of us"—Verlean looked at the other two women—"'bout one hundred dollars."

Tirzah was incredulous. "One hundred dollars?!"

Lavinia nodded. "We want our husbands to come home," she pleaded. "It's not safe for negro women wit a bunch of chirren livin' in de houses by ourselves. De white men already circlin' de property. Dey might take de land and us too."

Tirzah sighed. "I've heard enough. I need to see my son over at the jailhouse and get his side of things."

"You can't go by yourself," Miriam said. While she eventually accepted that gambling would always have a hold on Free, she could not imagine that he'd get into trouble such as this.

"A white guard doesn't scare me. I've been up against much worse."

"Ma, please," Novella said. "She's right."

Tirzah crossed her arms. "You got five minutes to come up with a better option or I'm going over there regardless."

Miriam, as always, managed to think on her feet. Novella's man may have been gone, but Miriam's wasn't.

Corinthian was at home pumicing his feet and keeping watch over a sleeping Temperance and Vera when Miriam burst through the front door.

"Corinthian, c'mon and get dressed," she said as soon as she entered, not mincing words. "Free's been taken to de jailhouse and we gotta take Tirzah to see him."

Corinthian sighed. He was expecting a quiet night, and going to see his wife's long-term boyfriend was not how he intended to bring in the new year. He moved slowly, taking time to dry his feet.

Miriam became visibly annoyed. This felt like a perfect illustration of their energies—she, hot and charged; he, glacially cool. She snapped her fingers three times at him. "C'mon nah. Make haste! You slower den molasses."

Corinthian walked right up to Miriam and stared. "You got some nerve askin' me to take de mother of dat man to de jail so she can see 'im like I don' know what dis all about."

Miriam's jaw dropped. He walked past her to check on the girls and returned to the living room. She was still standing there with a shocked look on her face.

"Ain't none of my business and it ain't none of yours either. Let dat man's wife go see about somebody takin' 'em. Your business is here at home wit me and your daughters. 'Member dem?"

Heat barreled through her entire body. The anger in his voice made Miriam believe that the remark had been fermenting inside him for quite some time.

Still, she managed to push back. "So you have no pity on an old woman, how godly of you."'

"Oh, I have plenty of pity for *her*. Plenty! She got a derelict for her only child so dat's all de burden right dere. No matter how much she try to dress 'im up as de light of de world, he ain't no good!"

Miriam was speechless, but Corinthian was not finished.

"Now everybody can't lie about what we already knew about 'im. His mama's good graces can only take a man so far before he gotta be a man on his own. Maybe him bein' away is a good thin' so he can stop sniffin' up and around you all de good cotdamn time. Mind your own, Miriam. Just mind your own."

She flinched. That was the first time she'd ever heard her husband curse.

"So you don' care dat Tirzah is ill?"

Corinthian's Adam's apple bobbed as the words he intended to say before that admission spoiled in his throat.

"I found blood in her handkerchief today at her party. She keep coughin' and coughin'. Somethin' wrong. She gotta go see him. You know de way of old folk: One day dey here, de next dey out."

No matter how little Corinthian cared for Free, he couldn't have that on his spirit, letting a mother die before her only son got to say goodbye. Corinthian himself couldn't remember his own mother. She was a myth of a woman only spoken about as a warning to young girls who clasped their hands together in church, but didn't do the same for their knees outside of it. The only time he'd seen what she looked like was at her funeral, attended by only him, his grandparents, and the local pastor. And Miriam learned this about him the night he cried on her chest as they lay together naked underneath the covers as newlyweds.

Together, they gathered Temperance and Vera and took them to Tirzah's home to be looked after while they went to the jail. From the moment Corinthian shone his lantern on her, he could see that Tirzah was worn down, clutching her handkerchief for dear life, and kept coughing into it. In her other hand, she held a wallet, which he recognized as Miriam's.

Corinthian said to Tirzah, "Now Mrs. Benjamin, I gotta ask you a question, okay?"

She nodded. "Go head, Cor."

"When de last time you been around white folk?"

Tirzah blinked and started laughing. "What?"

"I'm serious."

"The last time I've been around white folk," Tirzah said. "Been around them, been around them?"

"Yes'm. Not just sayin' hi and bye but actually bein' in conversation wit 'em."

"Besides them coming to Nicodemus looking—"

"No no, dat's on your own turf. Other den dat."

"Well," Tirzah scoffed. "It's been years. I've had no need for it."

"Well, you gon' need it now. Watch your step." He lifted her into the wagon and escorted his wife over into the passenger seat before hopping into the driver's. "Dese crackas ain't too kind to us, and especially not no negroes from Nicodemus. So don' be short wit 'em. State your piece and dat's it."

Tirzah chuckled into the dry air. No matter how long he lectured her about the potential dangers, he'd only be wearing out his tongue. She was going to see her son, and no white man could stop her.

They traveled along a dark dirt path where green wildflowers had been trampled by wagon wheels and possums scurried along to avoid the same fate. The stars were sparse on this night but there were enough to see the small towns along the way. She knew that they were out of Nicodemus and into the white part of town because the buildings were larger, brighter, and more striking. Their log cabin homes had electric lighting, even the awnings looked sturdier.

She could hardly look at the railroad passing through Hill City, its dark steeliness so modern, so distinct from the town's wooden buildings. Tirzah imagined how happy the residents must have been for this new development. More money and more people would keep pouring into this town, and prosperity was an inevitability. If only Nicodemus had gotten this railroad, people would be less bored and inclined to get into trouble, and her son wouldn't have sought pleasure and comfort outside of town.

The Graham County jail was located along Hill City's outskirts, and for good reason. The moment it came into view, one could hear the chains rattling from the inside. A faulty light bulb flickered at the entrance door, which was guarded by a white boy holding a rifle bigger than his entire body. As soon as he saw Corinthian's wagon coming, he reflexively pointed the gun at him but pulled back when Corinthian lifted both his hands in the air. But the boy's sweaty finger stroked the side of the trigger when he seemed to realize that he was outnumbered, even though the other passengers were women.

"What y'all comin' 'round here for? It's late," the guard said, and Corinthian noted that his voice was young.

"Here to see one of the people you got locked up in there. Dis here his mother, Tirzah," Corinthian said, placing a hand on Tirzah's back and gently nudging her toward the guard. "She ain't—isn't—feeling too well and she's gotta see him."

"You know how many times I've heard that excuse this week, boy?" the guard asked. "Ain't nothin' but a ruse for mothers to break their sons out of here."

"Now how would anyone be able to do that when you got a gun in your hand?" Tirzah said, then hacked into the handkerchief. Specks of blood splattered onto the ground near the guard's boots.

Disgusted, the guard took a few steps backward. "You best see a doctor about that. It's nasty."

Tirzah took a deep breath and pulled out a few dollars from her coat pocket. "I need to see my son."

The guard took it from her, then stepped aside to allow Tirzah to pass but placed his foot down when Corinthian and Miriam tried to follow behind.

"You gon' let an older woman be in dere by herself wit dose men?" Miriam asked.

"Miriam—" Corinthian warned.

"She can handle herself. Since she wanna see her son so badly," the guard replied and opened the door. He didn't bother to give Tirzah any light for her path, so Corinthian offered up his lantern.

Tirzah hesitated to fully cross the threshold; this was her first time inside the jail. But when she did, the stench damn near knocked her out. She didn't know if her eyes were tearing from the rancid odor or the sight of countless negro men crammed into cells like chickens stuffed into crates. She didn't know where one body started and another began, but in the darkness she saw dozens of pairs of eyes, looking like they were floating in air. Some of the men whistled, until the light shone on her face and they saw that she was old enough to be their mother.

"Free? Are you in here, baby?" she called out, then hacked into her handkerchief again.

There was a rhythmic rattling coming from the end of the hallway, and it didn't let up until the sound led her straight to him. Free was sitting on the ground with holes all in his shirt and trousers and dried blood on the top of his head. Both his hands and feet were bound with chains, and Tirzah silently begged God for help. While she was happy that Isaac wasn't alive to see his only child like this, she wasn't sure she had the strength to see her son through this mess without him.

Free lifted his head slowly, and Tirzah saw that his face had been bludgeoned to the point that one eye was sealed shut, his nose was bloody and crooked, his lip torn. She reached out a hand through the bars to touch his cheek gently, but he flinched. "Don't take pity on me, Mama. I deserve it."

"Deserve to be locked up in here like some animal?"

"I'm no better than anyone else in here."

Tirzah wanted to tell him that he was, but she sensed that the others could hear their conversation. Instead, she said, "I'm gonna get you out of here."

"No you won't. You're gonna let me stay till I learn my lesson."

"Free, you are my *son*. I'm never going to leave you."

"Mama, are you hearing me?" Free said, raising his voice. "I said I deserve to be here. You heard those women at your party. They weren't lying. I've done wrong. Now . . ." He shook his head. "I got out of hand and hurt people. I hurt a lot of people. . . . They got me and I deserve it."

"You're going to do right by everyone you wronged. You hear me? That's what you're going to do."

"I will."

"And why didn't you tell me that you were in that much trouble?

All this time, Free? All this time you kissed me on my forehead before you went off to what I thought was work, and bring home something for me? Why didn't you tell me before it got this bad?"

"Because I wanted to protect you. For your own sake."

"My own sake?" Tirzah asked. "So you're keeping your gallivanting around Graham County hush-hush for me? Tsk, how charitable."

"I wanted you to keep believing what you wanted to believe. That I was this good son of yours and that I lived up to my father's legacy. I didn't want to break your heart."

"You're breaking my heart right now! Look where all this hiding has gotten you!"

"If I would've told you the truth, you wouldn't have believed it. When we first got to Nicodemus, as much as you tried to deny it, you liked feeling important. You fell right in line after that first night and you wanted that image. I obeyed for a while because I owed you that because the thing about images is that that's all they are. There's no weight to them. But I liked feeling important too. And when I had those cards in my hand . . ." He rubbed his fingers together and sucked his teeth. "I felt like a god."

"I rebuke that! In Jesus's name."

"I wanted to be somebody, Ma. And I was. You saw me play before. You know how good I am. People knew me as Free Benjamin, the man with the quick hands—*the* Black Jack."

"But you didn't have to be that, Free. You could've been—"

"A what?" Free interrupted her. "A preacher?" His tone had turned mocking.

"You've always had a way with words—" she started.

"When my daddy was alive, I did. Not anymore."

"That's not true. How do you explain your way with women?"

Free smirked. "And the trouble it's gotten me into."

The jail door opened, and the guard ordered her to come out.

"You better go on home now. This isn't a place for a woman to be, especially not my mama."

Tirzah gripped one of the bars of the cell. "Now, I understand. All this time I thought it was me dealing with a broken heart and it's you. And because you hurt, your only means was to hurt other people— hurt those women, hurt your children. I named you Free and you are more weighed down than any person I know, even before those chains. But you remember this: I've been here. I'm always here, and if you don't hear anything else, know that I love you even still. Even right now. Because before you came from Nicodemus or Bogue or Shreveport, you came from me."

Just as the last words left her mouth, the guard yanked Tirzah's arm sharply and rushed her outside. As soon as she was back out in the open air, she started coughing and found she could not stop. Miriam, who was standing outside the vehicle, pressed one hand to Tirzah's chest and another to her back while encouraging her to take her time. Feeling woozy, Tirzah fell into Corinthian's arms, and he lifted her into the front passenger seat while Miriam sat in the back to prepare to return home.

Once the jail was a good distance behind them and there was a lull in her coughing, Corinthian took the moment to ask, "If dat money wouldn't have gotten you in, what would you have done?"

"Hmm," Tirzah replied. "I thought about going back home and pulling my pistol out from underneath my mattress."

Corinthian started to laugh, then saw that Tirzah had raised her eyebrow with an air of self-righteousness. A chill ran up his back, and not from the evening breeze.

"Free's father taught me how to shoot," she continued. "You know how rare it was for a man to teach a woman a skill like that? Then he was murdered, and we had to leave town."

"And dem white men just went on about dere lives." Corinthian sucked his teeth and shook his head. "Same ol', same ol'."

"No they didn't." Tirzah took a beat. "I shot the man who was the ringleader. Blew his head right off."

Corinthian pulled the wagon to a halt, and she stared back at him blankly. The night was silent, the air charged. Tirzah gazed at the starry sky, then at Corinthian and Miriam, who was also in shock, and smiled. Their postures relaxed, and then they smiled too, thinking Tirzah must be joking.

"A negro woman with a gun brandishin' it in front of a jail like dat? If we woulda made more noise, white folk woulda thought we was stagin' a rebellion," Corinthian said.

"Dey would've had us lynched before sunrise." Miriam cackled.

"Mm-hmm, before dere maids even made grits," Corinthian added to the macabre humor.

"Hmm." Tirzah looked off into the distance, more serious now. "They are more scared of us than you think."

"I can imagine."

"No. No, you can't. You two weren't born slaves, you don't know." Tirzah cleared her throat again into her handkerchief. "Did your parents or grandparents ever tell you things?"

"Not really," Miriam said.

"Ain't really spoke about it, I'm 'fraid. Just a few things here or dere," Corinthian admitted.

"Tsk, tsk, tsk." Tirzah shook her head. "We are losing our ways already. But I don't blame them. I barely told Free anything. Maybe if I'd scared him a little he wouldn't be in there."

"Don't go blamin' yourself nah. He a grown man. Tuh." Corinthian shook his head and tightened the reins of the horse.

"A grown man who's still wanting his father."

Corinthian didn't respond because he couldn't find it in him to express empathy for Free, his longtime romantic rival. But the truth was he knew what it was like to miss a parent. He ached for his mother, burdened by the weight of questions that would forever go unanswered earthside. But Tirzah kept going, speaking about Isaac in more depth than she ever had in Nicodemus. She told them about the trajectory of their relationship, and Free's formative years in Shreveport.

After a brief silence, Tirzah said, "Miriam, did you tell Corinthian about that wallet I have now? I saw you looking at it when you came to pick me up but you didn't even ask to have it back."

Corinthian looked over his shoulder at Miriam, who froze. "What? Your wallet with the *T* on it?"

"Yes," Tirzah said. "That *T* stands for my name."

"I thought the *T* stood for tomorrow, Miriam?"

"Dat's what I was told," Miriam meekly said.

"'What you were told,' Tirzah echoed. "It was never Miriam's—at least not at first. It was mines, the *T* stood for my name."

"But . . ." Corinthian glanced over his shoulder again, struggling to keep his eyes on the path. "Miriam, you told me your father gave it to you?"

Tirzah smiled. "I know who Miriam is. I know exactly who she is."

Corinthian contorted his face. "I know you know who she is, ma'am. You've known her longer than I have."

"No. I *know* who she is. I *know* who she is," she repeated emphatically. "I was right all along."

"Right about what?" When Corinthian turned to his wife a third time and saw how much she shrank in the back seat without the slightest protest, discomfort assailed his stomach and stretched throughout his body.

"She's as much a Waters as I am a Benjamin."

Corinthian chuckled uneasily. "She hasn't been a Waters since I married her."

Miriam clenched all the muscles in her body and closed her eyes. The rising tension had her wanting to leap out of the moving wagon. Miriam was fully seen by Tirzah. She knew that Tirzah knew who she was no matter how many years had gone by without approaching the subject of their lives prior to Nicodemus. They were both of Natchez stock, connected through Harrison, and the Mississippi had never left them. Just as the water always knows its direction no matter how many lakes and streams it pours into, so too these women were meant to find each other no matter the divergent routes required to bring them here together in this particular time and space.

Miriam held her tongue and Corinthian was at a loss for words, leading the conversation to gradually peter out. After dropping Tirzah off at her home, retrieving her children, and returning to her own home with her husband, Miriam couldn't sleep for several reasons. Corinthian slept on the far side of the bed. He didn't even kiss her good night, which was his usual behavior. In addition to worrying about his uncharacteristic coldness, Miriam could not stop thinking of Tirzah.

She must have fallen asleep eventually, because the next morning she woke to the sound of someone rapping on her front door. She got up from the bed, noticing Corinthian was already gone, and then walked out of the bedroom to find a teary-eyed Novella and a pitiful Corinthian making small talk in the living room.

Miriam tied the strap around her robe. "What's going on?" she asked.

Corinthian turned around. "We was just—" He couldn't finish his sentence.

"What's wrong?"

Her husband sighed.

"What?" Miriam asked again.

"I can't get Tirzah out of bed," Novella said. "She won' get up."

24

As soon as Corinthian's wagon left the grounds of the jail, the white man who guarded the Graham County jail felt compelled to deal another blow to the Benjamin family. He strode down the hallway and once he found Free in his cell, still weak from the beating on the day of his arrival, he said, "Sure picked a bad time to get in trouble with the law, boy. Your mother looked half past dead."

But the guard wasn't telling Free anything new. He'd heard his mother's cough, had heard the blood rising up her throat, how her words became clipped before she grabbed her handkerchief. There had been occasions over the past few months when he'd had to prop her up against his shoulder when those coughs knocked the wind out of her. Even so, he knew that she looked even worse tonight in the thin sliver of moonlight inside the jailhouse. Before the guard arrived to taunt him, he'd been preoccupied with thoughts of his mother. She was right. Before he came from Nicodemus or Shreveport, he'd come from her, and so he knew that something was wrong, very wrong. So instead of wearing his tongue out by pridefully engaging with the guard, he begged for his freedom. The guard relished the debasement.

Before the sun rose, the Nicodemus townsfolk were already gathering up their good plates and a handful of their best flowers to bring to Tirzah Benjamin's home. Corinthian agreed to stay behind with the children while Miriam went along with Novella to pay her last respects.

But first, Miriam ran into the bedroom, where she rummaged around in a drawer, then grabbed some envelopes, stuffing them into her pocket.

As the two women made their way down the mossy road, Novella spoke up: "I always knew that you and Free was lovers, Miriam."

Miriam dug her heels into the damp mud and stared at Novella. "What?"

"I may not have said anythin' all dese years but I'm not stupid. I seen de way he looked at you den and I see de way he look at you now."

"Novella, I—"

"Don' apologize 'cause you don' mean it. If you can lie down with somebody husband while married to your own, den you made your choices and were proud 'bout 'em."

"Why you tellin' me dis now den?"

Novella shrugged. "Somebody close to you bein' sick has a way of bringin' things outta you. Time is short and I don't wanna leave dis earth wit'out sayin' dis to you. Just for me to let you know dat I see you so dat you don' ever forget it."

"Is dat all? Dat was a pretty mild tongue-lashin'."

"No." Novella took a deep breath and tried to lighten her voice to a softer, higher pitch. "I have one last question." She closed her eyes. "Is your chirren Free's?"

She waited with bated breath for the answer. The clear sky turned overcast, and the breeze strengthened during the heavy pause. Finally, Miriam said, "No. No, dey not."

Novella searched Miriam's face for any hint of a lie, but the other woman stared back at her with peaceful, unwavering eyes.

"Now, I have a question of my own," Miriam volleyed.

"What?"

"Why did you come fetch me to see Tirzah since you know what you know?"

"She woulda wanted to see you. She sees you as family."

Despite the sad occasion, Miriam blushed and tried her best not to show teeth.

Novella continued: "She was my family first—de only mama I really knew. When we first came to dis town, she saw dat I traveled all dis way wit'out a fine dress for a party when I asked her if I could borrow one of hers. I promised to pay her back and she agreed and told me dat she wanted me to keep dat hardworking spirit so dat I always have something for me and only me." Novella paused. "I wish I woulda took more heed to dat advice. I been so wrapped up in Free's things dat I don' really know what's rightfully mine. I thought dat comin' to Kansas might mean a new life, a place to settle down and have babies. Two outta three ain't bad, I guess. But dat man wasn't ever de same since his pa died, and I didn' pay too close attention to it 'cause I wanted what I wanted. You and I are alike in dat way. When we want somethin', we go for it. But I can't understand how you have a husband like Corinthian and you sneakin' off wit mine. What you want wit him?"

Miriam blinked and stammered. "I just enjoyed him."

"Dat's all?" Novella replied, unimpressed. "You enjoyed him for years just because? You never thought you was gon' be together and he was gonna leave me?"

"I never wanted to be togetha wit him like you did. I didn't even wanna be married."

Novella jerked her neck out and blinked. "Why not?"

"'Cause I wanted me for mine alone. My ma told me dat life might be better if I stayed by myself for me. But now dat I'm older, I don't think any choice is better for a woman."

"Do you love him?"

All these years of their being together and Miriam hadn't ever asked herself this. She shrugged and moved her right foot in a circular motion on the ground.

"Does he love you?"

"I don' know."

"Well, he loves me. I know you know he loves me. And if you know dat a man loves another woman, den why would you try to stop what's already been felt?"

The revelation cut deep into Miriam's chest as everything began to make sense. Novella's question pulled her from the present and back to Natchez, when she belonged to the water and yearned for nothing more than to get away. Miriam had despised Tabithah for forcing her father into a union that should've never happened, but she was no different than her mother. She couldn't bear to tell Novella that Free told her that he loved her too, but only in secret passageways and under hot, sticky sheets. She was who she came from: a woman forcing herself into a space that wasn't hers.

Novella crossed her arms over her chest. She turned up her bottom lip and said, "You can't grow your own when you pluck from someone else garden. You already got enough of your own. You playin' on your own time and mine." She continued treading down the path to Tirzah's home and left Miriam right where she stood. Miriam allowed for Novella's words to settle into her body as sadness and shame overtook her. By the time Miriam advanced to catch up with Novella, she was already gone.

There at Tirzah's home, people were weaving in and out, coming in with steaming pots of food and leaving with small napkins pressed to their sorrowful faces. Elodie Williams approached Novella and Miriam in the kitchen, which was surprisingly empty. She squeezed them tightly. She had been assigned to watch over the home and make sure the children didn't peek into Tirzah's room while Novella fetched Miriam.

"How she doin'?" Miriam asked.

"She's quiet. Very quiet. I could hardly hear her breathe when the doctor checked for it. But she doesn't seem to be in pain." Elodie turned to Novella and said, "I didn't let anyone go inside, though everybody's asking to see her. I don't think she needs to be bothered unless you want to see if she'd like to take a few visitors."

"Maybe not yet."

The youngest of Novella's twelve children ran up to her and tugged at the fabric of her dress. "Ma, is Pa comin' home today?"

She held the back of the child's head and leaned her face into her hip. "I don' know, sweetheart. I don' know."

"I had a few of our men go and see about F-R-E-E. But they should've been back right now. I told them to hurry because we don't have much T-I-M-E," said Elodie.

"How much?" Miriam asked.

Novella bent down to her child's height and said, "Go on outside wit your sisters and brothers and let the grown folk talk."

The child did as she was told, and Elodie, who was never at a loss for words, began to fidget.

"Well?" Miriam asked.

"Tonight."

"Tonight?" Miriam and Novella said in unison.

Elodie nodded. "The doctor was going to wait till you got back, Miriam, but he's got other people to see around the county. Tuberculosis is what he said, and it's too far now. Whatever bit of lung she has left can't support her much longer."

"Oh!" Novella fell into Miriam's arms and started crying. Elodie huddled around them both, and no one let go until Novella pulled herself together. "I guess—" Novella straightened herself up. "I guess I have to call de chirren in."

Elodie nodded. "Have them see her, then send them out to keep running around. Don't let them see her when she's too close to the other side because it'll take an eternity to remove that picture from their mind."

Miriam took a seat in Tirzah's living room and greeted everyone who came through the door. From the window, she saw the trio of out-of-town ladies from the night watch loading up a wagon outside. Lavinia and Beatrice were already situated in the wagon but Verlean was making her way toward Miriam with a dozen carnations in her hands. "We didn' plan on stayin'," she said to Miriam as she pressed the flowers into her hand.

"Obviously." Miriam pursed her lips.

"We had no idea dat she was sick. If we woulda known we wouldn't have come around."

"But still you decided to stay here while people who actually cared about her came to pay dere last respects."

"You right about dat. It wasn't proper. We just were—"

"Desperate," Miriam replied. "I understand. Dis will all get straightened out. One way or another."

Verlean nodded and left.

After the women's wagon pulled away, Miriam headed back inside and sat on the sofa, realizing that she was just as much of an interloper as the others. She wasn't Tirzah's daughter-in-law, nor the mother of her grandchildren. Again, Miriam felt like her mother. They were both women who forced themselves into other people's stories and suffered for it. But unlike her mother toward her father, Miriam didn't know if she even really loved Free. He was attractive, yes, but he became irresistible because he was Tirzah's child and Miriam yearned to know her by way of her son. And maybe their union was what both of their parents could never achieve—a sense of togetherness at long last. But if she truly believed that, then why did she keep what she knew a secret?

The conversation around her quieted to a low murmur. She observed Novella fetching the children one by one—she wiping their sweaty faces and talking to them, them nodding but clearly out of breath and uninterested, she walking them into the room, and them emerging in tears, devoid of the energy they brought into the house. She felt the urge to go and grab her children so they could see Tirzah too, but she wasn't their grandmother. More guests floated in and out of the room as day transitioned into night.

All the while, Miriam remained in her one spot—silent and pensive. Her thoughts sent her away from the present moment, until Novella touched her shoulder and said, "She askin' for you."

Miriam reluctantly stood to her feet, and Novella gripped both of her wrists to pull her close. "Whatever you do, don' bring up Free. If she mention him, lie, and if you ain't a good liar, change de subject."

When Miriam twisted the doorknob to Tirzah's bedroom, she wasn't sure what to expect, but her heart raced when she heard the older woman struggling to breathe, wheezing as if spirits were tugging to pull the life out of her body. Slender white candles burned on the nightstands on both sides of the bed as well as along the windowsill. This was when Miriam realized that night had fallen. An owl hooted, and frogs croaked from the nearby marsh.

Miriam glanced at Tirzah and was taken aback by how beautiful she looked. Her face seemed less weighed down by wrinkles. Her hair, always dutifully styled into an updo or low bun, now lay loose on her pillows—thick, long, and curly. She was dressed in a long white slip like she was simply getting ready for bed, and she gazed at Miriam with sympathetic eyes.

"Were you afraid of what you'd find in here?" Tirzah rasped, but there was a lightness in her voice.

"No, ma'am. I just didn' expect you to look so . . . young. It feel like I'm gettin' a glimpse of who you were before . . ."

"Before?"

Miriam shrugged. "Everythin'. Before bein' a mother, before bein' married. Before."

"Yeah, I was very nice to look at when I was younger. I never heard any complaints."

They shared a small laugh.

Then Miriam sat by Tirzah's bedside and the proximity was overwhelming. She began to cry. Tirzah rubbed the top of her hand. "Go on ahead and let it out if you have to."

Miriam collected herself and said, "I'm sorry. I'm not just cryin' for you. I'm cryin' for my own mother."

"You never told me about her. What was she like?"

Miriam sniffed. "Beautiful. Stubborn. Strong-willed. Determined."

"Hmm. So many of us are. When's the last time you've seen her?"

Miriam looked to the adjacent wall and closed her eyes to ensure that she could get all her words out. "Since before I moved to Nicodemus. I don' know what happened to her. Rainfall came and de river was upset. She told me to run and I did, thinkin' she was gonna be behind me—or maybe I din't, I don' know. But . . . she din't make it. Neitha did my pa."

"Mercy," Tirzah said. "There were . . . many of us who never got to truly say goodbye to the ones we loved, and it caused us a great deal of heartache. We moved on because we had to, but somehow the past keeps biting the back of our necks."

"How do you move on? Really move on den?"

"If I knew that, I wouldn't be sitting here having my life come back to me in all kinds of waves. I don't just lie here because I'm tired, baby. I lie here because my memories put me flat on my back."

"Do you have any regrets?"

"Plenty. One regret I have is letting Free find my Bible with all my keepsakes in there."

"Why?"

"Because a man who I loved very much placed an ad looking for me, and I kept the ad. Good thing he didn't flip to any other pages or he would've found some notes." She leaned over and pointed at her nightstand on the right-hand side of her. Miriam pulled open the drawer and went directly to the page in the Bible where her keepsakes were held. The spot was easy to find because it jutted out farther than any of the other pages. She found a flimsy piece of paper—an advertisement from her father to Tirzah looking for her—and pressed it to her chest before tucking it back inside the Bible.

"I think Free changed when his father died, and he knew I loved someone before his father. He was never the same. Don't ever let Free get rid of my Bible or anything in it though."

"Why is dat?"

"Because if he gets rid of it, I'll really truly be gone."

"Yes'm. I make sure it's safe."

"Thank you." Tirzah laid her head back on the pillow and looked toward the ceiling. "I think about him still, you know."

Miriam sat back down on the edge of the bed. "What do you think about?"

Tirzah took a deep breath. "When my husband died, I knew I was loved but he also knew I loved another man alongside him. That other man, the man before my late husband, it's been one of the greatest mysteries of my life because I don't know. Whether or not he still loved me. Whether or not he stopped looking for me. Whether or not he forgot about me."

Miriam took both of Tirzah's hands into hers and planted a long, sustained kiss on both of them before wetting them with her tears. She slowly raised her face and said, "He did. He did still love you. He never stopped."

"Oh, baby." Tirzah caressed her damp cheek. "I never stopped believing it even if I had no proof."

"You do." Miriam took a beat. "You do have proof."

"You, you mean? I know you're Harrison's daughter. I was waiting... all these years for you to come out and say it. When you didn't, I had doubts, even thought I was crazy at one point. But the wallet . . . I knew."

Miriam shook her head. "Dere's more."

Tirzah raised her chin.

Miriam reached deep into her pocket for the envelopes she carried from home, opened them, and unfurled a few papers in front of Tirzah. "I saw your letters to him. I read as many as I could. I don't know how dese were able to be saved when de flood came but I had 'em and I dried 'em out as soon as I got to safe land." Miriam held the letters close to Tirzah's face. "He loved you. He loved you 'til the day he died."

"He did?"

"Yes."

Tirzah looked up at the ceiling and began to laugh. Her voice rang like an instrument tuned to perfection. "Oh, I'm so happy. I am so happy."

"Why?" Miriam's tears were so heavy she could hardly see in front of her. "I kept dem all dese years. You ain't mad at me?"

"Not at all." Tirzah stopped laughing. Her voice thinned. "I was loved and am loved. And God blessed me so much when he sent me you. You have ended the mystery of my life."

"But ain't you sad that you hadn't seen him before he died?"

"Why be sad? I'll be seeing him again. And again and again and again." She raised her chest and then her face stilled. The flame of the candles beside Tirzah's bed flickered powerfully and the outside winds rapped on the window glass.

Miriam kissed Tirzah's forehead just as the door flung open. Free stood at the threshold. Miriam looked at him in his breathless stance, and he at her, then down at his mother. Miriam held the Bible and letters close to her chest, as Free yelled, then choked, winded by a familiar grief that brought him to his knees.

2020

25

JANUARY 2020

SSSS.
  SSSSS.
SSSSS.
SSSSS.

Long drawn-out hisses were familiar to Oliver. He had heard them from the mouths of many patients at NewYork-Presbyterian. But this was different. In all his training as an emergency medicine physician, he had never heard a gasp for air like this from anyone until today.

In the waiting room, an elderly woman, whose emerald and gold rings seemed too big for her gangly hands, stood, all the chairs already occupied with sneezing and coughing New Yorkers. Her skin was black as the Madonna herself, and she had a mysterious air about her even as she struggled to remain upright. Oliver, who'd been passing by the receptionist's desk to check on the day's flow of patients, fortuitously spotted this woman out of the corner of his eye just as she was about to collapse.

Her name was Ms. Lunette, she told him, and she claimed that as soon as the triage team discovered that she had no insurance, they rebuffed her, rolling their eyes and mumbling that she should have gone to Harlem Hospital instead. Triage denied this and said that they had only asked her to wait in the waiting room like everyone else. Whatever the case, Ms. Lunette beamed with what little energy she had left when she saw a Black doctor come to her aid.

On any other day, Oliver might not have made such haste to assist her. It was flu season, and the entire staff knew the routine for inflected Manhattanites coming in at all hours of the day and night. He would've gently told this Black elderly woman to wait for her name to be called as was standard procedure. But the fragility of Ms. Lunette's breaths made plain the severity of the situation and propelled him to act quickly.

"Thank ya," she repeated in a whisper after he found her an empty bed. "It shouldn't be nothin' but a flu but I just had to be sure in my old age, ya know?"

When Oliver pressed a stethoscope to Ms. Lunette's chest, the crackling and rumbling feedback he received sounded like an eruption.

"Have you been anywhere besides New York recently?" Oliver asked.

"Not since I broke up with my boyfriend during a trip to Curaçao. That was back last fall."

He peered deeply into her sullen eyes, watching the gray rings around the cornea become darker under the fluorescent lighting, and ordered a respiratory panel. In a few hours, the results from the lab came back. Common cold, adenovirus, RSV, pneumonia, influenza: all negative. Oliver squinted at the results, read the panel left to right and right to left so many times his eyes started to cross, and slowly shook his head. Miss Lunette was sick, Oliver thought. But whatever she had was not registering on this standard exam.

DURING LUNCH, OLIVER WAS ABLE TO CATCH A FEW COWORKERS as they were making their way to the hospital cafeteria. He briefly brought them up to speed on Ms. Lunette and the negative respiratory panel before asking them, "Do you think we should test for the novel coronavirus?"

"Pfft. If you think you can get your hands on a test, I got a beach house to sell you in Iowa," a radiologist joked. "My girlfriend works at Mount Sinai and there's a shortage everywhere."

"Has she been to Wuhan, China, recently?" another emergency physician asked.

"No," Oliver told him.

"Italy?"

Oliver shook his head. "Nope. The last place she's been was the Caribbean last fall."

"Then why even swab her?" the radiologist asked, and the group left Oliver standing in the hallway, stumped. He slowly walked back to Ms. Lunette's room, where she'd pulled out the patient table to prop her feet up. She had her hands perched on her knees like she was waiting for him.

"Docta' Oliva'," Ms. Lunette said raspily. "Did you know I was a waitress at Minton's? Saw everyone from the finest pimps, the mob, Sarah Vaughan, Dizzy Gillespie, and Miles Davis! I always thought Miles was mean but that didn't stop him from pullin' all of the women." Oliver smiled and shook his head as she continued with her tales. Whatever could keep her spirits afloat would be good for her body, he thought. He was going to have to admit her, but as long as she kept talking, she was still breathing. As long as she kept talking, Oliver promised himself, he would be there to listen.

For days, Oliver would attempt to treat Ms. Lunette as though she had pneumonia, with intravenous fluids and antibiotics. But her symptoms weren't improving. Yet she still had the energy to tell Oliver about how before the age of forty, she had already traveled to Bamako, Dakar, Addis Ababa, and Alexandria—"the cradle rocks of humanity," she called them. The timbre of her voice was thin as she recounted the story of how she got kicked out of Spelman, then went straight to a cabaret stint in Vegas. Then a few days later, with a hoarse throat,

Ms. Lunette had to tell Oliver about her hitchhiking experience in Oregon, how she almost lost her life skiing in Vermont, and that she'd snorted so much cocaine at Studio 54 that her sense of smell had never been the same again. As her stories expanded further than the breath with which she had to sustain them, he saw there was no other option but to transfer Ms. Lunette to the ICU as her breathing was becoming shorter. Underneath his scrubs, Oliver sweated with a kind of panic he'd never experienced before.

He also found he couldn't leave the stress at work. If he'd been a single man, he could have gone home for a glass of whiskey to help him fall asleep, followed by a double or triple shot of espresso in the morning if that sleep hadn't been quite enough. A run through Central Park or some dumbbells at the gym could make the endorphins flood his body. But at the apartment he shared with his fiancée, Ardelia, it was hard to hide his anxiety, and she was starting to become concerned. Their wedding was in nine months. She needed to decide on a dress soon. Save-the-dates had to go out by the end of the month, and they still hadn't finalized their guest list. Correction: *Oliver* hadn't finalized his part of this list.

Ever since Ms. Lunette walked into NewYork-Presbyterian and her respiratory panel returned negative, Oliver became obsessed with figuring out what was wrong with her. He pored through medical textbooks, feverishly read the *New York Times* and BBC articles on the latest developments from Wuhan, and phoned medical school classmates from all over the country to see if they too had sick patients whose bodies rejected any of the traditional viral treatments. Emails started to pile up in his inbox, including urgent messages from Stacy, the wedding planner he and Ardelia had hired. Whenever Ardelia brought up another question about the wedding, Oliver promised her he'd get to it later and she'd silently wait for him to be present with her.

On the night following Ms. Lunette's transfer to the ICU, Oliver rushed home to take a shower, as he usually did after shifts. He dashed right past the kitchen and living room without saying a word. All of a sudden, Ardelia heard the water running and jumped to her feet. She marched over to the bathroom, flung the door open, and angrily pulled back the shower curtain, at which Oliver jumped and flinched.

"Jesus!" Oliver yelled. "You scared me. What was that for?"

"I had my dress fitting today and you haven't even asked me how it went."

Oliver relaxed his shoulders and stared at the water swirling down the drain. "I'm sorry, Ardelia. I completely forgot."

"Yeah, you did. And you just completely ignored me when you came in. You didn't even give me a kiss like you usually do."

He nodded. "You're right."

"And you haven't been responding to any of Stacy's emails! I feel like I'm planning this wedding all by myself here."

"Jesus, Ardelia! You know what's going on. I told you that I have a patient who's not doing well and I can't figure out why. I'm worried it might be the coronavirus."

"The Black woman you mentioned? Didn't you tell me that she hadn't been to China?"

Oliver sighed. "Yes. Can I get back to showering, please?"

"Fine." Ardelia pulled the curtains and was just about to march back out when his silhouette made her pause. His head hung low, his posture was weak. Intuition took hold: something was wrong. But because Ardelia could not place or name that wrong, she remained quiet, which only allowed her ire to take root.

MS. LUNETTE TRIED HER BEST TO CONTINUE TALKING AS OLIVER persisted in trying to find an appropriate cure. Sometimes she'd start and then the wheezing would ultimately have her doubling over, leaving her disoriented and forgetful of what she wanted to say in the first place. Other times, she'd stare at the fluorescent lighting and hum, allowing for all the unspoken words to metamorphose into a melody instead so that at least their essence could still be retained.

When Ms. Lunette's stay at NewYork-Presbyterian had hit two weeks, Oliver reluctantly went into her room and said, "I think we need to call some of your loved ones. Just so they know how you're doing."

"Mm-mm." Ms. Lunette shook her head. "It's just a flu."

Oliver closed his eyes as her denial gripped him. "Ms. Lunette," Oliver said, and reopened them. "Please."

"Do ya like Black history?" Ms. Lunette asked with more clarity in her voice than she'd had in days.

"I do. But my fiancée is the real history nerd. She works at the Schomburg."

"The Schomburg! Well, I'll be."

"And I mean . . . well . . ." Oliver blushed.

Ms. Lunette leaned forward. "What?"

Oliver wasted no time in telling Ms. Lunette about the letter he gave to Ardelia on the night of their engagement party, the family lore, and how said letter was his own piece of Black history. Once he finished, he realized that Ms. Lunette was losing color in her face. Yet she was smiling.

"I have something I have to show ya."

"Show me?"

Ms. Lunette rubbed her chest. "Yes. I—I can't go yet. I—got things I need to do. Things I've been . . . keepin' for years. Things I've collected in so many places I've been, on both sides of de Mississippi . . . people I've seen, I've talked about . . . I—" She choked back air. "Can't leave without showin' 'em to people. I—been plannin'—while now." Her voice tapered off and terror immobilized her face. She began to frantically wave her hands in front of her, and Oliver yelled for backup. Though his coworkers disagreed on what might be ailing Ms. Lunette, upon looking at her they knew that she needed to be put on a ventilator immediately. Once Ms. Lunette saw everyone moving quickly around her, she started to wriggle out of her bed, but she was no match for Oliver's reflexes. As he touched her arm, promising that everything would be okay, he could feel the heat surging through her skin. "I'll be right here," he assured her. "Remember, you got things to do. Remember? This will ensure you get back to them."

One of the doctors glanced at Oliver uneasily, but Ms. Lunette extended her right hand toward Oliver in such a way that made him feel as if he were splintering and dissolving across the entire room. Once Ms. Lunette was sedated and put on a ventilator, Oliver promptly went to the chief of the Department of Emergency Medicine and asked if he could take the rest of the day off to decompress.

His body was so shell-shocked that he didn't want to be around anyone on public transportation, and he called an Uber, which dropped him off right in front of his home on 138th and St. Nicholas Avenue. Mr. Johnson, one of his neighbors, was humming some kind of medley in front of the apartment building. He had to have been all of five-five, but carried the voice of a man twice his size. With his gray eyes and a salt-and-pepper beard, Mr. Johnson would sweep and sweep and sweep the stoop simply because he wanted to. Oliver groaned inwardly. He'd almost been home free.

"Hi, Mr. Johnson."

Mr. Johnson looked up and flashed a gap-toothed smile. "Hey there, young man!" He greeted Oliver like he'd just returned from a long voyage. "How you doin'?"

"It's a long story."

The elder leaned his broom against the stoop and squinted. "You don't look too good. Everythin' goin' okay?"

"Not really. I'm having a tough time at the hospital. One of my patients just got put on a ventilator."

"Huh. I don't mean to be crass but don't stuff like that happen all the time?"

"Naw, it's fine. They do, but this lady's different. I don't know why but I can't stop thinking about her. Not in the way you think, of course. She's an elder but . . . I don't know." Oliver shrugged.

"You have a lot of heart and a lot of empathy," Mr. Johnson said.

"But when you carry that much, you get run down quicker than others. What you think?"

"You might be right. I haven't been able to get good sleep in I don't know how long."

"I can tell by the way you look."

Oliver laughed and said his goodbyes. Before he knew it, his face was planted in a silk pillow, and after a single exhale, he was cruising through a deep slumber.

By the time he opened his eyes, turned on his side, and saw light through the crack of the door, he heard pots clanging, water running, and the TV playing at full volume. He took a deep breath and got to his feet, waiting a few moments to get his mind right. Ardelia spun around as soon as he emerged from the hallway.

"Hey," he weakly said.

"Hey." She leaned against the countertop and folded her arms over her chest. "You been working into the night for the past few weeks so I was shocked to see you napping in the middle of the day. Everything okay?"

"No. Well—" Oliver quickly caught himself. "Ms. Lunette is on the ventilator."

Ardelia sighed and turned her back on him to check on the boiling pots.

"What?" Oliver asked.

"Nothing. I hope she gets better," Ardelia said through pursed lips.

"Same. But I don't know anymore. I really don't."

Ardelia lifted the lids of the pots and stirred, trying to ease the awkwardness between them.

"What's the occasion?" he asked.

"No occasion," she said. "I figured that since you passed out in our bedroom, you could use some comfort food. And frankly, I could use some myself."

Ardelia always knew what to do to make Oliver smile. She saw him as a man, flesh and bone, and not as a doctor, white coat and stethoscope. Of course, she'd listen to him speak about his work, but she was more interested in the grooves and contour of his spirit.

A simple "How are you?" in the earliest parts of their dating life was the sweetest song to him. Her voice reached another depth when she posed it, her eyes shimmered as though his entire body could be consumed within her gaze—this was how he knew that he loved her.

As he gathered the utensils, placemats, and glasses to set the table, Ardelia pulled out a large box of vinyl records and placed one on the turntable. After the brief needle scratch, a woman's stirring voice issued from the player.

Oliver raised his chin toward the crooning and a smile grew on his face. "You sure do love this Violet singer, don't you?"

"Of course," Ardelia said as she took her seat across from him. "She's one of the tragically unsung heroes of blues music, I think. She was way ahead of her time."

They lowered themselves into their seats at the table and began to eat. "This is delicious," Oliver said with his mouth half full of mashed potatoes and string beans.

"Thanks. It's not as good as your cooking, but I'm getting there." He smiled. When they met, Ardelia had only known how to boil rice, but over the course of their relationship, became determined to add new foods to her repertoire.

"Hey, I have a question," Oliver said.

"Shoot."

"When's the last time you spoke to Sterling?"

A large spiderweb branched inside Ardelia's throat. Her body curled and shrank into itself the moment Oliver invoked her father's name. That name rang like a cymbal crash from the middle of her chest outward until she could not hear Violet on the record any longer—only the incessant ringing that began whenever Oliver pulled her most difficult trigger. Why did he want to disturb their dinner with a question about her father? Hadn't he been through enough today? Why would he invite the name of the man who first taught her what separation meant when all Ardelia wanted to do tonight was bond?

"Is that why you mentioned Violet? Because you knew that he gave me this record?"

Oliver leaned back in his seat, unsettled by how Ardelia's tone shifted from warm to biting in an instant. "You put the record on, not me." He half laughed to breach the blockade forming between them, but she did not return his smile.

"I'll speak to him when I speak to him. He can wait. He made me wait," Ardelia said, stabbing at a green bean.

"But he sends you letters all the time. Have you responded to any of them? Don't you wanna be on good standing with him for the wedding?"

Ardelia's face lifted from her plate. "This is the first time I've heard you talk about the wedding in I don't know how long, and it's about my dad?"

Oliver narrowed his eyes, confused. Wasn't he showing that he cared about their wedding as well as her family? Wasn't he showing that he cared, period?

"Just drop it, okay? I want to enjoy dinner with you." Ardelia sighed and shoveled a bite of mashed potatoes into her mouth.

Oliver quietly ate his food, though not without one last effort in mind. He pressed his feet deeper into the floor and scooched backward so that the sound of the legs dragging against the wood would snap Ardelia out of the anger she was stewing in from their exchange. She lifted her head and followed Oliver's movement around the table to her side, where he held out his hand. Roses bloomed on her cheeks when Ardelia touched his hand, and he swept her around the floor by keeping a firm hand on her waist. The top of her head rested underneath his chin as they rocked side to side to the music. Ardelia lifted her right hand to massage the side of his face and said, "Your beard is growing like crazy . . ." She moved her hand further up to rub his hair. "And your hair. When's the last time you went to the barber?"

Oliver caught his reflection in the mounted mirror on the wall beside their hallway and became spooked at how uneven and wild his appearance had become.

"Damn. I look a mess."

"Well . . . I didn't want to say anything. I know you've been going through a lot."

Without much thought, Oliver pressed Ardelia up against the mirror and kissed her until she softened in his arms. He was worried that she would break away from his embrace to ask him what he was doing, to which he wouldn't have an answer. His unkempt looks were embarrassing, and he didn't want to be reminded of it. But her body felt so good. She hadn't smiled this much in a while and neither had he. He was exhausted, yes, but something primal kicked up inside of him, to where he had Ardelia with her wrists pinned to the wall above their bed. Her moans further energized him to claw at every article of clothing she had on until she was stark naked. They kissed, nibbled on each other's earlobes, and gently bit down on each other's shoulders, but that wasn't enough for Oliver. He didn't want to consume her. He wanted to live inside of her. Taking up residence in the loveliest place he ever felt melted away his own life and responsibilities. If Ardelia were not breathless with her arms limp and hanging over the edge of the bed, only God and whoever lived down below would know how much longer Oliver could've remained in this place. He lay on his back beside Ardelia, staring up above until Ms. Lunette and her breathing tube began to appear in the tree-bark textures of the ceiling.

IN THE MIDDLE OF THE NIGHT, ALL THE EMOTIONS THAT OLIVER had kept tempered started to turn him loose. He hissed and convulsed in his sleep, rattled off all kinds of medical terms until the letters mashed together to form an entirely foreign tongue, and sweated until there were spots all over his ribbed T-shirt. If a pair of arms hadn't wrapped tightly around his rib cage, he could've fallen out of bed. Before he could scream, a sweet voice said, *Oliver.* Ardelia repeated his name, but he did not respond. A moan split the room in half. The sound carried so much agony that Ardelia released her grip on his body. Oliver slowly turned his sweaty hand to the other side of the bed and saw Ardelia sitting upright, staring at him—terrified. He didn't say a word. Instead, Oliver lay on his back and stared blankly at the ceiling with his mouth ajar.

"Oliver . . . are you okay?" Ardelia asked.

He turned to look at her, then back up at the ceiling. A single tear fell from his right eye.

"I don't know. I don't know what's happening to me."

The next morning, Ardelia made Oliver breakfast, but he couldn't eat. He ran the shower for all of thirty seconds before turning the faucet off. He trudged from the bathroom to the bedroom and back, and groaned every step of the way. When Ardelia leaned in for a kiss as he was making his way out the door, his cold lips barely connected with hers. Whatever happened at home faded once he boarded the bus. By the time he entered the hospital, unable to feel the ground underneath his feet, he'd forgotten how he'd even made it to work. And when Oliver went to check up on Ms. Lunette, her room was empty. The smell of disinfectant had replaced her scent of sandalwood and musk. He braced for the worst.

"Where is she?" Oliver called out in the hallway.

The residents stared at Oliver. He repeated himself, with bass in his voice. They told him to speak to the department chief. Dr. Peterson sat in his office, papers stacked in different columns on his desk.

"Oliver," he said. "Have a seat."

"No," Oliver replied curtly.

Dr. Peterson blinked once. "I'm sorry?"

"No, I'm not having a seat. No, I'm not going to talk about the stressors of this job. No, I'm not going to be harangued about the dangers of getting too close to a patient. No."

"Oliver, can I be honest with you?"

"I don't think I have much choice in the matter."

Dr. Peterson removed his glasses to rub his eyes and placed them back on the arch of his nose. "You seem to be losing focus."

"When did Ms. Lunette die?"

"Last night. Long after you went home."

"Was anyone with her when she passed?"

Dr. Peterson said nothing.

"You know something, doctor?" Oliver said. "When I graduated from medical school, my grandmother told me that back when doctors wouldn't see Black people, we could only rely on people in town. And she told me the story of her mother's mother or maybe her mother's mother's mother having to die at home because no hospital would see her. She had something wrong with her respiratory system too. Whether or not all of it is true, I don't know. But whoever that lady was in my family, she did not die alone."

Dr. Peterson did not so much as soften his shoulders. His expression made Oliver forget why he had even told that story in the first place. Oliver left without saying a word.

For the remainder of the day, Oliver was not in control of his faculties. People came up to him and they'd walk away. He could feel his lips moving and his throat vibrating with what he suspected to be words, but whatever was said, he could not remember. The tile floor underneath his sneakers melted away as he levitated higher and higher above every hallway, patient room, and elevator he occupied. Ms. Lunette was gone. In less than three weeks, she'd died. That was all he could think about—her gray eyes, her wanting to show him something, her outstretched right hand. If he hadn't gone home early yesterday afternoon, he probably could've saved her. And if he couldn't have, he could've at least kept his promise that he would be right there with her. He failed. In medical school, he was taught that he should never make promises to patients, but he did and he failed.

That night, he sat on the couch as Ardelia paced back and forth in front of him, listing name after name after name from her laptop screen. Soon, the words started to become painful and he began to soothe his eardrums. But from Ardelia's vantage point, Oliver was covering his ears and ignoring her again.

"Oliver," Ardelia whined. "Are you even paying attention? It's the guest list. This is crucial, honey."

"What?" he asked.

Ardelia placed her laptop down on the coffee table, ran down the corridor, and slammed their bedroom door shut. She didn't open it again that night, and Oliver could not get himself off the couch.

For the next week, more people began to come to the hospital presenting with symptoms like Ms. Lunette's. Respiratory panels would come back negative, bronchoscopies would be performed, tubes would be inserted. And they died just as quickly as she had—if not more quickly. Oliver would check on them one minute, and the next, he would find them still, cold to the touch, mouths open as if their spirits had been drawn out of their bodies. The hallways reeked of death. Even the medical workers seemed to exist in some liminal space, their bodies teetering toward the precipice of an unfamiliar terror. One by one, patients would expire in a manner that made Oliver doubt God. Still, he tried to remain a believer. He pictured a force higher than himself mercilessly barreling through the halls to collect its people. Everyday, it would be the same thing, and every night, Ardelia would want to talk about the wedding and Oliver would shut down, unable to hold space for the two of them, much less her and her anxieties.

Then one evening at the end of the month, though Oliver wasn't sure of the date itself, Ardelia was in the middle of asking Oliver if he'd like to do takeout for dinner, and he interrupted her, saying flatly, "I think I need to leave for a while."

Ardelia blinked and leaned back on the couch cushion upon which she sat. He flinched but stared directly ahead at the television screen, where CNN was blaring.

"What?"

"I think I need to get some space for a bit. I'm feeling overwhelmed."

"Is it me?" Ardelia nervously asked.

"It's everything. I need some space to get myself together."

"Are you breaking up with me?"

Oliver looked at Tirzah's letter framed on their mantelpiece and said, "Of course not, sweetheart. Of course not. Just . . . let me do this . . . okay?"

"When will you come back?"

"I don't know, Del. But I will be back. I promise. I love you."

"I love you too."

Oliver held her hands before raising them to his lips to kiss. Then he let her go and proceeded to the bedroom to pack.

He left the apartment without saying anything else and heard her weeping as soon as he closed the front door behind him.

Oliver stomped down to the first floor of the apartment building and breezed right past Mr. Johnson, who was leaning against the front stoop, eavesdropping. He watched Oliver till he turned the corner, then looked up at the light from their street-facing apartment and lit a blunt.

After blowing the thick smoke into the winter air, Mr. Johnson spoke to their window. "Just you hold on, Miss Ardelia child," he said. "He'll be back."

26

When Oliver decided to leave, Ardelia could feel from the middle of her forehead down to the pit of her stomach an unzipping of a tightly wound self she had fortified through years of therapy and introspection. She stood by the door long after Oliver closed it behind him to descend the staircase with his luggage. With her feet glued to the floor, Ardelia's chest became tight and the inside pockets of her mouth dried up like a desert. Her body shrank smaller and smaller until she imagined herself younger by at least two decades, waiting and waiting and waiting for her father to walk through the door of her grandmother's home on the South Side. The longer she froze in space in the present, the more severe his absence throughout her entire life became—a doorknob left unturned, a door still wanting to creak, footsteps yet to make advancements toward her. Yes, she loved him. She loved him down to the cellular up to the spiritual, but did he love her? If so, why exactly did she feel so small? Why was she standing here alone? Who exactly was the man Ardelia was waiting for? Ardelia eventually returned to her body and shook her head clean with the self-admonition that she better preoccupy herself as soon as possible or she'd spiral.

Luckily, she didn't have to look too far.

It was Black History Month and the Schomburg Center for Research in Black Culture planned to exhibit and coordinate events around the lives of Black Union soldiers. As associate curator of the Manuscripts, Archives, and Rare Books division, Ardelia was tasked with sifting through old pension paperwork, medical records, news reports, and photographs. Assignments like these excited her. Time travel was always available to her at the corner of West 135th and Malcolm X Boulevard. Some days, she'd travel to the Dahomey Kingdom, other times she'd hear folks gossip about W.E.B. Du Bois in their letters, or sit beside Ella Fitzgerald while she scatted. Each morning, she set up her station as she always did: a few books to the right, some stationery to the left, and her computer in the middle. But these days, she would crack her knuckles and take a large, deep breath, certain she was about to demolish her to-do list, only to find herself stunned at what she found: a sepia-toned photograph of a Black soldier whose eyes seemed to appear in her sleep and whose beauty followed her as she moved through her day.

He had prominent, sculpted cheekbones, a long neck, and skin as smooth and brown as opal. If she looked close enough, she could see that his lips were not completely closed, which made her think that he had wanted to speak to the photographer, that he had been captured just as he'd been about to communicate something important. There was no name on the photograph, which only heightened its allure. Handsome was an insufficient way to describe this unknown man. Otherworldly? Perhaps. He seemed to be both of another time and of this one. He was dressed in nineteenth-century garb, but he looked like the men who brushed Ardelia's shoulders on the subway platform.

She always assumed that in order for historians, archivists, and scholars to succeed, they had to be obsessive to some degree. But this was different. This was not about the pursuit of knowledge. It was something else, a haunting. Ardelia truly believed she had seen this man somewhere before. She imagined that one day the soldier's lips would part further, and he'd tell her whatever she'd wanted to know. Did the soldier have any family that was waiting for him? Did he have a woman, in particular, who was hoping to see him again? As soon as Ardelia thought of the second question, her mind didn't have to make a leap to connect her questions to her feelings surrounding her situation with Oliver. As a matter of fact, her mind neither leapt nor jumped to that connection; instead it moseyed right on over the next avenue in her processing of this sudden life change. But once she thought of Oliver, she grabbed her phone and saw that she had no new messages from him. Of course. Oliver worked day shifts, and historically never texted her during them because of how hectic his work was. But she could not rely on history any longer. His leaving set a new precedent and all bets were off. Soon, Ardelia felt like her brain was on fire with all the ceaselessly revolving thoughts: Was he thinking of her? Did he still love her? Did he still want to get married? Oliver was the most communicatively direct man she'd ever known, and yet she could not trust what he said any longer.

On her way home at the end of the day, Mr. Johnson waved her down just as she was turning the corner to her block. Ardelia winced because she was in no mood for small talk.

"Hey, hey, hey, look who it is!" Mr. Johnson straightened his back and smiled at her.

"Hi, Mr. Johnson," Ardelia said with a half smile. "You're always outside, huh?"

"Always. I like to see what's goin' on, talk to people like yourself. Keeps me young."

"Well, that's nice."

Mr. Johnson narrowed his eyes at her.

"Where you say you from again?"

"I'm from Chicago, remember? You've asked me that many times before," she responded in a playful tone.

"Yeah . . ." Mr. Johnson's voice tapered off, unconvinced. "You sound like my people from down South though . . ."

Ardelia didn't have the energy for Mr. Johnson today. "Gotta go, take care, Mr. Johnson!"

As soon as she turned her key in the lock, though, she regretted not chatting with Mr. Johnson a little while longer. She hated returning home after a long day at work, to an apartment in which the air didn't feel full in anticipation of Oliver being there in just a few hours. She didn't want to text him first. No. He left her. If anything, he should text her first. She was the injured party here. Injured she was. She was used to physiological responses to her worrying—sweating, finger biting, leg rubbing. But now, a stomachache had her doubling over the toilet before searching high and low in the kitchen cabinets for a probiotic or some Pepto Bismol. She was physically and emotionally hurt yet felt stupid, insecure, and desperate. Oliver had only been gone for a few days, and here she was getting sick like a loser. In between the walks to the bathroom, Ardelia was holding her stomach and attempting to calm herself down. He said he loved her before he left. That meant he was going to come back. But people say "I love you" all the time and leave anyway. Her father had. Her eyes unintentionally shifted to the letter on the mantelpiece, and the knots in her stomach loosened just a bit.

What a beautiful night their engagement party was, Ardelia thought as she held the frame in her hands. She read each line as slowly as she could. The knots loosened some more until she could finally breathe. Once Ardelia had read the last line, she started from the beginning. The process repeated until Ardelia started to say the lines more quickly than she read them and realized that she had committed them to memory. Hugging the letter to her chest, Ardelia reassured herself that he had to come back. If he was really going to leave, would he have left the letter? How did Tirzah retain hope for Harrison and he for her? And to think, Ardelia thought, she was already falling apart after a few days.

She would text him after all. "Thinking of you," Ardelia texted to Oliver, with a heart emoji.

He loved the message in a matter of seconds but didn't type any-thing back.

That should have been enough, but it wasn't. Why wasn't he thinking of her either? Sure, he was at work, but textual reciprocity was pretty low stakes, in her opinion. And if he had his phone on, why hadn't he texted her at any point until now? He could've been tired. Either from work or of her.

The cycle continued throughout the month: one of them would reach out to the other with a "good morning" or a "good evening," liking and loving messages, sending memes. No matter how much Oliver told her that he missed her or that he was thinking about her, those sweet words were not enough. The longer he went without giv-ing her a clue about when he'd be coming home, the more restless Ardelia became. Initially, she'd slip in a question about life at the hos-pital, hoping that he'd give some update on when the coast would be clear for him to come home, but he never got the hint, opting to keep professional affairs brief so as not to overwhelm her with gruesome details of all he was witnessing.

But it was with this withholding that a ravine formed between his words and her projections, and Ardelia could feel herself hurtling toward the bottom. Her fears were too anchored in her reality for her to be able to leap across this gap in mutual understanding to re-main close to him. Sometimes, she'd go into a bathroom stall at the Schomburg to cry whenever a coworker asked how Oliver was do-ing or how the wedding planning was coming along. On train rides, she'd listen to affirmations. At yoga, she'd remember her breathing. I'm doing everything I can, Ardelia thought to herself. I'm doing ev-erything I can and nothing feels enough. One night, without warn-ing, Ardelia stopped midway up the stairs to her apartment and had to lean on the rails to keep her balance. What if nothing is enough because I am not enough? she asked herself. Her body shrank again, but this time, this new stroke of self-flagellation flattened her into the wall. Her only desire was to be nonsentient—free of her anxious body, free of the exhaustion she carried from running herself ragged in her thoughts.

Then one night, the soldier appeared in her dreams. His back toward her, he stood on a dock above a wide body of water. She tapped him on his right shoulder, but the man who turned around was her father. His face was covered in sores and his skin was a blue-green hue. Upon waking up, Ardelia balled her fingers into a fist with anger at how everything began to make sense. She immediately reached for her nightstand and opened the drawer.

January 4, 2020

Dear Ardelia,

I know it's been a while since we've caught up with each other and I know you're a busy woman these days, but I still would love to see you. I know I made a ton of mistakes in my past, plenty of them being that I wasn't there for you as I should have been. What I've been trying to explain to you— but I suppose not good enough—is that I got demons, you see. Demons that been inside me longer than you've been alive. Longer than I've been alive. They're deep in this family and I was a victim to it. I hope you have leftover room in your heart to forgive me. But even if you don't, I still love you.

Winters in Chicago are getting chillier. Or maybe I'm just getting older. I can't stay outside for long because my chest gets to hurting and no tea or vapor rub seems to do the trick. I don't mind though. Not many people I wanna see and I'm sure people can say the same. I done messed up a lot of lives, baby. But at least yours is still as shiny as a pearl. That's my greatest achievement. God say he give beauty from the ashes and I take that literally.

How they treating you up in Harlem? Don't make me have to come up there if I have to. You keep your wits about you.

You a city girl with a southern heart. Don't let none of them
mens up there distract you. Not even Oliver. You hear what
I'm telling you?
    I'm proud of you, Delia.

                                        Love,
                                        Dad

Just like a man, Ardelia thought. Blaming his problems on everything and everyone else but himself. Sure, she grew up in the
church, but even she rejected the idea of "demons" coming for him,
unless they were a euphemism for drugs. To her, her father was taking no accountability for his actions. What did he mean that these
so-called demons were there before he was alive? That didn't make
sense. No one told him to do what he did. Even when her father was
apologizing, his contrition was laced with some bullshit. And Oliver
wondered why she didn't jump to respond to her father in a timely
manner.

Ardelia had read this letter so many times that it was marked with
grease spots and some of the letters were smeared. Now, she folded it
into quarters and stuffed it back inside her nightstand along with the
others, the drawer so full that she could never shut it completely. The
last time she could remember writing him a letter was when she was a
child, and he was in jail. But he couldn't understand her penmanship
nor she his, so they were ships passing in the night, acknowledging
each other without real recognition. She couldn't understand why he
insisted on writing letters when he had a phone now and could text
or send her an email.

She also couldn't understand why he called her "a city girl with a
southern heart" unless he meant the South Side of Chicago. He wasn't
no Southerner either no matter how many times he injected sayings
and proverbs that seemed inconsistent with his South Langley and
East Bowen Avenue upbringing. The older he got, the more she heard
his Southern drawl. She couldn't stand the affectation, one of many

he'd picked up during the moments in his life when his true self was too much to carry.

That's what she would do, Ardelia thought. If her father wanted a letter, then that's what he would get. But this letter would not go lightly. She would tell him about her and Oliver's separation, how she hadn't been able to think straight since he left, how she hated him for abandoning her and was now paying for it in adulthood. But when Ardelia sat down to write, her hand shook and the pen bled blue onto her composition paper. Tears dotted the margins. Thirty-four years of bitterness were no match for the width and weight of a fountain pen. Ardelia pushed her chair back with her feet and watched the pen roll off the table's surface. Just as she'd waited for him to show up in many events of her formative years, her father could wait for a response.

THE BLACK SOLDIERS EXHIBITION TO CLOSE BLACK HISTORY MONTH at the Schomburg went off without a hitch, but Ardelia couldn't enjoy any of the lectures, panels, or patron chatter buzzing around her. Her mind was elsewhere. Oliver left at the end of January and here she was on the last day of February. It had been a month—a short month, but a month no less—and he made no mention of moving back home. They still regularly checked in on each other, but the ring on her left hand had begun to feel less like a declaration and more like a fraud. She found herself obsessively rubbing at it in public as she conversed with visitors and colleagues, and some asked if there was something wrong with her fingers. The concern provided her cover to excuse herself from the crowd and catch her breath in a quiet corner on the employee-only floor. No, there wasn't anything wrong with her fingers. There was something wrong with her. Couldn't they tell? Couldn't they see how sad she was, or had she moisturized her hair too luxuriously, painted her lips too precisely, and smiled enough to fool everyone? Maybe, Ardelia thought, that was a part of the job, and she could pretend for a few hours that she would still be Mrs. Benjamin. So if someone were to ask about Oliver, she'd lift her chin and say that he was doing well and that the wedding planning was going well. All was well. The shambles would have to be confronted at home, as it was the only thing left waiting for her there anyway.

On top of this masquerade, her father's letter still bothered her. There weren't enough words to make up for his abandonment, and he knew it. Yet his letters were a special kind of effort. She could've called him, but she didn't want to speak to any man on the phone if it wasn't Oliver. Standing atop "the Rivers" cosmogram at the Schomburg, where Langston Hughes's ashes were interred and where which Amiri Baraka and Maya Angelou danced years ago, Ardelia could not feel that energy beneath her wide heels any longer. She was simply moving from place to place, group to group. On her walk home, Ardelia couldn't remember what happened. Her body could not gauge the appreciation of her and her coworkers' efforts. None of it mattered. How could she appreciate the dead when so much in her personal life was dying?

Then the next morning, as Ardelia was cracking eggs for a Florentine omelette, the TV blared with a breaking news report that moved her toward the screen:

The first COVID case in New York City had been confirmed.

27

MARCH 2020

Upon learning that coronavirus was now in New York and that the patient was a woman, Ardelia reminded herself of the tense moment when she'd interrupted Oliver in the shower weeks before. An elderly Black woman catching a virus all the way from Wuhan? Ardelia told Oliver not to run with that suspicion. In retrospect, a virus, just like any another infection, was going to spread and especially to a metropolis like New York. A Persian woman could've welcomed a relative into her Great Neck home and subsequently traveled to Grand Central so that she and Ms. Lunette could attend a show at Radio City Music Hall. One traveler from Wuhan could have returned to Canal Street where Ms. Lunette could've bought handbags and caught the illness while in the middle of her purchase. Or Ms. Lunette simply could've hugged a friend of a friend who had a friend who traveled to Avellino or Montreal or Punta del Este and sat on an airplane or train where someone coughed in her vicinity.

There were infinite possibilities as to how Ms. Lunette got the disease—if she did. Whatever the circumstance might have been, Ardelia didn't believe Oliver in that moment in the bathroom. She dismissed his hunches, and now she wondered if he might have been right all along. The first confirmed case did not mean that the virus could not have gone under the radar. Mistakes both global and granular happen all the time. She overburdened herself with her own mistakes she made while Oliver was by her side.

"Hey . . ." Ardelia texted him. "I just saw the news. That's crazy. How are you holding up?" She regretted her words as soon as she clicked "send." Though Ardelia wanted to tell Oliver that he might have been right, what use would that be now? Ms. Lunette was gone. He'd moved out. There was no going back; guilt and shame knotted her stomach all over again. Oliver did not respond quickly. For the first time in their relationship, he made her wait. Ardelia cried, practiced mindfulness meditation, and read aloud affirmations that she was deserving of love even if she was an imperfect person. His response finally came, three days later: "Hanging in there. More soon." No emojis, no liking or loving her message. The text was as sterile as the medical equipment he used at work.

To refrain from checking her phone or worrying about where Oliver's heart was, Ardelia intensified her schedule. She'd stay at the Schomburg till evening researching whatever suited her fancy that day, exercise, then binge-watch a show she was barely interested in. Fatigue was the only way for her mind not to drift to the state of her relationship. When Stacy, the wedding planner, started sending them both emails asking if the timeline for an October wedding needed some rejiggering, the gentle heads-up pained Ardelia, and she could not respond beyond "We'll discuss and circle back." She would be too embarrassed if Stacy, let alone anyone else in her life, knew that she and Oliver were together yet separated.

Then about halfway through March, Ardelia received word through an institution-wide email that in light of the increased COVID cases throughout the city, the New York Public Library would be closing its ninety-two locations, including the Schomburg. The seat upon which Ardelia sat in her home might as well have sunken to the floor. No work and no man. What was she going to do?

Deciding a walk around the neighborhood might be a good idea to clear her mind, she grabbed her keys and phone and headed outside. Harlem herself appeared usual on the surface—witty banter between aunties and uncles, loud music blaring from some speaker, fresh fish in the markets or chicken frying in back kitchens—but the more closely Ardelia scrutinized these spaces, the more she sensed that everyone was afraid. Locals seemed to be overcompensating by being out and about, filling restaurants and crowding sidewalks. Or maybe Ardelia was overthinking, as one with anxiety usually does. People moved and talked normally. Hardly anyone made mention of the virus. Still, Ardelia could feel that her environment was on edge. She walked for a mile, and then two.

By March 22, her environment had disappeared. Governor Cuomo's executive order for nonessential business to shut down would be going into effect. Everyone was urged to stay indoors unless absolutely necessary. That Sunday was the first time Ardelia did not see Mr. Johnson sweep the apartment building's front stoop. The first time she didn't hear tambourines and choral singing from the one of many churches in the area. The first time she heard more ambulance sirens screeching than humans chattering. *Now* what was she supposed to do? Ardelia thought. No work, no job, no sign of human life. She couldn't walk all day and night long to fill the gaps in her life, and there was only so much TV she could watch before she wouldn't be able to recall a character name or single plotline. The quieter Harlem was, the more idle Ardelia became, and that soundlessness was the worst because the worst thoughts began to take over.

How long would this all last? Whatever hope she had for Oliver to come home soon was dissipating. Her mind raced around the track of the last conversation they'd had in person. Oliver never told her when he'd be back, only that he would. In his texts, he never brought up missing their home or hinting when he might return. Now he couldn't. Impeccable timing. What if Oliver's plan all along had been to get as far away from her as possible? He must be relieved, Ardelia surmised. Now he could stay away from her for as long as he liked. She gripped the sides of a couch pillow and screamed into it as furiously as she could. When she came up for air, she saw the middle of the pillow was damp with her tears and sweat. This physical release made Ardelia suspect that she really was damaged beyond repair. No one could have predicted an epidemic would take over this city, not to mention the world. And Oliver wasn't faking those shivers he had in bed—the ones that scared them both. Why was she torturing herself with stories that would only ruin her?

So many times she reached for her phone and started to text Oliver before worrying she'd say the wrong thing. So she said nothing at all.

Several days after her office closed, Ardelia was finishing up her longest walk, from 110th and Central Park back to her home, when she saw that she'd missed a call from Oliver. Her heart raced. She ran up the stairs into her apartment to call him back and silently prayed that he'd pick up or else that would be another knot that would sprout in her belly.

"Hey . . ." Oliver's voice trailed off.

"Hey, baby." Ardelia huddled up on the couch. "How are you?"

"I'm hangin' in there. How are you holding up?"

"I'm . . . trying. Everyone at the libraries got sent home."

"I saw. I've been keeping up with the news."

"So have I."

Both were at a loss for what to say next, but their heavy breathing indicated they were both still on the line.

"I guess I should just come out and say it."

Ardelia sat up taller on the couch and began to soothe her chest.

"I can't come home yet."

She dropped her shoulders. "I know . . . I mean . . . I figured." He's not breaking up with me, Ardelia thought. At least that's something.

"I've been staying in an Airbnb, but we're hearing that a few hotels around the city are going to open up their rooms to health-care workers so . . . I figure I'd do it since I can get to the hospital quicker that way."

"Oh . . ."

"You don't want to be around me anyway right now. I don't want to get you sick. This way you'll be safe."

Why wouldn't he ask me what I want? Ardelia asked herself. "Thanks for being so considerate."

"Of course," Oliver said.

There wasn't much else to say after that so Ardelia made an excuse. "I have to get some work done tonight," she said. But both of them knew that she was lying. Not once had she ever left a phone call prematurely with Oliver because of work when she was at home. She couldn't bear to stay on the line any longer. Once they said goodbye to each other, Ardelia perused the internet for ways to bide her time.

She needed something that would take consistent effort with painstaking concentration: baking. With some flour and water, she'd prepare to make sourdough bread.

Days after her starter kit arrived in the mail, she began the new hobby. As she waited for the natural yeast to emerge within the mixture, she'd watch *Tiger King* on Netflix or read a history of bread making throughout human civilization. Initially, the dough would not cooperate. Just as Ardelia was about to place it into the oven, it would deflate like a whoopee cushion. The frustration allowed for her mind to focus even harder on the task at hand though. Yeast, as she discovered, was a living thing and, therefore, could be unpredictable.

There was fun in that unpredictability because there was no limit to how devoted Ardelia could be to bread making. Sure, she was working from home, but she had more freedom in her schedule. She bought meters and thermometers and probes and attended Zoom sessions on the fermentation process. After she finally figured out how to combat a deflated dough, then there was the task of knowing the exact right time to let the bread dough rise. Not since undergrad had Ardelia scientifically experimented with trial and error. But after she mastered that, she stared along the kitchen countertop at all the sourdough bread she'd baked without the slightest bit of hunger. All that food, and no one to share it with.

A cold epiphany struck her: nothing in the world could replace what needed to be addressed. She still missed Oliver. The knots in the sourdough bread were a physical manifestation of the knots in her belly. The aches in her fingers and the tension in her shoulders long after the baking was done were reminders that she needed to unburden herself.

At least, Ardelia thought, she and Oliver had spoken, whereas she and her father still had not, leading her to believe that this unevenness and lack of resolve could be additional causes for her restlessness. She rushed to grab her phone to call her father. Please don't pick up, please don't pick up, Ardelia said in her head. The anticipation was stressful. Finally, Sterling's voice was on the other line, and Ardelia said a rapid hello before realizing he was giving instructions on how to leave a message. "Of course he wouldn't answer. Of course," Ardelia scoffed, then closed her eyes so that her body would not get any ideas about crying. Yet in that suppression, she did not see darkness. Rather, she saw a clear image of herself as a child in her grandmother's home waiting yet again for her dad to come from somewhere by huddling up on the couch and abandoning anything and everyone until he showed up. He was the only parent she had left. Her mother, Charice, died from chronic kidney disease, spurred by lupus, at the age of thirty-three. Ardelia didn't remember much about her when she was alive because she was far too young to understand why she was being shuffled among family members. According to her paternal grandmother—who had a fondness for Charice—she ultimately took Ardelia in full-time when Charice exhausted her own biological family with her never-ending requests for help and assistance.

She dialed Sterling's number again. There seemed to be fewer rings before the voicemail this time. Whether or not this was actually the case was unimportant; her emotional truth consumed everything else. She closed her now burning eyes, seeing his big old smile. The third time she dialed, the call went straight to voicemail and the tears cascaded from her eyes with such force that she could barely see.

The only phone call Ardelia wound up receiving that day was from her wedding planner regrettably notifying her that the Brooklyn warehouse where her and Oliver's wedding and reception were scheduled to be held had canceled all social events due to New York now being the epicenter of the coronavirus. The venue was flexible with the deposits and an email notification would be sent to Ardelia and Oliver with an update, as well as an assurance that the staff would be monitoring the situation in case conditions changed. But Ardelia could not hold space for that kind of disappointment, since the one pertaining to her father eclipsed any other feeling she had.

What else could she do? For weeks, she'd read, she'd baked, she'd watched TV, she'd spent hours on the internet. Even her tears were not getting rid of the tension in her body. Her phone was going on "Do Not Disturb." She had to wean herself off obsessively looking for notifications. Her body needed a break, and she needed to move quickly or else she'd drown in her thoughts. Alcohol deliveries were being heavily promoted during lockdown, and Ardelia figured that she might as well help out a local business. One bottle of Roscato Rosso Dolce, a bottle of Chateau Ste. Michelle Riesling, a bottle of Black Girl Magic, and a bottle of Bartenura. In forty-five minutes or less, she would receive the delivery, pour herself a glass, grab some butter and olive oil from the kitchen, and have her wine with her sourdough bread. Once the wine was delivered, she didn't spend time chilling it, preferring to go on ahead and bring the Bartenura with her to the living room so she wouldn't have to go far to have another pour. Once the first sip slid down her throat and into her stomach, a few internal locks unlatched themselves in her brain. After a couple more sips, her shoulders loosened and a smile grew on her face. With the entire glass down, her mind was finally on autopilot.

The night was a blur. She cackled at something on TV, might have danced around her coffee table to a Spotify playlist. Maybe she spent too much time on social media. Not a single damn was given. For once in a great while, Ardelia felt good.

The next morning found her upside down with one of her feet dangling off the couch; it was like someone had mollywhopped her head with a mallet. With one hand over her eyes and the other tapping around the coffee table, she found her phone, thumbed in her passcode, and saw several missed calls and texts from her aunt Hazel, her uncle Charles, a few blood cousins, and a few play cousins from around the way. Each message started with "Your dad."

Ardelia snapped out of her hangover and dialed her aunt Hazel, her father's younger sister.

"My God, li'l girl!" Hazel yelled on the other end of the phone. She'd never heard Hazel's voice break, let alone her yell. "I've been trying to get in touch with you for hours!"

Ardelia stammered, "Is everything okay?"

"Your Uncle Charles went to go visit your father yesterday morning and he was having trouble breathing."

Ardelia held her breath, afraid to ask the most dreadful question.

Before she could, Hazel said, "He's on the ventilator. If you still pray, even if you haven't prayed in a while, you better start."

18

APRIL 2020

Something about Ardelia's screams obliterated the lingering thoughts about work in Oliver's mind and sent him straight to her street. He was at the entrance to the Four Seasons Hotel, waiting for an N95-masked nurse to take his temperature and inquire about his symptoms within the last seventy-two hours when he got the call. Everything whirled around him quickly. Another medical worker flinched and gasped when Oliver almost bumped into her trying to hail a cab. He could feel several pair of eyes on his back when he rattled off Ardelia's address to the driver. By the time Oliver stepped foot outside of his and Ardelia's apartment building and saw no one—not even Mr. Johnson—a chill traveled from the nape of his neck down his spine. This was the kind of silence that would make anyone suspect that something terrifying would happen at any moment. Only the terror had already arrived. They were all living in it as ambulance sirens blared in all directions. Oliver waited for a moment to dial Ardelia back. This was the first time he was seeing her since he moved out, and he was afraid of what he would see. Oliver wasn't one to overthink as much as Ardelia, because he believed that reality would never be as devastating as whatever the imagination could stir up. But this time, he was proven wrong.

As soon as Oliver told Ardelia to come to the window where he could see her, he saw her palm press against the glass and slowly slide down. Those beautiful curls of hers were matted and stretched over the crown of her head. And when she finally had the strength to pull her upper body up so that he could have a good look at her, another chill gripped his body with more violence. Grief had transformed his beloved's face. The words that tumbled out of her mouth were indecipherable. Her eyes were heavy with tears that made her red and inflamed cheeks glisten under the moonlight. "Oliver" was the only word he could make out as the hand that held the phone to her ear trembled uncontrollably. He decided to stay outside of her living-room window for as long as he could to see what was wrong. After all, nothing waited for him back at the Four Seasons besides a lonely, albeit luxurious, room.

"My dad . . . he. . . ." She pressed her face against the glass and cried into the phone.

"What about him? Is he all right?" Oliver straightened up and held the phone closer to his ear.

"He's on . . . a ventilator. Oh Oliver . . . I'm such a bad daughter. I'm so bad."

Oliver stood on the sidewalk until Ardelia seemed to quiet down. He looked down to check his phone battery and saw his reflection. His face was strong, straight, and emotionless. None of the sadness and compassion that he felt left any traces along his temples, eyes, nose, or mouth. If someone had looked at him like this while he was breaking down, he would worry that that person didn't care. Or worse—that they felt nothing. How could this be?

"You aren't a bad daughter. He will be okay, trust me." Oliver felt a pang in his chest as the words came out of his mouth. He didn't know if her dad would be okay, just like he hadn't known if Ms. Lunette was going to be okay. But what else was he supposed to say? He'd rather give her a sweet, empty promise than allow for the silence of uncertainty to persist. Most of all, Oliver wanted to be useful, and encouragement was all he could do in these circumstances.

"Look, I'll be back soon. Please keep me posted on what's happening. I love you," Oliver said, then pulled his collar up to his face and started walking away so that Ardelia could not see him any longer.

On the ride back to the Four Seasons in Midtown East, Oliver recalled how in their earliest stages of dating, Ardelia explained how her family differed from his own, like a warning rather than a statement. Oliver's family, the Benjamins, were a prestigious Kansan dynasty. Her family, the Gibbses, were regular Chicago Black folk. The Benjamins had made their name in education, while the Gibbses were a family of veterans, factory workers, and porters. When *Brown v. Board* came around, the Benjamin family fed Robert Carter and Jack Greenberg home-cooked meals before they argued the case in front of a district judge. An aunt assisted NAACP president McKinley Burnett in finding and encouraging thirteen Black families to enroll in all-white schools, and a great-great-cousin provided temporary legal counsel. The Gibbses, meanwhile, had been relegated to segregated schools long after the Civil Rights Act of 1964 passed.

By the end of the twentieth century, there was no Black organization in Topeka that did not have at least one Benjamin sitting on its board, and at least three Gibbs men in every generation had seen the inside of a jail cell. The Benjamin family was photographed by Gordon Parks and partied with Langston Hughes whenever his grandmother brought him into town. The Gibbses hung out around pimps, jazz players, and a few entrepreneurs. The Benjamins were churchgoers at St. John's AME and a part of Black elite organizations like the Jack and Jill set, the Links, and Freemasons. The Gibbses were too scattered, with too many unscrupulous characters among them, to be considered for these organizations. There were Cub Scouts and a few Deltas here and there, but that was all.

AT THE FOUR SEASONS, WHERE A NURSE CHECKED OLIVER'S TEMperature before he could go back to his room, Oliver's eyes became heavy, but with shame rather than grief. What kind of a man was he, to run out on his beloved, whose father was ill? What kind of a fiancé would run away from his beloved in the middle of a breakdown? After passing through the Art Deco–inspired passageway and waiting for the elevator to his floor, which would only take up one person at a time, Oliver wondered how he could dare show his face to her again.

Ardelia had never minced words when she spoke about Sterling, his absence throughout her childhood, and how it affected her dynamic with men. Oliver had only met Sterling a handful of times, and recognized, judging by Ardelia's comportment, that the meetings felt like an obligation to her. Oliver didn't think Sterling seemed like that bad a guy, per se. He had a sly sense of humor and clearly loved his daughter. At the same time, Oliver carried small stones of resentment because he felt that sometimes it was his burden to heal the pain that Sterling caused. How Oliver had to reassure Ardelia early on that his failure to text back quickly was not due to a lack of commitment but rather to the pace of his work. How he had to tell her that he wasn't cheating if he met an old female friend from residency for dinner. Ardelia was an insatiable spirit, a dragon that he had to keep feeding day in and day out. But he loved her all the same—her roar of ambition, her larger-than-life personality, her beauty. He always felt a deep sense of familiarity with her, one that other couples told him was a sign that they were meant to be in each other's lives. But he thought it was more than that. Hubris convinced him that his and Ardelia's bond was not like that of other couples they knew—they were different. Much like the earth and moon, Oliver liked to believe that he and Ardelia were held together by gravity. They orbited each other, their rhythms a secret language in and of itself. That's why he'd given her his ancestor's letter during their engagement party: to remind her that even if his words failed, there were those who came before him who had instilled in him a deep understanding of love and a triumph to come.

But now what? That letter haunted him. He was separated from her just as Harrison was from Tirzah. But that wasn't his doing, Oliver thought as he let himself into his room, stripped out of his clothes, and stepped into the shower. He'd just wanted a little space. Now they were forced to be apart. This wasn't the plan. This wasn't the plan at all. But what difference did it make now? As Oliver turned the shower knob all the way to the right for maximum warmth, he randomly remembered another correspondence of sorts—their wedding being canceled by the venue. He didn't even acknowledge it to Ardelia. Then again, neither did she. The stressors in their respective lives must've made all of that so peripheral. Or maybe they were afraid to talk about it because then they'd have to admit how much the distance was testing their bond. Their wedding was at least something to look forward to, and now, the couple had nothing.

After scrubbing himself so thoroughly that his skin turned red and raw, Oliver stared at himself in the bathroom mirror, flexing the muscles in his face—smiling and frowning, frowning then smiling, raising his eyebrows, wrinkling his nose. All these movements seemed foreign and strange. The reason transported him to a period of mourning too. His former self was nowhere to be found.

Each day, when the sun rose, he shoved his emotions inside, commuted to the hospital, put on his PPE, and began his shift. Oliver had always been warned by superiors to keep an emotional distance from his patients, but that caution was no longer necessary. He had become good at compartmentalizing, so good that his agility to switch on and off surprised him.

He hardly flinched or cast his eyes to the ground when another of his patients gasped for the last bit of air before expiring. He felt almost nothing when the nurses set up iPad stations so that patients could say goodbye to their relatives. Little stirred in his heart when he called people to tell them that their loved ones had died, and they shrieked so loudly on the other end that he had to soothe his ears after being the bearer of bad news. Sometimes he'd look at pictures of Ardelia on his phone or reread past messages full of affection and kindness as a way to pull his soul back into his body. Then he'd remember what he'd experienced that day at work and all the emotions he suppressed in the daylight would hold him hostage at night.

Yet on this night, his two selves could not have been more divergent. On the inside, his emotions were caught in a maelstrom. On the outside, he was a cool and collected shell. Perhaps, Oliver feared, he had pushed the part of his emotional self that made his personhood rich and connected so far into the recesses of his body that now he couldn't call it out into the open if he tried.

After moisturizing his skin and putting on his pajamas, Oliver walked out of the bathroom and toward the large windows facing the street. He yearned for the sounds of a prepandemic world. The wheels of a housekeeper's cart rolling down the hallway. Drunk hotel guests stumbling into their rooms after a night on the town. Cars honking. Pedestrians cursing out aggressive taxi drivers. Dogs barking. Birds chirping. The luxury of where he laid his head every night did not fill the void of human activity, and that reminder exacerbated his sadness.

He considered what would have happened if he was still at home. He could strip down every night before entering, and Ardelia would have definitely followed all the rules to keep both of them safe. Why'd he been so quick to stay away, if he truly loved her? The constant processing and reprocessing of current events kept him up for hours: if he had persevered and stayed with Ardelia as he grieved for Ms. Lunette, then his fiancée would not be alone in her devastation right at this moment. Yet he knew the separation was necessary, in order for him to collect himself. No matter how much he tried to justify his choices to himself, he came back to the same place: he wasn't a good partner away from her and he wasn't a good partner while lying beside her in bed. What good was he if he was not tending to patients? He was losing his humanity as his muscles were overexerted and his bones ached and death continued in spite of all his efforts.

19

APRIL 2020

A spirit woke Ardelia at the crack of dawn. That was the only way she could rationalize why she sprang up from her bed, walked straight out into the living room, and opened her laptop without any groans or sluggishness. She grabbed Tirzah's letter from the mantelpiece and briefly looked out the adjacent window—a burst of color from the fresh bloom of flowers growing in the small yards of brownstones, a stark contrast from the thick, gray clouds foreboding a spring shower. Tirzah's letter had to be near her as a talisman for what she felt compelled to do before the day began. She opened a blank Word document and began typing a letter to her father. Her fingers flew across the keyboard at the rate at which her mind worked. Anecdotes and missed opportunities, celebrations and disappointments were exorcized onto the page. Sometimes tears landed on her mouse pad, and other times she rubbed at the corners of her eyes so that her rhythm would not be sacrificed.

Suddenly, Ardelia closed her laptop and pushed it to the other side of the couch. No, she would not reread what she wrote. No, she was not going to edit her feelings to make them neat and refined. She'd had to tidy up her feelings toward her father for too long, and that had only led to the messiness of anxious thoughts, spiraling, and intermittent mental instability. He was going to hear what she had to say—even if he could not verbally respond. For about a week and some change, Ardelia and her father's nurses would coordinate to arrange FaceTime visits so that they could see each other. Sterling would blink, raise his eyebrows, or wiggle his nose whenever Ardelia would tell him about her long, languid days of lockdown. Sometimes she wondered if she were talking to herself as nurses informed her that he was very sleepy. But Sterling never took his gaze from her, his face always leaning toward the camera to acknowledge his daughter.

On the day she awoke at dawn, Ardelia was restless. So much energy whirled in her body that she could barely sit still, her father's face appearing in her mind on repeat.

The spirit possessed her again, and she grabbed her laptop to write another letter. Whatever this entity was had not finished its work the first time around. Now, the words flew out onto the page so rapidly that her fingers began to cramp up. There were friends and ex-boyfriends, places still in existence or overtaken by gentrification, soft memories and hard lessons, proverbs and riddles that had contributed to the woman she was today. Her father should know everything. Her father would know everything. Finally, she closed the laptop again, fell back onto the couch, and stared at the ceiling. Her head was throbbing at the Pandora's box she'd opened. Now rest seemed like a distant mirage. She wanted to tell him about what Harlem looked like this morning, Mr. Johnson, and her bread making.

Her phone rang and Ardelia soothed her forehead with her fingers. Now her senses were overwrought. The volume seemed louder than it had to be. But she answered without fully registering that she'd accepted a FaceTime call and snapped upright when she saw her father. His mouth was hung open and the bags underneath his eyes drooped more than usual.

Ardelia could hear herself hyperventilating and struggled to speak.

"Ardelia? Baby?" Her aunt Hazel was compressed to a small square on the bottom right-hand corner of her cell phone screen.

Ardelia wiped at the sides of her eyes.

"I wanted to get you on the line because—" Aunt Hazel turned her face away so quickly from the camera that her curly wig moved in the same direction. When she looked back at the screen, her hand was trembling over her mouth. "I wanted to get you on the line because I think it might be time, baby."

Time? Ardelia thought. Her eyes jumped to the microwave clock: 7:45 a.m. Time? The birds probably haven't started chirping in Chicago. The nurses probably hadn't bathed her father yet. Did he watch television? He always liked watching television. Did they tell him how it's springtime and describe the flowers to him?

She snatched her laptop and began reading from her first letter: "Dear Dad, I want to tell you that writing a letter has never been easy for me but I want to do it now . . ." She looked up at her father's face and saw that he wasn't responding in his usual way. So she read more quickly. She choked back tears as she tripped and tumbled over her words but kept on because there was no other alternative. Hazel encouraged her to pace herself, but Ardelia continued reading until she could do nothing but tuck her bottom lip into her mouth and patiently bear witness to the release that was under way. She would read one line and look up at her father, read another line, and look up at him to make sure he was still there. He was listening. Ardelia knew he was listening.

The last few words of her second letter contained the thing she didn't say in the first: I love you. With that declaration, Ardelia closed her eyes and her chest expanded as all her past selves collapsed into one. She didn't say "I love you" as a child would. She didn't say "I love you" to bait her father in some other time and space to care. Seeing him frail and speechless reminded her that he was human. When Ardelia said "I love you," every inch of herself could feel the hope and faith that her father always loved her, even if his capacity to show that love fell short. She loved him as anyone would love someone who was because he was. She loved him. And it felt good to say.

An incessant ringing spoiled the tender moment. Ardelia saw her aunt weeping and a team of doctors quickly entered into the frame of the video call, circling her father's body. The ringing stopped and the doctors slowly parted into two groups. Their faces were covered behind shields yet their slumped shoulders told the truth. In one ear, Ardelia could hear her aunt Hazel's echoing cries. In the other, the nurse was extending her condolences.

Darkness overtook her. When Ardelia reopened her eyes, she was lying on the rug beneath her coffee table. She gasped at the moment she woke up, her chest feeling so tight that she wished she could've set her heart free with a knife.

She'd pulled herself onto the couch to speak with her father, but now she stood, then fell to the ground once again. She was alone. All alone. How many times had she pushed her father away when he did make the effort of reaching out to her? What if he was just as hurt from her avoidance as she was by him? Everything fell into darkness again. She didn't know how much time she had passed on the rug, but when she came back to consciousness the birds were chirping outside. Soon after, ambulance sirens blared from somewhere down the block. Ardelia didn't even remember sleeping. Then it hit her: Her father was dead. He was gone. Gone. Dead. Those words might have been feathers drifting in the sky. Theoretically, she knew what they meant. Ardelia repeated the words in her head as she crawled to the bathroom and used the edge of the sink to hoist herself up to the mirror.

Her father was all over her. The shape of her eyes. Her nose. Her lips. She didn't know if it was the lackluster light coming through the window, her sleep deprivation, or a combination of the two, but it might as well have been him looking back at her in the mirror.

And then, she thought she saw someone else, not herself, not her father: the soldier. Work. She thought frantically of work. A place to hide from all of this. But there was no work. The Schomburg was closed indefinitely. She pressed her forehead into the mirror and groaned. She went back into the living room and found her phone wedged between her couch cushions.

The screen displayed a long list of missed calls and texts but the most recent one came from Oliver: "Hey. Just checking in. How's your father doing?"

Tears obscured her vision as she plopped down on the couch. For the first time since he'd moved out, Ardelia read Oliver's message and felt nothing. There was nothing for her to give. Nothing for her to say. She didn't care to talk to him or anyone, and she didn't care what that would mean for their relationship. At least her anxiety had wilted because the love of her father and the lamentation surrounding that were much stronger. Her fingers might've tapped on the screen and said something. She forgot whatever it was the moment she pulled her arm back and tossed it to the other side of the couch. Her phone began to buzz. And buzz and buzz and buzz. She wondered when those fretful thoughts about him and their relationship would come out of hiding. They didn't. He didn't matter and neither did she.

She notified her boss at the Schomburg that her father had suddenly died and was granted a weeklong bereavement leave, which she extended for an extra week using some of her PTO. The days that followed blurred together as Ardelia drew closer and closer to a sorrow that fermented and bubbled and fizzed with each minute that passed. There was nothing for her to do but sit down on her couch, watch TV, and mindlessly scroll on the internet. Her fridge was filled with all kinds of takeout: salads, quesadillas, Peruvian rotisserie chicken, macaroni and cheese from Melba's, Essentia water, Casamigos. She drank wine with dinner, sometimes more than she should.

One night, a few days after Sterling's passing, the phone buzzed and Ardelia drunkenly picked up.

"Hello?" she said, consternation swirling in her voice.

"Girl, have you lost your mind?" Hazel breathed heavily on the other end of the phone. "I been tryna get in touch with you for days."

"Oh. Sorry, Aunt Hazel. I've just been . . . not good."

"Neither of us are, baby. But you gotta check in wit us. You out there in New York by yourself. We gotta know you okay. You hear me?"

"Yes, ma'am."

"I need to talk to you about your father's funeral arrangements. There are a lot of things that need to be sorted out and the director of the funeral home only has certain days. Ain't never heard of anythin' like that in my life. But you know that virus goin' around. When can you get here?"

Ardelia sighed. "I can't get there, Aunt Hazel. It's not safe."

"Well, we don't have a choice! We always have homegoing services. That's our thing."

"Yeah, well, we have to make other arrangements. Look, I'll help you. We have to just get everybody on Zoom."

"Zoom. What's Zoom? I ain't never heard of no Zoom."

BY THE TIME ARDELIA SENT THE MASS EMAIL TO HER FAMILY WITH the details of her father's virtual homegoing service, she'd never felt so detached from her own body. Somewhere deep in her mind, though, she wanted to fly into a rage. Her father deserved more than an announcement of five lines written in Times New Roman and twelve-point font. But she, along with everyone else, was too tired to do any more.

When Ardelia was meant to present herself on camera for her father's funeral a week and a half after his death, she felt keenly that she didn't want to be there. The concept of a virtual homegoing service was absurd. The amount of time it took for the elders to learn how to mute themselves was a whole saga in and of itself where all kinds of dissonant sounds were happening the backgrounds and people were moving in and out of the frame trying to help one another but getting no closer to the result.

Everything was too truncated to commemorate a person's life. No drawn-out singing? No praise shouts? No repast chicken? The whole thing felt wrong. Still, she had been the one to insist on it, and she stood by that decision. She wasn't going to risk her life or those of the elders to congregate during a global pandemic, tradition or not.

Just as the pastor was about to close, Ardelia's grandmother waved her hand in the air. For as long as Ardelia could remember, Geraldine had been old. She had spider veins stretching from her elbows to her hands, deep wrinkles, and long, gray hair that wrapped around her arms like vines in a way that scared Ardelia. When Geraldine would yell at a young Ardelia for running in and out of her house, she feared that her grandmother's hair would snatch her up if she disobeyed. That's if Ardelia understood what was coming out of her mouth—either because she was old school, or too old to enunciate clearly, she was often incomprehensible.

"Wait!" Geraldine yelled as clear as a whistle as Aunt Hazel attempted to get her off-screen and allow the pastor to finish with the benediction. "He ain't gon' get no salute? No drummin'? No flag? No nothin'?"

Ardelia leaned forward toward the computer screen as Hazel lowered her head and said, "C'mon, Ma. Let the pastor finish."

"No! My son was a veteran. He sacrificed for dis country. We got a proud lineage of veterans in dis here family. I want him to have somethin'."

Ardelia blinked multiple times as everything in her body reactivated. She unmuted herself to ask a question, but as soon as she did, Geraldine's screen went black. A few seconds later, her square disappeared altogether.

Her father, a veteran?

For the rest of the day after the virtual homegoing service, Ardelia remembered the old soldier whose photo bewitched her during the exhibition planning for the Schomburg. That dream of the soldier transforming into her father had Ardelia believing that the imagery wasn't happenstance but rather destined. Her father was telling her about himself. Even her archival interests contained traces of him, and that connection was strangely comforting. Just what else—and how else—was her father trying to make his way to her, and would his voyage continue in the afterlife?

Two days later, she received part of an answer. While Ardelia was making lunch, the doorbell rang and two hard knocks shortly followed. "UPS!" a voice called out from the hallway. She opened the door and saw a delivery person standing far back behind seven carton boxes, each marked FRAGILE.

"You have these packages here," the delivery person said. "Because of COVID, we're not requiring signatures. I just need to see your ID."

Ardelia fetched her driver's license and held it out in front of her. The delivery person leaned forward, scribbled on the touch pad of his screen, and said, "Have a nice day."

"Thanks, you too."

Ardelia wasn't expecting any packages, especially any that needed her verification. Confused, she carefully brought both inside and placed them on top of the dining table. The return address was her aunt Hazel's. She raised her eyebrows with curiosity. It had been awhile since Aunt Hazel had sent her a care package, and those hadn't arrived in this kind of box. She grabbed the scissors and sliced open three boxes that were coded with the same yellow label. A series of oil paintings, one depicted a Black woman floating in a large tub in a small and narrow bathroom. There was a shadow on the tile floor, indicating a presence watching from a corner. But it was a small shadow—either from a door creaking open very gently or a child waiting here. In another, the main subject was a Black woman, apparently the same woman from the tub, standing in the middle of a grassy knoll with her mouth outlandishly large. Within that gaping hole, Ardelia saw the faces of two men, one gray and elderly, the other thin, toned, and youthful. The last work showed the same woman kneeling in a kitchen next to a table piled high with meat and bread, a crucifix hanging on the wall.

Ardelia slit open four other boxes with blue labels revealing abstract pieces. The colors were multitudinous, racing and spreading from all corners of the canvas. But there was always a grayish blob, or human face in profile, somewhere in the image, and sometimes clusters of them. The longer Ardelia stared at these paintings, the more she saw hands stretching and pulling toward or away from these gray entities. These gray shapes seemed to be overwhelmed by forces that swelled and swelled endlessly, helpless, immobile to the siege. What was the artist trying to say, she asked herself?

She ran to call her aunt, who answered right away. "Well, hello there! Did you get my packages yet?"

"I just did. Why didn't you tell me you were sending them?"

"I did. You never got back to me."

Ardelia didn't have to sort through her phone to know that her aunt was right. "Sorry."

"It's okay. We all need our time. But you gotta let someone know you're good, okay?"

"Yes'm."

"All right. So what'd you think? I remember you or Sterling saying you studied visual art or Black art history or something in school. Thought you would like 'em."

"These are beautiful. Whose are these? Are they yours? There aren't any signatures."

She cackled. "Those aren't mine, chile. They're your father's."

"My dad's?" Her heart jumped. A veteran *and* an artist, Ardelia thought. She smiled and held the phone closer to her face.

"Sure are. I know he wanted you to have them. He was quite the talent, wasn't he?"

"Quite indeed. But he never told me he was an artist."

"He hardly told anybody. I think us in the household growing up with our parents knew. He just . . . one day started working with his hands. But our mother didn't like his paintings—found them to be too much, I think, and he quit short after. But he always been good with his hands. That's my people, you know. We been good with our hands for a long, long time. Construction workers, carpenters, handymen, architects, artists. We got 'em all in our family."

"Wow."

"Mm-hmm. I thought you might want to hold on to 'em. I knew you would know what to do with it since you work with history and all that. Would you believe they were still intact all these years? Mm. A blessing."

"A blessing indeed. Auntie, why didn't you ever tell me this?"

"You ain't ever ask. Besides, I don't think he ever wanted you to see them till he was gone."

"Why?"

Hazel exhaled loudly. "I dunno. I suppose 'cause since you got all fancy with your degrees, he thought his work was no match for what you were seeing in the museums in Amsterdam and Paris and all that."

The two women said their goodbyes, but not before Ardelia repeated a string of sorrys for her silence and thank-yous for the invaluable gifts. Ardelia sat down in front of her dining-room table and closed her eyes. In a short span of time, she'd learned that her father was not only a veteran, but an artist—a talented one at that. She didn't know him at all. What if these paintings were other messages being communicated to her? What if the stories she had been telling herself about him were incomplete, or altogether wrong? There was no time like the present to figure it out.

But as she was thinking about what she could do with nothing other than the books in her apartment and a strong wireless connection, she heard Mr. Johnson singing outside and raced downstairs to catch him.

"Well, hello there, li'l lady!" he said from the front stoop.

"G'mornin', Mr. Johnson. Long time no see!" she said, remaining in the vestibule to keep her distance.

"Well, you know, I'm just tryna be safe. But I needed some fresh air. How you been?"

"Can I ask you just one quick question?"

He smiled. "I don't see why not."

"You always told me that you think I don't know the first thing about family, right?"

"Somethin' like that. I was talkin' 'bout that accent of yours."

"Where did you think I was from?"

Mr. Johnson rolled his tongue around in his mouth and briefly looked upward.

"I was thinkin' Mississippi or somewhere around there."

Instead of dismissing Mr. Johnson's hunch that her origins were much deeper than she thought, Ardelia decided to pursue the matter. After all, her assumptions about her father had already been upended. What if her understanding of her entire family needed a reassessment too?

30

MAY 2020

There wasn't a more ironic tragicomedy than a scholar of Black American art only learning after her own father's death that he'd pick up a paintbrush in his spare time. Ardelia would pace the hallway and scoff at the absurdity. She would brush her teeth in the bathroom mirror and avoid her own reflection because of her shame. Why hadn't her father told her? Despite their irregular communication, he could have mentioned his artistic work. Did he intentionally withhold this from her? A small voice slithered in: Did he intentionally withhold information about himself from her, just as she'd done to him?

She sank into her couch until one of the cushions beneath her jutted out. Perhaps they weren't so different from each other. There were signs she'd missed though. For God's sake, she thought, when he had a job, it always had to do with something with his hands: auto mechanic, handyman, neighborhood go-to guy to fix guns. Ardelia recalled that he repaired her Barbie Dream House in the time it took her to watch an episode of *All That!* He patched up her bike when everyone thought it was past the point of fixing. Her father was a dexterous man. How could she have been so blind?

At night, Ardelia lay in bed piecing together memories that now

began to make sense. Her father had never pushed her to be a doctor or a lawyer. While the rest of her family had expressed concern
about her financial stability when she decided to pursue a graduate
degree in art, he'd defend her. He always gave her space to be herself,
even if that space was often marked by his absence. Ardelia surveyed
all four corners of the bedroom, where her curtains and mirrors re-
fracted the moonlight, rendering some objects visible and obscuring
others. There were some things that were imperceptible in the dark
and would remain this way till dawn. Perhaps, Ardelia thought, this is
how life is—not a strict binary of black and white, but shades of gray
and milky hues that compose an expansive reality. This was how she
would know her father—not as *this* or *that*, but both. Otherwise, she
suspected that she wouldn't be able to hear him beyond the grave.

And when Ardelia closed her eyes once more to steady her
thoughts, she called out telepathically to him that she wasn't going
anywhere and she was ready to see. Once she opened her eyes, the
shadows in her room became apparent. Gray blobs, similar to the ones
in his paintings. She knew them. They were here with her, just as they
had been for him. Once more, Ardelia closed her eyes and thought of
the figurative paintings lying in the other room. That woman looked
familiar. That woman must have been her father's obsession, maybe
even as arresting as the soldier was to Ardelia months ago. Maybe
she was an older figure. Could she—was that? No. No way. Ardelia
pulled the covers up to her sternum and turned on her side. She reasoned that it was too late at night to get the gears in her brain to spin
or else she'd never get any sleep. But the answer was only several feet
away, and this idea was going to nag at her if she didn't get up right
this instant.

Ardelia walked out into her living room, turned on a lamp, and
pulled out her favorite blues record. She carried it over to one of her
father's figurative paintings and held them up, side by side. The woman's features were similar in both—same prominent nose, sultry lips,
feline eyes, slim frame. Ardelia was so spooked that she looked over

her shoulder to see if anyone was watching her. Her father was telling her a story and she was desperate to be enlightened.

The next day, she called Hazel again.

"Back-to-back calls from you? How could I be so lucky?"

Ardelia chuckled. "Hi, Aunt Hazel, how are you?"

"I'm good. What's going on? How you like that art I sent you?"

"I love them. They're very beautiful. Aunt Hazel, I have a question."

"What's up?"

"Dad had never been to Mississippi, right?"

"Naw, of course not. Chicago born and raised."

"We don't have any family from there, do we?"

"Mm-mm. Not that I know of. Why you ask?"

"I'm not sure. I guess I'm just trying to learn more about Dad through his art and I realize that I don't have much. All I know is his name, birthday, and where he lived. I hardly even know Grandma's story. Like what about her mother or her mother's mother?"

"My mum-mum?" Aunt Hazel took a beat. "Why you wanna know about that?"

"Because you never mentioned her."

"No one asked."

"Well, I'm asking now. Respectfully."

Aunt Hazel called for Geraldine to come to the phone and Ardelia took a deep breath before Geraldine greeted her with a "Hi, baby."

"Hi Grandma."

"What cha need?"

"What was your mother's name?"

"Temperance."

"Do you remember your aunts' or uncles' names?"

There was a long pause in which Ardelia could hear her grandmother's breathing on the other end and some indistinct commercial in the background.

"Baby, I'm ninety years old. I don't remember like I used to and it's not like we sat around talkin' 'bout everybody business. In fact, you probably de first of my grandchirren to ask me anythin' 'bout my life. Hazel?"

Ardelia's ears perked up at "chirren." She'd never heard any elder say "children" in this way and wondered if this dialect was due to her grandmother's old age or hinted at a life or at parents who lived somewhere beyond Chicago.

Ardelia could hear another person opening and closing cabinets on the other end and figured that it was one of her aunts or uncles helping her grandmother out. Hazel picked up on the other phone.

"Wait! Can you tell me more about Dad's art?"

"Your dad's art? Mm . . ." Her voice trailed off.

"Hello?" Ardelia asked.

"We still here," Aunt Hazel said.

Figuring that she wasn't going to get anywhere, Ardelia moved on. "I have something else to ask." She took a deep breath. "My dad gave me these blues records, some of which feature a woman named Violet. I think he put her into some of his paintings but I'm not sure. Do either of you know anything about that?"

"Violet?" Geraldine asked. "Oh Lord . . ." she moaned. She repeated the Lord's name over and over, but her voice sounded farther and farther away until her pleas were ghostlike.

"Ma—" Aunt Hazel called. Ardelia heard quick footsteps. A click. A dial tone.

Another darkness, Ardelia concluded, with the phone still pressed to her ear. Not only did she have to reckon with what her father had hidden from her, her aunt and grandmother were keeping secrets too. This family was like a house of mirrors, each relative reflecting a distorted image of another, either living or dead, and Ardelia wanted to be whole. Whatever distortions she had, whatever scraps she collected, she was going to do something with them. She recalled Geraldine's hesitation before she spoke her own mother's name: Temperance. A fragment of history, but nevertheless, something to go on.

She went over to her desk and searched on Ancestry.com via her laptop for a Temperance and Geraldine Gibbs on the South Side of Chicago and found a 1940 census. Geraldine was listed as ten years old, Temperance was thirty-seven years old, and they lived with a Thomas Gibbs, age thirty-nine. There were a few other small children listed in the same house on the 4100 block of South Michigan Avenue. Ardelia could've traced her father's lineage through his own father's name. It would've been easier since Gibbs was her own surname too. However, the female subjects in her father's paintings floated to the surface of her mind and her intuition spoke to her: "Follow the women. Follow the women." She typed in Temperance's name along with her estimated birth date—1903, based on the age listed for her in the 1940 census—and found a marriage record: a Temperance Stiruhlan and a Thomas Gibbs. Ardelia cocked her head to the side. Stiruhlan? Was that English? Scottish? She typed in a Temperance Stiruhlan born circa 1903 who lived in Chicago and there was a 1920 census. No Thomas Gibbs but there was another person listed besides Temperance. Her name was Vera Stiruhlan, age twelve—her sibling, their parents, listed above their names per usual household order—Miriam, fifty-four, and Corinthian, fifty-five.

Why hadn't Ardelia ever heard anyone mention this Vera? Sometimes genealogical data on the internet was unverified, but sometimes it was correct. The uncertainty only strengthened Ardelia's curiosity, and for a moment, grief had relaxed its grip on her mind and body.

The 4100 block of South Michigan Avenue. Vera. Geraldine. Stiruhlan. Paintings. Women. Her father. Herself. They were disjointed words that she had no idea how to streamline. She held up her hands and flexed her fingers directly underneath the light.

Frustration be damned, she knew that this was only the beginning.

31

1913

When Tirzah died, the sun shone a little less brightly in Nicodemus. Her death arriving so quickly after the new year began felt like a terrible omen of what was to come. A pillar of the community, Tirzah hadn't left behind any plans for how to continue bolstering the city's reputation and draw newcomers in. Her unwavering faith that Nicodemus could still thrive was not sufficient for someone else to carry the mantle of her many responsibilities. The truth was, the old folks were good and tired and vulnerable.

Tuberculosis is what the coroner said took Tirzah's life, and the disease soon claimed others too. The pine boxes started to fill up and the churches thought they'd run out of paper with which to print funeral programs. Like monuments crumbling into rubble, the older generation left Nicodemus.

Grief herself moved enough between the Benjamin and Sterling households to crack their foundations wide open, and Miriam and Free fell into the ravine. In the days leading up to Tirzah's funeral, Miriam hardly spoke. She'd sit outside and watch a nearby stream without moving for hours on end. Whenever one of her girls would try to get her attention, she'd remain still, tears flitting down her stoic face. Each nightfall, when Corinthian would escort her back into the house, he'd note how cold she was, how no number of compresses or blankets could warm her. He understood that Tirzah meant a lot to Miriam, as she did for many others in town, but he started to question whether her behavior was a bit extreme. From his perspective, Tirzah and Miriam weren't even that close. Sure, they had conversations after church and other social activities, but Tirzah had never visited their home, hadn't attended either of their children's births, and wasn't even there when Corinthian and Miriam got married. With the way Miriam was acting, Corinthian thought, it was like Tirzah had been her mother or something.

He attended the funeral with her, hoping that as soon as it was over, she would return to being his wife. The church was filled to the brim with people from all over Graham County. The choir sang with all their hearts, and the parishioners raised their arms to God. In the midst of all the organ strikes and tambourine sounds, somewhere in between the praise and shouting and the final prayer, Corinthian realized he didn't know where his wife was. He had no idea how she disappeared when she was sitting right beside him in the pew with their daughters. Something stirred within him. He asked a woman in their pew to watch over Temperance and Vera for a moment, and he maneuvered through the crowd to find his wife. As soon as he exited the entrance doors and walked behind the church, he found Miriam with her hands on Free's chest and Free's hands moving up underneath her skirt while he kissed her.

If it hadn't been the day of Tirzah's funeral, Corinthian would have put him in the ground right with his mother. But Free was no more than a buck fifty soaking wet, and Corinthian was almost twice his weight with hands as thick as leather. All he saw was a little boy with nothing to show for himself. So he allowed Free to walk past him with his head down. But Free didn't return to the sanctuary and instead continued into the fields where the cornstalks enveloped his body. As for Miriam, she stood there nervously rubbing at her upper arms. Corinthian said nothing. He wasn't the most eloquent of men, but what he had just seen tore apart the string of words he could've put together.

He remained quiet for weeks, and Miriam became even more shameless. She stopped cooking for the girls and hardly spoke to Corinthian. And she'd come into the house at ungodly hours of the night smelling of alcohol and cigar smoke, as if she wanted someone to see which vices she'd indulged in. How she was able to climb into bed next to Corinthian without so much as washing the stink off her, Corinthian didn't know. If he thought about her audacity for too long, he'd almost start to laugh. But when the anger didn't morph into laughter, he used that feeling to become even more productive.

On the bulletin board of Old First Baptist Church, Corinthian came across a flier from *The Chicago Defender* that advertised six-dollar-a-day jobs with potential for room and board as well as social services from the Chicago Urban League at 3719 South State Street. It was divine timing. If Miriam could have secrets, then so could he. He would pack his things little by little and stow them away in the closet and underneath the bed. When the girls were at school, he'd start to bundle their belongings, a little at a time, so they wouldn't panic. He started to put the word out to his friends in and around Graham County that he was leaving. He inventoried all the items in his house that were too large to bring to Chicago—furniture, farming tools, the wagon—with the intention of selling them. Each day, he planned to tell Miriam what was going on, rehearsing his lines in his head while fixing the children dinner or lying under the covers at night. But she might as well have been a ghost. After about two and a half weeks of logistical planning, the children picked up on what Corinthian was doing and he was surprised by how little they fussed. In fact, when they came home from school, they helped him pack items to be sold.

Whenever Corinthian had a moment to sit and think, he looked around his home. Every room and corner were as clean as the day that he and Miriam moved in. All this time, she hadn't noticed the difference, just floating in and out of the space. Corinthian wondered if he was just going to have to leave her behind. They hardly spoke to each other, and the girls had stopped yearning for her touch. Temperance was practicing her sewing, and Vera preoccupied herself in the flower fields out back. He didn't want to go without Miriam, but there was no turning back now. He checked the train times and planned the day of their departure down to the minute. The wagon and the furniture were already handled.

The biggest secret that Corinthian held in all of his planning was not the move itself but what was happening to their farmland. Twenty years ago, Nicodemus had suffered a series of droughts that ruined the harvest for quite some time. Though the crops recovered, farmers like him had slipped in and out of stability ever since. He'd pick up jobs at general stores and handle errands to make the money stretch whenever Vera needed a new pair of shoes or a pair of his pants was beyond patching. But he couldn't get a government loan, and none of the farm credit offices would offer help, so the family home would have no choice but to go into foreclosure. He could've told Miriam but there wasn't any time. Tirzah was sick, then Tirzah died. Miriam grieved, then Miriam rutted behind the church during Tirzah's funeral. The imminent foreclosure, Corinthian believed, was not the worst thing. It was time for him to leave Nicodemus anyway.

A few nights before he planned to depart, Miriam made a rare appearance at home at dinnertime, holding up a sign she'd found attached to the front door. "Sold? What is dis about, 'Rinthian?"

"Good evenin' to you too. Care to sit down and join us? 'S been a while since we ate togetha as a family." Corinthian looked at her and Miriam relented. She complimented the smell of the food and leaned over to kiss Vera, who moved her face away. Temperance, meanwhile, was too invested in her plate to lift up her head. To ease the embarrassment, Miriam grabbed Vera's chin and planted a wet one on her cheek and patted Temperance on the shoulder before sitting down.

"Dis look delicious," Miriam said, placing a napkin on her lap. "Did y'all say grace already?"

"We did. You was late," Temperance quipped.

"Temp—" Corinthian interjected. "Mm-mm."

"Oh." Miriam started to eat her cabbage and mashed potatoes. "Well—" She took a bite. "How was y'alls day? Everythin' fine?"

Her family stayed quiet.

"Is anyone gon' speak to me?"

Temperance slammed down her utensils, causing everyone to jump in their seat. "No! Where did you go, Mama?"

"Temperance!" Corinthian yelled.

"We leavin'! Wit or wit'out you, and I can't wait. I hate dis town and I hate you!"

Temperance ran out of the room before Corinthian could catch her and slammed her and Vera's bedroom door.

"Let her go," Miriam said. "Vera, go on wit your sister real quick."

Vera put her napkin down and did as she was told.

Once both girls were in their room, Miriam leaned toward Corinthian. "Leavin'? We leavin'?"

"Das right. Goin' to Chicago."

"Chicago! Pfft! What you know 'bout Chicago? You a country boy through 'n through."

"Well, dis country boy through."

Miriam decided to play along. "Fine. How we gettin' dere den?"

"We take de railroad from Bogue to Kansas City and den switch trains on to Chicago."

Miriam laughed. "Corinthian, you ain't never been on no train and neither have I or de girls!"

"It'll be an adventure den. Dere's a first time for everythin'."

She leaned back into her seat, stumped. "Just like dat, huh?"

"Just like dat. You saw de sign out dere. We gotta leave anyhow. Plus what good is dere to stay?"

"Plenty!"

"Like what? Free Benjamin?"

Miriam looked like she'd been slapped.

"You wanna stay here for dat man, den do it," Corinthian continued. "Do it and watch what happen to you. You get laughed at for sniffin' up underneath someone else husband when his mama just died, and I'll have another woman in six months."

"I don' want Free."

"Ha!" Corinthian tipped his head backward and laughed. "Do you really think I'm stupid?"

"No." Miriam shook her head slowly. "I don' want Free Benjamin."

"Lyin' again. Don' you forget I saw y'all ruttin' outside de damn church durin' her funeral?"

"You ain't see nothin'. I was tryna push Free offa me when you came around 'cause he was tryna tell me dat we still had somethin' and I told him no. I don' want him no more. And I don' know if I ever really wanted him. I think I wanted Tirzah. Das why I been out most days. Not for ruttin', for thinkin'."

"Den why you smelled like dat—alcohol and stuff?"

"'Cause . . . I din't say I ain't have help gettin' me to think. Calms my nerves."

Corinthian squinted. "So you wanted Tirzah? What you tryna lay up wit wimmen now?"

"No, you fool. She and my pa were lovers before I was born. Dey never got to see each other again. And I wanted to know more about her. Maybe das why Free and I got close to begin with—so I could be closer to her. I wanted to know why my pa loved her so much and I understood sooner den I thought. Free was just in de middle."

Corinthian sighed. "Why you ain' neva tell me any of dis?"

"Din't know how. Din't think you'd understand."

"Well, we got a long journey so you best get to talkin' when we on our way."

"And I don' have a say in any of dis."

"No, you don't. I'm de man of dis house and what I say go."

Miriam's mouth dropped.

"Ya better go 'head and be a mother and talk to ya chirren. De time tickin' and one already hate you." With a scoff, Miriam got up from the dining table and headed to the girls' room.

Miriam gently knocked on the door before pushing it open to find Vera cuddling her teddy bear and Temperance knitting a scarf, a new hobby that Miriam didn't even notice that her eldest was extremely good at.

"Temperance," Miriam said, but Temperance ignored her.

Miriam looked toward Vera, who clutched her teddy bear so tightly its eyes bulged. She could've slid to the floor in that moment. The two children she birthed could not stand to look at her. The freedom she sought for all these years for herself, and by extension, Free, had come at a cost to her family. She silently stood at the door watching the two girls in their own separate worlds and realized that this distance was what she deserved. Now, gazing upon the way Temperance pursed her lips, just like she did, and how Vera's nose crinkled up like hers, Miriam once again felt lost, lost and reckless.

"I never told you two about my mother."

The girls stopped what they were doing and looked up at her.

"She was strong, headstrong, and determined. She could keep up wit de men like you can keep up wit de boys 'round here. And she loved me. I was her only child and dat came wit a lot of pressure. But I thought dat she was too much sometime 'cause of it. I din't wanna grow up like dat. And while I was out there catchin' up on lost time of freedom, I forgot 'bout you two. I'm sorry."

Temperance put her needles and yarn down and Vera copied her with the teddy bear.

"Do you really wanna go to Chicago? Away from all your family and friends? Away from everythin' you know 'bout out here in de fields to dat big, wide city?"

The girls nodded.

There was nothing left to say. Miriam packed up her belongings and placed all the suitcases at the door. She did, however, ask Corinthian if she could make one important trip before they went on to Bogue. He wanted to be spared the details. As long as she was on the wagon by 9:00 a.m. sharp, it didn't matter where she'd go, but he, Vera, and Temperance would be leaving.

Much to his surprise, she came back short of breath just in the nick of time. He subtly sniffed her for any strange smells and checked her neck for any bruises, but she was unblemished. When they settled for the night, he would check the rest of her.

The family arrived at the railroad depot in Bogue. A few other negro families trickled in with their fine attire and suitcases. They nodded at one another, but the Sterling family stood in place, in awe of all the bustling activity around them. Each of them was dazzled by the men in their top hats and the women in their warm-colored dresses. There were voices overhead speaking to passengers about train times, engines blowing in the distance, and a lot of chatter heightened by the sharp acoustics of the station. The girls looked up to Corinthian to see what he'd do next, and he was thankful that he had on large enough clothes to cover his sweaty pits. Miriam was right: He ain't never been on no train. He didn't even know what to do. Would the train come right up to them?

He spotted a few people conversing with whites behind a glass and saw them exchange bills and white-colored paper. There was a large sign above the glass booths, and Corinthian had to sound out the words. Eventually, he grabbed one of the girls' hands and Miriam the other, and they marched up to the booth to take their chances.

The silver-haired white man behind the glass adjusted his spectacles and said, "Can I help you?"

"Hi. We takin' de train to Kansas City. De one at ten seventeen. We on our way to Chicago."

"You and every other negro," the man said. He spun around in his chair and returned to the glass with four tickets. "That'll be forty-six dollars for you two adults and twenty for the children. With tax, that'll be sixty-nine dollars."

Miriam balked. She couldn't recall the last time she heard a figure like that. But before she could say a thing, Corinthian had slipped a few bills in the slot through the glass and received the tickets.

After the family boarded the train and the whistling began, the train's wheels began to churn, and Temperance and Vera immediately turned toward the windows. The children watched how the landscape changed. Vera especially was saddened by how the wildflowers grew fewer with each passing mile. In a little over two hours, the train pulled into Kansas City, where a thick brush of heat overtook all the passengers. This station was about three times the size of the one at Bogue. There were more glass counters, more doors through which to enter and to exit, numbered signs all over the place, people speaking loudly, someone talking overhead but sounding muffled, birds swooping through to catch crumbs from someone's sandwich or to perch on top of trash cans.

There were more Black people in one place than Miriam had ever seen in her life, and they were moving in every direction as different city names were being called out: St. Paul, Minneapolis, Omaha, St. Louis, Los Angeles, Tulsa, Memphis, Colorado Springs, Milwaukee, Chicago. People were checking and double-checking their tickets, arguing with their loved ones about departure times and delays, straightening their bowties and patting down flyaway hairs, saying prayers and speaking affirmations, pressing heirlooms to their chests, crying, waiting. Every two or three feet another dramatic scene unfolded. Everyone was a character, and the many platforms were the stages.

"I thought we was goin' to Chicago?"

"We are. I guess dis just a stop along de way."

"Last call for Chicago on platform eight!" someone shouted, and the family rushed down the long hall. They had been standing by number two.

They climbed onto the train, out of breath and sweaty, just before all the doors closed. As the wheels squealed and screeched and the horn majestically blew into the open skies, the negro passengers whooped and hollered with joy before broadening into several rounds of applause.

Miriam leaned into Corinthian and placed her right pointer finger into her ear. "You would think we were headed to heaven, de way everyone carryin' on."

Corinthian tipped his head back and laughed. "Maybe not quite heaven, but we leavin' our Egypt for sure."

Temperance began to knit with a ball of yarn she packed in her suitcase, while Vera pressed her face up against the window because she didn't want to miss a thing. The wide plains, the wheat crops, the rivers, the farmers. Everything was moving fast. The family went through cycles of talking and eating and napping for what seemed like ages. Sometimes Vera would tug at her parents to ask when the trip would be over but they didn't have an answer. Other little girls were running up and down the aisles in between stops, and Corinthian and Miriam allowed Vera to do the same until she was good and tired and needed a nap again.

Once the train finally pulled into Chicago, and the Sterling family disembarked and entered the station, they thought they had stepped into a new world. Temperance couldn't close her mouth, staring at all the tall buildings rising high into the sky in the distance. Miriam had to stand still, trying to take in this station, which was the biggest of them all, and how the negroes themselves displayed more colors and affectations than she had ever heard or seen. Corinthian remained stoic, feeling the need to be the man of the family but deeply worried inside that he had no idea how to command his wife or children into this new place.

As for Vera, she could not take her eyes off a group of young boys playing a series of melodic and discordant notes that she had never heard before. Even when her mother tugged her along, Vera kept looking over her shoulder at them. What was that sound? What was that sound luring her in and never letting her go?

"Pa?" Corinthian peered down at Vera, who hadn't spoken in God knows how long. "What dey playin' over dere?"

Corinthian looked further down and turned up his lip. "Oh I don't know, Vera. It ain't nothin' though."

Dissatisfied, Vera yanked out of her mother's arms and ran over to the boys. She could hear her parents yelling her name far behind her but that only propelled her toward the musicians. One of them lowered his harmonica and the others did the same with their guitars. Once Vera had their attention, all she could do was stare until her parents caught her. Maybe her mother gave her a light tap on the behind; maybe her father scolded her. She didn't know. She didn't care. All she knew was that in this new land, she wanted to open her mouth and produce a sound like that.

32

JUNE 2020

As New Yorkers were marching in the streets to protest the police-related murders of George Floyd and Breonna Taylor, Ardelia and Oliver were breaking up. Oliver should've known it was coming, he chided himself. After Sterling died two months prior, they were like two ships passing in the night without a lighthouse to call them home. "My father died." The text was brief and matter-of-fact. Oliver called her multiple times and left voicemails, hoping that she'd tell him something—anything—about how she was doing. But she barely said a word. One night, when Ardelia did answer the phone and communicate with Oliver, she mentioned Sterling's Zoom funeral, and Oliver felt a pang at not having been invited. He could've brought it up then. He should've brought it up. But instead, Oliver remained quiet and nodded along. Ardelia obviously didn't want him there or else she would've told him.

Were they still even together? They hadn't spoken of their relationship ending. Oliver believed that even approaching the subject would be inappropriate given Ardelia's grief. Whenever they would text or FaceTime, though, he could see how quickly he was losing her. She refrained from looking at him head-on, heavily sighed as if she were bored, tired, or running out of air. Her texts were devoid of the usual goofiness she expressed through emojis and acronyms and turns of phrase. Though he had his own emotional debris to sift through, Oliver could still recognize that his beloved was not the same.

The only subjects that would inspire her to talk much at all was her family genealogy and internet sleuthing and art and Chicago and Mississippi and whatnot. On FaceTime, her hand gestures emphasized all the twists and turns in her research, and the only time she would allow Oliver to get a word in was when she had to take a breath. But every time he opened his mouth, Ardelia frowned as though she were expecting something different. What the fuck did she expect him to say? *I can't sleep. Sometimes I have to put my hand over my chest to calm my heart. I don't know whether it's Monday morning or Thursday afternoon. I don't know whether I'm coming or going. Sometimes when the room gets quiet, I replay the sounds patients make when they take their last breaths. I hate touching myself to wash my face or body because I'm warned every fucking day that I can't touch a single fucking thing without my PPE and now my own skin feels weird. A colleague died today. Another colleague died four days ago. Or was it three? No, there is absolutely nothing you can do to help. You're not a doctor and you can't bring anyone back to life. No, I don't want you to do anything. I want you. I miss you. There's nothing either of us can do to stop this ache. What do you want me to say?*

He could have said a fraction of these words and gotten his point across. But whenever he looked at the woman he loved, the next thing out of his mouth was fragmented and disjointed, and each word twisted her face further and further. Then one day on FaceTime, as Ardelia was telling Oliver about the genealogical research she was doing on her family, Oliver was zoning out while looking at the window.

Ardelia saw how the light shone on his face and said, "Wanna meet up in the park?"

"What? No," Oliver quickly replied. He couldn't imagine exposing her to the germs he'd been encountering at the hospital.

"Why not? We can socially distance. People are already starting to do that for outside gatherings. I masked up when I went to a Black Lives Matter protest near Central Park and so did everyone else."

"Ardelia—" Oliver rubbed his eyes and sighed. "The COVID rates are gonna spike again. You can be sure of it. It's not safe."

"It hasn't been safe for months though. Are we going to keep staying inside forever?"

"Well . . ." Oliver shrugged. "We're living in unprecedented times."

"You sound like a news anchor right now. Oliver, you're talking to your fiancée."

"Are we even still engaged at this point?" Oliver mouthed "fuck" to himself upon realizing how thoughtless his words were.

"What do you mean?" Ardelia's voice was higher pitched and quieter.

"I didn't mean it like that. It's just—look, our wedding was canceled and we didn't even talk about it."

"My dad was in the hospital, like, soon after that news."

"Right. But we never revisited it."

"What are you saying then? You don't wanna be engaged anymore?"

"Of course not! No. I wasn't saying that."

"Then what are you saying? What is it you want?"

He sighed. "I don't know. I don't know what I'm trying to say. Hell, I don't know what I want."

That last phrase rattled Ardelia's body. "I don't know what I want." How many times had she heard that line from a man she longed for? "I don't know what I want." How many times had she bent and kneeled and pretzeled herself into all kinds of shapes to give a man a choice of which version of her he preferred? "I don't know what I want." How many times could she wait around for someone to be sure of her? Ardelia thought that she had progressed past this stage when she met Oliver, a man who loved her and proposed to her, a man with whom she shared a life. But now she didn't know how much he could be there or invest.

All of this kicked up inside of her and Ardelia shot back: "Why don't you take all the time you need to figure out what you want? Alone."

Oliver almost choked on his spit. He started to say her name but she had already hung up. What did she mean, alone? Like . . . alone alone? Right this instant, or forever?

Later that night, Oliver heard Ardelia's cries instead of the patients' breaths, and before he could stop himself, he texted her: "I love you." Text bubbles on her end rose and fell, then rose and fell again. Then nothing at all. He deserved it, Oliver thought. He couldn't give her what she needed.

Oliver began to imagine that he was in a film. None of this was real, he repeated to himself. Was it? There he was, sitting on a firm chair across from Dr. Peterson, who was asking him if he had finished making new living arrangements. What? Oliver asked. What new living arrangements? Dr. Peterson sighed, took off his glasses, and reminded him that the Four Seasons wasn't going to host essential workers forever. They weren't? Oliver asked. The lines in Dr. Peterson's face deepened, and he said it would be best if Oliver took the day off to pull himself together.

And then Oliver was out in the open air, meandering until he saw a few runners coursing through a canopy of trees by Central Park. He blinked. He wouldn't be at the hotel anymore. He could finally go home. Yes, home. Oliver pulled out his phone and texted Ardelia so fast his fingers cramped: "Ardelia, I want to talk. I'm moving out of the Four Seasons soon and I want to come home. We'll figure out how to socially distance. You're right—I overreacted." He waited with bated breath and crossed one of the roads in Central Park to stand underneath the crape myrtle trees so that their smell would sweeten the response that would soon come. Again, the text bubbles rose and fell, rose and fell. "I don't want to talk to you. We'll make arrangements for you to move your stuff out."

His fingers hovered over the keys, but they were trembling, and he placed the phone on his lap. He couldn't just move out today. He'd need somewhere else to live. He'd heard that rents were dropping so the search might not be as arduous as usual. But it didn't have to start immediately. The sun hadn't reached its peak in the sky. He could sprawl out underneath the crape myrtles for a little while longer. Eventually, a few masked runners stopped to stare at Oliver, his legs covered in petals, and he got up, dusted himself off, and walked back to his hotel room. After stripping down and putting his clothes into a bag, Oliver collapsed facefirst into bed. He took as much air into his chest as he could until the strain on his body made him exhale.

When Oliver awakened, it was dark outside. He could not have slept that long, could he? He opened his laptop and started to search for apartment rentals, soon finding countless units near the hospital advertising AVAILABLE FOR IMMEDIATE MOVE IN. He put in requests for virtual visits and got responses within the hour. "I did what you want," Oliver texted Ardelia. "Can I at least see you when I move out? We can be safe." He sent a face-masked emoji. He held his breath. A thumbs-up over his last message. He exhaled.

Within the week, he secured an apartment in Murray Hill after viewing the unit via FaceTime. On the day he arrived by taxi to the apartment he'd shared with Ardelia to meet the movers he'd hired, Mr. Johnson was outside sweeping, his back to the street. He turned and straightened his spine as he squinted through the glass. Mr. Johnson beamed when he saw Oliver step out of the car, but his smile faded once Oliver got closer.

"My oh my, look at chu," Mr. Johnson said. "You look like you haven't eaten good in a while."

"I've been all right."

"No you haven't."

Oliver could feel the tears rising and hung his head so his former neighbor wouldn't see.

"Yeah . . ." Mr. Johnson said softly. "I know you ain't all right.

You work in those hospitals so I know you ain't okay. And 'Delia ain't either. She been worried sick 'bout chu."

Oliver lifted his head. "She has?"

"Of course. Sometimes I go check on her 'cause she a young, single woman and lost her daddy and all. And if she don't talk to me 'bout chu, I hear her talkin' to somebody on the phone about chu."

Oliver took a deep breath. "But I'm moving out today. . . ."

Mr. Johnson gripped his broom handle. "Why?"

"We broke up."

"Boy . . ." Mr. Johnson started, and Oliver shut his eyes. He could feel the air sharpen between them. He recognized the tone his daddy and his uncles used whenever a swift tongue lashing was about to occur. "I never pegged you for someone who was dumb."

"She broke up with me!" Oliver took a pause. "Technically."

"Now you young, I get it. But don't be dumb. Don't be like me. I was young once too, you know. Rippin' and runnin' the streets. Thought a young woman was always gonna be there until she wasn't. Worst mistake I ever made in my life."

"There's no one else, Mr. Johnson."

"Oh yes there is. You. You gettin' in your own way." Mr. Johnson stepped to one side and nodded toward the steps. "Let me get outta yours so you can handle your business."

Oliver hesitated to enter the apartment building, but straightened himself too so that he could do what needed to be done. He wondered if Ardelia missed him and whether her hair still smelled of mango butter and jasmine. Did she still listen to her blues records? Did she still place her pen behind one ear when she was thinking hard about something?

Oliver opened their front door, and the home was nothing like he remembered. Papers were strewn all over the countertops and floors. Post-its with her inscrutable scrawl were stuck to the coffee table, the refrigerator. Beneath a large heap of notes on the dining-room table were several provocative paintings.

A sneeze came from the bathroom. Oliver snapped upright and froze by the dining-room table, waiting for Ardelia to say something.

He quietly walked into the dark hallway leading to the bedroom and stopped outside the bathroom door. "Are you all right?" Oliver asked. He held his breath. Now there weren't any bubbles between them, only empty space and memories of their shared life.

"I'm fine," Ardelia said curtly from the other side. "Do you have disinfectant and gloves?"

"I do."

"Good. Are you wearing a mask?"

"Yes, of course." Oliver took a deep breath. "Can I at least see you?"

She didn't respond.

"Okay," he said. "I get it."

He started on the bedroom and stuffed all his belongings into cardboard boxes, periodically checking over his shoulder to see if or when Ardelia would emerge from the bathroom.

"I'm finished up," Oliver called from the hallway after about half an hour, but then he halted when he realized that he was mistaken. On the mantelpiece, he saw that one of Sterling's letters to Ardelia was framed right alongside Tirzah's letter. This time when Oliver looked over his shoulder, he was relieved that Ardelia wasn't watching him. There was no way that she would have situated her father's letter next to Tirzah's, and kept Tirzah's in pride of place, if Oliver were not still important to her. She could've shoved it into a box in the closet. She wasn't slick, he thought to himself as the lines in his mouth curled into the very beginnings of a smile.

After he'd pushed the last box of his into the stairwell, Oliver took one last look at the two letters side by side on the mantelpiece.

"That's the last of it!" he called out to Ardelia, closed the door, and continued on smiling.

33

SEPTEMBER 2020

Mr. Johnson had been watching them from his station near the stoop. He saw how quickly Ardelia would try to hide to cover her flustered, red face from him in the mornings or race inside the vestibule with what he assumed was a whole bunch of snacks. At the beginning of lockdown, Mr. Johnson had retreated into his home like everyone else, even though the disruption in his schedule aggravated him. He was close to eighty, but he felt that his senses had never been so acute. Ardelia's mourning rose above the sirens, and her sunken silhouette cast a shadow on the curtains. As the months progressed and people were outside a bit more, Mr. Johnson would sit on the bottom step or lean against the ironwork, listen to Ardelia, and grip his broom handle with both hands, his bottom lip trembling. He thought the cries would haunt him for the rest of his days if he didn't intervene.

So one day that fall, Mr. Johnson put on his mask, grabbed his gloves, and kept a miniature disinfectant spray in one of his back pockets. He raised his fist to knock on Ardelia's front door but stopped when he heard her moving around inside. There was a soft record scratch before a track came through the walls, then a long har- monica solo before a man jumped on the beat with his guitar and lyrics. Ardelia was singing along word for word without missing a key change or phrase.

"Say, you got you a fine voice there," Mr. Johnson said through the door.

Ardelia's feet shifted quickly away from the door.

The music lowered. He heard her steps approach the door. "Do you mind if I keep the door closed?" she said, sounding as though she were pressed against the wood.

"Of course, I get it. And I know you wasn't expectin' me. If you were gonna open the door for anyone, it'd be Oliver, I know." Mr. Johnson heard Ardelia sniffling and added: "You love that man. And he love you too. Whatever y'all got goin' on, that love don't just go away. But cry it out if you need to for you—it's never good to hold it in."

"I ain't just cryin' 'bout him. It's my Dad passing. It's . . . everything." Her voice cracked and she cried.

Mr. Johnson pressed a hand to the door. "You got a lot goin' on, Miss 'Delia, I understand. A whole lot goin' on." She remained silent, which he took as his cue to continue. "I remember the first day I met Oliver. His clothes coulda used some ironin' but he was sharp still. His eyes were always lookin' somewhere I couldn't follow though. Until you came along. I saw his eyes find yours like a bee finds pollen. You understand?"

"Yes," she said quietly from the other side of the door.

"I wouldn't lie to you, 'Delia. I always felt close to that boy, and I don't know. Maybe he remind me of kin. You remind me of kin too, honestly."

He heard a soft chuckle. "Maybe we are . . . I haven't forgotten about that Mississippi comment you made a while back."

The music coming from inside Ardelia's apartment changed and his eyes opened wide. "Is that Muddy Waters I hear?"

She flung open the front door and looked at him, a mask covering the bottom half of her face. "How do you know Muddy Waters?"

"Li'l girl, ha! What do YOU know about Muddy Waters?"

They laughed, and Ardelia, seeing that he'd come protected, then stepped aside to let him in.

Immediately, he saw three vases full of roses in and around her kitchen and smirked. "Y'all ain't together, huh?"

Ardelia sighed. "He won't leave me alone. You should've seen the chocolates he sent a few weeks ago. Almost gave me a toothache. I thank him and then I move on."

"If that's the case, then why don't you throw these flowers out?"

"Throw out roses? Are you kidding me?"

"Uh-huh . . ." Mr. Johnson was unconvinced, and they both knew that her excuse wouldn't work on him.

"So tell me, why you playin' the blues, young lady?"

"Honestly . . . I grew up on it. Listen to this." Ardelia walked over to switch the record to a more seductively haunting sound produced by a few guitar chords. A man's strained voice slithered from the speakers. "This man right here? Name's Booker Stone."

"Booker Stone? Mm. Never heard of him."

"You wouldn't have. He never got as big as the others."

"Mm. He good."

"Ooh listen—" A woman's voice floated above Booker's, their harmonies sweet, fluid, and powerful."

"Who is that?"

"This lady? Her name is Violet, no last name. My father introduced me to her music. She's only on Booker's earlier tracks but suddenly disappears from any of the later records. She never hit it big herself. Maybe she just gave up on music earlier than he did."

Ardelia's phone began to vibrate on the dining-room table, and she grabbed it before Mr. Johnson could see the name that appeared on the screen. She sighed, pressed a button, and slammed it facedown on the kitchen countertop.

"Careful, girl, those iPhones ain't cheap."

Ardelia shook her head. "He won't stop reaching out. I told him that if we're gonna be broken up then we need a proper break, which means no contact. I just . . . I don't need this confusion in my life."

"If a man is doing all of this—sending gifts, reaching out—seems like he's not the one confused."

Ardelia could feel her cheeks turn red.

"So anyway, this Booker Stone. How do you know his music?"

"Also from my dad. Sometimes I think he may've been a relative because my family has so much of his discography that I haven't been able to find in one place elsewhere," Ardelia said.

"Your people from the South Side of Chicago. Right? That was the bedrock of dis kind of blues. Where'd you say Booker was from?"

"Chicago."

"No no, before that—his people."

"Oh, I don't know none of that. Why?"

"Well, you probably already know this but blues came to Chicago by way of Mississippi. Musicians left the delta for the Windy City. I done told you before your people ain't all Chicago."

"True," she said. "But I don't even know if Booker Stone is his real name. Hell, I gotta crack one name before I even think about moving on to researching Booker's and wherever that may lead."

"What name?"

"Stiruhlan. My last name is Gibbs. But I know Stiruhlan was my great-grandmother's maiden name on my dad's side. It doesn't exist in Chicago before 1920."

"I don't think I'm followin'," Mr. Johnson said.

"So . . ." Ardelia began to pace around her dining-room table as Mr. Johnson pulled out a chair and sat. "I've always thought my family had been in Chicago since . . . forever. If no Stiruhlans existed in Chicago before 1920 then that means that my family didn't exist either, which makes no logical sense."

"I told you that—"

"Yes, yes—" Ardelia held her palms out in front of her. "I know, I know. Migration, I know. But I can't find any Stiruhlans before the 1920s anywhere in Illinois, or in Mississippi either. I can't tackle the entire country, that could take ages."

"Hmm . . ." Mr. Johnson raised his chin to the ceiling. "Spell the name for me."

"S-t-i-r-u-h-l-a-n."

He shook his head. "I ain't never hear of no Black folk wit that last name."

"Neither have I," Ardelia said, and laughed.

"You know . . ." Mr. Johnson stood up from his chair. "It could be a misspelling. White folks used to take down our names back in the day and got them wrong all the time."

"Hmm . . . could be. But where would they get that spelling from?"

"Who's to say?"

"I had a crazy thought right before you came over. I thought Stiruhlan sounded like my father's name: Sterling."

"Steer-uh-lan. Stir-oo-lan." He looked past Ardelia and repeated the different pronunciations until they collided. He blinked at her. "Say your father's name slow."

She sighed. Ster-ling. Ster . . . ling. Ster . . . ling." The more slowly she said it, the more she could hear the hill between the first and second syllables. A speaker could bumble along that hill and create another syllable altogether. "Ster . . . uh—"

"There it is." Mr. Johnson pointed at her. "Say it slower."

"Ster . . . uh . . . ling. Stir—oh my God." She released a hearty laugh. "Oh my God!"

"It's similar, right?" Mr. Johnson asked.

"Always too similar to be believable."

"Do you have any great-grandparents' names?"

"Miriam and Corinthian Stiruhlan."

"Look up Miriam and Corinthian Sterling and see what pops up."

"I will." Ardelia grabbed her laptop off the couch and looked up over her screen. "Do you mind if I do this alone? It's a lot to wrap my head around."

"Of course." Mr. Johnson rose to his feet. "Just remember: Sometimes we overthink what's right in front of us." He turned his head and leaned forward toward the blues streaming from the vinyl player. "I love that lady's voice."

34

1922

Blues music streamed into the Stiruhlan household no matter how hard Corinthian and Miriam tried to block its flow. Every time a door or window was open, the sound of a harmonica or guitar came from somewhere outside. Whenever any of them went as far as the corner, there was someone singing about their troubles to anyone who'd listen. Corinthian and Miriam would not have despised the genre so much if they hadn't feared that Vera was being infected by it. Temperance had already gone off to college. The word itself felt thick in their mouths when Temperance brought up the idea. But Wilberforce University would be offering her free tuition, and she would be able to achieve more than what her parents did. Miriam agreed and convinced Corinthian to do the same.

Vera was different. She wasn't talking about her plans for the future. Instead, her parents saw something stir up inside of her whenever the blues started coming through. Miriam would catch Vera tapping her foot to the beat at the dinner table or Corinthian would bust her swaying her growing hips to the music coming from beyond her bedroom window. He'd berate her for leaving it open, warning her it was unsafe, but she knew that she would throw caution to the wind so long as she could hear that music. And no amount of sequestering her in a Baptist Church sanctuary with all-night revivals, Bible study classes, and Sunday school and service could drive out the rhythm in her soul.

They lived on 4184 South Michigan Avenue, in the heart of the Bronzeville section of Chicago, an area their neighbors would later call "the Black Metropolis." Miriam observed soon after their arrival that the clothes on their backs and in their suitcases would be insufficient to keep up with the glamour around them. Not even Elodie Williams, God rest her soul, could compare to the city ladies with their tailored blazers and skirts. And there was so much to do: The nightlife lit up the neighborhood with its neon signs and renowned performers; the theater entertained generations young and old; and negro-owned, negro-served businesses were booming. In the beginning, Corinthian and Miriam frequented some of these spots. There, Miriam found the thrill and excitement she'd experienced with Free, but it was even better this time around. This was a new place where she would not be the subject of gossip—though from the looks of what she saw inside these places, no one was in any position to judge. Besides, the look on Corinthian's face when they strolled around town was one she hadn't seen since they were courting. He was indeed happy, and Miriam wanted to keep him that way.

Though Corinthian was Kansas bred through and through, the longer he stayed in Chicago, the more it felt like home. Soon after the family's arrival, the negro YMCA on Wabash Avenue helped him find a job and a home quicker than he expected. Every morning, Corinthian left before sunup for work. Whether by foot or by bus (during inclement weather), he was a part of a mass influx of negro Chicagoan men employed by the handful of mills on the South Side. If it wasn't Acme Steel, it was Wisconsin or Republic or Youngstown Sheet & Tube or South Works. Wives would pack their husbands' lunches and see them out the door. They would pray that their husbands wouldn't get maimed on the job, that their husbands' bosses wouldn't stiff them on their checks, and that if they did, their husbands wouldn't come home angry and take it out on them.

Though Corinthian was satisfied with his job because it kept a roof over his family's heads and food on the table, he despaired about how small their home was, on a piece of land so small he couldn't do the math to figure out its fraction of an acre. His only consolation was the patch in the backyard where he could grow some beans, tomatoes, and summer squash. The women in his life were uninterested in his garden. Miriam's defense was that her fingers were too sore from the domestic labor in their house and someone else's to be gentle with the plants. Temperance was too busy studying, and Vera, who had once been enamored by the beauty of the flowers of Kansas, had become a city girl. She didn't want to hear nothing about what could manifest from dirt and water when mom-and-pop grocery stores and restaurants were around the corner.

From the time she was fourteen, Vera's beauty seized attention no matter how conservatively she dressed. She was the object of much discussion and many arguments at home. Even though Vera obeyed every stringent rule he had in place, Corinthian was never pleased. But so long as Vera was mindful of who her savior was, Miriam didn't mind if she went to see a film or get a scoop of ice cream after sundown with a friend. She didn't want Vera missing out on everything all the other teenagers were doing in spite of the threat of the devil. And even in church, that blues music was slithering its way to the altar and pulpit, Miriam knew. There weren't enough hours of praying and preaching that could separate parishioners from that sweet, secular sound. Not in any northern city and especially not in Chicago.

It was on one of her free afternoons with her girlfriends that Vera found Booker Stone. She heard his guitar strumming one afternoon while window-shopping and followed the sound down an alleyway where gangsters and hookers roamed. Everything looked and felt different. The large brick buildings that bordered the alleyway created only a narrow space for the sunlight to break through. Vera wondered if any of the people who hung around these parts could tell whether it was day or night. The air was so thick she tugged at her collar to get some more air, but it didn't stop her from finding out who was producing this siren call from somewhere down Maxwell Street.

She followed the sound down that alleyway and found the owner of that voice. It was a light-skinned boy about a foot and a half taller than her, and he was a part of a quintet that was performing under the shade of the awning of an adjacent boardinghouse. The singer's sad eyes and pallid skin made the hairs on her arm stand at attention. He wore a fedora that could hardly contain his greased curls, and his shirt and trousers were too big for his gangly frame. The voice he directed at the players who accompanied him was deep and full of bass. No light-skinned boy she knew ever held a voice like that in his throat. They were always much softer, more gloss than grit. And then when he gave the eight count and began singing, she felt he was the most handsome man she'd ever seen. Thousands of souls were unleashed from the first note. His lyrics circled Vera's entire body, moving and twisting it in ways she didn't think possible. She closed her eyes and dreamt of places near and far—no road maps, no signs, just wide-open space where he'd play and she'd sing. Her throat vibrated and her chest got warm. A melody issued out of her mouth.

The music abruptly stopped.

She opened her eyes and saw all the musicians staring at her.

"Oh." Vera wished that the earth would crack open and swallow her whole. "I'm sorry," she said, and slowly began to walk backward.

"Wait, don't go!" Booker said with an outstretched hand, and she halted. "You sounded good. Dat harmony you did. You got a good voice, you know dat?"

"Oh. Thank you." Vera turned beet red and moved one of her curls behind her right ear.

"Where you sing at?"

"Sometime at church. Sometime in the bathroom."

All the musicians except Booker laughed until he raised a hand to silence them. "You never really *sang* sang before? With a voice like dat?"

Vera shook her head.

"What's your name?"

"Vera."

"You from de North Side or somethin'?"

"No, not at all! I live on South Michigan Avenue."

"South Michigan?" Booker leaned forward. "Hell, wit de way you talk, I thought you woulda been from Winthrop Ave, surrounded by all dem white folk." The rest of the guys laughed.

"Well, where I come from, there was nothing but negroes. No white people for miles." She held her chin high. "I'm from Kansas. Nicodemus, Kansas."

"Never heard of it but Niggademus sound nice. Well"—he cleared his throat—"I'm Booker Stone. Dese here my boys—Cats, Fats, Gee, and Scoop."

"Where you boys from?"

He smiled and did a quick melody on his guitar. "Mississippi."

"Where in Mississippi?" Vera asked.

"A place too rough for someone as pretty as you to know anythin' about."

"Okay . . ." Vera trailed off. "You all up here for work?"

"Somethin' like dat. You a Christian, Miss Vera?"

"Of course."

"Well, you know in de good book, it say God made man from de dust of de ground and breathed life into his nose, right? Well, God gathered me from de mud of de Mississippi Delta and breathed blues into my bones." He resumed strumming a tune.

"That's really poetic."

"It's poetic 'cause it's true. Every bit of it. No exaggeration."

She could feel herself blushing.

"What? You ain't think a country boy like me knew such a big word like 'exaggeration,' huh?"

"That's not it—"

Before she could finish, one of Vera's girlfriends called her name, and she ran out of the alleyway without saying goodbye. As soon as she reached the street, Vera worried she'd offended the stranger. And then she wondered why she cared. On her walk home, she heard Booker everywhere. A key in someone's voice or a rumble of a passing car reminded her of him. Her humdrum life had been awakened with an infusion of romance.

For a week, Vera could not stop thinking about Booker and orchestrated a plan to see him again by inviting the same girlfriends to hang out on Maxwell Street. Not too long after they arrived, Vera heard his voice and lied to her friends about having to use the bathroom so that she could continue down that alleyway and see him again. There, Booker asked her where she lived, because he wanted to take her out for ice cream, and Vera told him her address but warned him that her father would never allow it. And besides, a musician wasn't what Corinthian had in mind for his daughter, unless he played the organ at church.

Later that evening, half asleep, Vera heard music playing and walked toward her window, wondering why she didn't shut the windows tight before bed when the winds from the Calumet River were quite fierce. She rubbed the crust from her eyes and saw him— standing in the middle of the street, alternating between playing the guitar and harmonica. He was singing about some girl who slipped away from his fingertips, and each time he sang the word "girl," he lifted his fedora to reveal his otherwise shadowed face. She was the girl who slipped away, and he was coming for her.

From a dark corner of the hallway, Miriam was watching Vera watch him. She was moved by how the moonlight shone upon her daughter's face and how the curtains fluttered, heightening her beauty. And the music. It was similar to the beat of the tunes she'd heard at the juke joint in Natchez with her own parents. Before she knew it, Miriam teared up thinking about her mother.

"Vera," Miriam said softly.

Vera jumped and moved away from the window. Her eyes were repentant, and she stood with her arms straight at her sides. "I'm sorry. I—"

"Don't worry about it." Miriam walked over to the window and peeked out. "Oh he's a looker. What is his name?"

Vera blushed. "Booker." She lowered her head to hide her smile. "He's a blues player from Mississippi."

Miriam's heart fluttered. "Mississippi?" She lifted Vera's chin, then placed her hands on both of the girl's shoulders. "Did I ever tell you dat I lived dere?"

Vera shook her head.

"I came to Kansas when I was young like you. So you got more in common wit dis Booker fella den you think."

Vera's smile stretched so wide that the sides of her face hurt. "He said I can sing, Mama. And I like him. I like music. I like him and his music. And . . . I wanna perform with him. Just to see . . ." Her voice tapered off.

Miriam looked at Booker through the window and her apprehension rose from somewhere deep in her stomach. He was a good-looking young man for sure. Too good-looking. His hands gently slid up and down his instrument, and Miriam guessed what he could do with a woman's skirt. The way his eyebrows lifted high as he landed each note indicated he was a confident man. Couldn't tell him nothing. And he was from the Deep South. Of course Vera was enamored. She wasn't used to the soil down there that made men like him. In a city like Chicago, Booker could take Vera on a ride. But Miriam was certain that her daughter couldn't handle the speed.

Miriam decided to offer a gentle warning: "My mother was very much in love wit my father. She woulda done anythin' for him. But he was in love wit someone else."

Vera's eyes got large. "Really?"

"Mm-hmm. Problem was they couldn't be together."

"Why?"

"Because life, baby. You lucky. You always knew freedom even while you were readyin' in my womb. Your grandparents—people from dat generation can't say de same. Dey mighta wanted one thing but circumstances beyond dere control kept 'em from it."

"Oh," Vera said, her eyes downcast.

"I'm tellin' you dis 'cause I don't want dat for you. Now I don' know 'bout dis young man, but I know how he already got you actin'. I saw de way you jumped when you saw me watchin' you. Even though I'm worried 'bout you 'cause you quite sheltered, I'm not gon' keep you from your freedom to love either. I'm just worried."

"About what?"

"Oh baby . . ." Miriam looked at her daughter with pity in her eyes. "Dere's so much you don' know 'bout de world, 'bout men. And I don' want you gettin' so wrapped up in one man so young. Go after ya dreams first like ya sister did."

Vera sighed.

"I just want you to be safe, dat's all."

"I will be safe."

Miriam pursed her lips. "Dere are ways to stop disease, you know. And pregnancy. Did you and him . . ."

"Mom! No! I—I wasn't even thinkin' 'bout dat."

"Well, you will be. And I want you to come to me before you do. Don't let no man teach you everythin' to know 'bout your own body." She sighed. "Now get to bed soon before ya daddy wakes up and catch you. He might just go and get his shotgun."

From that night on, Booker and Vera found their way to each other again and again. As soon as she knew her father was asleep, she'd meet Booker on the side of her house, and he'd play her a few notes before asking her to join in with her singing. After school, she'd hang out with her friends before cutting away to watch Booker practice with Cats, Fats, Gee, and Scoop. In time, she became their sixth bandmate, learning how to improvise and scat better than the rest of them. Booker would never admit that she was better than him, though, which she felt only made her work harder and smarter.

Booker was intriguing. He hadn't even tried to kiss her yet. Every time Vera thought he was about to, he'd give her a correction on how to sing or command a stage. Whenever he patted her on the back or shoulder for a job well done, her body held fire and water at the same time. He had to have known what he was doing to her. His calloused, veiny hands bore the markings of a man far more experienced than his nineteen years. Those fingers strummed more than the strings of a guitar. He wielded the universe every time he looked at her. But her patience was wearing thin. Soon she would be graduating. She could do domestic work like her mother or maybe learn how to become a seamstress. She could marry a deacon or someone who worked in the steel mills like her dad and live a congenial life. But it wasn't what she wanted.

One late afternoon during a basement rehearsal, Vera had just about had it. She stamped her foot midway through a song and wouldn't go any further.

"What's de matter, V?" Booker asked.

"What is the point of all this? Why am I singing and singing and singing and that's it?"

Cats, Fats, Gee, and Scoop leaned in toward one another, ready for a full-on lovers' quarrel.

"What you mean, what is de point of all dis? We goin' professional, dat's what."

"W-W-W-What?" Vera stammered.

Booker laughed. "You think we just doin' dis for fun?"

"You want me to really sing with y'all, in clubs and stuff?"

"Of course. We doin' all dis to get you ready."

"But I can't. My dad. He don' like blues or any secular stuff. He'd kill me."

"Well, den don' tell him."

"But—"

"Ah c'mon girl. You do everythin' your folks say?"

"If I did, would I be here?" Vera asked.

The band whistled and laughed. Booker slowly grinned.

"What about a stage name?" Scoop chimed in. "Somethin' dat no one will know you by if we put it on a flyer."

Booker's eyes roamed around the room as he brainstormed.

"I got it," Vera said.

The boys looked up at her.

Vera raised her eyes to the ceiling, then announced: "Violet."

"Why Violet?" Booker asked with a disapproving stare.

"Because dere were a lot of violets where I'm from in Kansas. Dey ain't got wildflowers in Mississippi?"

The boys laughed, and Booker's lips gradually curved into a smile. "Wildflower, huh? All right den. Let's see how wild you can get."

35

The humbling happened for Oliver. He'd assumed that since Ardelia had kept Tirzah's letter in pride of place that she still had strong feelings for him. He'd assumed that Sterling's framed letter next to it meant that they were still going to be family. He assumed that it wouldn't be long until they would get back together. They were still in touch after he moved into the new apartment in Murray Hill. He'd bring up memories of their shared life together, and she'd reply swiftly and thank him graciously each time. After a little while, however, she stopped replying as quickly, often leaving him on read for hours. If he asked to FaceTime, she'd tell him she preferred a phone call—a brief one—or text. She was "trying to focus"—her job and family research were taking up much of her time. The further Ardelia pulled away, the more Oliver pursued her: sending her dinner via UberEats, extra masks in the mail, aromatherapy sets, flowers, and chocolates.

Eventually, Oliver got tired of being the one who was doing most if not all of the reaching out. He couldn't understand. Isn't this what Ardelia wanted: for him to take the initiative? He was opening up about his life, filling her in on minutiae as much as he could. By some miracle, COVID rates didn't spike when people were gathering outside during the summer, and this relief provided space for Oliver to see glimmers of his former self. His feelings were not foreign to him any longer. His body started to feel like a home again.

What Oliver decided to do next was manipulative, but he saw no other option. He was determined that he was not going to reach out to Ardelia for a week and see whether she'd come toward him. On the first day, Oliver didn't hear from her, but it was too soon to cause him any alarm. On day two, he started to wonder if Ardelia had noticed that the pattern had been broken. By day three, Oliver knew that she must have, and his heart began to sink. By the end of his weeklong test, Oliver felt like a failure when he broke to reach out to say hello, to which she only responded with a "Hey, how are you?" Though they made small talk, Ardelia didn't care that he was gone, clearly, and he had too much pride to ask her why. They weren't in a relationship. He was the one who couldn't let go. But why hadn't she asked him to take Tirzah's letter when he packed his things? Why didn't she message him on the day he moved out when she realized that he'd left some belongings behind? What kind of game was she playing with him, and why was it working? He'd never been so bothered by another woman evidently being unbothered by him. He kept his phone on "Do Not Disturb" because each notification that didn't come from her only hurt him more.

Finally, as December was under way, Ardelia sent him a long message, saying that if he truly cared about her, he'd leave her alone. Completely. So she could heal.

Upon reading her words, Oliver sank into his desk chair at home, every part of his body reeling. He missed her. Oh, how he missed her. In the days that followed, he would sleep on the left side of the bed, as he once had when he lay beside Ardelia. In the morning, he would wake up, stretch out his arms, and turn toward the other side of the mattress to see that there was nothing in front of him but a stack of boxes still waiting to be unpacked and broken down. In the bathroom, he would sniff for hints of jasmine, rosemary oil, or peppermint oil but only detect the faint earthy smell of running water or Windex. Any music he heard could not overpower the vibrant memories of Ardelia playing her blues for them during dinnertime. No meal tasted as sweet if she were not beside him to share in the abundance. And worst of all, there was no one who he wanted to talk to in the morning or after a long day of working. There was no one who delighted him more to see. But she was gone. She really was, and the more he acknowledged it, the more he sensed a festering illness from which he was afraid he'd never recover.

On a Saturday morning, Oliver had exhausted himself with thinking of Ardelia and decided to reach out to his parents, who were usually the last people he want to talk to about his feelings.

Irene snatched the phone on the first ring and shrieked with glee when she saw Oliver on the FaceTime screen.

"Hi, Mom," Oliver said.

"Oh, baby . . ." Irene's silvery pixie cut shimmered in the light. In the background, Marshall was moving across the kitchen, adding ingredients to a sizzling cast-iron skillet. "It's so good to see you, even though you look mighty tired."

"I am . . ."

"Why don't you FaceTime us more often? You almost had me and Dad flying to New York just to check if you're okay."

Oliver weakly smiled.

"You okay, baby?" she asked.

"Just been goin' through it. Tired. Because of workin' in the hospitals, you know."

"It looks like more than that. Wait—" Irene scanned the screen. "Where are you right now?"

Oliver took a deep breath and caught his mother up on what had happened between him and Ardelia, starting from the beginning. By the time he got to his moving out, Irene had migrated into the kitchen so that Marshall could be in the conversation too. As Oliver went on, his parents' faces rose and fell and twisted and dropped so much that he wondered if they'd wake up the next morning with aching jaws. And then, suddenly, Oliver burst into tears. He covered his entire face with both hands and said nothing as his whole body trembled. After a few moments of reassurance from his parents that it was okay, Oliver removed his hands. His embarrassment was overcome by the relief of having released months upon months of disappointment, words said at the wrong time, words that could've been said at the right time, the touch starvation, the grieving, the yearning . . . all of the yearning. He cried until his voice almost gave out and his sleeves were too wet to catch any more tears. Once Oliver's tears stopped and his vision was clear, he saw his parents sitting there lovingly and patiently, concerned yet still present.

"Baby . . . you've been holding that in for a while, haven't you?" Irene asked.

Oliver nodded.

"I should've known something was up. I know you mentioned months ago that the venue canceled your wedding but it was a simple text. No follow-up, nothing. You didn't even let us know if you two were gonna reschedule it. I didn't want to pry but I knew it."

"Don't be no fool nah," Marshall chimed in. "That Ardelia is a good woman. A good, good woman—and that's hard to come by."

"And Oliver is a good man," his wife shot back.

"I didn't say he wasn't."

"I know, but I'm just sayin' . . . he's a good man. And he's good enough to see good too."

"That's right," Marshall concluded.

"What about Tirzah's letter?" Irene asked.

"It's still there on Ardelia's mantel," Oliver asked.

"Well, if y'all aren't going to be together then you need it back!"

"Irene . . ." Marshall interjected.

"No, nah-uh. A break needs to be a clean break. Besides, that's a family heirloom. It needs to be returned to us."

"Can't you see he still loves her?" Marshall asked.

"Of course I can, but love is not enough to sustain a relationship."

Oliver sighed. "I left the letter there with her because I thought we'd get back together. That this separation we had—me leaving first, then her breaking up with me—was all supposed to be temporary. We'd be back together just like Tirzah and Harrison were. It was a message I was sending to her."

Irene and Marshall stared at Oliver, confusion in their eyes.

"Why are y'all looking at me like that?"

"I . . . don't think that's true, son," Marshall said.

"What? What's not true?"

"I don't think Tirzah and Harrison ever got together," Irene said. "At least that's not the story I was told." She looked to her husband for reassurance.

"You're right. That wasn't the story," Marshall said.

"No," Oliver said, nervously laughing. Before he could question why he was reacting so strongly to this, he began blabbering and sputtering like a vehicle on its way out. "No but—no. No. You said—wait, I remember you saying—when-when-when-when I was young and you—you told me. Wait you told me—no." Oliver went over to his laptop and typed in Ancestry.com, a database that Ardelia often referenced in conversation, in a Google Chrome tab. Upon seeing the search results for "Tirzah Benjamin" and "Kansas," he pointed at the screen and yelled "Aha!" so loud it made Irene and Marshall jump. "See here?"

But when he scrolled down a little he saw that there was no Harrison Benjamin or any Harrison at all next to a Tirzah on any Kansas census. The only other man "near" Tirzah in the census pages was one named Free Benjamin who was married to a Novella Benjamin. He pored through other results of this Tirzah in Kansas, who lived in the same time period as this young man Free, and discovered two obituary copies. Strange, Oliver thought as he inched closer to the screen. There were two obituaries for the Tirzah with identical birth dates. However, one was listed as a Tirzah Benjamin and the other as a Tirzah Levi. Levi? Who was Levi? It soon dawned on him that Levi was the surname of the man who Tirzah referenced in her letter to Harrison, the one Oliver gifted to Ardelia.

Oliver got quiet and leaned back in his seat. "They never did it," he finally said. "They never got back together."

"Sad," Irene said. "But not surprising, given the era. Families were separated all the time."

"Mom, I'll call y'all back later," Oliver said suddenly. Irene and Marshall protested, but he promised repeatedly that he wouldn't go back on his word. All this time, he'd believed that Harrison was his great-great-great-grandfather, married to his great-great-great-grandmother, Tirzah. He didn't know if he misremembered the story his parents had told him, or if he'd crafted this whole story in his head, but that's what he'd believed and clung to.

Oliver looked out the window facing the street corner and watched pedestrians passing to and fro. Something about this reminded him of his visit outside Ardelia's apartment after she told him about Sterling's declining health. He could not imagine how lonely she'd felt, watching her father die through a phone screen, as she could not touch, let alone reach the man she was planning to marry. Oliver blinked. All this time, he believed Tirzah's letter to be an amulet that would safekeep his and Ardelia's bond from the moment he placed it in his then fiancée's hands. Though he'd tried so hard to win Ardelia back, perhaps that wasn't the point. Their relationship was in jeopardy from the moment he left her standing there in shock as he packed to leave their home. He'd been too confident, too wrapped up in his head that day. But now he was going to reach out again to Ardelia, even if he was violating a boundary.

"Hi" wasn't enough. She wouldn't respond to that. "I know I shouldn't be reaching out" might be met with a block. Instead, "Tirzah and Harrison never made it," Oliver texted her.

His phone rang immediately. All Oliver had to see was the letter "A" and he immediately picked up.

"Hey . . ." he said, his voice suddenly full of doubt.

"Hey . . ." Ardelia said. "Did you send that message because I'm such a research buff, you knew it would be like a bat signal to get me to respond?"

Oliver swallowed a large ball of saliva. "Kinda . . . but that's not all."

"Oh?"

"When I left you back in January, you really didn't think I was coming back, did you?"

"What does it matter now?"

"It matters to me."

Ardelia sighed. "I didn't. No matter what you said, I didn't."

"Do you think I took you for granted?"

"Oh wow. Uh . . ." Ardelia sounded nervous. "A little bit, I think. But what does this have to do with Tirzah and Harrison?"

Oliver recounted what his parents had told him and that he'd confirmed online. "All this time I thought they found each other again, just like we would. I know it doesn't make sense, but I was wrong. I focused so much on the end of their story, which never was the truth in the first place, rather than thinking about Tirzah's loss, and maybe even . . . your loss."

"It really makes me feel good to hear you say that," she said softly. "Loss is why I'm doing what I'm doing right now—running myself ragged with all these censuses and death certificates, and all this other shit."

"How is it going?"

"It's going. I'm just hitting some blocks that I feel like my grandmother could clear up for me, if she weren't putting up so much of a wall. She's the oldest person in my family and no matter how much I try to get her to talk, I come up with nothing."

"So go to her."

"What?"

"Go to her. Vaccines are being rolled out. Plan a visit."

"Back to Chicago? I don't know, man. . . . Chicago is not . . . my favorite place. It's just . . . too much. Too many memories, for one."

"Precisely. Just think about it."

"Oliver?"

"What's up?"

"If Tirzah and Harrison didn't reunite, then where did Harrison go?"

"I'm about as clueless about that as I am about my own last name."

36

1913

Novella knew that Miriam and Free had to be doing something during Tirzah's funeral. As soon as she saw Corinthian walk out the door as the grievers lined up for one last look at Tirzah's body, she knew. Novella tried to put it out of her mind as she approached Tirzah's casket. When she reached it, she was startled by how beautifully the funeral home people had prepared her face; she looked like she was simply resting. Novella hoped that the fact that death hadn't altered her looks meant she must have gone to heaven. That lady had been through enough—she'd survived slavery and the murder of her husband, avenged his death, and moved hundreds of miles away to start a new life. If anyone deserved paradise, Tirzah did.

Novella was saddened that Tirzah had gone off to the Lord yet felt blessed to have had her for as long as she did. If it were not for Tirzah's instruction in the kitchen, Novella wouldn't have known how to feed her babies properly. If it weren't for Tirzah's discipline, the children would have run wild in and out of the house. If it weren't for Tirzah's insight, Novella would've gone crazy over Free's wandering a long time ago. That last one had been the most difficult. There were many nights when Novella would've chased him in any direction on earth to see what was driving him away from the beautiful home they'd built together. To keep her happy, he didn't have to do anything but help take care of their children, eat the food she cooked for him, and lay his head down beside her at night. But he couldn't even give her that.

As a matter of fact, Novella thought, Free had never really given her anything. The wind passing through a cracked window stayed longer than he did. When Tirzah died, Free had buried his head on his mother's still lap and done something Novella had never seen him do before: cry. He cried and cried, though no amount of tears would bring her back to pat him on the head or kiss him in the space between his eyebrows. But Tirzah's body wasn't even in the ground yet before her only son was back to his usual behavior. Briefly, Novella sat in the pew enraged by Free's audacity during his mother's funeral. But when the organist struck a chord that motivated everyone to whoop and holler, Novella readjusted herself and relief settled in. She held on tight to her youngest children seated on either side of her and realized that Free was never hers. Tirzah was. The babies Novella carried and held in her arms were. The tears came, and she cried with abandon until a group of older women crowded around her and laid hands on her shoulders. But the weeping felt good. She cried for the mother she had. She cried for her marriage. Once she was all out of tears, she sat upright and felt a strange sense of self-possession.

The night following the funeral, Novella found herself taking an evening stroll through the fields behind her home with only the full moon to illuminate her path. She stretched out her arms to graze the tall cornstalks, and her bare feet touched the dirt. She smiled and laughed as if she were a young girl again, remembering what it felt like to have so many fewer cares, to lose track of time, to be concerned only with being alive. But actually, it wasn't true. Novella had been a child of mourning, a child without parents, a wanderer. This feeling of lightness had to have been from an ancient time, a past life. But this was what it felt like: freedom.

"What are you doin' here?"

Novella stopped and looked up to realize that she'd reached Miriam's home, where Corinthian was standing with a lantern on his porch. She looked at her dirtied feet and the dirt on her dress, then back up at him.

"I . . ." Novella opened her arms, then dropped them at her sides. "I think I might have lost my mind. Or freed it." She laughed.

"You definitely look like you done lost your mind. Wit all due respect, ma'am."

"Don't call me ma'am, Corinthian. Your wife and my husband been in de bed together for years. We practically family."

Corinthian quickly looked over his shoulder, then shut the front door behind him before moving a few steps closer to her. "Where you get off talkin' like dat now?"

Novella shrugged. "I don't care anymore. I don't. . . . Dere's nothin' else left to care about. Tirzah gone. My husband gone. It's best I be gone wit my chirren. We gotta sell de house anyway to pay off Free's debts."

"Better you sell den have it taken from you."

Novella widened her eyes. "Not you too, Corinthian."

"Yep. Loan denied. Credit denied. Don't you be goin' around tellin' people dat."

"'S not like you de only one. It's happenin' to so many of us, it's like dey want us to leave." She sighed. "Miriam know?"

Corinthian scoffed. "I ain't tell her yet. She ain't sat down long enough for me to."

"Oh." Novella walked up to the porch and grabbed ahold of the rail. "How you do it?"

"Do what?"

"Handle it all dese years. 'S different for me 'cause I'm a woman. But you as a man?" Novella shook her head. "I don't know how you didn' kill her and him both."

"And send dem both to eternity together? Not a chance."

Novella laughed before he continued.

"But what am I s'posed to do, Novella?"

"You coulda left her. Married someone else."

"Same goes for you," he said, and Novella raised her eyebrows. "We more alike den you think. We just two people who fell in love wit de wrong people."

"You think dey was always wrong for us even wit all de chirren and everythin'?"

"I ain't say all dat, nah. Because wrong don't always lead to more wrong. We got our chirren out of it. But I'm talkin' wrong for us—" Corinthian pointed to his chest. "Us. Not no one else. Even wit all de good dat mighta come outta dat wrong."

"I mighta forced Free too much. I always wanted to get married to him. Always. Maybe I shouldn't have."

"Don't go feelin' bad for yourself 'bout things dat happened years ago. Free's doin' what he did when he met you at de altar: used his free will. God given us all free will, and we decide what to do wit it."

"Choices."

"Indeed. Just as much as I choose to stand here talkin' to you and you beside my porch talkin' to me."

Novella fantasized about seducing Corinthian. She could see Corinthian quite clearly with the help of his lantern, and she liked what she saw. He was handsome with a wide chest and thick hands. And she was sure the sex would have been explosive right there, where every rustling sound in the nearby fields would only drive him further into her body with excitement. She could've had him. She understood the ways a man held a woman in his gaze if he wanted her. But Novella wished Corinthian a good night and disappeared in the fields with the knowledge that he was watching her every step of the way.

In the days that followed, Novella's ears became less attuned to Free's comings and goings, and thought more of the community. Now that Tirzah was gone, Novella saw Nicodemus with eyes more aligned with reality. Grief may have been a part of it, but she couldn't deny that she was getting that itch to move again. That adolescent urge to flee she'd felt years ago in Shreveport reignited in her body, and she experienced fleeting moments of excitement at the most random moments. In all the thoughts, she never imagined Free beside her, and she felt better for that. How easy the decision was for her not to care about where he landed at the end of the night. How liberating the surrendering of him to the world. But she was not alone. She had her dreams.

She'd continued to work occasionally as a stenographer around town, but the opportunities had started dwindling as more businesses shuttered and friends moved away. Her lifeline was the church, and it was there that she came across the *Kansas Baptist Herald*, where her eyes were soon drawn to a full-page advertisement: Shiloh Baptist Church of Tennessee Town in Topeka had job openings for secretaries, stenographers, custodians, and Sunday school teachers. Novella thought that maybe Topeka would be the best place to move. The transition might not be that hard. She wrote to the church and told them how she was from Nicodemus and the daughter-in-law to the late Tirzah Benjamin. The church secretary responded by telling her of the Colored Women's Club, the many schools, the fur stores, the haberdasheries there in Topeka, along with a route on how to get there. Novella put a plan into motion.

She told the children to start packing their things, and sent mail to her adult children of the upcoming move. Free was gone most days and nights, and the longer he stayed away, the more she realized how little she needed him, how little she ever had. Everything and everyone underneath the roof was just fine, and she began to entertain the thought of leaving him behind. For good.

Until one night, while the children were fast asleep and Novella was having tea, she heard a stomping near the front door. Before she could run to the bedroom closet to pull out Tirzah's pistol, the door swung open and Free was standing in the threshold with a large bag slung over his shoulder.

"Ain't you happy to see me?" Free said, his breath heavy and his expression proud.

"Not really," Novella said.

"Well, you will be once I show you what I got."

Free walked over to the table and plopped the bag down on its surface, giving his wife a sly look. Curious, Novella followed. Free opened the bag and pulled the sides down to expose wads of cash.

She gasped and looked around. "Where'd you get all dat money?"

"I won it. What do you think I've been doing all this time?"

"Climbin' between Miriam's legs, dat's what."

"I've been doing nothing of the sort."

Novella sucked her teeth and flicked her right hand at him.

"Anyway. I won this money for us. So we don't have to sell the house."

"It don't matter."

"What you mean, it don't matter?"

"Me and de chirren movin' to Topeka. You can stay in Nicodemus wit whoever you want but we goin'."

Free took a few steps back and started to laugh. "Woman, what the hell do you mean?"

"Just what I said."

"And what about this house?"

"Tirzah told me she wanted dis house sold to pay off your debts."

"Didn't you hear what I just said? Look at this money!"

"How I know you ain't get dat money some other kind of way? You already been to jail once." Novella cut her eyes at him. "And you been nothin' but a disappointment your whole life."

Free lunged at Novella and raised his hand at her but she puffed out her chest, like she was inviting him to strike. He looked at his palm underneath the strong light, then back at Novella, and shuddered. Then he backed away and stumbled out the door, and returned into the night from whence he came.

Most mornings, Novella woke up waiting to wonder about Free and his whereabouts. But she was surprised by how easily she could go about her day without thinking about her husband. After all, he had left that bag of cash behind, which she'd hidden under the bed.

Then one day, Miriam came knocking on her door with envelopes in her hands. She handed them to Novella and told her that she was leaving for Chicago soon with Corinthian and their daughters. As Miriam ran back down the front steps, Novella called out to her, asking what the envelopes were. Miriam stopped, turned around, and shouted back, "Don't give it away! Whatever you do, do not give it away!" Then she disappeared into the fields.

It was soon evident to Novella that Miriam and her family had already left Nicodemus because Free started coming around their house more often. His boots dragged on the floor, and he barely raised his chin to acknowledge anyone. Not like the children cared. The last of their twelve children were in adolescence and fully preoccupied with exploring the town, gossiping, and spending time in nature. Novella didn't give a good Goddamn about Free either. He could fix his own plate and wash and iron his own clothes. Sometimes he would slip his hand under the covers at night and caress her waist, but Novella would turn further toward the window and feign a snore until Free returned to his side of the bed. In the daytime, Novella would sometimes find Free packing his belongings, but they never spoke about the move. She had everything in place, and Free knew it. Whenever Free wasn't around, Novella would get acquainted and reacquainted with the envelopes Miriam left her.

They were letters, revealing that Tirzah was in love with someone other than the late Isaac Levi, and she loved him deeply. Often, Novella sensed the details were too intimate for anyone's eyes other than those of this man Tirzah called Harrison. However, Tirzah was honored to be able to recognize a level of zeal that she never experienced—not even for her own husband. Novella would press these letters to her heart and feel as though Tirzah was standing right beside her. She'd lose track of time and frequently leave parts

of these keepsakes in different areas of the home where she last en-
grossed herself in them. The fact that no one—neither Free nor her
children—tampered with them wherever they wound up in the house
only strengthened Novella's belief that Tirzah was here, protecting
these invaluable objects.

The day before the Benjamins were set to move—about a month
after Tirzah's passing—when everything had been sold, discarded, or
packed, Novella went out to the mailbox and saw that the editors of the
local newspaper had sent a copy of Tirzah's obituary for fact-checking.
She pressed the envelope to her chest and smiled. A keepsake, Novella
thought, so that they could keep some part of Tirzah close as they
made their new home in Topeka. She'd drafted all the words herself
for the paper, but couldn't wait to see the details of Tirzah's life. But
as soon as she unfolded the paper, she saw an egregious error in the
first line: Tirzah's last name was listed as Levi. Tirzah Levi. She went
inside of the house to see Free fortuitously passing by the front door.

"Tirzah Levi?!" Novella shook the paper in his face. "Don't nobody but you, me, and God know dat was her name."

He exploded. "*Is* her name! That's her name! That's been her
name ever since the day she married my pa. She ain't never left him
so she leaves the earth with that name."

"She is a Benjamin! We all are! We been dat way ever since we
came to Nicodemus."

"But it ain't real! And besides, she was my ma!" Free smacked his
chest and his voice sounded like that of a child. "Mine! Not yours! And
besides, I'm the man of this house and I get final say!"

"'De man of dis house,'" Novella said, her tone mocking. "I been
more of de man of dis house den you for a long time and you know it."

"Woman—"

"So you done went behind my back and tried to undo all dat I
did, huh?" Novella said. "You ain't got enough time to be dere for ya
chirren but you got enough time to change a goddamn last name?"

"It's my pa's last name!" Free yelled. Their youngest children peeked their heads out from their bedroom. "Am I the only one who cares about his legacy? My own mama barely spoke a word about him since we moved here and—" He shook his head.

"Nuh-uh, go on. You finish what you started sayin'."

Free took a deep breath and briefly shut his eyes. He took a seat at the kitchen table and leaned forward. "Novella . . . sometimes I wonder if she ever loved him. You remember when I found all that stuff in her Bible? That advertisement?"

Novella looked down at the ground and bit her tongue for a moment. "You still thinkin' bout dat?" She pulled out a chair and sat down across from him. "But dat was years ago."

"I think about it all the time."

"Why ain't you never tell me?"

"Because . . . you were so focused on gettin' married."

She exhaled with resignation. "I was. Dat I was."

"That you were. You were so focused on getting married, and I was sitting there—just some boy—wondering if his parents, the two people who loved him most in the world, ever really loved each other."

Novella gripped both of Free's arms and pulled him closer to her. "Listen," she said, "I saw your mother shoot Spencer Ambrose in de face. His blood and skin and his insides splatterin' on de wall. I saw it. Wit my own two eyes. And I saw how proud Tirzah was when she did it. If love ain't killin' a man, knowin' all dat we know about what Spencer was capable of after what he did to your pa, den no, Tirzah never loved your father."

He shook his head. "Why didn't she ever tell me?"

She shrugged. "We had to move so quickly. You were so mad at her and at de world. Maybe she thought it was too much at de time and you'd go tellin' everybody in Nicodemus wit'out thinkin'."

Something shifted in Free's eyes. They seemed alleviated of their burden, as though they belonged to a child rather than a grown man. "She really killed him?" he asked, his voice sounding like a child's too.

"Yes. Dat's why we had to change our name—to get away, Free. De

Ambrose family is rich. Dey woulda came lookin' for her. We became Benjamins not in spite of your daddy but *because* of what she did in his name. You understand?"

Free nodded. "But it's been years. Who would go looking for Levis in Kansas of all places?"

"You wanna take dat chance? And risk us and our chirren?"

He sighed. "No, of course not. You're right."

"Right." Novella rose to her feet. "Now lemme go on down to de church house and see if we can change dis for de records. We don't need to be leavin' a trail like dis behind."

Free stood up too and gently took the paper out of her hand. "This stays here. That's my only request. You can change whatever you need to change over there but this right here?" He held up the paper. "I need to remember that she was a Levi. That she was my father's wife. It's one of the only things I have left of her."

How Novella wanted to tell him that that wasn't the only thing that was left. That there were letters that Miriam left behind. But in that moment, she nodded and left. Now she had a secret. She would tell him in time, but it would not be today.

37

FEBRUARY 2021

"The Cold Food Blues"

I waited up all night for you to come home
I waited up all night for you to come home
Just for you to leave me here all alone

Bought me the best meat and bread a woman could buy
For a busy man who run around and tell me a lie
Sitting here at the table with your cold food
Wondering where you are as I cry

My dear daddy never did this to mama
And my mama never did this to daddy
They been together for years
And they always been happy

Figure I take a train out of here
And find me a better man
Off on 4th street and south ave
Is where I'll stand

Bought me the best meat and bread a woman could buy
For a busy man who run around and tell me a lie
Sitting here at the table with your cold food
Wondering where you are as I cry

Jesus waiting on me to come home
He say I been gone too long
He waiting on 4th and south ave
Begging me to leave this life alone

We done moved away as exodus
Instead of leaning further on him
We done moved away as exodus
And that's why life been so grim

I wanted everything fast
I want everything now
I sing this song

When my knees shoulda bowed
'Cause my daddy was ready to go
But my momma didn't wanna leave
And I wanted something different
But I can't handle what I done received

'Cause we done moved away as exodus
Instead of leaning further on him
We done moved away as exodus
And that's why life been so grim

Ardelia had pored over these lyrics with such acute focus that she could recite the lines forward and backward. These words that

Violet sang were without any accompaniment from Booker Stone, one of two songs in which Violet had the sole writing credit.

These days, Ardelia felt doubtful about pretty much everything. She'd gone back on her word and resumed talking to Oliver. Healing might not come soon enough, if at all, she feared. And yet, him reaching out meant he still cared about her, that she still held some kind of power over him. Tirzah's letter still sat on her mantelpiece. Who was she kidding? She hadn't even bothered to tell him to pick it up after all these months, and he never brought it up either. Ardelia winced, thinking of how she and Oliver were becoming *those* kinds of people, those whose relationships were once built, later broken, and now wafted along without clarity because the murkiness provided safe cover from fears left unspoken. When Ardelia listened to Violet's music, she figured she didn't want to be with Oliver. He left her and she knew too much about men leaving. But she could not help but look toward the front door as she replayed "Cold Food Blues," believing that she was a woman-in-waiting, like a singer almost a century older than her.

She'd been listening to these records since she was a child. But now, the lyrics carried a deeper, much more painful resonance given the conditions of her own romantic life. She missed touch. Hips bumping each other in the kitchen, legs brushing up against each other on the couch.

New York never lacked for men, but she wasn't sure that was a good thing. Before Oliver, Ardelia had found herself in situations where the attraction was there, but the commitment was not. The men's names and faces blurred together. She found a way to be okay with drifting beneath someone who had good conversation, a good job, good looks. But the men, she knew, believed that there might be someone better across the Brooklyn Bridge, waiting for the L train at Union Square, sitting beside them at Corner Social, or behind them in line at the Trader Joe's on Columbus—and sometimes she believed this too.

Before she met Oliver, she hadn't known that men like him truly existed. Her family worried that someone as attractive and intelligent as she was by herself was a problem. No matter how much the aunties smiled in her face, they expressed their concerns more gravely with each year that passed, and that unease rubbed off on her. What good was a nuclear family, anyway, if she hadn't had one and turned out just fine? Her family was full of wives, husbands, mistresses, and backdoor lovers; children and side children; siblings, half siblings, and siblings disguised as cousins. Her family had splintered off and sutured with others so many times that no one she knew was ever sure of their original line. Then again, she never asked. Her father was enough of a mystery as it was.

Ardelia would spin like this and lose track of time. But then she'd stop herself and return to the lyrics in search of biographical clues instead of emotional resonance. Many blues artists referenced their backgrounds in their songs. Robert Johnson sang about Mississippi and Arkansas in "Last Fair Deal Gone Down" and "Terraplane Blues." "Levee Camp Moan" by Son House, "Muddy Water" by Bessie Smith, and "Highway 49" by Howlin' Wolf revealed the artists' Mississippi connections. But Violet was different. First, she went by only one name, which set her apart from her contemporaries. Second, she didn't reference Mississippi in her songs—only Booker did. The only location that she mentioned twice was the corner of Fourth Street and South Avenue.

Ardelia spent weeks poring over Chicago maps from the first half of the twentieth century, telephoned many a historian and urban planner, and came away with the knowledge that there had never been a Fourth Street intersecting South Avenue in Chicago at any time, and perhaps anywhere else in Illinois, for that matter. If Violet hadn't wanted people to know who she really was, she'd done a good job. Almost a century later, a professional researcher with a huge library and archive center like the Schomburg at her disposal *and* the whole internet still couldn't come up with much.

What Ardelia could find were bits and pieces scattered across obscure online blues forums and scanned copies of materials from the blues archives at Ole Miss. Violet and Booker Stone had never made it big. More details about Booker Stone were discovered through Ardelia's discussions with music historians from New York City to Sunflower County, Mississippi: his date and place of birth, his parents' names and occupations, his work in Mississippi before moving to Chicago, and his death at the age of forty-seven. Violet died at twenty-nine, a fact that chilled her. All the secondary sources that Ardelia gathered through books, interview transcripts, and newspaper articles made her suspect that Violet was born in Chicago. But Ardelia couldn't detect a Chicago inflection in Violet's voice, nor a hint of a Mississippi accent. Ardelia wondered if this had been held against her. She wasn't talking about Clarksdale or Gulfport or levee camps or the fast life in the streets of Chicago in her songs. Her music might've been alluding to a place with a small reputation for rhythm and blues compared to the aforementioned places.

Ardelia would have to go to Chicago. Oliver had been right, though she wouldn't remind him of this. If she could resituate herself in the Windy City, she could perhaps understand or get a sense of what Violet had seen, and maybe what her own grandmother didn't want her to see. Ardelia spoke of her plans to visit her aunt and grandmother, and they were happy to have her home. But Ardelia wanted one condition to be clear first: as senior citizens, they would both get the vaccine when it became available to Illinois senior citizens in early March. Despite their reservations about the vaccine in general, they agreed.

Meanwhile, signs of life were reemerging in New York. More people filled the streets, and restaurants created more outdoor dining sheds to save business. Ardelia, along with her colleagues, were permitted to be back on site. Event programming resumed with strict restrictions on capacity and safety protocols, and the Schomburg allowed more visitors to venture in and study within its walls during limited hours. From behind her desk, Ardelia could sense the lingering fear and hesitation in the people who smiled at her while they quietly walked to an empty table or cubicle on the far side of the room.

When she wasn't researching Violet or retrieving a book for a visitor, Ardelia would return to the last exhibit the Schomburg put on before lockdown—the Black Soldiers. She thought of how sad and unmoored she was then; now her mind had sharpened with focus on her family research that began with a curiosity about her father being a soldier himself. Ardelia liked to check out the Black Soldiers exhibition pieces to remind herself of that time before anyone knew what was coming. Then she returned to that unnamed soldier who stirred her attention a year ago. His photo was preserved inside of an acid-free folder in the second drawer on the left-hand side of her desk. She placed him on the surface of her worktable and stared at him under the fullness of the overhead lights.

"Excuse me?"

Ardelia jumped backward in her seat. An older Black woman in loose, neutral clothing and gold baubles adorning her neck and wrists stood in front of her. Her large hips pressed against the edge of the desk and her pixie wig was lopsided. The acrylic nails on her fingers were chipped and she had a few gold caps on her bottom teeth.

"Hello," Ardelia said. "How can I help you?"

"I wanted to ask you a question."

"Sure."

"An old friend of mine passed away some time ago and I know she collected a ton of things."

Oh boy, Ardelia thought. She had to stop herself from taking an exhausted breath. It was not unusual for an older person to ask if the Schomburg was interested in archiving their families' whatchamacallits in order to get some money. She should've known that as more family members died off, the number of inquiries would spike.

"And I wanted to know the steps to take for the Schomburg to consider storing the materials."

Ardelia nodded. "Have you had these items organized and labeled?"

"Yes, ma'am. We got them stored in acid-free cardboard boxes and they've been kept for over a year. But purposefully. We know these things are precious."

Ardelia smiled, impressed. "And how many materials are we talking about?"

"Oh whew." The lady itched the nape of her neck, then patted down the back of her wig. "Could be hundreds. This was my dear friend's wealth, you see. But we were thinking of showing her things to the Harlem community first and then maybe after, sending them along to y'all."

"Have you drafted a proposal for us yet?"

"A proposal?"

"Oh. Yes, this is standard. Here, let me show you," Ardelia said. Close but not quite there, she thought. She directed the woman to the part of the institution's website where she could submit a proposal.

"Ah, I see," the woman said. "And what is your name?"

"Ardelia Gibbs."

"Thank you, Ardelia. I'll get on it." Ardelia rose to shake her hand, and the woman was about to turn in the direction of the elevator when she did a double take at the black-and-white image on the desk. "The U.S. Colored Infantry."

"I'm sorry?" Ardelia was already sitting back down.

"The U.S. Colored Infantry." The woman pointed at the man's uniform. "That's a Civil War soldier. See there?" She pointed to the top of the man's head. "That's a forage cap. The style of it makes me think it's a Union soldier. And that . . ." The lady leaned her head to the side. Ardelia pushed the photo closer to her. "That . . . could be Hill City in the background. You see how all the ground keeps going up behind him. And he looks like he's near water. That there could be a steamboat. Maybe he was a part of the Seventieth Regiment. Vicksburg, Mississippi. But you'd know better than me."

Her jaw dropped. "How are you making these guesses?"

"My dear old friend. She taught me a lot about how to look for these kinds of clues."

"Was your friend a historian?"

"Not a traditionally trained one, but I'd like to think that she was."

"What did you say your name was?" Ardelia asked.

"Sherrie. Do you have a piece of paper and a pen?"

"Sure."

Sherrie scribbled her name and number and email address and passed it to Ardelia. "Here's my contact information."

"Well, Miss Sherrie, it was a pleasure meeting you. I'll email you so we can stay in touch."

"You do that."

As the elevator doors shut and transported her away, Ardelia wondered, Who was that lady really?

And why did Mississippi keep finding her?

38

MARCH 2021

The day Ardelia arrived in Chicago, Geraldine sat in her bathtub for hours. Even in her nineties, Geraldine had her wits about her and retained her dignity by bathing herself. She may have moved a little slower, but she refused to let anyone help her so much as make a plate at a BBQ. Aunt Hazel would tell folks out in public that she was her caretaker, and Geraldine allowed her only to save face. Hazel was divorced and her children had careers and families of their own, so once she retired, there wasn't much else for her to do besides yoga and water aerobics two or three times a week. And besides, Geraldine didn't mind the company. They would watch reruns of *Judge Judy*, *Golden Girls*, and *Good Times* together, cook dinner on Sundays, and go for walks through Lake Shore Park if the temperature was bearable. They planned to pick Ardelia up from the airport as they'd been doing since she came home from Bryn Mawr for school breaks. But about an hour and a half or so before they needed to leave the house, Geraldine went into the bathroom and did not come out.

At first, Hazel didn't notice because she was too busy double-checking that she had all of Ardelia's favorite snacks and that the spare room was properly outfitted with extra blankets. But when she went to check that the basket of spare toiletries she'd placed in the bathroom was complete, she discovered that the door was locked. "Ma?" She knocked a few times. No answer. She knocked again and heard nothing, not even the water swishing and lapping. Hazel flew into a panic, but thinking fast, pulled a bobby pin out of her hair and jammed it into the doorknob. Her hands were shaking, but she got the knob to turn and almost fell into the bathroom. There was Geraldine sitting in the tub, totally fine, staring back at her, bewildered.

"Ma!" Hazel yelled. "You didn't hear me screaming for you? I thought you were dead!"

Geraldine's eyes fixed on the floral curtains and she exhaled heavily.

Hazel was worried. Geraldine didn't say a word even after she helped her out of the tub and into some fresh clothes. She greeted Ardelia when the girl got into the car at the airport, but dipped into the background while Hazel and Ardelia chatted away about anything and everything under the sun. But Geraldine wasn't having a cognitive slip; she wasn't speaking because she was watching. She knew exactly why Ardelia had returned to Chicago. Hazel had told her of her intention to send Ardelia Sterling's artwork so that her granddaughter could have sweet memories of her father's talent to balance those of his addiction, imprisonment, and abandonment. She hadn't imagined, however, that Ardelia would become obsessed with learning more and more and more. Geraldine hoped that if she stayed quiet, Ardelia wouldn't ask her any questions about Violet or Booker Stone or blues or none of that. Seeing the records peeking out from Ardelia's tote bag, she worried that she was in for the third degree.

That night, both Hazel and Ardelia were kept up by Geraldine's gentle pacing around the house; she floated in and out of rooms, the ends of her white slip fluttering in the air. Ardelia was still up, skimming through more forums and academic journals, and she heard the water running in another part of the house, footsteps advancing and receding, and at one point, some humming.

Alone with her own thoughts, Ardelia stared at the ceiling and thought about how much her grandmother and father were alike, both unhelpful. Over the course of a week, try as she might to squeeze those thoughts out of her mind, the exhaustion of running around the South Side of Chicago without any success only heightened her feeling of hopelessness.

She'd tried to begin with Maxwell Street Market, a place where she'd read that many Chicago blues artists got their start by playing outside for anyone to hear. It no longer existed. What stood in its place were athletic fields owned by the University of Illinois. Ardelia was able to sift through the school's collections and found some black-and-white photographs of Maxwell Street in the 1930s and '40s, but there was no sign of Violet. She thought she might've seen Booker Stone in one of the images, but couldn't be sure. That man could've been anyone. And besides, he wasn't even playing his guitar in the photograph.

Then she headed to Gatewood Tavern, also known as "the Gates." Any blues artist worth their salt would've performed at that nightclub. According to some folkway recordings Ardelia had found through the Smithsonian, the club was located on West Lake Street and North Artesian Avenue. But when she got there, she saw nothing besides supply stores, a currency exchange shop, a few parking lots, and some social service organizations. There was no sign indicating the area's important role in blues history. No plaque. No nothing. The same went for the famous Metropolitan Theater on 4644 South King Drive, where all kinds of heavy hitters like Bessie Smith, Louis Armstrong, and Cab Calloway performed—a large, unmarked plot of land between an insurance company and cleaners. At times, Ardelia would stand on a corner, close her eyes, and steady her breath in hopes that she would be able to hear Violet crooning or Booker Stone strumming his guitar somewhere down the avenue. But she was only met by the sound of cars honking or engines blowing.

"Don't worry," Hazel said at the dining-room table one night when

Geraldine had already gone off to sleep. Ardelia had hardly touched the fried catfish, cabbage, and wild rice that her aunt had cooked, just moving her food around with her fork, dramatically sighing. "My oh my," Hazel continued. "I don't think I've seen you look like that since you were a teenager hung up on some boy."

"Sorry," Ardelia said. "It's just so frustrating. It's like whatever idea I have or any reference to her no longer exists in Chicago. You would think I'd find more in this city since there's so much history here."

Hazel took her plate to the kitchen and returned with a stemmed wineglass and a bottle of Pinot Noir. She uncorked the wine and poured Ardelia a glass. "To calm your nerves."

"What about for yourself?"

"Well . . ." Hazel looked over her shoulder. "Might as well. I tend to drink when Mom isn't around anyway." She went back into the kitchen and got a glass for herself.

After the two women clinked glasses and took a sip, Ardelia leaned in toward her. "Lemme ask you something: you've lived in Chicago all your life and you're in your seventies."

"All right nah, where you goin' with this?"

"There's never been a South Avenue and Fourth Street—has there? No sense in me going on a wild-goose chase tomorrow."

"On the South Side? Absolutely not."

"I just wish Grandma would tell me something, anything. It's strange how she has such a good memory, but she doesn't remember this."

"Maybe she doesn't want to remember."

"What do you mean?"

"The older you get, the more guarded you become about certain details of your life. Your generation is different. Maybe 'cause of the internet or something, but y'all like to tell and let everything hang out."

Ardelia snorted. "All right, I can see that. Well, I don't have much time. My job is allowing me to work remotely for another two weeks and then that's it, I think. I'm not sure I can get an extension."

"You're doing all that you can. I'm impressed, if that counts for anything."

"Thanks. It's just that I've already been here for a week, and I've done nothing besides get in my ten thousand steps a day walking around Bronzeville."

"You'll find something, Ardelia. Have you tried the churches? What about Olivet Baptist?"

"Oh wow . . ." A light bulb went off in Ardelia's head. Olivet's four walls held a massive repository of information about those who'd settled in or drifted in and out of the neighborhood.

"It had occurred to me before, but I dropped the idea," she said. "Because why would they have anything on her when blues was considered the devil's music when she was alive?"

"Oh girl." Hazel sipped her wine. "The ones playing 'the devil's music' were usually the people who got to Sunday service the earliest. Someone there can point you in the right direction."

Ardelia hadn't been to Olivet in a while and she rehearsed what she was going to say to any Olivet staff members if they asked about New York. It's fine. I'm doing well. Work's good. Hanging in there. A nod, smile, a Christian hug with a light pat on the shoulder. And if one of them were so much as to ask about her bare ring finger, she'd tell them that she was getting her band resized because she lost weight.

No matter how long Ardelia had been away from Olivet, she always admired its architecture, which was styled in the French Gothic tradition. She couldn't deny that this place was special not only to her family but also to Black Chicago at large, her family never letting her forget that this sanctuary was a place of peace and mobilization during the 1919 race riots so they'd always be safe there.

But there was no Violet in their files either. Adjacent to the pastor's office, the impressively sized repository was air-conditioned, the boxes it contained all properly sealed.

"Nothing?" the secretary, who could not have been much older than Ardelia, asked.

Ardelia flipped through the index tabs of the obituary binder associated with the year of Violet's death, 1937, as well one year ahead or below just in case. "No Violet here . . ."

"Well, it was a pseudonym, you said. You're not looking for the name Violet, are you?"

Ardelia sighed, exhausted. "I think it's a pseudonym, but I could be wrong. But I assume that some obituary would mention a singer of note passing."

"Not necessarily," the woman told her. "I've heard that families sometimes obscured what someone did for a living if it was in any way tied to their deaths. Like, let's say, someone was a great pool player and got shot in an alleyway after they beat the wrong guy in a game. No one would want to bring it up."

Ardelia hadn't consider that. "Hmm . . ."

"How old was she when you said she died?"

"Twenty-nine, I believe."

"Oh that's young. No children?"

"Not that I know of."

"And she was a blues singer who never made it big?"

Ardelia nodded. "Correct."

"Oh, chile. It don't take a rocket scientist to figure that out."

Ardelia lifted her head from the binder. "What do you mean?"

"Drugs."

A storm swirled inside of Ardelia's body, and her fingers moved like lightning across the obituary pages. She stumbled, and the secretary pulled out a chair and helped her into it.

"This was it. This was it all along."

"What was it?" the secretary asked, making her way over to the water fountain to fill up a cup for Ardelia.

"Daddy," Ardelia uttered. This was what Daddy had wanted to tell her her entire life. Violet was in Sterling's blood. Violet was part of the problem that preceded his being born. If drugs were the reason for her demise, then maybe those were the same demons he was referring to in his last letter to Ardelia. This was why Daddy had gifted Ardelia Violet's records. They were family heirlooms—siren songs hearkening back to past lives in her lineage that she had overlooked. She'd overlooked them because she had overlooked Daddy, or expected him to behave in a certain manner. All this time, all that music playing in her apartment when she was cleaning, while she and Oliver had dinner, while she was getting ready for work . . . He was speaking to her. They were speaking to her.

As soon as the secretary handed her the water, Ardelia downed it, thanked the woman, and dashed out of the church. The South Side appeared novel and familiar all at once. She looked to her left, then her right, to capture any small details that she might have missed on her way in. She had never felt so rooted to a place and yet desiring to take flight with this breakthrough. Instead of taking the bus home, Ardelia walked until she gradually picked up speed to a run. Tears flew out of her eyes and her chest ached from the cold, but that only motivated her to keep going until she turned the corner to her grandmother's home. As soon as she approached the driveway, she looked up to see Geraldine sitting near the window staring back at her. Ardelia slowed down and marched up the front steps.

When Ardelia came inside, she silently removed her shoes and knelt next to the sofa upon which Geraldine sat. She cupped her grandmother's hands and said, "Daddy gave me Violet's music not because he simply liked her as an artist, right?"

Geraldine started to tear up and looked out the window.

"I couldn't find her in many records. Aunt Hazel told me to go to the Olivet and I find out that Violet might have succumbed to drugs, just like Daddy. That's why you didn't want to talk about her. That's why you didn't want to talk about his art, because he painted her."

Geraldine said nothing.

"Grandma, please . . ." Ardelia begged, her voice cracking with desperation.

After a moment, Geraldine attempted to speak, but it came out as a croak. "It was on my birthday," she said. Then she took a breath, ready to begin her story.

39

1929-2021

When the stock market crashed, Chicago was dealt an even worse blow than New York. The city relied on manufacturing, and when it was time to slash jobs, negro men like Corinthian, as well as Mexican workers who had moved to the city, were some of the first to be let go. When they weren't organizing to fight against evictions, relief cuts, and labor protections, the unemployed were forced to stand in line every day with hundreds of others to get bread or soup at a local food pantry, or else starve. Corinthian refused to allow Miriam to join him in line. Even without money, Corinthian had pride, and he was not going to let the whole neighborhood see his wife out there waiting. He hated receiving government assistance because he didn't trust it after he was denied a loan back in Kansas, and the taste of the soup he got at the pantry was tainted by the knowledge that the kitchen was run by one of the biggest mobsters in the country. It was only by the grace of God, Corinthian believed, that the family was able to keep their house. Other families they knew, with whom they'd sat in church and dined at the best restaurants on the South Side, had had to move into cramped boardinghouses so that they wouldn't be out on the street.

The slick suits and shiny dresses favored by many of the Black
people in the neighborhood quickly vanished as Black-owned enter-
prises went out of business. Each day that he was not at the steel mill,
Corinthian felt restless. He became unmoored and surly, and he had
nowhere to direct that anger but back in his house.

The primary target of his ire was Vera. It hadn't taken him long
to recognize that the small yet mighty voice on the radio he'd heard
while running errands on Maxwell Street belonged to his daughter. He spun around wondering where her voice was coming from,
but the sound got smaller as a Henry Ford model car drove out of
sight. It happened so quickly that Corinthian thought maybe he'd
imagined it. In the nights that followed, he stared up at the ceiling
wondering if his own daughter was really getting involved in "that"
music. She never showed any signs of subversive behavior. She kept
her manners, dressed modestly, and respected curfew. But there was
a knot in his belly that made him wonder if she'd inherited her mother's ability to maintain a secret better than the devil himself. Then,
little by little, Corinthian noticed a new bracelet hanging around
Vera's wrist, a new brooch fastened to one of Miriam's church outfits, a sparkling piece of porcelain in the kitchen cabinet. He was
at the drugstore when he saw demos featuring some pretty little
thing named Violet, who looked just like his daughter, and some
man by the name of Booker Stone beside her. He bought one copy
as evidence.

Later that night, when Vera returned home to what she thought
was a sleeping house, Corinthian turned on one of the lamps in the
living room and held up the demo. Vera didn't deny it.

"I love music and I love makin' music," she said after a moment.
"And I'm goin' to keep makin' music. I'm good at it."

Corinthian encouraged her to try another profession. Maybe she
could be a choir director for Olivet, but she refused. "If you like music
so much," he insisted, "become a schoolteacher like your sister. You
can teach music to children and earn a decent living."

Vera was adamant. She didn't want to teach children and she didn't want to arrange gospel songs for Baptist services. She wanted to live. She wanted to be a star, drive a Cadillac, and tour the country with the man she loved.

"Dat man ain't no good, Vera," he shouted, his voice booming, at which point Miriam came running out of the bedroom in her robe.

"You haven't even met him!" Vera said.

"I don't need to," Corinthian shot back. "Dat man ain't no good and he takin' advantage of your innocence and he gon' leave you high and dry once he done had his fill."

She adjusted her coat collar and turned her lip up at her father. "I ain't as innocent as you think."

Corinthian lunged at Vera and was just about to grip both of her arms when Miriam got between them.

"Out! I want her out!" Corinthian said.

Vera held on to the sash of her mother's robe while Miriam held on to her. But when Vera looked at her mother, imploring her to intervene, Miriam remained quiet. She had already put Corinthian through too much in their marriage. And so Miriam fell in line with her husband and helped Vera pack, though she assured her daughter through her tears that now she would be free to do whatever she wanted. Now, Miriam said, Vera could fully explore her love with this new man. If things didn't work out, Vera could always come home, she promised, even though both women knew that option was not guaranteed. And when Miriam saw Vera off after a long, quiet bus ride to the club that night, watching her small frame seemingly evaporate into the red, hazy glow of the interior, she worried that she'd made a mistake by going along with Corinthian. For his part, he'd refused to say goodbye, believing that if Vera wanted to ruin her life, he couldn't be a part of it.

At first, life on her own was good for Vera. She and Booker were able to afford a cozy love nest only a few blocks down from where they recorded. The only downside was that most nights traveling musician friends of Booker's slept on their floor and couch, and Vera was expected to feed everyone. The money she earned from performing was enough for her to send money to her mother and buy herself some nice things every other month. In a matter of weeks after J. Mayo Williams, a scout for Black Swan Records, saw the pair perform at the Gates, she and Booker signed a recording contract. It was their big break, but Vera found herself struggling to keep up with the demands of being a recording artist and a live-in girlfriend. There was always dinner to cook, clothes to wash, a corner to sweep, a countertop to dust, and a shoe to shine.

Gradually, Booker's expressions of gratitude grew less frequent—flowers every Friday, then every other, then not at all. He wanted her to work harder and sing more about city life rather than Kansas—to sing with more grit and sorrow in her voice—and he was going to do whatever he could to draw it out of her. If that meant taking her to the most sordid places, where the people looked like zombies and screwed like rabid animals and their mouths were as fast as they were profane, so be it. If that meant entertaining a woman for too long so that jealousy would kick up in Vera's spirit, then he would play the game. He wanted to toughen her up, and that he did until the only thing that made her stand tall with pride and a smile was a needle to the arm or a line up the nose.

In their earlier years, Vera had seen Booker sniff and rub his nose, and assumed his Mississippi body was vulnerable to the extreme Chicago cold. One day, though, one of his nostrils was closed and nothing anyone could do would pry it open. When Vera asked Booker what ailed him, he showed her his bag of heroin, encouraging her to give it a try, which she refused. The first time she tried it, less than two months after her father's rejection, was after she found a woman in their bed. The pain and betrayal were far too great to carry, and she needed to escape. Her high conjured images of wildflower fields in Kansas, the first time she heard blues as a child, Booker, God, the devil, heaven, hell, her invincibility, and the disastrous beauty of life.

It was only supposed to be one time. But the women never stopped coming. The friends wouldn't stop squatting on their floor. The records were never quite right, and though her mother sent her letters, Corinthian never came for her. She wanted to recreate the family she'd lost but nothing ever grew in her womb. Booker's resentment for their difficulties having children came through his barbed words and fists to her face. He threatened that he would have babies with other women instead and did just that. Eventually Vera's one time became a habit that took over her entire life. She stopped showing up to recording sessions, figuring she'd never be a big star like Ma Rainey or Bessie Smith anyway. Whenever Vera managed to make it to a studio, she was either out of her mind or battered from Booker's retaliation during a petty fight. But then Paramount bought Black Swan Records, and then that company went under, and Vera and Booker were left with nothing. Booker disappeared without a word, and she stayed in their apartment for as long as she could before the landlord put her out. From there, she found abandoned homes to squat in or slept in the beds of men with whom she did unspeakable things to keep a roof over her head and her habit maintained.

Word got around about Miriam and Corinthian's daughter. From the pews of Olivet Baptist to the street bazaars, people whispered about how bad she'd looked when they saw her hanging out on a corner or walking through a dark neighborhood at night. Though Vera was only one of countless other young people who got wrapped up in fast living, it didn't make her parents feel any better. Corinthian hated being right about the path Booker had led her down, but he wasn't going to bring her back into the house. She made her choice, he told Miriam repeatedly when she could not sleep at night. And besides, she wasn't Vera. She went by Violet now, and he didn't know no woman named Violet. Most nights, when Corinthian was asleep, Miriam would kneel in her prayer closet and pray for some resolution.

That resolution came in the form of a granddaughter, the first of Temperance's after a string of grandsons. Over Thanksgiving dinner at Miriam and Corinthian's home, the new baby in her arms, Temperance said, "I want Vera to meet Geraldine."

"What for?" Corinthian asked with his mouth half full of turkey and gravy.

"What for?" she asked. "I want my daughter to know that I have a sister. She's my only sibling."

"You didn't care at all when the boys were born, so what's the change now?" her father asked.

"Pa, please—"

"She on drugs," he warned her. "No young child need to see dat."

Temperance didn't say another word about it, but as she helped her mother with the dishes in the kitchen, they spoke quietly about Vera and tried to guess her whereabouts. Then when all the men and boys were fast asleep, Temperance gathered a restless baby Geraldine, and they walked out the door with Miriam. En route to the local bus stop, they turned the corner and passed by a bony woman and would have continued going on had that woman not addressed them both by name.

They turned around and Temperance gasped at what they saw under the street lights. She turned to her mother, who was at a loss for words. Vera looked older than her mother—her skin dry and flaky, eyes dark and sullen, teeth yellow, hair frayed and stringy. Miriam held back tears and said, "Vera?"

The woman nodded.

"I didn't know you was dis close. What you doin'?"

Vera shook her head. "I'm always around. Sometimes I even pass down our block. You just hadn't bothered to look out the window. But I was there. Or maybe y'all didn't recognize me."

Ashamed, Miriam lowered her eyes and Vera moved her attention to the chubby-faced baby squirming in her sister's arms.

"Who is that?" she asked.

"Your niece, Geraldine," Temperance replied. "Do you want to hold her?"

Vera looked down at her hands and then at her tattered jacket. "I'm too dirty. I'll mess up her pretty clothes."

Temperance held out the baby to her. "I can always wash them."

Vera looked down at the fussy infant, then up at Temperance, who reassured her with a nod, and so she took Geraldine and cradled her in her arms. As soon as the baby gazed at this new person, she quieted, studying every aspect of her aunt's face. Immediately, Vera fell in love. She could not remember the last time she had held something so precious, if she ever had at all. This love was pure. It wasn't attached to music, which had disappointed her, or to a man, who'd hurt her. This love was of her blood, reminding her that she could be a part of something beautiful again.

"Can we see each other again? Please?" Vera asked.

They decided that every last Thursday of the month, they would meet in the cafeteria at the high school where Temperance worked, after class had been let out for the day. If Temperance felt that Vera was clean, she allowed her to hold the baby. The incentive was enough for Vera to stay away from drugs at least for a few hours so she could be near her niece.

This routine carried on for years—sometimes they'd meet in the cafeteria, other times it would be at a nearby diner, until Geraldine was approaching her seventh birthday, and Corinthian proposed that they hold a celebration at the house on the day itself, a Thursday. Temperance and Miriam wanted to see Vera but they knew that Corinthian would not allow her to come. To distract him, Temperance and Miriam fashioned a plan: they'd invite the entire neighborhood to the party. If enough people came, they figured, then Corinthian would be less inclined to act out when Temperance and Miriam snuck Vera in. They'd already picked out a nice dress and shoes for her to wear, and Vera promised that she'd fix her hair up real nice. In the meantime, Vera had crafted a plan of her own. She was not going to fade into the crowd as Miriam and Temperance had intended. She was not going to spoil her dear niece's day, but she was not going to avoid her father either.

Miriam and Temperance were in the kitchen getting the potato salad and macaroni salad out of the refrigerator when Vera hesitatingly walked up behind her father, who was fixing the music outside on the front lawn. Little Geraldine was watching what was going on as her friends played nearby. She wanted to run up to her auntie and wrap her small arms around her waist until she saw how quickly Vera's face changed when her grandfather spun around, pointing a strong finger at her.

"What the hell are you doing here?"

It was the first time Vera heard Corinthian say a curse word, and she was too shocked to speak.

"This is a kid's party. It's not appropriate for you to be here."

She composed herself. "It is my niece's birthday."

"At my house. I didn't invite you." Corinthian sized her up with a scowl and sniffed a few times. "You stink." He shook his head before turning his back on her.

Vera went into the house, running into Temperance and Miriam, who were walking out with the bowls. Geraldine saw her aunt mouth a few words, to which the other women nodded. As the guests crowded near the food table to fill their plates, Geraldine could not remove her eyes from the front door, which had been left open. She waited for Vera to come out again, but there was no sign of her. Unable to wait any longer, Geraldine decided to go and get Vera herself so that she wouldn't miss the birthday cake.

Water pooled around Geraldine's shoes as she stepped further into the house. She followed the trail all the way to the crack underneath the bathroom door and gently nudged it open. Steam fogged the mirror and Geraldine swatted at the clouds so that she could better see. Vera's feet were arched over the tub faucet as the water overflowed onto the floor. Dots of blood speckled the tile. "Aunt V?" Geraldine called out to her, but she didn't respond. She tiptoed further into the bathroom and saw her beloved auntie in a body of water sleeping peacefully, a syringe floating near her right arm.

Geraldine walked over to the tub, reached one of her hands into the water, and attempted to shake Vera awake, to no avail. Rapid footsteps advanced behind her, then an ear-splitting scream that caused all the chatter outside to come to an abrupt halt. Geraldine was gathered up, her eyes shielded, her face buried into the bosom of a body that smelled like her mother. Chairs were folded up, people had scattered, the adults were running circles around each other. And all the while, Geraldine didn't have the slightest idea what was going on. All she'd wanted was to make sure her Aunt V got a piece of cake. Why wasn't anyone waking her up?

• • •

"For as long as I lived," Geraldine said to Ardelia and Hazel, who were both moved to tears, "I was never able to get that image of her in the bathroom out of my head."

"That's who Daddy painted. It was her, right?"

Geraldine nodded. "When he was a teenager, I told him about my beloved aunt because I saw that he was curious like you and he was getting to be rebellious like her. And . . . he wound up just like Vera."

"But Daddy didn't die from drugs, Grandma." Ardelia gently grabbed Geraldine's wrist. "It was COVID."

"I didn't say he died from drugs, baby. And my aunt Vera ain't die from drugs neither. She died from a broken heart—from a daddy who wouldn't see her. But dey ain't know no better. Her own mother, my grandmother, was born from a woman who felt abandoned by her own husband. I was told he loved somebody else but I can't be too sure. And then all these years later, my son wound up abandoning you." Geraldine laced her fingers between Ardelia's and rocked back and forth. "Now look at you . . . you in the family way too."

"What do you mean? I'm not pregnant."

Geraldine gave her a look. "I know. But don't think I ain't realize that you haven't brought up your fiancé not one time since you been here. When am I gonna see you get married?"

Ardelia sighed. "We've broken up, Grandma. It's a long story."

"Who broke up with who?"

"It was me."

"Was it because of someone else?" Hazel interjected.

"No, it wasn't like that."

"Does he still care for you?" Geraldine asked.

"He does."

"Does he reach out?" she pried, to which Ardelia widened her eyes. "What? You think you can come to my house and ask me all sorts of questions and I can't ask you none?"

"He does." Ardelia refrained from telling her relatives that he'd been wishing her good luck via text each day that she'd been in Chicago, to which she'd replied with a thumbs-up or a simple "thanks" but nothing more.

"Hmm . . ." Geraldine hummed. "You come all this way to Chicago to learn about the family. And you're so quick with your mind—you're just racing and running back toward us, trying to recover something from your father. And all the while, you've been running away from a good man who loves you. I remember how he looked at you at your engagement party."

"I'm not running!" Ardelia raised her voice, then minded her tone. "I'm sorry. I'm not, Grandma. He left me first."

"Are you tryna to be together or are you tryna win?"

She remained quiet.

"Hmph." Geraldine nodded. "I had hoped that with you and

Oliver, this heartbreak that seems to follow our family from genera-tion to generation would end. But it hasn't. And least not yet."

"Not yet?"

Geraldine took a beat before grinning with a degree of warmth that only an elder can bestow.

"You did what our family did not and suffered 'cause of it."

"What's that?"

"You came on back. Now you gotta move forward."

40

APRIL 2021

Oliver had just gotten a chopped cheese from a nearby bodega when his phone buzzed in his pocket. He nonchalantly pulled it out to see a text from Ardelia and stopped in the middle of the street, barely missing being hit by an MTA bus. Once he was safely on the opposite sidewalk, he took a deep breath and opened her message. "Kansas." That was it. He smiled.

If this were bait—Oliver looked around and shuffled his feet a bit—then he was taking it. He hit "call" and hoped his heavy breathing wouldn't mess up the chill vibe that he was going for.

Ardelia picked up on the third ring. "Hello?"

"Hey. . . ." His voice came out labored and uncertain.

"Hi. . . ." Ardelia drew out hers.

"That was a random thing to message me," he joked.

She laughed. "Yeah it was."

"But I mean . . . when I randomly messaged *you* about Tirzah and Harrison, it worked. So . . . you got me." Ardelia was quiet but Oliver trusted that she was still on the line.

"What's this about Kansas? Are you trying to tell me that you've been thinking of me by referencing my home state?" Oliver winced as soon as the words were out, fearing that he was coming on too strong.

"Not quite, actually." She told him everything: from how Chicago looked in the springtime to Geraldine's habits to her going on a wild-goose chase all across the South Side only to find that her home church had the clue that she needed. The blues records that she played weren't just cultural items passed down from her elders. They were familial keepsakes. Violet was Geraldine's aunt Vera. Their last name, Stiruhlan, was actually Sterling. Chicago was not their origin city, and Violet's reference to South and Fourth were to streets in a small town in Kansas called Nicodemus. A 1910 Census record confirmed a Vera, Temperance, Corinthian, and Miriam Sterling lived there, and their birth years matched up with those in Chicago.

"So, Kansas," Ardelia said, short of breath.

"Wow," Oliver said. "You've been pretty busy."

"I have been. And I've been wondering: What if my people knew your people?"

"Heh. That would be something, wouldn't it?" he said. "Did you only text me because I'm the only person from Kansas you know?"

"Yeah . . . well, no . . ."

He held the phone closer to his face and waited.

"Oliver . . . do you think that I . . . left you hanging at any point in our relationship?"

"Oh wow." He looked around to see how much privacy he had from passersby, then proceeded to walk to a nearby park. "Uhh . . . heh. That's a lot to think about for the years we've been together."

"When you moved out—I mean, in January of last year, did you feel like I was . . . pulling away?"

Oliver took a deep breath and squeezed all the muscles in his face. "Not right then. If anything, I was the one pulling away. But eventually . . . yeah . . ." He exhaled. "But I didn't want to say anything."

"Why?"

"Because I knew where it came from. I knew your history with your dad and all, that it wasn't just about me. I left, then your dad died, and then you got wrapped up in the research and I was happy you had something to occupy your time but . . . I did think I was losing you."

"Oh," she said softly.

"But I'm glad you've kept me updated on everything. It feels nice to hear you speak like this."

"I didn't know who else to tell. I still need to figure out if there is a Mississippi connection because I keep getting all these signs and I don't know. I got excited and—" She sighed.

Her fast talking reminded him how much he missed her passion, and the honor he'd felt sitting beside her in the midst of that excitement. There was a silence. Each of them wanted to say something. Ardelia wanted to ask him if Kansas meant that they were meant to be together, but didn't want to get ahead of herself. Oliver wanted to blurt out that he loved her, but he didn't want to make things awkward. They existed in the in-between.

There was no one else but her for him, and there was no one else but him for her. Maybe they didn't need to explain anything. But if not now, when? Spring had finally arrived in New York again, reminding its inhabitants why they chose to build their lives in this difficult city. The days were longer, the breezes lighter, there were even flowers in Central Park, beautiful ones. More people were spending time outdoors, and the hospitals were no longer overflowing with COVID patients. Oliver's anxiety had mostly abated, but he remembered that just last year, the summer—when all this socialization first resumed—marked the demise of his and Ardelia's relationship.

"When will you be coming back to New York?" he asked.

"Soon. I needed to come home, and I feel like there are still loose ends to tie up here, stories I need to hear."

Oliver could feel the sweat under his armpits and a lump in his throat. He wanted to ask her how soon but didn't want to appear clingy. Yet again, that answer was vague. Would she really be coming back?

"Understood," Oliver said finally. "Well, keep me posted. I'm really proud of all of your efforts."

Ardelia was taken aback by the formality of his tone, but she bit her tongue and thanked him before hanging up.

Oliver noted that Ardelia had left him with a "take care" that could have been friendly or could have been passive-aggressive. He decided that the next morning, he was going to grab his mask and go see about Mr. Johnson.

WHEN HE ARRIVED, MR. JOHNSON WAS SWEEPING OUTSIDE AS usual, slowing his broom when he saw Oliver approaching. "Hey, look who it is! Long time no see."

"Hi, Mr. Johnson. How are you?"

"Can't complain, can't complain. How you been? If you're lookin' for Ardelia, she been gone for a while. Off to see her folks in Chicago."

"Yes, I know. Do you have any idea when she'll be coming back?"

The older man shook his head. "Not a clue. She seemed to be in a hurry to get out the door though. Musta been missing her people a lot."

"I see . . ." Oliver's voice dipped.

Mr. Johnson leaned his head to the side. "You okay?"

"Not really." Oliver sat down on the stoop, and Mr. Johnson joined him. "I don't know, Mr. Johnson. I just have this worry that she may never come back."

"Heh. Now why does that sound familiar?"

"Ouch." Oliver rubbed the nape of his neck.

"Oh no no no. Don't you start beating up on yourself." He placed a hand on Oliver's back.

"But I drove her away."

"Hmm. . . . It's more complicated, but that was a part of it, I'm sure."

"I thought you were trying to make me feel better."

"My boy, in order for you to get better, you gotta see better. Understand?"

"Yes, sir." The two men looked straight ahead and watched neighbors passing by on the sidewalk. Then he said, "My people never wound up being together."

"What, now?"

"This family letter that I gave Ardelia, it's been in my family for God knows how long. I thought it was a love letter, but I found out they never wound up together."

"What's that gotta do with you and 'Delia?"

"There I was thinking it was a gift, and now I feel like it's an omen."

"Oh Lawd," Mr. Johnson said, cackling. "You young people are so dramatic. Y'all think text messages and Facebook and all that compares to what my generation and older had to go through. Y'all have it so much easier, and you keep gettin' in your own way."

Oliver sighed.

"All I'm sayin' is . . . whatever happened in the past—there were so many more obstacles back then. You have more in your control now."

"Funny you say that because I feel out of control."

"Naw, not one bit. You wanna know why? Because"—Mr. Johnson swung his knees around to face him—"you have your freedom. Now what you gon' do with it?"

Oliver knew exactly what he was going to do with it. He thanked Mr. Johnson and gave him a proper goodbye. Then, he returned home. There would be no quick text message to ask if Ardelia could hop on a phone call—none of that. He was going to write her a proper email to ask if she was willing to talk. But not before he told her how much he loved her and how he'd like to see when they'd be able to get things back on track, if she still wanted that.

Before Oliver could compose a single sentence, though, he saw a new email at the top of his inbox from an address he didn't recognize. He was about to send it to spam when he saw the subject line: "Harlem Exhibition - A Personal Invitation."

Dear Oliver,

My name is Elizia McWashington and I am writing to you because you took care of one of my dearest and oldest friends in her last days. Her name was Lunette. I remember her speaking fondly about the young, handsome doctor who checked in on her every day. I'm glad her end was not as lonely as it could have been.

Ever since her passing, a couple of her friends and I have been trying to handle her belongings in her Harlem apartment where, as I'm sure she might have told you, she'd been planning on doing an exhibition to show the community all the Black history in her trunks and other storage places.

I'm thrilled to say that we've been able to put on a little gathering of sorts and I'd be honored if you'd come. It's on Saturday, May 8th at 1 p.m., 218 Edgecombe Avenue, Apt #1.

I hope to see you there.

Best regards,
Elizia McWashington

• • •

The day of Ms. Lunette's home exhibition did not start well. Despite the sunny weather and the sound of late '90s R&B from passing cars, Oliver woke feeling uneasy. He hadn't been to any kind of social event for more than a year, and he worried that even with proof of vaccination being required before entry, he or the other guests might get sick. But he did not want to keep hiding. The world was beginning to move on, and besides, the event was for a good cause. His will overtook his concerns, and he began to ready himself. Then the phone rang. Ardelia had taken the initiative to reach out to him, and her squeals were sweet nectar. She told him of her plans for the day, which involved, as usual, digging deeper into her roots. Miriam, as Ardelia discovered, had listed her birthplace as Mississippi on census records. Now where exactly in the state that might be wasn't clear, and she was hoping to scour the internet for copies of some death certificates to be sure.

This lead sounded exciting, but then Oliver heard Donell Jones's "Where I Wanna Be" playing in the distance, followed by honking and ambulance sirens. She remained quiet and so did he. Oliver had gotten distracted by the email from Ms. Lunette's friend, then lost his nerve and never sent Ardelia the email pouring out his feelings. Now he wondered if he made the right decision. She was back in New York, and the recognizable city noise confirmed it. She was back in New York, and she hadn't told him—a swift blow to the chest. He wasn't going to ask why, but he knew by the way she moved on to asking about his day that she wasn't going to talk about it. Oliver lied and said that he might go for a run in the park, then go see some friends for dinner. He didn't want to mention Ms. Lunette—who'd been occupying his thoughts from the time he received that invitation—since Ardelia hadn't liked hearing about her even when they were together.

Hamilton Heights wasn't a part of uptown that Oliver had explored much, and when he exited the subway into a busy intersection, he noticed that there were signs about the late Ms. Lunette's exhibition, complete with a black-and-white image of a finely dressed woman taped to the poles on every corner. When Oliver turned down West 144th Street toward Edgecombe Avenue, he noticed a few others walking in the same direction. Either there was a party going on, or everyone was going to the same place as he was. When he reached the entrance of Ms. Lunette's apartment building, he saw that the door had been left open, and dozens of people milled around the entrance.

Inside the apartment, the air was full and there were quite a few women, some waving Chinese fans, others church fans, in their faces, as they brushed past Oliver. Heels click-clacked on the checkerboard tile floor. Miles Davis and his trumpet blew from some corner of the apartment. He couldn't help but smile beneath his mask. Maybe Ms. Lunette had lived as colorful a life as she'd told him. If only she could see the turnout. One part of his brain wondered why he wasn't panicking. He hadn't been this close to so many people in so long, but curiosity took over.

As he took it all in, her apartment astounded him. The artwork that adorned the walls, the large open space displaying historical artifacts on top of a fine linen tablecloth, the abundant light streaming in through the windows. Had to be rent stabilized, Oliver guessed. Even still, how had Ms. Lunette had all of this and still wound up alone? Small children held their parents' hands as they looked at old vinyl records and program announcements for Carmen de Lavallade and Geoffrey Holder, Cicely Tyson and Josephine Baker. They didn't understand the value of what they saw, he knew, but the twinkle in their eyes gave him hope that one day they would reassess and sit back in wonder. He wished that Ardelia was there, had even held out a little bit of hope that she would've found out about it by word of mouth. But he could not stand in the corner for much longer. He had to take advantage of the event or else there'd have been no point in him leaving his home in the first place.

Oliver moved toward the outer edges to take in some of the finery: a dress designed by Stephen Burrows, sketches by Ann Lowe, editorials written by Romare Bearden in *The Chicago Defender*, Soviet posters from the 1920s and '30s designed to lure African Americans to Russia, photographs and newspaper clippings from Juneteenth celebrations back in the 1880s. These precious items weren't put in any specific chronology, but Oliver found the lack of organization gave them an even deeper meaning. Time collapsed in this apartment. The young and old mingled in the home of a woman who'd passed before any of them knew the virus was coming. And yet her presence pulsated within these walls. Each time Oliver gazed at some part of history, he liked to imagine what a younger Ms. Lunette had been

doing that caused her to come in contact with the object, recognize
its value, and hold on to it no matter how far and wide she traveled.

Out of the corner of his eye, he saw others were crowding around
something on a stand in the middle of the room, which he couldn't
see. As people moved out of the way, they were wiping the corners
of their eyes. Oliver's curiosity was piqued, but instead of making his
way right over, he surrendered to the waves of voices and bodies moving to and fro, yielding to the melody, hoping to find the rhythm. It
was undeniable that he'd missed this community, the cackles, the cacophony, the curls, the cues, the cadences. Whenever someone would
brush up against his shoulder, a wave of emotion took him under.
How long it had been since he touched someone. How long it had
been since someone touched him. Ardelia returned to the forefront
of his mind, and he wished to kneel at the altar of her body. Never
would Oliver have expected to have his spirit push and pull, stretch
and contort, at an exhibition, as though he were swept up in an ec-
static church service. But if God was once made of flesh, and Black
was the first thing they saw before the world began, then this place
was as divine as anyplace could be.

The air was getting hotter the closer he got to the mysterious
object. At last, a couple moved from their position and gave him an
opening. He moved up closer to the plexiglass, behind which lay a
large Bible whose spine was hanging on by a few measly threads. The
book itself was open, and there were scraps of written notes pieced together on one brown, tattered page, and notes pieced together on the
other side. He inched forward toward the Bible and squinted through
the glass:

June 24th, 1865

Dear Harrison,

*The war is finally over. The day you went off with the Union Army I
swore I'd never see you again. But now we have a chance. Spencer*

*Ambrose made me and a half dozen other slave women to go to
Shreveport. I'd been working for another mistress because I assumed
his pa hadn't come through with enough money to support his
lifestyle so he had to rent us out one by one. I hope you're in Natchez
by the time you get this letter. I sent it through the Freedmen's Bureau
here in town and I'm led to believe by my good friend Isaac that
Natchez has one too.*

*I'm going to find my way back to you. I know you haven't
broken your promise. I know you came looking for me back at
the plantation. I know you're alive too. I can feel it every time
I think about you. I know you're thinking about me too. I pray
you find someone to read this for you and assure you that your
beloved is coming back.*

*Folks around here think I need to get married and forget
about you. But I haven't forgotten about you and I will not
forget about you. I love you and that's as true and unshaken as
the sun rising in the east and setting in the west. Wait for me. So
that we can begin our lives together now as freedpeople.*

Love,
Tirzah

Oliver lost his steadiness of breath as he heard someone saying his name.

He followed the sound to Ardelia staring right at him through the plexiglass on the other side. A mask obscured most of her face, but he recognized those jubilant eyes, now surging with water, and the way her curly hair hung over her forehead. She slowly walked over and the two estranged lovers stood in front of each other. Passersby watched the scene unfold behind their fans and pamphlets, whispering and smiling at the pure affection flowing from them, the energy filling the entire room with joy that was alive and well.

"Look at you," Ardelia said. She extended her hand toward his face and he inched forward for her to touch him. "You need a haircut."

Oliver rubbed his head. "Now you tell me. I didn't think you'd be here. But now it makes all the sense in the world."

"What do you mean?"

"You probably heard about it from one of your colleagues, right?"

"Close. A woman named Sherrie came by the Schomburg and told me that a friend of hers was having an exhibition before her archives went somewhere, maybe to us. We emailed a few times but it wasn't until I got the invitation that I found out it was for Ms. Lunette. I didn't plan on going, but then I thought, since she was so interesting you never stopped talking about her when she was alive, I might as well check it out."

Oliver beamed. "I came by the apartment looking for you," he told her.

"You did?"

"Yeah. I thought you might stay in Chicago forever."

"Forever?" Ardelia laughed. "Why would I do that?"

"I don't know . . . I just . . . I was scared I'd really lost you forever."

"I know the feeling. But I'm at fault too."

"I moved out first."

"But I was so focused on getting married and cementing that we were together. And then I wanted to leave you before you had a chance to leave me. I was scared."

"Me too."

Moved by her sincerity, Oliver quickly wiped his eyes and pointed to the plexiglass. "Have you seen this yet?"

"No. When I came in, there was such a huge crowd that I went to the back to check out the rest of her collection."

A wide grin emerged. "Have a look." Ardelia walked slowly to the plexiglass while Oliver patiently stood to her right, watching her eyes move from left and right. Gradually, her eyes got bigger and bigger.

"Oh my God."

"Crazy, right? How would Ms. Lunette—"

"No. You have to come with me right now. Right now."

Seeing that letter along with Ardelia at Ms. Lunette's home, of all places, was enough of a surprise to keep him levitating all the way to the vestibule of their apartment building and upstairs to their unit.

Once they were inside, Ardelia went into the bedroom and returned holding a large, white binder to her chest. She opened and held the binder out in front of Oliver so that he could see its contents. There was a death certificate for a Miriam Stiruhlan, who'd listed her husband as Corinthian Strihulan. Her father and mother were listed as Harrison and Tabithah Ambrose from Mississippi. There were census records going all the way back to 1870. She found Vera, Miriam, and finally, Harrison, listed as a strong talent with his hands—a carpenter in an 1860 slave record under the Ambrose Family in Natchez, Mississippi. She flipped the pages over one by one so Oliver could see everything, until they reached the last page: an advertisement from the Freedmen's Bureau of a Harrison Ambrose seeking his beloved Tirzah Ambrose in the missing person's section of a Southern Black newspaper.

Now it was Ardelia's turn to watch Oliver's face light up with the revelation of the stories and stories before them.

• • •

Moments before Tirzah's death, Miriam thought of how she kept Tirzah's love letters to her father and regretted that she held on to them for so long without saying a word until now.

"Why be sad?" Tirzah's radiant beauty shone from the candlelight when she lovingly stared at Miriam, with no trace of any anger over the secret she'd kept for so many years. "I'll be seeing him again. And again and again and again."

She was confident in her tone and serene in her face as her chest rose and fell slower and slower.

Before Novella and Free dashed into the room to say their final goodbyes, Miriam quickly slipped the letters into Tirzah's Bible, only to find several more letters addressed to a Harrison there. She kept the book close to her body on her silent walk home in the bitter cold. She thought of her mother when she crept back into her marital bed and hid the Bible among her undergarments. Every time she left and returned to her bedroom, no matter how long she'd been away, she would check the drawer to see if everything was still there. When Miriam was alone, she read and reread the letters.

Her initial plan was to give the Bible to Free as a way to explain why she had been drawn to him in the first place. But she didn't admire him so much anymore, no longer thought so fondly of their so-called love, whatever had caused them to almost ruin their families. And the more Miriam thought about it, she figured that he wasn't the best person to leave the letters with. He didn't know if he was coming or going even when Tirzah was alive. No. These letters had to be kept among women, a tradition that Tabithah had started without knowing it.

When Corinthian told her their family was leaving for Chicago, Miriam realized that she would have to make haste to Novella. She risked being left behind by her husband and children but took her chances sprinting across the fields. Through one of the front-facing windows, she could see Novella cooking, dejectedly dropping the ladle into a steaming pot. Miriam rapped on the door and had just enough strength to push out a greeting before doubling over to catch her breath.

"What's going on, Miriam? Free ain't here if dat's who you're askin' 'bout."

"No, ma'am." Miriam shook her head and kept her hand on her hip as she leaned on the doorjamb for support.

Novella was surprised by Miriam's deferential tone and loosened her stance. "Are you okay?"

"I'm fine. I'm just—whew." She fanned herself.

Novella grabbed her hand to escort her into the house, but Miriam resisted. "I can'. I don' have de time. I'm leavin'."

"Leavin'? You just got here and you barely said a word."

"No, Novella. I'm leavin'. Corinthian and I are goin' to Chicago and I don' think we comin' back either."

"I know."

"You know?"

"He and I talked about it one night." Novella recognized the admission was a petty one but the look of shock upon Miriam's face gave her a small, redeeming pleasure.

"Oh . . . Well, maybe you and Free should consider it. Nicodemus ain't gon' change. It's not like when we was young and we gotta go where it's at, you know?"

"So . . . you ran all de way over here to say goodbye."

"I did. But I wanted to give you somethin'." Miriam took both of her hands and placed a Bible into them.

"I already got one of dese."

"Open it."

Novella did it and immediately had to grab the envelopes before they flew out of it. "What's dis?"

"Letters from Tirzah to her beloved."

"Pastor Levi?"

"No. To my father, Harrison."

"Your father?" Novella asked. "How would she know about your father?"

"Look, I don' have time to explain dis, dat, and de third. Just know dat she never got to see him again and she wrote it to him 'cause she was still in love wit him right to the end. And I need for you to keep it for her. Not for me, for her."

"But why?"

Miriam sighed. "Novella, you got any keepsakes from your people?"

"Not really. I was very young when I lost my parents."

"Den dis is important. And wit Tirzah gone, dis what unites us in our memory, what ties us togetha. Probably de only thing of hers dat has a chance of lastin'. You get rid of dis and my people and your people just gon' be circling around and around each other wit'out no peace and no resolution. Our children and dey children's children gon' have de lot we had and who wants dat?"

Novella stayed silent but peered down at the letters.

"Promise me—" Miriam held both of the other woman's shoulders. "Promise me dat no matter what happens, no matter if y'all stay or go, dat you keep dis in your family. I don' care if you tell your children de reason or not. Keep dis and keep it right. Understand?"

Novella nodded. With one hand still clutching the Bible, Novella wrapped her arms around Miriam before bursting into tears. "You don' forget about us when you all live big and lavish in some city, you hear?"

Miriam squeezed her back. "We won'. You don' forget about us neither. 'Cause regardless of what happened, we family."

Novella watched Miriam run back across the fields until she became nothing but a tiny speck. Then she removed the letters from their envelopes and was so enraptured by the first few lines that she took a seat in the rocking chair on their front porch to read the rest. When one of her children started calling her name, she stuffed them into her apron pocket, patted the exterior, and went back into the kitchen to tend to her pots.

"Oh Tirzah," she whispered to herself as she stirred. "Tirzah, you are loved. You are, you are, you are."

She was.

When it was time for Novella and Free to pack up and leave, only one letter remained in one of their suitcases. The rest were scattered in places around the house, where Novella read them in Tirzah's honor. Decades later, one of them wound up in the hands of a vibrant nomad named Ms. Lunette, who was trying to buy clothes and decor at a Black Kansan family's estate sale and wound up walking away with something far more valuable than fabric or pieces of furniture.

Tirzah's children, their children's children, the children of those children, and Oliver all reacted the same way when they held the fragile, browned letter in their hands. Small tears started to fall, then the water gushed from their eyes. For Novella and Free's children, the surviving letter was kept in an old Bible. For their grandchildren, in the bottom of a large trunk stored in the attic. For their great-grandchildren, in a scrapbook. For Oliver's parents, the letter was placed behind a secret door in the back of their wine cellar.

Oliver stretched out his arms to Ardelia, but didn't step too close in case she wanted to move slow. But to his surprise, Ardelia sank into his chest, and their breath and heartbeats moved in unison. They said nothing to each other because enough had already been said. Neither of them knew how long they stood there embracing, but there would be no more leaving, no more running, no more abandoning.

They cried into each other's shoulders before the crying evolved into an uproarious laughter that made the apartment vibrate with ecstasy. They laughed at the sheer absurdity of them finding each other and finding each other again and again. They laughed as their people had to have been doing on a different plane.

Once their lungs gave out from all that laughing, Ardelia looked at Oliver. She whispered, "Welcome home."

ACKNOWLEDGMENTS

Thank you to the Most High and the ancestors who spoke to me in dreams that this manuscript would get done on tearful nights where I doubted myself.

Thank you to Barrye Brown for your assistance and for showing me the love letter that started it all.

To the linguists, historians, and other star academics—Taylor Jones and Hiram Smith, Gary Joiner, Samuel Hyde, Martha Jane Brazy, Joshua D. Rothman, John Baugh, Namwali Serpell, and David Wondrich—your kindness, brilliance, and accessibility are such treasures.

Thank you to my mother, Sybil, my father, Jon, my sisters, Trenair, Courtney, Taylor, and Logan, as well as the rest of my family for keeping me grounded and wrapped in love.

Thank you to Monica Odom for selling this novel, Emily Griffin for editing the hell out of it, Sharon Pelletier for carrying the mantle of representing me and my work, and Adenike Olanrewaju for getting this to the finish line, editorially and emotionally. It truly takes a village.

Thank you to Maya Baran and Lauren Cerand for publicity; your excitement for this book kept me excited even though my anxiety put up a fight!

Also to the rest of the team: Liz Velez, Katie O'Callaghan, and

Zaynah Ahmed—I couldn't have asked for better advocates for this story.

Thank you to Elon Green, Sarah Weinman, Lyz Lenz, Joe Osmundson, and Denne Michele Norris for the writerly group chats full of gossip, guidance, and laughter.

Thank you to Brigitte M., Jasmine G., Sire, Devin L., Jen G., Brandon Z., Logan H., Maraiya H., Genay J., Liz C., Jade J., Ty M. . . .

Thank you to my scholarly inspiration, W. Caleb McDaniel, for your intensive research on the Forks of the Road slave market and Natchez, Mississippi, during the antebellum era.

Thank you to RB for the experience of you and the recognition of a safety that I'd never imagined that I'd have.

ABOUT THE AUTHOR

MORGAN JERKINS is the author of *Caul Baby*, *Wandering in Strange Lands*, and the *New York Times* bestseller *This Will Be My Undoing*. Jerkins has taught at Columbia and Princeton Universities, and has written for the *New Yorker*, the *New York Times*, the *Atlantic*, *Rolling Stone*, *Vanity Fair*, and the *Guardian*, among many other publications. She lives in New York.